SIN LIKE THE DEVIL

HARROWDEAN MANOR #1

J ROSE

WILTED ROSE PUBLISHING LTD

ISBN (eBook): 978-1-915987-25-9
ISBN (Model Paperback): 978-1-915987-26-6
ISBN: (Discreet Paperback): 978-1-915987-27-3

www.jroseauthor.com

For all the lovers of antiheroes.
Let's allow the women to be baddies too, eh?

TRIGGER WARNING

Sin Like The Devil (Harrowdean Manor #1) is a why choose, reverse harem romance, so the main character will have multiple love interests that she will not have to choose between.

This book is very dark and contains scenes that may be triggering for some readers. These include strong mental health themes, drug addiction and overdose, graphic violence, attempted murder, psychological torture, mentions of self-harm, allusions to childhood sexual abuse, and suicide.

There is explicit language throughout and sexual scenes involving dubious consent, blood play, breath play, knife play and orgasm denial.

If you are easily offended or triggered by any of this content, please do not read this book. This is dark romance, and therefore, not for the faint of heart.

Additionally, this book is written for entertainment and is not intended to accurately represent the treatment of mental health issues.

J ROSE SHARED UNIVERSE

All of J Rose's contemporary, dark romance books are set in the same shared universe. From the walls of Blackwood Institute and Harrowdean Manor, to Sabre Security's HQ and the small town of Briar Valley, all of the characters inhabit the same world and feature in Easter egg cameos in each other's books.

You can read these books in any order, dipping in and out of different series and stories, but here is the recommended order for the full effect of the shared universe and the ties between the books.

For more information:
www.jroseauthor.com/readingorder

AUTHOR'S NOTE

Dear Reader,

I'm excited to be bringing you another story in the Blackwood Institute world. If you're new here, thank you for picking up Sin Like The Devil. You're in for a wild, toxic, violent ride.

For housekeeping purposes, this book takes place during Sacrificial Sinners (Blackwood Institute #2) and spans some of Desecrated Saints (Blackwood Institute #3). However, you do not have to read Blackwood Institute first, though I would strongly recommend it.

Next, I'm going to issue a warning. I don't usually hand hold in this way, but this is an enemies-to-lovers romance, through and through. Please read the TW and enter with caution.

Our leading lady is a morally corrupt antihero who has made a lot of controversial choices. Because why should only the male love interests be antiheroes? Let's give our women the chance to be baddies too.

Speaking of which—the male love interests. This is a complicated story fuelled by hatred and revenge. The guys aren't here to be heroes. They're broken, traumatised and make very ethically questionable decisions.

I don't write straightforward romance. This shared universe is sinister. Imperfect. Flawed. It explores humanity in all its most disturbing forms. If you're up for a challenge, read on. But don't expect redemption to come quickly or easily.

Thank you for being here. Grab a blanket, make an iced coffee, and look after your mental health while reading dark romance. Most of all, enjoy Sin Like The Devil.

Love always,

J Rose

"Maybe we feel empty because we leave pieces of ourselves in everything we used to love."

- R.M. Drake

Established in 1984, a world-first experimental program pioneered by global investment group, Incendia Corporation, founded six private psychiatric institutes across the United Kingdom.

Blackwood Institute
Harrowdean Manor
Priory Lane
Compton Hall
Hazelthorn House
Kirkwood Lodge

Hidden behind multimillion pound, state-of-the-art facilities and slick marketing campaigns, these institutes hide a far more harrowing reality. To find the truth, you must enter the gates of hell with the other patients assigned to Incendia's care.

These are their stories.

PROLOGUE

RIPLEY

Present Day

Did you survive a tragedy if you never speak about it?

Some people would argue not. Well, they're assholes. The lot of them.

Personally, I don't give a fuck whether you want to air your dirty laundry for the entire world to pick apart or not. That's your call. We all survive the aftermath of total self-destruction in our own ways.

But we've been programmed to view survival as being contingent on our later success—the capitalistic drive to monetise your demons and sell them to the highest bidder in the name of bullshit self-improvement.

There are survivors out there who remain silent. Invisible. Slipped through the cracks of society's broken fringes, watching the parade of inspirational figureheads championing their own resilience.

We don't all talk about our pasts. Nor do we all want to

remember the struggle. The fight. The breaking. The cost of survival. These things are left unsaid in the shadows while the loud ones toot their own horns.

I've spent my life running from cameras and film crews, bloodthirsty reporters and foolhardy journalists, all determined to get the scoop on what happened ten years ago when the whole country burned. The fuse was lit inside the country's psychiatric institutes. I had the honour of being incarcerated in one.

Harrowdean Manor.

It's the last unsolved mystery.

When the biggest failed experiment in modern medical history was dismantled and exposed, the six private institutes embroiled in the conspiracy fell into ruinous violence.

Some made it out alive.

Others didn't survive.

Already uncomfortable, I shift my short, barely five feet body in the stiff leather armchair that I've been assigned to after having my hair and makeup done. The blinking eye of the camera set up catches every sharp breath I suck into my lungs.

Tucked off to the side, Elliot O'Hare—the eagle-eyed investigative journalist who's spent the best part of a decade harassing me—is fiddling with the microphone attached to his grey lapel.

Any sane person would be nervous for this interview. But any sane person wouldn't have survived what I did. Perhaps that's what shielded us from harm—the poisonous cloak of our insanity.

It protected us from the horrors we endured because we were already broken in the first place. That's the whole reason we were all trapped inside of Harrowdean Manor. Society deemed us all unfit for their picture-perfect world of falsehoods.

"Okay, then." Elliot straightens his narrow frame, an

overflowing notebook clasped in his wrinkle-lined hands. "Are you ready to start, Miss Bennet?"

Staring down at the oil paint-stained tips of my fingers, I absently pick at my chipped purple nail varnish. "As ready as I'll ever be."

"If you'd like to stop for a break at any time, please let me know. I understand this will be difficult for you. We'll go at your own pace."

Difficult.

The word weighs heavy on my tongue like acrid cigarette ash. Escaping Harrowdean wasn't difficult. It wasn't even hard. In the end, it extracted a simple toll. I left one thing behind.

My broken heart.

The splintered remains... *they* took with them.

"Three... Two... One. The camera is rolling."

When the blinking red light of the camera begins to strike its deathly knoll, I sit up straighter, attempting to conceal my anxiety. My heart has been trying to tear free from my ribcage ever since I arrived.

After spending hours trawling through my meagre wardrobe this morning, looking for something other than my studio clothes, I shed my usual sweatpants in favour of plain black jeans and an off-white blouse that complements my tawny hair and pale complexion.

It's rare that I emerge from my combined apartment and art studio. The real world is unpalatable to me. I prefer the safety of my canvases and the slick of oil paint wielded as a weapon by my brush. No one can ever get close enough to hurt me as long as I live in isolation.

"Please state your name and age for the record," Elliot prompts.

I clear my scratchy throat. "Ripley Bennet. Thirty-six years old."

"Thank you for agreeing to speak to me, Miss Bennet.

We've spoken to many ex-detainees of this cruel regime, but your story in particular has always fascinated us."

Summoning a lifeless nod, I remain silent.

"We've been working on this documentary series for several years now." Elliot tells the viewers what I already know. "Incendia Corporation was officially disbanded a decade ago by the prestigious security firm, Sabre Security."

The London-based, private security company has become a household name. It was taken over by ex-inmates of Blackwood Institute four years ago. I choked on a mouthful of cereal when I read that headline. Now there's a hell of a story.

"We're releasing this documentary series to commemorate the anniversary of the disbandment," Elliot continues. "This is our chance to give the victims back their voices."

The past echoes inside my head. *Drip, drip.* Bloodstained corridors stretch out around me. *Slash, slash.* The knife is cold in my grip. *Stab, stab.* The cries of death and agony compose a sinister soundtrack. I'm still caught in Harrowdean's web of contradictions.

Illusion and distortion.

Patient and exploiter.

Innocent and culpable.

"Miss Bennet." Elliot's professional voice draws me back.

Shaking the rising haze from my head, I stuff the memories back into their internal prison. My therapist says they're safer in there. *Safe, Ripley. You're safe.* Harrowdean is long gone. Even on those dark days when a twisted part of me wishes it still existed.

"Sorry," I mutter.

"It's quite alright. I understand this must be a difficult subject for you, even after all these years. You lost people in Harrowdean, correct?"

All I can manage is another jerky nod that ruffles my unruly, jaw-length mop of curly hair. The words are caught in a barbed wire trap in my throat, unable to tear themselves free.

Fingers twisting together, I focus on the layers of ink that wrap around my arms in intricate tattoo sleeves. But even that isn't a distraction—the tattoos on my left arm are disfigured by puckered scarring. Another reminder of my time inside.

"We've spoken to many ex-detainees and heard shocking stories of medical malpractice, psychological torture and abuse."

"That's what they kept us in there for." I shrug. "We were never meant to be more than their playthings, all for the sake of medical experimentation."

"Quite," he hums.

That's the thing most people don't get. Not what happened inside of Harrowdean Manor and the other institutes—that's a matter of public record now. But the involvement of the patients themselves in the abuse. And those of us who enabled it.

The infamous story that's printed in the history books is only half of the truth. The other half lies buried in our broken minds, waiting to eventually see the light of day. That's why I'm here. After a decade, the time has come for me to reveal mine.

"Perhaps, you'll tell us about how you came to be incarcerated in Harrowdean, one of six experimental institutes owned by Incendia Corporation that were shut down and demolished—"

"Harrowdean wasn't just an institute," I interrupt.

Elliot taps his pen against his chin thoughtfully. "How so?"

"Well, that's just what the world wanted to see. It made it easier to ignore the truth that was staring them in the face for so many years."

My eyes stray back to the blinking camera, capturing every last traitorous syllable. In the years since Harrowdean, I swore I'd never tell. As long as I kept Harrowdean's secrets, my life was safe. But that didn't protect those I sacrificed for my own selfish purposes.

"We're here for the truth," Elliot states simply.

"I'm not sure the world is ready to hear it."

"But are you ready to tell it?"

Hesitating, years of silence hold my tongue hostage. I've never told my story before, and for good reason. The world feels no sympathy for people like me. Speaking up now will unleash hell upon me, but after years of torment, I've finally taken my therapist's advice. I can no longer live my life in the shadows. This is how I'll heal.

I need to exist.

I need to speak up.

I need... salvation.

Nodding cautiously, I refocus on my clenched fists. "Yes."

"Then tell us, Ripley. What was Harrowdean?"

"For me?"

Elliot's mouth lifts into a kind smile. "Yes."

Trawling back through years of torrid memories, dipped in spilt blood and dusted in the substances I peddled for my own benefit, the truth is a simple admittance of guilt. I find the awful words far too easily.

"Harrowdean Manor was my kingdom to rule."

CHAPTER 1
RIPLEY

PUNCHING BAG – SET IT OFF

Ten Years Earlier

BIPOLAR DISORDER IS A FUCKING BITCH.

Shit, sorry. I meant that to come out better. More hopeful, maybe? But you don't need me to do that. There are plenty of others who write articles for mental health blogs and wear their stability as a badge of honour.

Fuck. Okay, too dark.

Let me start again. My brain has zero filter before a minimum of three macchiatos, and I haven't had caffeine since the day I was taken into custody. Like a simple fucking coffee is going to make us any crazier? I've never heard such crap.

Anyway, I'll amend my statement since we're just talking between friends here. You can handle God's honest truth, right?

Bipolar disorder is a motherfucking cunt.

Better?

Awesome.

Don't get me wrong... The highs are high. Feverishly so. In those bright, otherworldly periods, you become a deity-like figure of supreme power and excellence. A god with all the power and almighty importance such a role would entail.

Those are the good times that doctors don't like to advertise. When they talk about bipolar, they make it sound bad to be so high, you believe that your eyeballs are two giant marshmallows in your head, just waiting to be melted over a campfire.

But the lows?

They're the real kicker.

I once read that when technical divers go deep into the ocean, they have to take several decompression stops on the way back up to prevent themselves from being paralysed by the pressure that's built within their body. That's what the lows feel like to me.

Total paralysis.

The weight of the whole world is pressing down on you— crushing, splintering, overtaking every breath until it feels like you're attempting to breathe fire rather than air. When that pressure builds, it's impossible to avoid the depressive stasis that follows.

I was always an odd child. The lonely orphan, rattling around her absent uncle's cold, impersonal four-story townhouse. I've been on antipsychotics and mood stabilisers ever since the housekeeper found me having a midnight birthday party for my friends on the balcony.

The overpaid London doctors said I was hallucinating my fourteen-year-old ass off and too manic to realise that my so-called friends weren't even real. My horrified uncle, Jonathan, swept me off to an expensive psychiatrist who slapped a nice, neat label on my forehead.

That was it.

Bipolar.

End of story.

From that day forward, a handful of brightly coloured pills converted me into a semi-functional human being who graduated from art school at twenty-one and established her own life. And it worked for several years, until I relapsed and had an episode so bad, I landed myself in here.

After thinking that Martians were attempting to take me away, and if I left my two-bedroom flat in Hackney, I'd break an air lock that surrounded my apartment, Uncle Jonathan signed off on a generous donation to ensure I'd be dealt with quietly.

He easily handed me over to avoid any damage to his public image. Being a prolific financier and investor in the city might have afforded him a luxurious lifestyle that I benefited from growing up, but it didn't allow for a batshit crazy niece, assaulting the pizza delivery guy while manic.

Leaning against an oak tree located off the green quad at the centre of Harrowdean Manor, I await the gaggle of patients making their way towards me. Right on time, as per usual. Everyone knows what day it is. I run a tight ship and never stray from the schedule.

Wednesday afternoon is our designated time slot for contraband collection. Santa Claus is here with gifts, and someone is about to get shit-rich on their self-destructive tendencies. Being the self-proclaimed queen of Harrowdean has its benefits, but I'm just an intermediary. My payment for the illegal crap I peddle comes in other forms.

"Hi, Ripley." Santos reaches me first, his bleary eyes downturned. "My usual, please."

Reaching into my sock, I pull the small plastic wrapper of cocaine from its hiding place. He checks in for more every day or two, and as long as my contraband lines hold steady, I regularly fulfil his order.

"Usual price."

"Uh, well…" He avoids eye contact, shuffling his worn shoes.

"Come on, man. Don't give me that."

"My girlfriend's behind on rent," he rushes to explain.

"She's gonna smuggle the cash in at tomorrow afternoon's visitation after she gets paid. Can I settle up then?"

"Tomorrow?" I raise an eyebrow.

His washed-out eyes finally meet mine, brimming with panic. "Please, Ripley."

"You know the deal."

"It's just one day——"

"No payment, no coke."

"No!" he begs again, dragging his palms down his face. "I need to re-up."

"I'm not a charity. Pay up or fuck off."

Hands trembling, he seizes a handful of my oversized anime t-shirt. "All I'm asking for is twenty-four hours."

Unbothered, I inspect my cuticles. "Not going to happen."

"What is wrong with you, bitch?"

Now he's pissing me off.

Sliding a hand into the waistband of my worn grey sweats, I grasp the metal switchblade I keep stashed at all times for my own protection. Santos's eyes widen as I draw the weapon free and flick out the blade, gesturing with a wave. He quickly releases my shirt.

"Back off or I'll happily paint the ground with your innards and let the guards find your body. They'll take great pleasure in covering it up to avoid filing the damn paperwork."

Cursing under his breath, he raises his hands in surrender, taking several large steps backwards. My blade remains drawn until he slinks away, muttering his displeasure.

I squash the faintest crack of pity trying to grow roots in my heart. Nothing is free in this world. Not even illegal contraband passed between patients like we're fucking prisoners trapped on death row.

My regulars slowly appear over the course of the next hour. Requests vary, week by week. Harrowdean is small enough for me to know all the other patients by name with a maximum occupancy of just sixty people spread across two floors of private bedrooms.

Rae requests blades. Always. She cuts herself until the razors turn blunt then barters for whatever cash she can scrounge in here to buy herself more. Usually by sucking dicks.

We're on friendly terms, but I keep her at arm's length after what happened before I came here. I learned that lesson the day the last person I cared about met a grisly end. Finding my best friend swinging from the ceiling was the worst day of my life.

I've been haunted ever since.

For most patients, it's drugs. Cigarettes. Alcohol. Sometimes weird shit, like the time our resident nympho, Tania, paid me in stolen jewellery for a nine-inch pink dildo complete with ribbed veins. Like I said, weird shit. That isn't even the half of it.

Taking a pack of cigarettes from me, Rick hands over a crumpled ten-pound note while unashamedly checking me out. He's a douchebag, through and through. I hate his guts, but he's a good customer. I'll tolerate his sleaziness for the repeat business his nicotine addiction provides.

"Eyes up, pal."

"You're looking good, Ripley. Nice t-shirt."

Eyes narrowed, I don't take the bait. Unlike some who attempt to escape the reality of being locked in here by dressing fancy as fuck, I'm rarely caught out of my favourite well-washed t-shirts or paint-splattered sweats. I'm not here to impress anyone.

"You hear about Priory Lane?" he asks conversationally.

A deathly chill races down my spine. "What about it?"

Rick tucks the cigarettes into his jeans pocket. "It's under official investigation. Everyone's being relocated until the heat dies down."

The mention of a place I'd love to forget is enough to sour

my stomach. I spent twelve months in Priory Lane before being transferred here to live out the rest of my three-year psychiatric sentence. Not even leaving that hellhole scrubbed away the memory of finding Holly's corpse there.

"Priory Lane will be open again by the end of the week." I huff in derision. "These investigations never last."

"You're not interested in what the authorities may find?"

Suppressing a laugh, I can't help but find his optimism entertaining. We all know these institutes are corrupt as hell and more about profit than the treatment of the unwell.

But they'll never find any dirt in Priory Lane. Hush money shuffled in all the right places will see to that. The truth about our dire circumstances is more known here at Harrowdean, but if anything, the situation is bleaker. No one ever comes here or asks questions.

"I couldn't give a shit." Irritation leaks into my tone.

He lowers his voice. "Scared?"

"Fuck off, Rick."

Feet spread, he eyes me with amusement. I hate the way his tongue skates over his teeth as if he's deep in thought, contemplating how best to get in my head. The dickhead loves to play mind games.

"If these places go under, your little reign of terror comes to an end. You don't mean shit out there in the real world. We all know you're just the warden's bitch."

"Feel free to source your ciggies elsewhere if you have a problem with me."

He straightens, a nasty sneer painted across his lips. "Like where? You own us all."

Damn straight, I do. Everyone in this place belongs to me. Even the ones who don't buy contraband fear the power I have.

"You know, I hope when the police do come knocking to tear this hellhole down, you're the first one they throw under the bus for enabling it all."

"You chose to come here. I heard about what you did." I scan him up and down in disgust. "Did it feel good? Beating that guy to death?"

"Like you're so innocent, psycho."

Humiliation curdles in my gut. "I didn't kill anyone."

"Not for a lack of trying, though. I've heard the gossip. Besides, I'd rather be locked inside a real prison than this twisted shit show."

"You took the deal," I point out.

"If I could go back, I'd never agree to come here. None of us would."

I'm sure Rick and so many of his criminal pals spew the same shit. It makes them feel better, like they can forget they signed up for Harrowdean's glittering rehabilitation program. Duped like the rest of us.

"You committed a crime. It's not my fault you're doing the time."

"People come here to be helped," he argues, two red splotches forming on his cheeks. "This is supposed to be a treatment program. We all know that's a sham, though. Soon, the world will too."

Cruel laughter bubbles out of me. Now he's really starting to piss me off. I'm not above kicking his ass in front of everyone to teach him a lesson about respect.

"Whatever, man." I dismiss him with a wave. "Get out of my face."

"Watch your back, Ripley. I wouldn't want a knife to slip into it."

With a wink, he disappears to smoke and join his friends. I school a perfectly blank expression into place. No one can know the effect his words really have on me. I hate to admit it, but Rick's right.

I've spent the last year building a reputation for myself. Doling out contraband and inflicting a beating where necessary has earned me this hard-ass image. But I can lose it just as quickly. Perhaps it's time I taught these sheep a lesson to remind them who's in charge.

My eyes connect with Noah's pale brown orbs from across the lawn. He's slumped over at his usual picnic bench, mouthing the words *half an hour* with a raised brow.

I shoot him a thumb's up, anticipation already rolling down my spine. This new friends with benefits arrangement is working nicely. What? A girl's gotta eat. Especially when the excess energy grows too unbearable, inching its way into mania-territory.

Noah is a gangly, fellow manic depressive who got transferred here less than a month ago. He's tolerable for now. The others all want to fuck me too, I'm not denying that. But only to score themselves some free gear.

Noah's different. Lengthy periods of depression will do that to you. He's far too numb to mastermind an elaborate scheme to win me over to score himself a free spliff or whatever shit he's into.

I like that about him. The brokenness hidden behind his sad eyes and slumped shoulders is its own safety net. He's incapable of feeling anything too deeply. Therefore, he can't get attached. This arrangement is only temporary.

By the time I've offloaded this week's deliveries with no further incident, it's almost time for my dick appointment. I cast Elon—my least favourite grunt and assigned guard—a nod as I pass him on the way to my room on the fifth floor.

"Any problems?" he queries.

There's no sense lying to him. His gunmetal eyes catch everything. He's stocky and well-built, his closely cropped hair accentuating the harshness of his features. The man is as ugly and rough around the edges as they come.

"Nothing I can't handle."

"What does that mean?" His voice is a lazy drawl.

"It's been taken care of."

"You're supposed to keep them under control, inmate. Fail to do that and alternative arrangements can be made."

"That won't be necessary." I swallow the trepidation bubbling in my throat.

"For your sake, I hope not."

Grinning creepily, he gestures for me to continue up the winding, mahogany staircase that services the east wing. The beady, painted eyes of countless original paintings follow me, denoting various long-dead old bastards in white wigs and frilly suits.

Harrowdean Manor is the smallest of six privately-owned institutes spread across the United Kingdom. Nestled in the quiet, inconspicuous countryside of the rural midlands, it's a sprawling, Victoria-era manor house straight off the pages of history books that tell the tale of long-gone asylums.

Only, this one isn't long gone.

Far from it.

Hidden in a secretive forest of juniper and willow trees, Harrowdean is a gothic monster split across four huge wings—dorms, classes, therapy rooms and utilities like the cafeteria and library. It's a whole world locked behind dramatic stained glass, tall archways and crisscrossed bay windows.

Decades ago, it was converted into a home for the mentally unstable, including those deemed too fucked for prison.

Most people end up here one of two ways. Some are criminals, offered a shiny lifeline that enables them to escape jail time by agreeing to a three-year sentence in the experimental program.

But the rest of us? We're genuinely insane.

And I'm talking fucking *clinical*.

I didn't joyride in a celebrity's limo or burn a handsy relative alive. Yes, both true stories I've heard. I wish my story was that interesting. Instead, my manic ramblings were silenced, and I was shipped off to avoid causing my uncle more bad press.

Harrowdean wasn't even my first stop on the crazy train. Sedated and restrained, I was taken to the bigger, northern branch first—the infamous, and apparently under threat, Priory Lane. Fuck, how I'd love to see that slice of hell burn along with everyone in it.

Passing other patients in the carpet-lined halls, most avert their eyes. They all know I'm top dog. If you want anything illegal in here, I'm the girl to speak to. And that role grants me the respect, and more importantly, the fear, that I relish in without shame.

"Rip!"

Sighing, I halt outside my bedroom door, *Room Seventeen*. Rae is several doors down on the same floor. Dark-brown, almost black eyes lined with thick kohl, she flashes me a toothy smile from beneath her voluminous auburn curls.

"You know my name," I drone back, gripping the door handle. "At least bother to finish it."

With an eye roll, she lays her deep, raspy voice on thick. "Ripley. Satisfied?"

"Overjoyed." I begrudgingly release the knob and turn to face her. "What do you want?"

"I'm out. The last pack you gave me were dull."

"It's not like I can just nip down to the drug store and find the good, sharp razor blades for you to slice yourself up with. I'm beholden to others too."

"Yeah, whatever. I want the good ones."

Darkness creeps in. It blooms in the pits of my mind, metastasising with the weight of my guilt. I prefer the days when I'm too fucking high—or even better, too fucking depressed—to give a shit what she does with those razors.

But those in-between periods of lucidity as I wait for the bipolar roller coaster to regain speed are the most destructive.

The days when I have to contend with the consequences of my decisions. At least when I'm off my head on imbalanced dopamine, I don't care who gets hurt.

Semi-sane Ripley cares.

Way too much.

"Ripley?" she whines. "You with me?"

Licking my lips, I force moisture into my mouth. "Fine, I'll figure it out. Now fuck off, Rae."

She grins back. "Love you too, doll face."

"Uh-huh."

Flipping her off, I quickly scan the keycard that unlocks my bedroom door and escape into the cool comfort. Early January daylight barely penetrates the darkness inside.

I keep the curtains drawn over the barred window. The dark drapes rest on an anti-ligature rack, held up by magnets. I keep minimal personal effects around, but the folding photo frame depicting the last family trip with my parents rests at my bedside.

Safely hidden, my eyes burn, but I refuse to release the moisture swelling inside. Looking at that photograph, I can still remember when the social worker sat me down and told me my mum wasn't coming home.

It was a hit and run. Dead on collision. I didn't discover those details until years later when I was old enough to pry into her death. Dad had passed a little over a year earlier from heart failure. Faster than blinking, I became an orphan.

Don't think, don't feel.

That's how to survive, Ripley.

I've lived by those words since my childhood. But part of me wonders how liberating it would be to let all the pain and grief I've been quelling since I stared at that social worker overwhelm me.

If I was consumed by that wave, perhaps I wouldn't float back to the surface again. Perhaps I'd finally be free of Holly's ghost still haunting me. I may rule this kingdom, but I built it for her.

Finding her dead ruined me.

They ruined me.

CHAPTER 2
LENNOX

HATEFUL – POST MALONE

"ARE WE THERE YET?"

Jerked out of my simmering anger that's built over the hours-long drive through the midlands, I focus on the view outside the window. Concrete motorways and impoverished cities have been swallowed by empty countryside.

We're surrounded by frost-bitten fields, dotted with the occasional livestock. Even the sheep look miserable. It's a little more built up than the north of the country, but we're far from the nearest town or city.

"Not yet," I grunt back.

"We've been driving for hours."

"Just be grateful we're being transferred together."

Sighing through his nostrils, Raine tilts his head back and lets it hit the chair cushion. His long fingers are tangled together, wringing and twisting. He'd never admit to it, but I know he's nervous as hell.

It fucking pisses me off. I hate that everything he knows, the safety systems he's put in place that allow him to function, have all been torn away.

Priory Lane is being ripped apart as we speak. Some ex-patient talked, probably thinking they were doing us a favour.

That couldn't be further from the truth. Our files were stamped for immediate relocation when the institute's doors closed.

Glancing across the narrow aisle that separates the transfer van, I try to catch my best friend's eye. Xander stares straight ahead, a bored look on his face.

He's utterly unfazed, as per usual. Some days, I'd happily beat him black and blue just to elicit a hint of emotion. His lack of concern or even annoyance is infuriating.

The handful of others all cuffed and shoved onto this rattling piece of scrap emblazoned with Priory Lane's coat of arms don't dare speak in our presence. It's good to see that our authority is upheld even outside our territory.

We'll need that dog-like obedience to continue if we're to survive whatever lays ahead. If it's anything like the last place, this institute is just another torture chamber hidden by slick marketing and the public's disinterest in the mentally ill.

We will take it just like we took Priory Lane—hard, fast and with force.

Cuffed hands gripping the back of the chair in front of me, I clench the cheap plastic until it creaks and splits. That gains Xander's attention. He spares me a cold glance, his midnight-blue eyes devoid of understanding. My emotions run hot, much to his disdain.

"Don't say it," I bark at him.

"Pull yourself together, Nox."

"How are you not freaking out about this transfer?"

He shrugs nonchalantly. "I'm not concerned."

"You should be!"

Nothing rattles Xander. Not after what we endured together, months before Raine came along. Xander has always had little empathy, but the slivers of human vulnerability that remained were quickly beaten out of him in Priory Lane.

Returning his attention to the mist-soaked scenery outside the window, Xander ignores me. I didn't actually expect a response. But fuck if it wouldn't feel good to see his airtight control falter, even for a second.

Silence reigns until the winding road ends at the entrance to the rural estate. We drive through a huge, wrought-iron archway sandwiched between brick pillars.

Adorned with twisted vines and perfectly formed roses, the garish crest at the apex of the gate denotes two letters: HM. A signed death warrant that's stamped on our thick case files.

Harrowdean Manor.

"We're here," I whisper to Raine.

Adjusting the round, blacked-out glasses balancing on his straight nose, he nods detachedly. His hands are trembling, despite his poor attempts to hide it by forming fists. A thin sheen of sweat coats his forehead too.

With the long journey and constant supervision, he hasn't been able to get high today. I should've known this would happen. But dealing with his inevitable withdrawals is low on my list of concerns right now.

This is our new home.

The kingdom we must conquer to survive.

Along the winding, cobblestone driveway, weeping willows sway in the cool winter air. Up ahead, Harrowdean looks pretty small in comparison to the institute we've unwillingly left behind.

Relief momentarily extinguishes the furious fire that's constantly burning in my veins. Hell, this will be easy. It's tiny in comparison to Priory Lane's sprawling compound of buildings.

"Small," Xander comments.

"Good news for us. We can figure shit out fast and get back on top."

Quickly counting six floors marked by dark windows and glossy ivy strangling the red-brick exterior, a smile tugs at my mouth. This will be even easier than I thought.

The whole institute appears to be based in one huge

manor house with the odd smaller building dotted around. Most of the offshoots look abandoned. If everyone is housed inside, we can take control of such a small population easily.

Parking outside the wide-set entrance steps flanked by more pillars, a tall, narrow-shouldered man awaits with the usual black-clad security presence. His fine suit and prominent gold tie pin betray his identity.

I recognise him from those expensive brochures that always seem to be floating around in the institutes. This guy features in all the phony marketing materials.

The warden's here to greet his newest arrivals.

"Hold onto me," I mutter.

"I'm fine," Raine murmurs back.

"Jesus, man. Just hold my fucking sleeve or something."

"I said I'm fine."

Biting back the urge to cave his head in, I grab his hand and move it to my arm, forcing him to grip my coat sleeve. His lips are pressed in a tight line as I guide him down from the van with Xander leading the way.

The others fall behind us without a single word uttered. No one dares move before we do. After disembarking, we're quickly scanned with wands to search for weapons, and our bags are confiscated to be searched.

I play close attention to Raine's violin case as it's scanned and combed through. If anyone dares cause trouble for him, it'll be the last thing they do. I don't let anyone give Raine shit.

The warden plasters on a smile that doesn't reach his eyes. "Morning all. I'm Mr Abbott Davis, the warden here at Harrowdean."

There's a murmur of greetings.

"So who do we have here?"

"Xander Beck, *Warden*."

Davis studies Xander with an appraising look. "Mr Beck."

Lifting his slim wrists to be un-cuffed, Xander doesn't flinch beneath Davis's watchful stare. The warden's lip curls at the power move. He knows exactly who we are and what we were to Priory Lane's regime.

"Sir." A blonde-haired guard approaches with a clipboard. "All inmates accounted for. These six complete our arrivals from Priory Lane."

Davis nods, still staring down Xander's icy glare. "Excellent. Please show our new arrivals inside."

Gritting my teeth hard enough to physically hurt, I swallow down the barrage of abuse that wants to escape. Being cuffed and dragged about like sacks of meat feels fucking degrading after all we've done for the powers that be behind our captors.

"What's happening?" Raine grunts.

"Stick with me."

"I can walk alone."

"Doesn't mean you have to."

Awkwardly gripping his guide stick in one cuffed hand, he purses his lips. He's at a disadvantage without the gift of sight, but no matter his pride, Raine knows we'd never let anyone set a damn hand on him. Not while I'm breathing. I've lost enough people I care about.

We all follow the guards inside. Xander will have a plan. I trust his judgement. The tap of Raine's stick against the interior's hardwood floors breaks the oppressive silence as he searches for obstacles.

Harrowdean is as lush as expected. It's all dark, stained wood, glinting crystal chandeliers and panelled walls covered in fancy as fuck artwork. The well-lit reception is small and leads to a grand staircase, splitting off in different directions.

CCTV cameras are fixed at multiple strategic angles, of course. Heaven forbid management fail to capture the material they're so desperately seeking. That's another dark secret, though. One of many.

"Stick." A guard stops at Raine's side.

He tilts his head. "Nope."

"Not a request, little freak."

Forcing Raine behind me, I move to block the guard's approach. "You really gonna stoop that low?"

The asshole sneers at me. "Just doin' my job. Lord knows what illegal contraband he's got stashed in that thing."

"There's nothing in it," Raine defends.

"Hand it over, inmate."

Meeting Xander's eyes, his mouth is a flat line, the only hint at his underlying emotions. The fucking robot isn't going to intervene? Fine. He may wield his words as a bloodless weapon, but these wankers don't listen to reason.

"Nox," Raine warns, doing his weird, mind-reading perceptive shit.

How he somehow manages to read us despite not being able to see our bodies or facial expressions, I'll never know. Raine's perceptive by necessity and highly attuned to other people's emotions.

He sees beyond the usual social cues the rest of us are so easily distracted by. But I don't need analysing right now. Ignoring him, I seize a handful of the guard's black t-shirt and wrench him closer.

My movements are limited with the cuffs cinched tight around my wrists, but I can still smash my forehead into his nose to elicit a delicious *crack* that makes me drool with satisfaction.

"Leave him the fuck alone," I threaten.

The guard's wail of pain is music to my ears. I manage to lift my hands quickly enough to get two awkward punches in, causing him to fall flat on his ass, blood dribbling down his chin.

Tackled from the side by another guard, I'm soon eating a faceful of the polished wood floor. My entire body hums with electric rage, setting my nerves alight and incinerating all sense of reason.

I buck and thrash, attempting to throw off whoever is

pinning me to the floor. I'll kill them all. If we're not gonna rule this place, then we'll burn it to the ground instead. I won't go back to being a specimen.

"Ah. Mr Nash, I presume?" Davis crouches down on my left. "Your reputation precedes you."

"Gee, thanks." I turn my head to look at him.

"It isn't a compliment. Are you that determined to spend your first night here in solitary confinement?"

"You wouldn't dare. Don't you know who we are?"

He casts a critical eye over me. "I think it's quite clear that I do."

"Then why the hell are we still here?"

"Because you are my patient like anyone else now. Your previous arrangement is null. We run our own operations at Harrowdean Manor."

"Warden Aldrich assured us this would be a smooth transition." Xander hasn't moved an inch, still wearing that inscrutable look. "We had an *agreement* after the events of last year."

Davis scoffs in genuine amusement. "I don't care how Aldrich ruled his patients. He's under investigation now, isn't he? This is my institute, and you are under my care. Fall in line or face the repercussions."

Fuck, fuck, fuck.

After losing everything, we survived Priory Lane by taking the lifeline we were offered. A chance to escape the clinician's sadistic program and serve a greater purpose. Without that, we're as vulnerable as the rest of these lunatics.

Gaze connecting with Xander's dead eyes, he offers the tiniest shake of his head. *Fucking fine, dickhead.* He wants to play this smart instead of smashing shit. We'll see how well that strategy works.

"Sure," I grit out. "Care to call your attack dog off?"

Smiling thinly, Davis stands and smooths his charcoal suit

.trousers. "At ease, Langley. Our angry friend here will keep a lid on his temper."

The heavy weight on my back vanishes. I'm free to awkwardly stand. Hands white-knuckled on his guide stick, Raine is staring straight ahead behind his black lenses, appearing checked out.

I know he's hanging on to every verbal clue to decipher what's happening. Most assume he's zoned out when he does this, but he's actually picking apart every last sound and scent.

"Let's get this show on the road, shall we?" Davis looks between us all. "Much like Priory Lane, classes and weekly therapy are mandatory. Your previously chosen educational subjects will be accommodated."

"Where are the dorms?" a quieter patient asks.

"The east wing is assigned for residential use. Utilities can be found in the west wing, with classes and therapy rooms spread between the north and south. Other buildings are off-limits."

The urge to ask sizzles through me. What about the rest? We know from first-hand experience what he's deliberately omitting from his explanation. More lies beyond this whistle-stop tour. The real purpose behind this institute.

"Your previous IDs will suffice," Davis continues. "Keycards will be issued for your assigned rooms along with schedules. Some of you will have to bunk up."

Our bags, now searched and declared clear of any contraband, are dumped back at our feet by more of Davis's obedient lapdogs. Scooping up mine and Raine's bags, I touch his hand to guide it back to his violin case. He wouldn't dare entrust anyone else with his precious baby's safety.

Sparing us all an authoritative glower, Davis adjusts his silk tie. "Heed the lessons learned from your last incarceration. I won't tolerate any trouble."

I swear, the corner of Xander's mouth twitches infinitesimally. But it's gone so quickly; I have to wonder if I imagined it. Beneath his iceman persona, we all know that trouble is his fucking middle name.

"Follow the rules, complete your sentence and go home." Davis nods like it's that easy. "Welcome to Harrowdean Manor."

Yeah… Fucking welcome.

CHAPTER 3
RIPLEY
DEAD OR ALIVE – STILETO & MADALEN DUKE

QUAKING WITH ANXIETY, *I tentatively step out of the dorms and peer around the quad. It's my first day here. Priory Lane is truly massive. Countless antiquated Victorian buildings are dotted around, looming and oppressive in the frigid winter air.*

Curious eyes stray my way from other patients lingering nearby, chatting and basking in a rare blast of cold sunshine. It's colder here than I'm used to. London usually retains some of its sweatbox status in the winter. I think it may actually snow here.

"Hey! Newbie. Over here."

Squinting, I catch a flash of bouncy hair. A tall, willowy woman is waving at me from across the grass. Her oval-shaped face is pretty in a fairy-like way. She's rugged, visibly several years older than me. When she sees me hesitating, she rolls her eyes.

"I don't bite. Just saying hey, neighbour."

"Neighbour?" I inch down the stone steps.

"Your room's across from mine."

"Oh."

Another patient sidles up to the woman, eyes nervously darting from side to side. She reaches out a hand, and they exchange a quick, perfunctory shake. Something is passed between them before the other patient scuttles away with a muttered, "Thank you."

I'm shocked to silence. I thought this place was meant to be some kind of rehabilitation program, yet here this chick is, dealing drugs in broad daylight without a single care. It's hard not to be impressed.

"Can I get ya something?"

I stop at the edge of the grass, close enough to see the calculating gleam in her eyes. "Like what?"

"Anything you want."

The relentless itching in my veins forces me to ask, despite my determination to remain invisible for the next three years. If I don't paint or sketch soon, I'll be staring down the barrel of yet another manic episode.

"Charcoal pencils? And a sketchpad?"

Snorting, she doubles over with a short laugh. "Do I look like a fucking art supply store?"

"You said anything I want."

"People usually ask for stuff that's a little more… irregular."

I shrug dismissively. "I'll pass on the hard stuff, thanks. I didn't get time to pack all my supplies before they took me away, and my useless uncle has pretty much disowned me. So pencils it is."

"What did you do?" she chortles.

Biting my lip, a smile breaks free. "Might've accused the pizza guy of being a Martian and gone on a rampage that made the news. You know, the usual world-ending stuff for prissy family members."

"Clearly." Considering for a moment, she looks me over. "Fuck your family. I can get your damn pencils."

"How much?"

"Consider it a welcome gift. You got a name?"

"It's Ripley."

She outstretches her wrinkled hand for me to clasp. "Holly. Stick with me, kid. You'll be alright."

Quickly shaking her hand, I catch sight of two other patients hanging nearby in the shadows of the tree line. Rather than approaching to strike up a deal with her, they're silent, creepily watching us.

Two pairs of contrasting eyes track our every move—one belonging to an over-muscled boulder of a man. His eyes are filled with burning anger that corrupts his pale seafoam irises visible beneath his mop of tousled, chocolate hair.

The other is a stark comparison. Where his companion is all muscles and rage, he's slim and birdlike, his platinum hair paler than fresh snow. He wears his midnight-blue eyes with absolute detachment. Not a single hint of emotion belies his intense stare.

"Friends of yours?" I whisper, unnerved by the attention.

When Holly tracks my line of sight back to the pair, her easy-going persona falters, showing a glimpse of something darker. It flickers across her features like bubbling storm clouds, casting a foreboding shadow that promises retribution.

The broad mountain with fiery eyes offers a smirk before walking away, his ghostly pale friend following behind. Nothing that passes between them and Holly could be classed as friendly; I feel like I've inadvertently stepped into a minefield between two enemy lines.

"Hell no," Holly mutters curtly. "If you know what's good for you, kid, you'll stay the fuck away from those two."

Jerking upright, a cold sweat clings to my skin. I'm shaking so hard, it feels like my body is vibrating. The memory rests at the forefront of my mind after clawing its way out of my mental lockbox while I fitfully slept.

My nightmares are usually reserved for high-definition retellings of my parents' deaths. Not so much Dad's heart attack. My mind prefers to imagine how Mum's car crash unfolded while I was safely at home with a babysitter as she travelled back from a girls' night.

But not tonight.

Instead, Holly is haunting me.

I can feel salty droplets clinging to my body in the darkness of my bedroom. Scrubbing my face, I drag in a breath. She isn't here. I'm alone in my room at Harrowdean, far from the clinging horrors of last year.

Being turned over to the care of Priory Lane was the most terrifying moment I've ever experienced. Far scarier than losing my family, being confronted by my own delusions or even the resignation in my uncle's eyes as I shared my diagnosis.

It was the moment I lost all control.

My life no longer belonged to me.

The moment I stepped out of Uncle Jonathan's town car and into the northern chill, I knew my life was over. Three-year rehabilitative program or not. There was no coming back from being practically disowned by your only remaining family and forcibly confined to a psych ward.

Shoving back the bedsheets, I try to sit up but waver. My limbs are heavy and feel like they're wrapped in cotton wool. Numbing paralysis pumps through my veins, cutting off feeling to my extremities.

Depression is a silent but deadly weight that I know all too well. It's been a few weeks since my last down episode, but I recognise my own warning signs. The ups and downs are a regular part of my life now.

While others may feel the darkness creeping into their minds, the first thing to go is my ability to move like a normal human being. It's the technical diving effect playing out in real time.

Just get up, Ripley.

Fucking move.

You're in control of your own body.

But the awful truth is… I'm not. I haven't been for a long time. My brain doesn't belong to me; it belongs to my illness. That cruel bitch calls all the shots around here. I'm just along for the ride. Powerless to the rising tide approaching to decimate my self-control all over again.

"Come on," I whisper weakly. "Please, just move."

By the time I've worked up the will to move my leaden limbs, the sun is almost threatening to rise. I struggle to remain upright as I stumble through scattered art supplies to the attached ensuite, hands outstretched to stop myself from falling.

The plastic surface of the mirror above the sink distorts my reflection as I wait for the shower to heat up. I've always kept my hair short. More often than not, half the tight curls are shoved up in a sloppy knot and secured with a paintbrush, leaving stray, tawny-brown ringlets to tickle my jawline.

My wide, round, hazel eyes are more green than brown, framed by thick lashes that cast shadows across my lightly freckled cheeks and slightly upturned button nose. I straighten my silver septum ring with a sigh then step into the shower.

It takes scrubbing my ink-swirled skin to within an inch of its life with my favourite papaya body wash to remove the remnants of my nightmare. Holly sometimes infiltrates my dreams, but those two demons haven't shown their faces for a while.

Teeth gritted, I scrub hard enough to leave dark purple lines from my nails. *Bastards. Bastards. Bastards.* My mental chant accompanies my scrubbing, on and on, until I'm bright-red and aching from my own bodily assault. But at least I can feel my limbs again.

Making myself step out of the spray, I wince at the sting of cool air against my abused skin. I'm not like Rae. Pain isn't my thing. But hating every inch of myself sure as hell is, and a violent shower helps tame the thoughts of self-loathing long enough to reconstruct my mask each day.

I've convinced myself that if one day I scrub hard enough, I'll be able to rip the very skin from my bones and tear free from this carcass holding me prisoner. If I leave this body behind, perhaps I can leave my sins with it.

Until then, I must live with the monstrous person I've become. Some days that's easier than others. I can slip into a human skin suit and play the role I've been given. But other times, it's excruciating.

After drying off, I grab my discarded grey sweatpants from the floor and throw on a loose, acid-wash t-shirt. With each breath, I piece my careful façade back together. Another section of my armour is replaced, layer by layer, until the vulnerable version of Ripley is safely hidden.

The world can never know she exists.

Weakness would be my downfall.

By the time I grab my keycard and throw on a hoodie, my familiar, hard-faced scowl is safely back in place. I've got a date with a to-go breakfast and the unfinished canvas sitting in Harrowdean's studio. Aside from the weekly art therapy sessions, I usually get the place to myself.

It's early enough for only the non-sedated patients to be braving the cafeteria. The usual breakfast rush doesn't hit until at least nine o'clock when the previous night's court-sanctioned sedation inevitably wears off for everyone else.

Down the winding staircase that descends from the fifth floor of the east wing, the lavish decor and glimmering chandeliers fail to impress me. That's how they suck you in—a luxurious, well-polished exterior, crafted to conceal the truth.

That doesn't stop the private sponsors from lavishing the institute with donations so they can proudly pronounce themselves as mental health advocates. It's all shallow. Performative. No one actually cares if we're rehabilitated or not, as long as we're safely out of sight, and therefore, out of mind.

"Langley," I greet stiffly.

One foot propped behind him, the usual morning guard spares me a glance. He's tall and well-built, his tanned biceps straining against the soft material of his black shirt.

He's always been friendly to me. Sometimes suspiciously so. He's cute in a boyish way with his dark hair and fuzz-covered jawline.

"Morning, Rip. You're up early."

"Got a project calling my name in the studio."

Bright-blue eyes scanning over me, he frowns slightly. "Anyone causing ya trouble?"

"Nothing I can't handle on my own."

When his aquamarine eyes soften, I cast a cursory look around, ensuring no one is watching. I like Langley. Unlike some of the warden's well-paid thugs, he has a heart. Shame I can't afford to have any form of attachment in this place.

But in here, I don't get to have friends. Connections. *Weaknesses.* There's a reason why I keep everyone at arm's length. I'm here to do one thing. Survive. And I'll take myself out long before I let anyone break me again.

"Anyone gives you shit, I want to know about it." He moves to rest a hand on the baton strapped to his hip. "Contrary to what you may think, you're not alone in here."

"I've been alone for a long time," I say matter-of-factly. "It has nothing to do with this damn place. Do me a favour and mind your fucking business."

Waiting for the hurt to fill his eyes, I stare for a second longer before walking away. The sooner he stops seeing me as some tragic experiment that's somehow his to protect—from his employer no less—the better.

The cafeteria is located on the ground floor of the west wing. Traipsing down plush corridors adorned with more priceless artwork, I force my exhausted body to obey. Food. Paint. Forget. That's how I'll get through today.

With freshly waxed hardwood floors, cream walls and several long, rectangular tables to house the small patient population, it's practically empty at this hour.

Food awaits on the service line in the uppermost corner. I bypass the hot option and grab some fruit to take away. As I'm grabbing a juice box in lieu of the macchiato I'd rather be drinking, something hard shoves into my shoulder.

I trip and stumble, catching myself on the service line before I faceplant on the floor. Rick offers me an innocent smirk before he turns away with his breakfast tray in hand.

"Sorry, didn't see you there," he coos over his shoulder.

"Seriously?"

"What's up, Rip? No guard dog to kiss your ass today?"

Placing my food down, I snatch the back of his loose blue shirt and yank. He's dragged to a halt long enough for me to slip a foot around his ankle and shove his shoulder, causing him to go flying.

Food splatters across the floor as he lands unceremoniously on his ass. Rick bellows in shock and pain. I stare down at him pathetically rolling around.

"Sorry," I snap angrily. "Didn't see you there either."

"Motherfucker!" he screeches.

"You seem to have egg on your shirt."

Swiping spilt milk from his face, Rick eyes me furiously. "You have a fucking death wish or what?"

"I was perfectly happy minding my own business until you showed up." I tilt my head to stare down at him. "You're cut off. I don't sell to assholes. Spread the word."

Before he can respond, I grab my apple and saunter away with a wink delivered to an open-mouthed Langley, watching everything unfold from his post. He shakes his head at me, lips quirked up as he fights his amusement. What? I told him I could handle myself. Maybe next time, he'll believe me.

The art studio is located in the deserted south wing, at the end of another seemingly endless corridor surrounded by locked classrooms. I swipe my keycard to let myself into the large, shaded space.

Flicking the lights on, the comforting surroundings of my happy place are revealed. No one touches my canvases or supplies—not even Lena, the resident hippy art therapist—so I have a whole corner all to myself.

Everyone knows better than to fuck with my artwork. Like Rick said, being the warden's bitch has its perks. It only cost my soul.

Pulling out my oil paints, I begin to set up. My

paintbrushes are clean and waiting for me. The only exception to people touching my shit is when I use my leverage to get someone to clean up after me. Again, *perks*.

The canvas I'm working on is a disturbing sight. Violent sprays of black, dark-green and crimson form the bleak landscape I'm crafting. It's a horrifying scene, and in the eye of the storm, a single shadowy figure stands.

She's alone. Trapped. Powerless to escape the endless tragedy all around her. My hand flicks, bends and swoops, splattering paint in an unrestrained torrent of previously suppressed rage.

All the emotions I spent my shower time shoving down come rushing back to the surface. I'm not sure where the two additional shadow figures come from in the background, but my hand soon creates them.

Throat parched and stomach rumbling, I barely stop to shove an apple into my mouth. Once I slip into that trance-like state of deep focus, it's impossible to come back to reality. Not until the painting is done and I've spilled my guts onto the canvas.

The lights in the art studio seem to grow brighter, and I distractedly register the sun setting through the room's bay windows. Not even the promise of dinner is enough to release me from my frenzy. It's pitch-black outside by the time I add the final flick of paint and deflate.

Jesus.

Fucking.

Christ.

It takes a lot to scare me after all I've seen, but even I can admit that what I've created is downright terrifying. It looks like a scene from Dante's inferno. The final layer of saturated flames on top of the greyscale shadows completes the hellish landscape.

Bleak.

Apocalyptic.

Beautiful.

Studying my work, I realise that I've been gently swaying to the rhythm of haunting violin music this entire time. Glancing around trying to gauge the source, it sounds distant, leaking through the partially open door leading to the corridor.

My stiff body protests as I move close to the doorway, following the melody. As it's a Sunday, there are no classes taking place. This wing should be deserted. But a few doors down, I can see that one of the classrooms is unlocked, the door slightly ajar.

I've only been into the music room once. A long since discharged patient bent me over the piano and fucked me senseless during one of my hypersexual manic episodes. He was a good lay.

Curiosity drives me to walk towards the classroom. Peeking around the door, I find the room in almost darkness. The only light is from the moon, a waxing crescent spilling through the arched window and illuminating a single figure sat alone in the shadows.

The violinist.

It's… a guy.

With an exquisite instrument tucked beneath his chin, he stares straight ahead into nothingness while playing with masterful control. I have no idea how he can see what he's playing with such dim lighting, but the notes spilling from his fingertips are pure perfection.

I can't make out much beyond the golden sheen of his hair that's illuminated by the moonlight, the strands long on top and roughly shoved back from his lowered face. He's slim but built, his limbs poised to strum the next note. I'm certain that he's new—I don't recognise him and Harrowdean is small enough for me to know everyone.

When the newbie hits a bad note and softly curses, I study his nimble fingers, realising his hands are shaking. It's a familiar tremble. I've seen it enough in my customers when they can't afford to re-up for a few days and go through withdrawals.

Is that why his music is so hauntingly sad?

Am I hearing the ache to shoot himself full of poison?

Hands freezing on the instrument, he tilts his head ever so slightly. It's a subtle cocking motion, like he's listening for the patter of approaching prey, inching closer to his hunting trap.

My heart is beating so loud, I can hear it roaring in my ears. When he speaks, his rough voice slices into my skin like razor blades. There's a delicious raspiness to his intonation.

"Hear something you like?"

Inhaling sharply, I look around like a complete idiot, convinced he's talking to someone else. How the hell does he know I'm listening? I've barely poked my head around the door.

Before I can offer a smart remark, my throat closes up. I don't know if it's the deep, gut-wrenching pain entangled in his music or the raw tenor of his voice, but any clever response I had dries up in my mouth.

"Well?" the violinist prompts.

He still hasn't lifted his head. Not even a glance in my direction. Hands scrunched, my nails dig into my palms. I want to yell at him for breaking my peace when I banked on this wing being empty. Yet not a single syllable spills from my tongue.

"If you're here to gawp, feel free to fuck off." His voice is resigned as he resumes playing the violin. "Your breathing is ruining my concentration."

My... breathing?

"Sorry," I mutter.

Disturbed by this strange creature, I turn on my heel and race away without a second glance. The sound of his crooning instrument hitting every last chord with finesse follows my retreating footsteps.

I return to my canvas to finish up, the sound of his music continuing. Lilting. Anguished. Hitting every note with well-timed perfection. If I wanted to, I could get a guard to heave him away for distracting me.

But I don't.

Instead, I find myself swaying again.

Although we are both lost in our own worlds, we're only metres apart, separated by the thin walls between us. The evocative violin music continues late into the night, long after I've tidied up, stacked the canvas and run out of unnecessary jobs to do.

I mentally scold myself and leave the art studio. As I pass the music room, the door left ajar, I catch another glimpse. The violinist has paused briefly, his instrument in his lap. I watch him lift the back of his hand to his nose.

He snorts up whatever is there, a relieved sigh slipping out of him. His bowed shoulders seem to perk up, and when he returns to his violin, the melody has lightened to a more joyful rhythm. I quickly turn and walk away.

Survival is a personal thing.

Sometimes, it looks a whole lot like self-destruction.

CHAPTER 4
RIPLEY
I'M NOT YOURS – THE HAUNT

"RIPLEY BENNET!"

Startled out of my numb daze at the sound of my name being called, I shuffle forward. The line is moving at a snail's pace this morning. It's always the same on Mondays, when classes and therapy sessions resume.

Harrowdean runs like any other secure unit—relying on a tried and tested combination of regimen, strict order and regular poking and prodding by the on-site clinical staff. All the usual day-to-day banalities of life on a psych ward, at least to the average Joe.

What goes on behind closed doors is a whole other ball game. One that not everyone has to bear witness to. They're blissfully unaware of their privileged position as one of the protected. Patients too risky to be targeted, often with families and loved ones who would notice their turmoil. Not all of us have that benefit.

"Rip." Rae nudges my shoulder. "Hurry the fuck up, would ya?"

"Alright. Don't get your panties in a bunch."

I force myself to approach the nurse's station to collect my meds. The swaying, zombified line of patients behind me all watch with varying degrees of interest.

Some are desperate for their daily dose of sanity, while others are dragged into line by the ever-present guards. The nurse slides a small paper cup brimming with tablets through the hole in the metal grate to me.

They have to keep the pharmacy strictly under lock and key, for obvious reasons. I've lost count of the number of attempted break-ins I've witnessed. Not everyone can afford my services.

One thing Harrowdean has no shortage of are desperate bastards searching for any way to remove themselves from the chess board of life. Pills. Blades. Rope. It's all the same to them.

A quick fix. An easy escape.

Who wouldn't want that?

Hell, everyone heard the story about Blackwood Institute's incident a few months ago. Gossip gets around, even behind bars. From what I hear, some asshole threw himself off the roof.

Bang.

Splat.

Goodnight.

One scrambled set of brains on the hard concrete, and it's game over. They must've been well-connected to even get access to a rooftop. Hearing that news brought my precarious arrangement into sharp focus.

The power my position provides may be keeping me alive right now, but I'm not the only one feeding this toxic machine of exploitation and abuse. Every institute has one of me.

Have you figured out what I am yet?

No spoilers…

Studying the lurid selection of pills in the paper cup, I quickly swallow them down then stick out my tongue to be inspected. The nurse dismisses me with a waved hand.

"Next!"

I'm not on their radar. If I wanted to kill myself, I could do it a lot more quickly and efficiently than by stashing my meds. I haven't lasted this long only to go and throw it all away now. Annihilation isn't my end game here. Survival is, plain and simple.

Watching Rae take her medication, it's obvious the staff are keeping a keen eye on her. I'm pretty sure that she wound up in here after a serious attempt on her life. And here I am, wilfully arming her with more ammunition to continue harming herself.

You can hate me.

It still won't compare to how much I hate myself.

"Gross." Rae shudders, sparing me a puzzled look. "What are you staring at?"

I roll my eyes at her. "None of your business."

"Weirdo. You eat already?"

"Yeah, I've got my session with Doctor Galloway. You off to class?"

Flicking fiery auburn hair over her shoulder, she shrugs. "Maybe. You get my next shipment?"

Shame curling around my internal organs like a poisonous cancer that I'll never hope to cure, I nod back.

"Slipped under your door."

"Sweet. What do I owe you?"

"The usual."

Bouncing on her feet, she's eager to escape. "Can I get you later?"

Glancing around, I ensure no one is listening. Rae is the only exception I'll make to my own personal rules. Call it sentiment or stupidity, but I care about her. Even if I'd never admit it out loud.

"Not like I'm going anywhere."

"You're the best, Rip."

Trust me, I'm really fucking not.

At the promise of a fresh stash of razor blades, her face has transformed. The heavy weight of defeat has evaporated, like darkness lifting after a solar eclipse to reveal the cold light of day once more.

My coping mechanism is detachment. But Rae's? It's the power to inflict pain so great, it offers a twisted form of relief. We are night and day yet bound by the same infallible sickness that trapped us in this purgatory together.

Rushing away to skip class and lock herself in the bathroom until she blunts her newest toys, I'm left with the gut-punching pain of knowing whatever damage she inflicts, I shall forever bear the responsibility. Everything I've done is at the expense of her slow death along with all the others I've armed to destroy themselves.

Walking past the remaining patients picking up their morning meds, I meet a few eyes, taking note of their visible fear and respect. Both emotions inextricably entwined. Luka, an anorexic from the sixth floor, even steps out of line to open the exit door for me.

Doctor Galloway's office is located on the left side of the north wing, past admin rooms filled with dull-eyed staff and the heavy guard presence lingering in the reception area. I'm early as usual.

Leaning against the wall, I'm lost in the intricate swirls of ink that make up the landscape canvas mounted outside her office when the door clicks open. Her familiar lilting voice leaks out from inside.

"You know where to find me if you require additional assistance settling into life here at Harrowdean."

"That won't be necessary," a rough drawl responds.

"We can make adjustments to accommodate your specific needs."

"I managed fine in the last place. I'll be alright here."

"Well, as you wish."

When the door swings open, Doctor Galloway spots me

lingering outside. She's mid-fifties at best, her wrinkled face usually pulled taut in a grimace that deepens her crow's feet. Wearing her silver-streaked hair in a slicked back bun does her ageing appearance no favours.

Today's outfit is another ill-fitting pantsuit and tweed blazer. This woman needs to hire a stylist already. Harrowdean must pay her enough to afford one. Silence is expensive, after all.

"Be right with you, Ripley."

"Sure, doc."

Summoning a tight smile of acknowledgement, she holds open the door to release her last patient. The moment he's unveiled, my heart spasms in my chest. As he makes his way out into the corridor, the bright chandeliers overhead reveal all the details I couldn't make out last night.

His haunting violin music has played on a loop in my mind ever since I found him in the music room. Staring at my mystery violinist, my breath falters. Goddamn, what a sight he is.

Golden hair slicked back, his perfectly proportioned nose and full, thick lips are front and centre. The razor-edge of his jawline is sharp enough to cut metal like it's butter and covered in a light blonde scruff.

A pair of blacked-out glasses on the tip of his nose, his caramel-coloured eyes flick upwards for a brief moment. They're unfocused. Darting around the corridor without ever daring to grace me with their honeyed magnificence.

He rushes to slide the glasses back into place and takes a deep inhale. I don't know why I bite my lip and hold my breath, like somehow if I don't dare steal a single inhale for myself, he won't recognise me.

"No live performance today, babe." The corner of his mouth quirks in an amused smirk. "You'll have to gawp elsewhere."

Eyes hidden from sight, he unclips a folded, plastic stick

that was clasped in one hand. It reaches mid-chest, and the tip is red, extended to reach the floor. That's when the penny drops.

The comforting darkness.

His unfocused gaze.

A strange awareness of my breathing.

He's *blind*.

"See you next week for your next session, Mr Starling."

"Raine is fine."

Doctor Galloway continues to prop the door open for him. "Okay, Raine. Do you need assistance finding the exit?"

"I'll manage," he responds easily. "My friend is meeting me."

"Oh, good. I'm glad you were all transferred together."

"We got lucky," he comments vaguely.

The unusual name befits everything I find weirdly fascinating about this golden-haired man. His seemingly perfect, almost angelic appearance tempered by the memory of his anguished music, played alone and in the shadows. Nothing but his violin and loneliness to hold his hand.

My curiosity is only heightened by the fact that he played like fucking Vivaldi without being able to even see where to place his fingertips. But as I scrutinise him, silently berating myself for being foolish enough to show an ounce of interest, I realise he *can* see.

Perhaps more than I can.

Perhaps more than any of us can.

"Hmm." Raine tilts his head again in that strange, calculating way as he stares in my general direction. "Is it guava?"

"I'm sorry?" I splutter.

His mouth twitches again. "Your body wash. I couldn't place it last night."

I watch his tongue dart out to wet his full lips, almost like he's tasting the air. Brain still short-circuiting, I mentally slap myself hard enough to knock myself back into gear.

"So?" he presses.

"I'm not sure how my choice of body wash is any concern of yours."

Doctor Galloway is watching us like we're some fascinating car crash unfolding. That doesn't stop Raine from studying me with every sense available to him from behind those odd glasses.

"When you disturb my violin practise smelling like a walking smoothie, it becomes my business."

Cocky son of a bitch.

"Then find somewhere else to practise," I snap back.

Steeling my shoulders, I'm about to push past him when footsteps march down the corridor towards us. My back is turned to whoever is approaching as I move to escape into the therapy room.

I can't see the newcomer—I only hear a sonorous, low-pitched bark.

"Raine! You done, man?"

No.

It can't be.

"Yes," Raine replies.

With the creeping agony of ice filling my veins, I'm forced to slowly turn to confirm the nightmare I'm living. As soon as I look, I'll know it's just my imagination.

Wake the fuck up, Ripley.

He isn't here. He can't be here.

I made sure of it the day I left Priory Lane and all its bad memories behind. Those two demons showing up in my dreams can't have been an omen. I made sure they'd never see the light of day again for what they did.

The son of a bitch I buried alive is walking right towards me, those muscle-carved shoulders as broad as ever, bearing the weight of his sadistic cruelty. My demons have escaped their state-funded prison.

I'm staring at Lennox Nash.

Gorgeous.

Insane.

Categorically evil.

When his pale, seafoam eyes land on me, I have the pleasure of seeing his utter shock. Clearly, he also didn't expect to be running into a ghost this morning. I have a split second to summon a perfectly blank expression.

"Lennox." My voice is flat and emotionless. "It's been a long time."

We've played this game before. It doesn't take long for his shock to vanish, replaced with his ever-present rage. Lennox is the definition of angry man syndrome.

He's furious with the whole fucking world and out to solve all his problems with his fists. Those muscles weren't made in the gym, though he spends most of his time in it. Lennox's strength comes from a lifetime of fist fights.

Long overdue for a shave, his round jaw is smothered in dark-chocolate hair. Those furious, deep-lidded eyes sit above a slightly upturned nose, marred by a small bump above the bridge. No doubt cracked beneath knuckles during one of his countless fights.

A small silver ring glints in his left ear, matching the silver chains peeking out of his white t-shirt. The fitted sweatpants that hug his tight ass and bulging thighs should be prohibited. I hate that he's so goddamn attractive.

"Tell me this is a joke." He halts several metres away. "For your sake, I better be imagining this shit."

My hands curl into balls at my sides. I'll fight my way out of this if I have to. Make no mistake, Lennox isn't the kind of man to allow his enemies to escape unscathed.

I went for the jugular the day I left Priory Lane behind, uncaring of the consequences of my actions. If he didn't hate me before, he sure as fuck does now. I made sure they knew who arranged their misfortune.

"Shouldn't you be dead by now?" I clip out.

Lennox's lip curls, baring his perfect teeth in a snarl. "Was that your plan?"

"I'm disappointed that you thought I intended anything else."

Our audience looks as bemused as I feel by his sudden appearance. Doctor Galloway is lingering in the doorway to her office, seeming conflicted as to whether she should intervene or not. Raine's head swivels back and forth, tracking the sound of our voices.

Arms folded across his barrel chest, Lennox glares at me with enough fury to melt the skin from my bones. I can almost feel the individual skin cells catching alight and turning to liquid mulch.

Those light-green eyes once terrified me. But I needn't have feared him or his best friend. In the end, it wasn't my blood they wanted. They settled for stealing my soul and trampling it to pathetic, irreparable pieces.

"We were almost killed!" he yells.

"Well, Nox..." I unleash a sadistic smile. "*You* killed *me* first."

"Clearly, I didn't do a good enough job of it." Nostrils flaring, his voice is a spine-chilling warning.

"Clearly."

"Don't worry, Rip. I won't make the same mistake again."

It happens so fast, Doctor Galloway is powerless to intervene. He closes the distance between us in a flash. Raine is shoved aside as Lennox lunges forward to attack, his huge hands easily finding my throat.

Slammed against the wall, pain radiates through my skull when the back of my head connects with the hard brick. His scarred hands are two huge clamps squeezing the very air from my windpipe, worsened by the sharp bite of his nails digging into my flesh.

I grab his wrists, attempting to wrestle myself free. My lungs are on fire. Burning. Smouldering. A scorching torrent blazing ever stronger behind my ribcage. He's actually going to kill me this time.

Maybe I'll enjoy it.

My empire of sin will die with me.

"Nox!" Raine yells.

At the same time, Doctor Galloway speaks up. "Stop it!"

But still, my attacker refuses to relent. He's determined to choke me to death for every last ounce of pain I arranged to be inflicted upon him. I doubt any achievement of mine will ever compare.

"Do you have any idea what they did to us?" Lennox spits, his saliva hitting my face. "Or the twisted shit I had to watch them do to my best friend?"

Abandoning my futile attempts to overpower him, I settle for kneeing him in the dick instead. Thankfully, it's far more effective, causing him to finally release me so I can breathe. Each inhale is an excruciating wheeze.

"He d-deserved to have his insides p-plucked out and examined!" I huff between gulps of air. "I h-hope they tore him apart and m-made you watch the show."

Cupping his sore Crown Jewels, Lennox shoots me a glare. "I'm going to enjoy doing the exact same thing to you."

The old Ripley would've run away screaming and locked herself in her dorm room. She would've let Holly protect her from the Big Bad Wolf and comforted herself with falsehoods like *it'll be okay.*

But not this Ripley.

She isn't the victim.

She's the fucking predator now.

Catching my breath, I force my voice to steady. "I'm not a

scared girl anymore. That person died alongside her best friend. But you'd know all about that, wouldn't you?"

The smug grin that overtakes his expression is yet another kick in the teeth. I'll surrender every ounce of power I've carefully cultivated here for the chance to wipe it from his goddamn face.

"How is your precious friend?" Lennox taunts as he straightens. "What was her name again?"

Not even the distant sound of Doctor Galloway calling for security stops me. Hurling myself at him, I'm determined to drain every last drop of life from his veins.

Just like he did to me.

Just like he did to *her*.

"You know her name!" I tackle him to the thickly carpeted floor. "I hope her memory haunts you both!"

The sound of Raine's shouts doesn't stop us from battling. We tangle together and roll, both grappling for the upper hand. I know he won't go down without a fight, but any ounce of self-preservation I had has been obliterated.

I don't care about survival right now. Fuck the countless lives I've sacrificed to protect my own worthless hide. I'll give it all up for the chance to draw blood. To repay him for the life he so cruelly stole.

Lennox Nash deserves to die.

And I want the privilege of claiming the kill.

Knuckles crunching and skin splitting, I inflict as many blows as I can before the thunder of security approaching causes me to falter. Lennox is beneath me, a stunning curtain of blood pouring from his split eyebrow.

"You're in my institute now." I lean close to whisper menacingly. "This time, I'll be the one to take everything from you."

"Like hell!" he roars.

"Be afraid, Nox. Be fucking afraid."

With my parting shot fired, I let my body go limp. I'm

easily plucked off him and dragged backwards by two guards. A bubble of hysterical laughter inches up my throat, and I gladly release it.

"Take her to the warden's office!" Doctor Galloway demands. "Now!"

"She's a psychopath." Lennox swipes dribbles of blood from his face. "Put her in solitary and throw away the damn key."

"You'll be joining her for inciting violence, Mr Nash!"

Poor, foolish Galloway.

She has no idea what she's dealing with. Lennox and his sadistic best friend only speak the language of violence, and a night in a padded cell won't ever change that.

A pair of hands loop under my arms, then my ankles are seized. Lifted into the air, I don't even fight it. Trying to run from Harrowdean is futile. Its irrevocable sickness gets us all in the end.

As I'm carried away to whatever punishment lies ahead, all I can see is the slight upturn of Raine's lips. It isn't happiness contorting his features. Not even amusement. He just heard me attempt to kill his friend.

And somehow…

He looks impressed.

CHAPTER 5
RAINE

ALL THE WAYS I COULD DIE –
ARROWS IN ACTION

TAP. *Tap. Tap.*

Lost in the vast expanse of blackness that paints my vision, I rely on the ever-present beat of my guide stick. My life has been reduced to that incessant, steering tap, counting out each pace to be committed to memory.

Fourteen steps forward. Five left. Rough cotton bedsheets. Three steps right. The sleek metal of a built-in lamp. Six steps back. Smooth wooden wardrobe doors. More cotton folded neatly inside.

That's how I know Xander unpacked my shit for me. The obsessively folded piles. He's as meticulous about his space as he is his carefully chosen words.

Tap. Tap. Tap.

You know, "experts" say that eighty percent of human perception comes from the eyes. Vision. It's by far the most important sense of the five. When our other senses fail us, our eyes will always protect us from danger.

But who can see the incoming threat, the approaching tiger salivating over its prospective prey, when your eyeballs are two useless lumps of meat in your skull? I may as well be walking around with two empty sockets where my eyes should be.

Fingertips gliding over stacked clothing, I explore the over-washed fabric, searching for signs of my favourite t-shirt. It's a remnant of a past life. The memory of its charcoal-grey colour and neon band slogan are fuzzy in my memory after five years of nothingness.

There.

I can feel the frayed edges and smattering of holes in the fabric. Unlike some, I couldn't give a fuck what I look like to others. You quickly stop caring about being judged when your whole existence is ripped away by a doctor in a white coat that you can no longer see.

Tugging the t-shirt over my head, I smooth my mop of hair away from my eyes. I keep it longer on top but shoved back as the strands distract me when they tickle my face. It used to be golden-blonde, brighter than the sun, but I haven't seen my reflection since I was eighteen.

I'm sure for a lot of people, losing their vision two days after coming of age would be the end of their life. And in some ways, it was for me. But the narcotic abuse I put my body through, and continue to do, started long before a dirty needle stole my entire basis for existence.

"Raine? You up?" A fist thumps on the door.

Quickly yanking a pair of skinny jeans into place, I fumble my way back towards the bedroom door. This room is smaller than the last one I had. It'll take some time to remember the correct paces to cross the space. I've already stubbed my toe twice.

Swiping under my nose, I make sure any remnants of the pill I awkwardly crushed and snorted in the bathroom are gone. I'm sure Lennox has already noticed the shakes and cold sweats.

I'm trying to stretch out the last of my stash for as long as possible. After my morning hit, I feel all warm and tingly.

Navigating a pitch-black world is just a little less terrifying when my mind is swimming in happy chemicals.

"Password?" I drone.

There's a pissed-off exhale.

"How about open the fucking door before I break it down?"

I feel for the handle then swing the door open. "You're such a morning person, Nox."

I don't know what my friend looks like. We shared a particularly awkward encounter early on in our friendship when I requested to run my hands all over him to produce a mental picture of his appearance.

I know he's big. Burly. Grumpy. And a certified, grade A asshole. Except to me and maybe Xander. Lennox doesn't care about anyone or anything but those he considers family. It's his modus operandi.

Thunderous footsteps thumping past me, he barges into my bedroom with a low growl. I slam the door shut behind him then resume fastening my jeans. Though he's seen me in far less.

"To what do I owe the pleasure?"

"Family meeting," he grumbles. "The almighty one is on his way."

"Now, now. Don't go inflating Xander's ego any more than it already is."

I hear the creak of expanding bedsprings as Lennox takes a seat. "Hardly."

"Does this family meeting have something to do with your guava-scented girlfriend?"

"Jesus, Raine. Do you know how weird it is to hear how you categorise us in your head?"

I drop my shoulder against the wall and unleash a smirk. "Alright, Mr…" I take a deep inhale. "Hm. Burning wood? Campfires, maybe? Or is that tobacco? I thought you quit smoking."

Lennox softly curses. "Trust us to pick the weirdest fucking stray out there to adopt."

"No backsies. So what's the deal with guava girl?"

"It's papaya, genius."

I feel my eyebrows raise to my hairline as surprise washes over me. "How do you know what kind of body wash she uses? Feels like more than an educated guess."

"Xander." His tone is thick with amusement. "And believe me, you don't want to know how he got that information."

"Why not?"

"Leave it, Raine."

It's not like the infamous Lennox Nash to keep secrets from me. He may be a knucklehead with the world's shortest fuse, but he's loyal to a fault and never shies away from telling you exactly what he thinks. If Lennox hates your guts, you'll damn well know it.

"You get taken to the warden too, then?"

"Nah," he rumbles. "They just wanted her. Haven't seen the bitch since."

Ignoring the way that makes my insides twist uncomfortably, I retrace my careful steps across the room. *Tap. Tap. Tap.* When my guide stick connects with what I think is the desk, I feel for the chair then spin it around to sit down.

"Technically, you started it."

"How would you know?"

"My ears work perfectly fine." I flip him the bird, hoping it's in the right direction. "You gonna fill me in on this little feud?"

"Little." He laughs, but it's bitter and strained. "There's nothing *little* about the purgatory that evil cunt left us in. She wanted us dead."

"It obviously didn't work."

"Obviously," he mutters.

"What happened before I came to Priory Lane?"

Before he can respond, there's a terse, all-business knock

on the door. I hear Lennox move to open it, letting Xander step inside. I'd recognise his trademark spearmint scent from a mile off without needing to see his face.

Our fearless leader has to be the most cold-hearted bastard I've ever had the displeasure of meeting. Xander is the kind of person to stop next to a car wreck just to take photos rather than call the police.

Last time I touched him, his features felt narrow and bird-like. I bet the iceman looks like a breakable China doll. Pair that with his short, cropped hair, so soft I'd wonder if he bought shares in a hair product company, and he's the full picture of elegance.

"Where have you been?" Lennox demands angrily.

Xander silently pads into the room, the rustling of paper being unwrapped telling me he's pulling out a stick of gum. Oh, yes. The iceman is always minty fresh.

"Have you seen her?" Lennox asks. "Xan?"

After a long beat of silence, his flat response comes. "No. Are you sure it's her?"

"You think I'd forget?" Lennox hurls back. "She kicked me in the fucking ball sack."

"Doesn't sound much like her," Xander challenges coldly, his voice as lifeless as ever. "I think you're seeing ghosts, Nox."

"It. Was. Fucking. Her."

I can just imagine the pair of them glaring daggers at each other right now. For two men who claim to be best friends, family even, they fight just as hard as they love. Though Xander would never admit such a thing. He shows love in far more violent and sadistic ways.

I wave a finger in the air. "If it helps, I witnessed the whole thing. This chick knew who Lennox was and sure didn't sound happy to see him."

"You hear her name?" Xander asks in a loud exhale.

"Yeah. Ripley."

He hesitates before his voice changes, almost like he's

speaking around a smile. "So she's here, then. And the little toy has found a backbone."

"Ripley ran off here to hide after she fed us to the wolves!" Lennox explodes.

They lapse into loaded silence, though I can hear someone cracking their knuckles. I like to think I'm a patient guy—I have to be to simply communicate these days—but being left out of non-verbal conversations drives me fucking insane.

"Still waiting for my debriefing." I clear my throat pointedly.

My bed protests beneath the weight of someone sitting down. By the sounds of the groaning springs, it's Lennox's over-muscled frame. I'm surprised the bed supports him.

"Ripley Bennet was a patient in Priory Lane before you arrived." He speaks in a clipped tone.

"So what? You guys fucked her?"

Xander tsks. "It's hardly something so juvenile."

That's not an outright denial. Seems like Lennox isn't the only one keeping secrets.

"Is that a yes?" I push.

"Why do you care?" Lennox fires back.

Mouth clicking shut, I shrug it off. "Just want to know what we're dealing with."

"Trust me, Raine. Stay far away from Ripley," Lennox warns. "She's psycho with a capital P, and not in a cute way."

She smelled pretty damn cute to me.

"We earned our place in Priory Lane through brute force." Xander states matter-of-factly. "But the contraband lines that flowed through the institute once belonged to someone else."

"Someone else?" I repeat. "Her?"

"No."

The question of who hangs between us. I caught on quick when I arrived in Priory Lane, realising Lennox and Xander were the fucking kingpins of the institute.

"We did what we had to do to survive. Plain and simple," Lennox justifies. "Not everyone sees it that way."

Several pieces of the puzzle simultaneously click together. Whatever you wanted—smack, booze, blades—they could get it for you. It's how we met in the first place.

I was on my fifth stint in rehab after showing up to a scheduled gig too incoherent to remember my own name. The ultimatum came from my manager... Get clean, or my career in the music industry would be over.

After rehab failed, he dangled this golden lifeline instead. That same day, I walked straight into Priory Lane's arms. It seemed like a sweet deal to escape more rehab and appease the bastard profiting off the one thing that makes my life worth living.

My violin.

Of course, I didn't get clean. Lennox refused to sell to me at first. But when I made it pretty clear that I'd find a way to get high with or without their help, Xander was the one who caved. At least that way they could keep an eye on me.

"What did you do to her?"

"Ripley?" Lennox scoffs. "Not a damn thing."

"No, asshole. Her friend. Whoever the hell she accused you of hurting."

Lennox hesitates before answering. "Absolutely nothing. She did it to herself."

There's another beat of awkward silence, broken by the sound of feet shuffling. I can feel the tension skyrocketing between them.

"With enough encouragement," Xander adds.

"Wow. Fuck." I knead the back of my neck, which is feeling tighter the more they speak.

"It's really not how it sounds," Lennox protests.

"Isn't it?"

"Yes," Xander interjects. "It's exactly how it sounds."

Processing that, I wish I could say that I'm surprised. Out

of us all, I'm generally the most level-headed. Even for a smackhead. These two have a list of issues longer than my arm that not even my penchant for opiates can compete with.

Grumbling to himself, Lennox moves again to begin pacing the room. I know it's him—his footsteps are heavy and furious. The man has fucking ants in his pants today, this Ripley chick has him all riled up.

"What exactly did she do to you?" I ask carefully. "For you to hate her so much, I mean. I sure as hell get why she hates both of y—"

"Ripley Bennet must be dealt with." Xander cuts over me, completely ignoring the question.

Lennox's pacing halts. "I don't think it's that simple."

"And why not?"

"She said something after she kicked my ass." Lennox pauses, presumably reaching for the memory. *"You're in my institute now."*

"What does that mean?" I lift and drop a hand.

Neither responds for a loaded second, filled with enough tension for me to taste its cloying bitterness on the tip of my tongue. Someone huffs, while another taps their feet. It's weird as fuck to see my friends so unnerved. Well, not see. More like sense.

I've taught myself to recognise their emotional cues—even Xander, who barely has any. Spend enough time with someone and their tells become like clockwork. Sighing. Pacing. Huffing. This is the eighty percent of my perception now.

"It means… she thinks she's untouchable." Xander makes a small, almost amused noise in the back of his throat.

"So?" Lennox sighs.

"So that will be her downfall."

CHAPTER 6
RIPLEY

MISFITS – MAGNOLIA PARK & TAYLOR ACORN

LAYING on my back with my feet above me, resting on the padded interior of the cell, I toss the apple I was given for breakfast up in the air. Do they seriously expect this pointless, solitary shit to work on me?

I get it. *Bad Ripley*. My role here is simple. Incite violence, addiction, fights—whatever the fuck I want—and supply all these worthless sons of bitches with enough self-destructive shit to fan the flames, but do not get involved. I'm supposed to remain neutral.

The perfect inside man.

An inconspicuous weapon.

My role definitely doesn't entail beating the crap out of someone and almost revealing my hand. Secrets and subterfuge, remember? That's the name of the game. Instead, I ran my mouth and threatened to kick Lennox's well-toned ass.

In front of a clinician, no less.

Real fucking clever.

Catching the apple, my hand stills mid-throw when a loud shriek lances through the morning's peace. Even through the walls of my padded cell, I can hear it. The terror. Fear so horrifying in its intensity, it would make a grown man run like a scared puppy.

Taking a big bite of the apple, I crunch through the sharp tartness, unfazed by whatever is unfolding around me. Better them than me. You don't get far in a place like this by having an ounce of sympathy.

But as the shrieks continue to grow in pitch and intensity, feeling soon slinks back in. Ever the deadly assassin. What if it were Rae in there? Or Holly? Everyone is somebody to someone.

A brother. Lover.

Father. Sister.

Just because I don't give a shit about the screamer one cell over doesn't mean they don't have family out there, praying for their safe return from the brink of insanity.

How different would this world be if we all cared a little bit more? Or allowed ourselves to admit that we give a shit about other people, even when they refuse to care about us?

No, Ripley.

I cared before.

Look where that got me.

To pass the time, I imagine Lennox in there instead. Screaming like a red-faced toddler begging for a snack. Hmm, nope. What about Lennox attached to electrodes, convulsing as he's shocked repeatedly?

Much better.

Add in some bulging eyes and wet sweats too. What an awesome image. I'd pay to see that motherfucker torn apart for someone else's entertainment. I don't even want the leftover pieces. I just want to see him suffer while his limbs are removed.

I've yet to see the almighty keeper of his short leash. Xander was the only person who could ever keep that rabid dog in check. If Lennox is here, then his psychopathic overlord won't be far behind.

I meant what I said.

This time, I will be the one to take everything from them. As soon as they let me out of this goddamned cell, I'll plaster on a pretty smile to get myself back in management's good books, then let the games begin.

A sharp rap on the steel door is my only warning before it's unlocked and clanks open. I jut out my bottom lip, pouting like a child at Elon's displeased glower.

"Poor, Elon. Sent to babysit the naughty patient."

"Get the fuck up, Ripley."

"Maybe I quite like it here."

"You wanna stay another night?" he snorts. "Be my guest."

Turning his back to leave me here, I quickly scramble, finding my feet. He tosses my confiscated shoes at me to put on. They took them when I was dragged here, like I'd attempt to use the laces to string myself up or something.

"That wasn't so hard, was it?" he sneers.

Shoes slid on, I surrender my wrists to be cuffed. "Whatever."

He easily restrains me, then I'm dragged from the padded cell, out into a well-lit corridor surrounded by other occupied cells. This is the wing rolled out for clinical inspections and investors' tours.

Trust me—if you're taken into the *other* wing, you don't walk out. Cuffed or not. And that circle of hell sure doesn't make it into the fancy brochures laid out in the reception area.

"I thought you were smart enough to keep your head down," Elon says disdainfully. "You want to lose the privileges you've been given, inmate?"

"Nothing about this life is fucking privileged."

With a hiss, he spins and slams me up against the white-painted wall. I squeak in shock as his hand clenches around my already sore throat, squeezing on top of the fresh bruising inflicted by Lennox.

"You want to see the real horror show, Ripley? Don't think for a second that you have it hard here. Watch your goddamn mouth, or you'll lose it all."

He tightens his grip until I nod, admitting defeat. I slump forward when he releases me, rubbing my aching throat. I'm going to be walking around like some kind of bruised up sex doll at the rate I'm pissing people off.

"Come on. The warden wants a word."

"Fabulous," I rasp.

He flashes me another warning look. "Attitude, inmate."

This time, I have the sense of mind to keep my mouth shut.

I'm towed onwards, past the solitary confinement wing to the offices beyond. Warden Davis prefers to keep to himself far from the clinicians and patients alike. He's paid far too much to lower himself to our level.

Gleaming linoleum turns to thick carpet as we enter the administrative side of the wing. At the third door to the left, marked with a small bronze plaque, Elon knocks politely then waits to be called in.

"Enter," Davis calls out.

Inside, it's as lush and pretentious as you'd imagine. Hardwood floors and thick, patterned rugs. A sprawling dark-wood desk littered with organised paperwork and framed photographs. Not to mention the middle-aged man of the hour in his fine grey suit and usual gold tie pin.

With salt-and-pepper hair, a neatly trimmed beard and deep set, coal-black eyes, Abbott Davis is the corporate dream. I'm sure Harrowdean's PR team popped a fat boner the day he walked in. He's the perfect poster boy for their pet project.

"Ah, Miss Bennet." Davis's usually professional tone is marked with annoyance today. "Take a seat."

I have to bite back a sardonic response. "Warden."

"I hear there has been some commotion." His incisive gaze sweeps over me. "Care to explain yourself?"

Taking a seat opposite the desk, I wait for Elon to find his place in the corner of the room before responding. "It was nothing."

"By Doctor Galloway's account, you had an altercation with one of our new arrivals."

Glancing out the window behind him, I try to act unaffected. I don't want him to know how much power he holds over me. The fear he can so easily provoke. Before long, my eyes stray back to him though.

"Just... a little misunderstanding."

"Is that so?" he hums with a slightly quirked lip. "Perhaps you're also misunderstanding your role here, Miss Bennet."

My heart hammers behind my ribcage. "No, sir."

"When you transferred to Harrowdean Manor, I saw an opportunity for you. Has your time here not been... productive?"

The urge to scream in his picture-perfect face almost overwhelms me. Productive. I doubt the bereaved families of patients I've sold gear to would care for that choice of word. Frankly, I don't either.

"Yes... sir," I choke out.

"I'd hate to have to report back to one of my best investors that his niece isn't behaving."

I swallow hard, forcing down the hot ball of nausea making its way up my throat. Most days, I can forget that my uncle is the one who put me here. Or rather, his money did. He may be an investment banker by name, but that doesn't mean all his enterprises feature on the FTSE 100.

Harrowdean and its sister branches run off the dirty money bankrolling their depravity and the carelessness of those splashing the cash while turning a blind eye. I just so happen to be related to one such piece of shit.

"If it wasn't for Jonathan's generous donation to facilitate your transfer, I doubt we would've accommodated such a volatile subject in this position." Davis continues to study me. "I need someone I can count on."

Panic takes root. I can feel my carefully laid plan unfolding. After losing Holly, I knew I had to do something. Anything to escape Priory Lane and the demons who took it from her. Begging my uncle for a quick transfer was a level I felt willing to stoop to.

Priory Lane could keep its new kings. I didn't care enough to stop their ascension. But I wanted them broken, smashed to pieces and ground to a paste before they took their thrones. Then the world would see them as I did.

"I understand," I reply.

"Do you?" He inclines his head, eyes narrowing.

"Yes, sir."

"Then remind me. What is the purpose of a stooge?"

Lacing his fingers together, he props his chin on top and gives me his undivided attention. Does he want me to lay it out for him? Every last way I've corrupted my soul to avoid the torture I've seen inflicted on others?

If you haven't figured it out yet, grab the fucking popcorn. How far does the depravity go? The answer would take far longer to explain than even I think I have left on this godforsaken planet.

And it starts right here. At the top.

"To be a secret participant."

"In what?" Davis asks pointedly.

I lick my suddenly dry lips. "In a psychological experiment."

He smiles slyly. "The stooge acts like one of the patients, but their loyalties lie elsewhere. To further the aims of the research team and perform whatever task they may require of them."

Tasks like selling drugs. Blades. Contraband. Whatever volatile elements the clinicians fancy throwing into the mix to elicit a new result. The more accelerant, the hotter the flames.

That's good for research and good for business. As long as it remains a secret. That's why it's all controlled from within by surveillance and the placement of a stooge to gain the patients' trust.

I choose the perfect candidates.

Then sell to them so the clinicians can study the result.

I'm not just allowing them to hurt the vulnerable people in here for their own scientific purposes. No. Far worse. I'm the one hurting the patients here, people just like me, to avoid being hurt myself. Their pain is my protection.

The ultimate selfishness.

But don't the selfish ones always survive the longest?

"You've been given a very comfortable life here, Miss Bennet. A lot of allowances have been made."

"I understand that."

"Then tell me why you're attacking other patients and threatening Lord knows what?" Davis frowns like this whole conversation is an inconvenience. "When you've been explicitly told to keep your nose clean?"

I don't respond. He doesn't want to hear anything I have to say. It'll only buy me a one-way ticket back into that padded cell. Or somewhere far worse. A useless stooge is a dead stooge. Rich uncle or not.

"We have to keep the program running as discreetly as possible. You signed yourself over to us the day you agreed to work for us."

"Yes, sir," I repeat monotonously.

What I wouldn't give to puppeteer him the same way that I do every other crazed, medicated patient in this place. I'm their God. But management? They're mine.

"No more fighting." He straightens, palms landing on his desk. "Do your job. I don't want to see you in here again. Do you understand?"

His harsh tone brooks no argument. And fuck, do I want to argue. That broken, pitiful part of me, still convinced that we can piece the jagged shards of our morality back together, wants to stop this once and for all.

But I won't walk away from Harrowdean if I do. This job offers me protection from the sickness the others must face. The truth behind the story everyone else is told about these institutes.

This isn't just an experiment.

It's far more sinister than that.

Behind the façade—a successful, rehabilitative regimen for criminals and the insane alike—lies its true purpose. Camouflage for the program. An experiment of the sickest sort. The same torture I signed Xander and Lennox up for as a parting gift.

"Miss Bennet," he barks, jerking me from my thoughts.

Nodding, I bite my tongue hard enough to draw blood.

"Good. One more strike and I'll be forced to re-evaluate your place here."

It takes all of my self-control to summon a pretty fucking smile and plaster it in place. If I'm removed by management and subjected to God knows what, Lennox and Xander won't hesitate to take my place.

It wouldn't be the first time they've grabbed power. They saw what Holly was, the control she had. She didn't stand a chance against them once they decided to take it from her. To become the stooges themselves.

"Get out of my sight." Davis dismisses me with a terse nod. "And heed my warning, Miss Bennet."

Keeping my lips sealed, I stand then scuttle from the room. He has to think that he's subjugated me. That the threat of punishment is far greater than my desire for revenge. Little does he know, I'd sacrifice it all to taste blood.

The lives I've traded for my own mean nothing while those monsters continue to breathe air. I thought they were gone. Lost in the system. Broken by whatever the fuck Priory

Lane's *special wing* decided to do with them once I arranged their induction.

Yet they live.

But not for long.

I'll have to do it myself. Tear them apart, chunk by blood slick chunk, until they beg to return to the purgatory they crawled out of. It will look like paradise in comparison to what I spent my night in solitary planning for them.

Leading me back out to the reception, Elon pauses to unlock my handcuffs. The handful of patients floating around avert their eyes when I glower at them.

"See something that interests you?"

The onlookers quickly dissipate.

Elon snickers at the fear that fills their expressions as they scurry away. Rubbing my sore wrists, I spare him a nod then leave before he can change his mind.

The stairs leading up towards the residential floors feel endless. My legs are two concrete-filled pillars attached to my body after a sleepless night. Halfway up to the second floor, I hear their voices descending.

Familiarity is another sharp and unwelcome slap in the face. After a year spent trying to erase the memories that haunt me, hearing them so close feels like living a nightmare.

"The dickhead started it." Lennox's voice is a low grumble. "Who takes five minutes to decide which damn cereal to eat?"

"You can't just go around punching people, Nox."

"Says who?"

"Erm, the fucking law?" I recognise the raspy tenor of Raine responding. "Are you looking for trouble?"

"He doesn't even have to look for it," a voice responds.

The third voice causes a chill to break out across my skin. As if a snowstorm has swept over the staircase, the air is laced with frigid anticipation of his arrival. I knew he was here. But hearing him takes me right back to that night.

It was before my entire world changed. His cool, clinical touch brought me to life. A lash of pain. Soft, wet swipes of his tongue soothing the sting. Limbs pinned and spreadeagled. Powerless. At his utter, irrevocable mercy.

Fuck!

I turn and bolt back down the stairs before they can spot me. I'm no coward, but I have to play this smart. Facing off against Xander fucking Beck in this state will win me no awards. Plotting how to take down the king of cold calculation already took me several hours of pondering.

Ducking behind a tall potted plant at the bottom of the staircase, I hold my breath and wait. It doesn't take long for them to descend. Xander walks at the head of the group. Lennox stomps behind, a hand grasping the cute violinist's elbow.

"You know," Raine begins. "If she—"

"Not here," Xander clips out.

Lennox steers his friend towards the south wing where the daily classes are located. They trade conspiratorial whispers that I can't make out, and I keep my breath held until they disappear.

Shit.

I'll never get close enough to inflict any amount of damage when they're all together. Lennox has already had his hands around my throat. And I have no doubt Xander would happily give him another chance to choke me to death. As long as he could watch.

Breaking outside into the quad, it's a bright but freezing cold January day. Those not in therapy or classes mill about, wrapped in wool scarves and bobble hats. Guards bounce on their feet, red hands cupped over their mouths in attempts to warm up.

I have a plan.

All I need is a sacrificial lamb.

Scanning the smattering of picnic benches, he's in his

usual spot. Noah likes the bite of cold air. He once told me it makes him feel something, if only for a second. His depressive episodes come more frequently than mine.

"Look alive," I greet wearily.

His head snaps up as I approach. "Ripley. Heard you got taken to the hole."

"News travels fast, huh?"

"In this place?" He lifts a shoulder in a shrug. "Nothing much else to do than gossip."

"Well, people better not get too excited. I'm back now."

"They were probably more concerned about where to source their shit from than excited."

I loop a leg over the bench seat. "Were you concerned about that too?"

"I'm not a junkie." Noah sighs. "I have no interest in buying drugs."

"Well, I don't just sell drugs. Interested in a trade?"

A sparkle briefly lights his sad, lifeless eyes. Everyone has that one thing. A pressure point. Find it and you'll own them, head to fucking toe. I just need to know what Noah's crutch is beyond meaningless one-night stands with batshit crazy drug dealers.

"I have a job that needs doing." I lower my voice, subtly glancing around. "You see the newbie yet?"

"Which one?" he replies. "I counted several."

"Big. Bulky. A sour-faced bastard with a bad attitude."

Noah snorts. "Saw him punch someone in the breakfast line this morning. That your guy?"

Fucking Lennox.

"Bingo."

"What about him?"

"I want you to pick a fight. Make it look like he started it. You're gonna get hurt, enough to get him thrown into the hole for a good while."

His brow line raises. "Why would I do that?"

"Name the price. It's yours."

Noah's mouth opens and closes several times before he finally responds. "You're serious?"

One day, people will stop underestimating me. Until then, I have to justify myself to idiots like Noah who see nothing but a mousy girl playing a game she doesn't understand.

"Do I look like I'm kidding around?" I gesture angrily.

While he chews over my proposal, I feel my plan begin to solidify. I can't get to Xander while his rabid pet is around. He serves his master too well. Remove Lennox from the picture, and Xander is free game.

That is how I'll win.

Break their family, and I break them.

"Well?" I push anxiously. "What'll it be?"

Gnawing on his lip, Noah seems to decide something. He nods to himself, not quite in defeat but with a look of satisfied resignation. I tap my fingers against the wooden bench and sigh.

"Noah?"

"I don't care what it is, but I want enough of it to OD. That's my price."

Taken aback, I feel my spine stiffen as shock coils within me. "To overdose?"

He watches me stoically. "Yes. In exchange, I'll let him fuck me up so bad, he never sees the light of day again."

My mind whirls. "So this OD... We talking hospitalisation or... you know, night-night?"

The corner of his mouth lifts in what is almost a smile. "Well, let's just say we better make our next booty call the last."

With icy dread pulsating through me, I simply stare. Not at my hook-up. Not even at my fellow patient. He's just another human, another sufferer, without an ounce more to give to this world. He wants me to kill him.

A life for a life.

Is revenge worth that price?

"Noah…"

"Whatever you're going to say, don't bother."

"But—"

"No." Noah holds up a hand. "I know you've been where I am."

"Look, this isn't—"

"I said no. I'm done, Rip."

"I can get you anything. Just… not that."

"That's what I want," he reiterates.

Taking a moment to consider, I stare at him. Every last telling detail. Who am I to tell him what he should do? I'm nothing to him. Not really.

Only someone who's been at the bottom of that black pit, the crushing weight of the earth pulverising their bones to ash as it bears down on them can understand how truly bleak it feels.

Like I said, doctors don't want to advertise the benefits of being high, and feeling invincible, like the whole world is your oyster. But at least when you're manic as fuck, you don't want to kill yourself. I'll take that sweet deal any day.

If I take his life, am I depriving him of the chance to feel that euphoria again? To find hope, peace or even a life without all this misery? Can I live with myself knowing that he'll never have the chance to find out?

Yes.

Yes, I can.

Because I told you… I'm not the good guy. I'm not even the misunderstood but morally redeemable fuck-up. The troubled kid with a good heart. There are enough stories out there about that person—go to the damn library and see for yourself.

I'm the monster they made me. Born from blood and thirsty for revenge, enough to sacrifice an innocent to achieve that goal. For some, redemption isn't realistic. All we have is our rage to keep us warm at night.

"If we do this… I can't have it lead back to me."

"I'm sure you can figure out the details," he replies in a bored tone. "Not like I'm gonna be here to deal with the repercussions."

"Yeah, hilarious."

But Noah isn't laughing. He holds out his hand towards me. Would you hate me less if I say I hesitate? Because I don't. Not even for a second. Our hands link as we seal the deal.

It'll take a while to sneak enough of what he needs from incoming batches of contraband. I can't exactly request a nice little cocktail on his behalf. Even Harrowdean has its standards, and typically, test subjects have to be alive to be helpful.

"I'll need a while to source everything. When it's go time, you better be ready."

"Not like I'm going anywhere, is it?" he counters.

"I guess not." Feeling like I need to say more, I dare to allow a sliver of emotion into my voice. "I'll remember you."

Lips thinning, he shakes his head.

"Please don't. Not like this."

CHAPTER 7
RIPLEY

MEET YOU AT THE GRAVEYARD –
CLEFFY

ONE HAND TRAILING along the staircase's balustrade, I will my body to respond. It's another down day, but this one feels different. Not even the paper cup of coloured pills from the nurse's station alleviated the weight bearing down on me.

I tried to sleep the feeling away this morning, but this isn't physical exhaustion. No amount of sleep will cure the crashing chemicals in my brain dragging me back down. More often than not, it only makes me feel worse.

What is it my old psychiatrist used to say to me? *Each step is a small victory.* Even if that's only to the bathroom and back. I suppose he wanted to make me feel better about ending up with a UTI when in the height of a depressive episode, I didn't move for three days.

"Ripley!"

Internally groaning, I ignore Langley abandoning his post to follow me as I reach the bottom of the staircase.

"Hey, Rip. Wait up."

"Not today," I reply tersely.

"Are you okay?" Langley's hand hovers just above my arm.

"Fucking brilliant. Leave me alone."

"Just doing my job." He scowls.

"Are you?" I look up into his baby blues.

After my brief stint in solitary, I'm keenly aware of every eye laser-focused on me. If the warden even suspects that Langley is overstepping his duties, a dismissal is the best-case scenario. I dare not think of the worst.

His gaze is soft with concern. "I'm trying to look out for you."

"And I told you—"

"It's alright, Jayden," a sneering voice interrupts. "I can take it from here."

Thick-soled boots stopping next to us, Elon's ever-present, phony grin is firmly in place. His blue eyes narrowed suspiciously, I can tell that not even Langley is convinced by it. He has no choice but to step aside.

Elon takes his place next to me, tightly clutching my wrist. "Shouldn't you be in class, inmate?"

Asshole. He knows I don't attend classes like everyone else. Yet another perk. If only my privileges could get me out of weekly therapy too.

"Just off to the studio," I force out.

"How opportune. I can escort you."

"Oh, fabulous."

Ignoring the sarcasm dripping from my voice, Elon frogmarches me through reception and towards the south wing. I don't bother looking back at Langley. That man needs to learn when to give up.

Once we're in an empty corridor, Elon drops his voice. "You're late on inventory."

"Yeah."

"That's it? Yeah? Unacceptable."

Wrangling my wrist from his crushing grip, I pull a folded piece of paper from my sweatpants. Elon quickly takes it from me, his thin lips pursed. He scans over the neatly scribed lines of items with his steely gunmetal gaze.

Folding my arms below my chest, I don't let my

apprehension show. I've only added a few extras to my usual contraband order, small quantities I can sneak into a stockpile for my arrangement with Noah. Anything in large amounts would rouse suspicion.

Elon quickly refolds and pockets the list. "Don't be late again. We say jump, you say how high. Got that?"

"It was a couple of days. Cool off, will you?"

Grey eyes hardening, he takes a step closer. "Did you not learn your lesson? I've got a padded cell with your name on it if not."

I should be playing this smart, but fuck it. Today is not the day to be all up in my business. I'm already struggling to stay afloat.

"If you lock me up in solitary, who is gonna sell your shit?"

His nose wrinkles in disgust. "You think we can't find another desperate bitch to do our bidding?"

"I imagine you'd only have to look in the mirror to find that."

"You little—"

Tap. Tap. Tap.

"Is there a problem here?"

That raspy voice, filled with palpable self-assurance, apparently shocks Elon out of his rage. He glances over his shoulder to find Raine in the middle of the corridor, one hand holding a violin case, the other wrapped around the guide stick clasped in front of him.

Gleaming blonde hair slicked back, his blacked-out glasses rest above his full lips, stretched in a smirk. I don't know who puts his outfits together, but between the glasses, ripped grey jeans and loose tee, he looks every part the violin-toting rockstar.

"Keep moving," Elon barks.

Raine readjusts his grip on the guide stick. "I was actually on my way to see Ripley here."

"You were?" I gape at him.

His grin widens at my surprised tone. "Still got time to help me with that art project? It's uh, rather urgent."

The subtle cocking of his brow would be humorous if I didn't know who this guy is friends with. I don't know what's worse… a run in with Elon or accepting help from Lennox's latest puppet.

"Sure," I say uneasily. "I have some time."

"Great. Lead the way."

Sauntering up to me with his stick tapping away, he offers his elbow. I quickly step out of Elon's reach and take the proffered arm. Raine follows without question, letting me guide him down the thick carpet towards the classrooms.

Out the corner of my eye, I see Elon ball his fists and glower at Raine. He quickly abandons any plan to follow us, probably disappearing to take care of his list. When he vanishes, I breathe a sigh of relief.

"You're welcome, guava girl," Raine whispers.

I quickly release his elbow. "My body wash is papaya, alright?"

"Oh, I've been made aware. Doesn't have quite the same ring to it though, does it?"

"You've been discussing my choice of body wash?" I ask incredulously.

Raine chuckles, deep and throaty. "Gotta pass the time somehow."

"Sounds thrilling."

"A conversation with me?" he replies slyly. "It always is."

Avoiding the arc of his stick clacking out a clear path, I fight to keep my eyes off him. Something about Raine intrigues me. He's full of conflicts—vulnerable yet confident, a silver-tongued flirt hiding behind glasses and scruffy t-shirts.

Nothing about him makes sense. Yet nothing can erase the memory of him caressing his violin's strings alone in the music room. I've found my mind replaying that scene over several times, attempting to comprehend what I saw.

"Well, thanks for the save," I begrudgingly admit. "Feel free to go back to whatever you were doing."

"Actually, we're going in the same direction." He lifts his violin case. "Can you tolerate me for a bit longer?"

Fighting a smile, I keep my voice disinterested. "Suppose I'll have to."

"Promise I'm a lot more civilised than the company I keep. Though if you want to tackle me like you did Lennox, you have my full consent. It sounded hot."

"Your *friend* deserved what he got."

Raine snorts. "Of that I have no doubt."

Keeping his elbow to himself, he follows me at a leisurely pace. I sneak glances at him every few steps, but his slight grin remains sealed in place. How can someone capable of such mournful music have such a normal outward appearance?

"Did you know that your breathing changes every time you're about to ask something?" Raine enquires conversationally.

"I wasn't going to ask anything."

"But everyone always wants to. Stop hesitating, it's annoying. Ask."

I suck in my bottom lip, nibbling on it as we pass several classrooms. "I suppose everyone wants to know the same, right?"

"More often than not." An amused chuff bursts from him. "Short answer? No, I wasn't born blind."

When a door opens and patients begin to spill out in search of lunch, the first cracks in Raine's exterior begin to show. His jaw clenches, betraying a slight tic. Each tap of his guide stick becomes a little more forceful, like firing warning shots.

Someone rushes out with their head down, focused on a sheath of papers. Before they can collide with Raine, I quickly grasp his wrist and tug him aside. His skin is hot to the touch, almost feverishly so, and silky-soft beneath golden fuzz.

His hard body brushes mine, head tilted downwards and turned towards me like he's seeking safety. For a brief second, I savour the warmth of him pressed right up against my side.

He's surprisingly firm. Chiselled. Muscular beneath his revolving door of frayed t-shirts and skinny jeans. A lump forms in my throat at his sudden close proximity.

"Now we're even."

He releases a short breath. "You keeping count?"

"I don't like owing people."

I'm close enough to get a waft of his scent. The intoxicating combination of freshly squeezed orange juice and salty seawater overwhelms my senses. He smells like lazy mornings on the beach, sharing breakfast picnics before catching the next surf.

"Get a good sniff?" Raine snickers.

I flinch away, releasing him once more. "Your good hearing is creepy."

"Oh, I've been told. But it comes in handy."

Feeling exposed, I train my gaze on the art studio at the end of the corridor and move faster. Somehow, Raine is able to see far past the tactics I've long since perfected to portray my indifference.

He doesn't need his sight to read me like a book. That's a scary realisation. Even my breathing can betray the lie I live to him. No amount of bravado will stop him from discovering the version of myself that I refuse to let the world see.

"Music room is on your right." I deliberately don't stop for him. "Door's open."

Entering the art studio—deserted as usual on a Thursday —I'm flustered as I approach my covered canvas from last week which still needs signing and varnishing. I'm gathering my supplies when the sound of a stool scraping against the wooden floor fractures the peace.

After placing his violin case on a workbench, Raine hops up onto the stool and crosses his jean-clad legs at the ankles.

He's facing the window, so I clear my throat and watch his head turn towards me.

"Why are you following me?"

Tilting his body, he repositions himself to face my direction. "We're supposed to be working on an art project."

"There is no project."

"And if your friendly resident stalker returns, looking to continue your conversation?" he counters. "You're going to need that alibi."

Slamming down my tin of varnish and brushes, I brace my hands on my hips. "What's your deal? Did Lennox or Xander put you up to this?"

"Nope." He pops the P exaggeratedly. "And I doubt they'd approve."

"Then what's the motive here?"

"Does there have to be one?" Rolling his lips, Raine looks like he's fighting laughter. "Sounds like people give you a wide berth. Maybe I just want some peace and quiet."

Despite by brimming curiosity for this mysterious man, I keep my voice level. "You're disturbing mine right now."

"Say no more." He mimes locking his mouth and tossing the key. "Pretend I'm not here."

Staring at him incredulously for several seconds, I quickly realise he isn't going to move. I'm keenly aware of his presence mere metres away as I suppress a growl, turning back to my canvas. I'm not used to sharing my personal space.

Beneath the paint-flecked white sheet, my finished canvas sits untouched. I sign it off with my signature in the bottom right corner then methodically begin varnishing, quickly becoming engrossed in my task.

Not even the sound of Raine unlatching his violin case and setting up his instrument disturbs me. I'm lost to the swirls of oil paint and varnish, sucking me back into the terrifying landscape that poured from my brush.

By the end of the first coat, my body has started to sway

along to the muted chords Raine is plucking out as he tunes his violin. It's a stripped-back rhythm, light and oddly reticent, never quite betraying the raw emotion I heard him perform in private.

I still, laying down my brush. "When did you learn to play?"

"Before I lost my vision. I was around nine." The plucking continues. "My school's music program was wildly unpopular. Just like me. I fit right in."

"You were unpopular?"

"No one likes the junkies' son. I didn't have the latest clothes or mobile phone like everyone else. Everyone knew my folks were crackheads."

Still staring at my canvas, I wrestle with my conflicting emotions. "Why the violin?"

"I stumbled into the classroom one day while running from some bullies and found this ancient, battered violin. The rest is history."

"How old are you now?"

"What's with the third degree, guava girl?"

"You're the one who followed me in here."

"I guess that's fair. I'm twenty-three."

Turning on my stool, I allow myself another glimpse. He's a year younger than Lennox, while Xander is twenty-six, the same as me. That makes Raine the baby of their friendship group.

"You continued to play after you lost your vision?"

Raine nods hesitantly. "Took some practise, but I never stopped playing after it happened. Music gave me something to focus on."

I bite back the urge to ask what happened to him. No wonder he can play the chords by heart without the need for a single glance. Those wound metal strings are an extension of him, and he strokes them like it's second nature. Easier than breathing, almost.

"When was that?"

"This?" He gestures towards his eyes. "A little over five years ago."

An internal voice is telling me to stop asking rapid-fire questions, but he's like a puzzle I can't help piecing together. I want to know how this smooth-talking violinist with the filthiest smile ended up becoming friends with people like Lennox or Xander.

I hear him inhale before he speaks. "My turn. Do you always work with… Is that oil paint I can smell?"

"Yes it is, and that depends," I answer honestly.

"On what?"

"Sometimes, I prefer the richness of this medium and its saturated colours. Other times, the piece requires a lighter touch. Pastels, watercolour, sometimes pencil."

"What is it that you paint?" His head tilts in interest.

"Mostly landscapes or abstracts. But I dabble."

Fingertips still dancing over the neck of his violin, his pale brows knit together, like he's willing his mind to conjure some clue as to what I've painted.

"Can you describe it to me?"

Despite his confidence, there's a slight, almost unnoticeable crack in his voice. A hint of vulnerability. Something tells me that he wouldn't let it show by accident.

Ignoring every last warning bell telling me to put distance between us, I shift my stool to the left.

"Come closer."

Raine places his violin back in its velvet-lined case then walks towards me. After abandoning his guide stick, his steps are slow and hesitant. Another snippet of the person behind the mask. The same mask that I find myself wearing every day too.

We both put on a show. Play pretend. Bury any hints of weakness to survive in a world that doesn't allow for fragility.

Perhaps Lennox and Xander are part of that show. Even monsters make good allies when it's convenient.

I reach out and snag his shirt sleeve. Raine lets me steer him into place, standing directly in front of the still-wet canvas. His lips are parted, breathing slightly unsteadily. He feels it too, then. The fear of flaws being exposed to another person.

"The canvas is about three feet in front of you," I explain, my voice breathless. "Imagine the ocean. Raging, wild, uncontrollable. There are sprays of deep forest-green and hints of crimson against the waves."

His throat bobs, the muscles in his neck tensing, but he remains silent. Despite feeling exposed by the emotion passing between us, I decide to continue.

"In the eye of the storm, shadows form a solitary figure. Trapped. Powerless. She's unaware of the others behind her, two larger silhouettes lurking in the background. They're all imprisoned by saturated flames, eating up the ocean."

Still holding his shirt sleeve, my hand grasps his bicep, feeling that same burning heat emanating from his skin. He isn't trembling like last time, but I know a withdrawal fever when I see one. He's in the early stages.

"Why is she trapped?" he asks quietly.

I consider the varnished canvas. "Because who isn't trapped by something? None of us are free. Especially not from ourselves."

After a long beat of silence, Raine replies in a thick voice. "What about the others in the painting?"

"They're trapped too."

"So they aren't the bad guys?"

Unnamed pain lashes against my breastbone. "Being trapped by the same evil doesn't automatically make them good people. Victims can still be monsters."

"Doesn't make them bad either."

"Circumstance excuses nothing," I reply hotly, irritation bleeding from my words.

"Sorry, Ripley." His tone lacks its usual playful lilt. "Circumstance is everything, isn't it? You don't blame soldiers for the price they paid to survive the battlefield."

For a split second, I almost give him the benefit of doubt. Part of me actually thought that we were the same. But anyone willing to condone their friends' violence is cut from the same fucked up cloth. He's just like them.

You're a hypocrite, Ripley.

Stop lying to yourself.

If I follow through and help Noah end his life, will I be any better than them? Willing to shed blood, to sacrifice another living, breathing human being, simply to achieve my own goal?

If they're the villains in my story... am I the villain in theirs?

Circumstance. It's a real bitch.

"Well, it's a good thing that it's just a painting." My voice trembles with the torment clawing at my insides.

"Is it?" Raine challenges.

When I shift, trying to put a safe distance between us again, he manages to blindly snag my wrist. His thumb presses above the furious pounding of my pulse. Even I can feel it's going wild.

"You're angry." He gently runs his calloused thumb across the thick veins protruding beneath my skin.

"You needed to feel my pulse to figure that out?"

"Look, I don't know what happened between you and the guys, but—"

"No. You don't know what they did." The words escape my gritted teeth. "To me. To *her*."

"I know." Raine's chest rises with his inhale. "They hurt someone you cared about."

My heart is a dead lump, entombed behind my ribcage. "They destroyed someone I cared about."

"And? Isn't what you did to them payback enough?"

"Someone's been gossiping."

Raine shrugs dismissively. "I know shit went down before I showed up. Xander doesn't talk about it. Lennox punches a wall if I bring it up."

Huh. Perhaps they didn't escape as unscathed as I thought. I'd still like to know how the pair of them wrangled their way out of the deadly trap I laid for them.

"I'm going to hurt your friends, Raine. If you don't want to get hurt too, keep your distance from them and me."

Head dipping lower, his salty, citrus scent assaults me. "Is that a warning?"

"It's a threat."

"I'm not the type to abandon my friends. So you'll have to hurt me too."

Is he grinning at the mere thought?

Staring into the black depths of his lenses, I can't decide if I want to punch this cocky shit or find out if the taste of sunshine also dances on his tongue. I must've finally lost it to even be contemplating the latter.

"I think I'm starting to understand why you're here."

Chuckling, he resumes stroking the sensitive skin of my tattooed inner wrist, causing the hairs on my arms to lift. I internally scold myself for enjoying the featherlight touch.

"This place is a hell of a lot more interesting than rehab ever was."

I feel the hum of his rising fever once more. "You were in rehab?"

"Spent more time in than out. Five stints."

"That wasn't enough to keep you out of this place?"

"Apparently not." He laughs humourlessly.

I never give a shit about customers. It's the price of doing business. Yet I find my heart cracking open and bleeding for this broken boy, hiding a deadly addiction behind smirks and over-exaggerated bravado.

Does anyone else see how hard he's faking it?

This Raine isn't real.

His entire act is an illusion.

"This isn't a game." I push away the empathy trying to gnaw through my resolve, redirecting us back to safe ground. "I meant what I said. If I have to kill you to get to them, that's exactly what I'll do."

"We've progressed to killing?"

"I won't let them hurt anyone else."

Rough fingertips dancing upwards from my wrist, he traverses my ink-covered forearm, leaving a blazing trail in his wake. I find my breath stuttering. Luckily, he can't see me biting my lip hard enough to sting.

Those sure fingertips feel like tasers against my flushed skin. His thumb tugs my shirt sleeve, testing the rough cotton before he moves higher and wraps my loose, brown curls around his digits.

"What are you doing?" I ask nervously.

He fingers the coarse strands of hair. "What colour is it?"

"Um, dark-brown."

"The curls are natural?"

His laser focus is making nervous sweat bead on my forehead. I feel like I'm being inspected. He lightly tugs on a strand, measuring the length against my jawline like he's taking mental notes to better construct an idea of my appearance.

"Yes," I squeak.

"What about your eyes? Colour?"

"Uh, hazel."

Releasing the ringlet clasped in his fingers, Raine's hand hovers close to my face. "Do you mind? It helps me to form a mental picture of who I'm talking to."

"I bet you say that to all the girls."

"Most don't complain about me wanting to touch them." He sighs in a long-suffering way.

I want to tell him to get lost. Instead, I find myself suppressing a snort.

"I should've known the whole blind thing was a flirting tactic."

"You caught me." Chest rumbling with laughter, Raine seems to consider me behind those blacked-out lenses. "Feel free to do whatever you'd like in return. I'm an open book."

"Um." My throat seizes. "I don't kn…"

An invisible hand wraps tight around my windpipe before I can say no. That damn curiosity is too strong to ignore. As my voice trails off, Raine waits expectantly. Not daring to touch my face yet, his hand hangs in limbo as I deliberate.

For once, I don't want to run. Those violin-toughened fingertips promise salvation, and the smirking man bulldozing my self-imposed boundaries knows it.

Instead of answering, I lift an unsteady hand and grasp his glasses. Raine's throat spasms as I carefully slide them from his face. All I want is another glimpse of the honeycomb jewels he keeps hidden.

If it wasn't for them or the telltale bouncing of his eyes from side to side, never finding a target to land on, I wouldn't know he's blind. His irises are golden pools of treacle.

It isn't always dramatic like how it's shown in the movies— clouded over eyeballs or obvious, gnarly scarring. Even his pupils still dilate, untouched by whatever stole his eyesight. They're a regular size. He must've run out of whatever I caught him snorting the other night. That explains the lack of intoxication.

"Satisfied?" Raine murmurs.

Gently placing his glasses down, I stare into his unfocused eyes. "Seems only fair."

"Agreed. Now, hold still."

Fingers connecting with my left cheek, he gingerly caresses

my skin, following the slope of my features. His index finger traces the outline of my jaw, while his thumb swipes over my lips, tugging the bottom one down ever so slightly.

Travelling upwards, Raine strokes beneath my eye, as if feeling for the sunken ravines that provide evidence of my exhaustion. My heart gallops painfully when he traces my eyebrows and cupid's bow before following my narrow, upturned nose.

"What do you see?" I breathe out.

Inspection complete, he brushes the backs of his knuckles against my cheek. "Well, I can hazard a guess why Lennox and Xander are so obsessed with you."

"I could've told you that. They hate my guts."

His hand falls away. "Even if they hadn't told me the bitch who set them up is hot as fuck, I would've guessed so. But it doesn't matter to me either way. I have a different concept of beauty now."

I'm not sure what's more entertaining—the fact that pair of assholes willingly said something semi-nice about me or Raine's back-handed compliment. The feel of my face tells him I'm hot. People have said a lot worse to me, so I'll take it.

"What do you find attractive?"

Tongue darting out to wet his lips, those honeyed orbs dart around, searching for the forever out of reach.

"Conversation. Laughter, but only the genuine kind. The way someone breathes. Footsteps. Nervous tics like teeth grinding or fidgeting. The slightest change in tone or intonation."

"You pick up on all of that?"

Raine hesitates, the corners of his eyes crinkling in thought, before he answers. "I have to. I live my life in the margins of a full page. All I've got is subtext."

Hand searching the nearby table for his glasses, Raine locates them, then his gaze vanishes once more. Retreating back behind the relative safety of his lenses and a scripted persona.

"Thanks for the art lesson." He changes the subject.

"Raine—"

"I should go."

Fumbling back to his abandoned violin case and guide stick, he gathers his belongings to leave. My muscles twitch with the urge to chase after him and break those fucking glasses so he has no ability to hide anymore. Not from me, at least.

"And good luck with the grand revenge plan," he adds. "Perhaps you'll feel differently about circumstance when your so-called enemies are dead and you're left to deal with the consequences."

Tap. Tap. Tap.

I'm left staring after him, my face still tingling from the tender caress of his fingers mapping its topography.

CHAPTER 8
RIPLEY
DEVIL – LOWBORN

"OI! BITCH!"

I release Luka's hand, a small bundle of laxatives passed between us. He takes one look at the impending hothead barrelling towards us then books it with a muttered *thank you*.

"Welcome," I grumble.

My Wednesday deliveries are almost complete. The usual suspects have scuttled up to accept their packages and deliver payment or hopelessly barter for a grace period they should know I'll never give.

Blowing out a long breath, my skin prickles with pins and needles. It feels too tight. Stretched thin over my bones, like the groaning, rusted springs of a used trampoline being pummelled by an overexcited child. Mania always begins physically for me.

Another warning sign.

The upward swing is coming.

After my intense encounter with Raine, I spent a two-day stint in bed. Leaden and immovable. I only moved to use the bathroom and drink water from the tap. Not even my stomach could fight the weight of depression and force me to eat this time.

Tossing and turning, his words tormented me on a sleep-deprived loop. *You don't blame soldiers for the price they paid to survive the battlefield.* Maybe not. But shouldn't the survivor feel some remorse? Shouldn't they mourn the blood on their hands?

Lennox and Xander don't feel remorse. They have no regret for their cruelty, only pride at the position they stole in the most heinous of ways. Some villains cannot be redeemed. Especially those who refuse to acknowledge their own crimes.

"Ripley!" the voice hollers again.

Sighing, I scratch at my irritated inner arms beneath my jacket. I should've known that Rick would send one of his lackeys to fetch his usual smokes, like I'd somehow surrender the goods if he didn't show his face again.

The poor bastard looked scared shitless when I told him to trot back to his friend to deliver the bad news. I ain't selling shit to Rick ever again. Not after the stunt he pulled. But apparently, he's going down swinging.

"Morning to you too," I greet cheerily.

Stopping short, Rick holds back a snarl. "Where the fuck are my smokes?"

"As I told your little pet, Carlos, I have nothing for you."

His hands curl into fists at his sides. I don't give a shit about the lines of olive-toned muscle bulging beneath his t-shirt. If he makes a single move, I'll unleash hell on him.

"We have a standing order!" he insists, nostrils flaring.

"Like I explained in the cafeteria, I don't sell to assholes. Clearly, you didn't heed my words."

"You cannot be serious."

"People keep doubting me." I lay on an exaggerated pout. "Am I not being clear enough?"

Rick's face is slowly turning a beetroot shade of red. It's not an attractive look. No one's here to pay attention to us in the abandoned quad, it's too cold to brace the icy wind and impending snowstorm today.

I'd prefer an audience; I can't have people thinking they can talk to me like I owe them shit. Rick's been inching ever closer to crossing that line for a while now. My authority over the patient population can't be challenged without consequence.

"You don't want to do this," he warns in what I'm sure he thinks is a threatening tone. "I don't care what people here think of you. I'll bury you all the same."

"For refusing to sell you some cigarettes?" I laugh at him.

"For disrespecting me!" His lips curl back in a grimace. "And for being a bitch!"

Laughter dying, I let him see exactly how pathetic I think he is. "Tell me who the hell would respect someone like you?"

"Back off, Ripley. Final warning."

"Or what?" I challenge. "You gonna teach me a lesson, tough guy?"

His shoulders hunch in preparation. "Maybe I will."

I see the blow coming from a mile away, ducking before his fist can connect. However, a punch to my stomach comes too soon after for me to avoid. Pain flaring in my midsection, I wheeze through a choked breath.

"Still wanna laugh at me, bitch?" he shouts.

Rick takes advantage of my momentary surprise and goes for another hit. This one connects with my left cheekbone. My head whips to the side, a delicious sizzle of agony racing through my extremities.

But there's no satisfaction to give him.

Pain doesn't shut me down.

It wakes me up like a lightning bolt to the heart, reminding me why I've spent years fighting to survive in the first place. To hurt. To feel pain. To be unequivocally alive. I'm living for Holly too, and every ounce of agony I can secure further repays my debt to her ghost.

It's no less than I deserve. A life of immeasurable pain and suffering. Perhaps then, when I ascend the steep slopes into the devil's lair, he'll take pity on me and send me straight back up. Doesn't seem likely though, does it?

"You walk around this place like you own it, but I see through you," Rick hisses, his spit flying. "You're worthless."

Shaking the dizziness from my head, I glare up at him. "You're right. I'm nothing."

"Too right!"

"But you know what?" My feet spread into an even stance. "That also means I have nothing to lose."

When I lunge, Rick tracks the move and attempts to block the blow. Exactly as I knew he would. I pivot at the last second, my Converse-covered feet sliding on the lawn as I land a low punch to his kidney instead.

The air whooshes out of him, choked off by a second punch to his ribcage. As he attempts to cover himself, I switch stances and hit upwards, clipping him straight in his square jaw.

Pain cracks across my knuckles, but he stumbles backwards, a second from falling flat on his backside. I take a moment to enjoy the show. Watching him flail about is fucking hilarious after all his bravado.

"You asked for this!" he bellows.

I shrug nonchalantly. "Do your worst, hot shot."

With an angry scream, he barrels towards me. I won't tackle him like I did Lennox. That would be too easy. I want to enjoy this oh-so sweet victory before I bury this son of a bitch once and for all.

Down we go.

Twisting, punching, we're a violent tangle of limbs. Rick's legs find my waist, and as I make impact with the ground, he manoeuvres himself on top to straddle me. His triumphant grin only makes me even more giddy.

I feel a hot slick of blood trailing from my mouth, the ache sharpening my awareness. His eyes latch on to the sticky ribbon. As he inspects his handiwork, I fight the urge to buck him off.

"Wasn't so hard, was it?" he leers. "Whores like you belong on their backs."

"I suppose this is the only way you can get a girl to touch you, huh?"

Fingertips sliding over cold grass, I inch my hand down my oversized tee and into my waistband. He's far too distracted by peacocking his fragile masculinity to pay any attention to my movements.

"Believe me, I'd need a hell of an incentive to touch you." He looks over my face with exaggerated disgust. "Who could ever want you?"

"Is that supposed to hurt my precious, girly feelings? Fuck off, Rick."

He grips my biceps, keeping me pinned. "Not until you learn some damn respect!"

As I'm wrapping my fingers around the handle of my switchblade with full intent to stab him in the liver and be done with this already, the weight pressing into me instantly vanishes.

"Argh!" Rick screeches.

He's tossed aside like little more than a sack of potatoes, tumbling before landing on the ground with a pained curse. In his place, a slim but wiry shadow blots out the winter sun beaming through snow-filled clouds.

The shadow crouches, bringing his midnight-blue, almost black gaze level with mine. His appearance steals the oxygen from my lungs. Such devilishly familiar eyes. A frozen wasteland, bereft of all human emotion and empathy. Nothing but cruelty stares back at me.

I'm sucked into that desolate black hole without warning, despite the years since I first found myself caught in his spider's web. I couldn't help it back then; his savagery intrigued me. But now, I know what kind of monster I'm up against.

I won't survive a second round.

One already broke my soul in half.

"This guy bothering you?" he asks crisply.

"Xander."

"Hello, Ripley."

Nothing escapes his all-consuming orbit. Not even the promises I made to myself that if we ever came face to face again, I'd be more than the submissive toy he saw me to be, standing in the way of his grand master plan.

A mere obstacle.

And one he could destroy.

That's what put me in Xander's line of fire. It was never personal. Not even sexual. He wanted power, and to get to Holly, he had to eliminate me. Even if that meant reaping my soul and devouring it whole, like a fucking appetiser.

It was just one night.

One fateful, agonising, fucking *liberating* night.

That's all it took to leave her exposed.

"Cat got your tongue, little toy?" He raises a single, platinum-blonde eyebrow. "I wondered when our paths would cross."

Unable to stand the sight of him looming over me, I ignore Rick's pained whimpering and clamber to my feet. "I hoped they never would."

"I bet you did. Have you been hiding from me?"

Yes.

"Don't flatter yourself," I grind out instead.

Tall and compact, Xander doesn't pack his threatening prowess in bulk like Lennox does. He's still ripped beneath his starched polo shirt and jeans, but he could raze entire armies with nothing more than his intelligence and sharp tongue.

Those soulless orbs are framed by long, luscious lashes, a

stark contrast to his spotless alabaster skin pulled taut over exaggerated cheekbones and thin lips. He's beautiful in that ethereal, masculine way only those blessed by the DNA lottery can be.

His hair, kept neat and short, is the purest shade of snow-white. It gleams like pale moonlight. Oh, the fucking irony. How can this walking, talking incarnation of the devil so closely resemble an angel?

And he knows it.

But his victims never do.

"Back off." I force some steel into my voice. "He's mine."

Xander's brow is still raised. "Were you under the impression that anyone but myself is allowed to steal those exquisite sounds of pain from your tongue?"

Goddamn. Fucking. Psychopath.

"I'll be giving you no such thing," I snap back. "Exquisite or otherwise."

"It seems you're mistaking me for giving you a choice in the matter."

It takes all of my willpower to force back a barrage of desire-tinged memories. Wrists throbbing beneath the tight constrict of restraints. Shoulders burning from being pinned, powerless and vulnerable during the hours of torment he inflicted.

I wish I could say that he forced me. But even as I protested and writhed, terrified by his clinical, sadistic approach to sex, a traitorous part of me wanted the pain he was so fascinated by inflicting.

"I'm rather busy right now." I brush myself off. "Find another time to annoy me."

Casting Rick's still-slumped form a disdainful look, Xander lowers his voice. "As enjoyable as watching you bleed is, I don't take too kindly to others playing with my toys."

Wiping my split lip with the back of my hand, I narrow my eyes in challenge. Xander stares back for several seconds like he's waiting for me to cower and obey. Not this time. When I don't back down, he gestures for me to go ahead.

"But by all means."

"That's what I thought," I mumble.

Turning, I find Rick still on the ground, struggling to catch his breath. Xander may not look the part, but I know how strong he is. Even if he feels no need to advertise it like other men do, he could've broken Rick's back without a smidge of remorse.

Conscious of the iceman himself still watching, I finish pulling my switchblade from its hiding place and flick out the knife. It's sharp. Glinting. Begging for a drop of blood to embellish its metallic surface. Rick's eyes widen as he sees me approach.

"Listen, Rip."

"So where do I belong?" I gesture wildly with the blade. "What was it, hmm? On my back?"

"You can't do this to me!"

With a cursory glance around, I note the nearby CCTV camera. We're just out of shot in my usual delivery spot. No one will ever know if I rough him up, especially if I can scare Rick enough to keep his mouth shut.

I place a foot either side of his waist. "No one is coming to save you."

When he begins to tremble in fear at the blade moving ever closer to him, I lift a foot and smash it down on his face. The satisfying crunch of his nose smashing beneath my shoe is truly a glorious thing.

Blood is a riotous explosion pouring from his busted nose as I peer down at him. Still, it doesn't sate me. I usually tame this side of myself with the violent outpouring of artistic rage that I inflict upon my canvases. But not today.

Knees bending, I hover over his torso, dragging the sharpened tip of my blade along his clavicle. His t-shirt is flecked with blood beneath the grass stains and mud from his fall. Digging a little deeper, I slice into his skin.

"The only one who needs to learn respect here is you," I whisper sweetly. "You've forgotten who's in charge here."

"That's what y-you th-think," he splutters. "You're d-deluded, Ripley."

Digging it in deeper, I watch his eyes blow wide with pain. "Want to say that again?"

"This... isn't your institute. You're just an experiment... Fuck!" He yelps in pain. "Just like the rest of us."

Hearing Xander shift on his feet behind me, I refuse to let even a crack of concern for Rick's words show. I'm more than that. Harrowdean needs me. I'm valued here. Important. In control. They'd never successfully run their program without me.

Would they?

"You're... replaceable," Rick spits out. "We all are."

"Shut the fuck up, Rick."

"No. Like you, I also have nothing to lose." He smiles through the blood running down his chin.

Repositioning my grip on the switchblade, I stab it down into the earth an inch away from his head. He flinches, his eyes darting to the cool kiss of steel so close to impaling his face.

"Stay away from my business, and keep your mouth shut. Or next time, I won't miss. Understood?"

"It's only a matter of time until this whole thing is exposed to the world." His teeth are stained bright-red. "Priory Lane's already under investigation. Who will they blame for Harrowdean?"

I hang over him. "Stop. Fucking. Talking."

"The corporate masks hiding behind their fancy lawyers, or the unhinged nutcase on the ground, peddling drugs for profit?"

Patience expired, I yank the knife from the ground and

raise it above my head. Rick yells as it swooshes towards him, burying handle-deep in the soft flesh of his thigh.

"I am not deluded," I hiss in his face as his screams reach a fever pitch. "This is my kingdom, my institute, and you belong to me."

"Fucking lunatic! My leg!"

Grasping the switchblade, I drag it out of his thigh with a sick pop. "You slipped and fell, right? Better go and get stitched up. I'd hate for you to bleed out and fail to spread the word that I'm still in charge here."

After wiping the blade on his t-shirt, I climb off him and inch backwards. Rick presses a shaking hand to the wound in his leg as he wobbles to his feet. With a final filthy glare, he limps away towards the west wing.

My entire body is vibrating with vehement rage. Seeing the trails of blood left in his wake does little to appease me. I rebuilt my life after Holly's death on pillars of control—choosing Harrowdean, becoming their stooge, discarding everything I believed in for the same job she once did.

I took the deal.

I sacrificed it all.

But am I the one to blame?

Hands clamp down on my shoulders from behind, two steely traps preventing me from fleeing the scene of the crime. The scent of spearmint brushes over me as a soft, cold pair of lips teases the shell of my ear.

"Old Ripley was a delight to break," Xander murmurs. "But you, little toy? You're going to be my favourite project of all."

A sick shiver curls down my spine. "Let go of me, Xan."

"You know, it was quite the surprise to hear who arranged for us to be admitted into the program before vanishing from Priory Lane. I didn't think you had it in you."

Fury boils in my gut. "It clearly didn't work."

"Oh, but it did." His tongue flicks out to tease my

fluttering pulse point. "They broke us, dearest Ripley. Every day for months. But that's what you wanted, right?"

"I dreamed about it every night," I spit, acutely aware of his tongue lashing my skin. "I imagined you bleeding and in pain. Locked in a cell. Cold. Alone. Maybe dead."

He sucks in a breath at my words. "Did you enjoy your revenge?"

When his teeth scratch my earlobe, sinking in with a sharp bite that feels deep enough to draw blood, I gasp. He'd tear my throat out with his bare teeth if he felt so inclined. Probably without blinking.

"Answer me," he demands.

My body still remembers its ordeal. Obeying his every command to obtain even an ounce of relief. I'm powerless to stop it from surrendering once more.

"Yes."

"There's a good girl," he purrs.

Slipping a hand into my short hair, he grasps the messy strands then tugs so hard, it causes tears to burn in my eyes. My head is pulled back, exposing my throat to his fingertips. He trails them over my skin, a gentle caress yet full of threat.

"Then you know why I must now repay the favour," Xander says coolly. "I'm going to enjoy breaking you all over again. And I won't stop until you're begging for death."

"I don't beg for anything. Not anymore."

"But you will for me."

I hate him so fucking much, it's searing my insides like I've swallowed acid. Yet I can't convince my body to respond. Nor does it stop the hot flush of want from curling in my core. I know just how it feels to be broken by him.

"Your institute won't protect you from me, Ripley. I'll take everything you've built here and burn it all to the ground long before I let you escape again."

Releasing my hair and throat, his hot breath vanishes from

my ear. I stand stock-still, paralysed by too many conflicting emotions to make any logical decisions.

"Run. You know I love the chase."

As much as I want to stand my ground, defend the life I've spent rebuilding to never be that weak, submissive girl again, she never truly left me. Not beneath the shields and defences I've constructed.

So I run.

CHAPTER 9
XANDER

RAIN – GRANDSON & JESSIE
REYEZ

PEN TAPPING against her leather-bound notebook, Doctor Chesterfield stares. She looks frustrated. Even a little bemused. I drag a single fingertip up and down the soft velvet of the armchair I've spent an hour sitting in.

"Your notes from Priory Lane were… enlightening."

I simply stare back.

"You're in the final nine months of your sentence now. How do you feel about that?"

Stare. Blink. Wait.

She'll have to admit defeat eventually. Baiting me to speak has never worked before, and it certainly won't now. I vowed to never again allow a shrink into my head after the third round of hydrotherapy in Priory Lane's *special wing*.

Admittedly, I was curious to know how long it would take for frostbite to set in. A twelve-hour session chained in sub-zero water finally did the trick. I carried around a toe of dead tissue for a week before they did me the kindness of removing it.

Can't have a product limping, can they?

That wouldn't appeal to buyers.

Doctor Chesterfield leafs through a thick binder of notes.

"Have you enjoyed studying maths in our program? I know you like computers."

Now she's really fishing. When that doesn't work, the doc decides to get personal instead. It never takes them long to reach for that old line of attack.

"Seventeen is a young age to be diagnosed with antisocial personality disorder, clinically speaking. It's noted that your childhood symptoms worsened with age."

Gazing straight through her, I burrow into the cold emptiness that flows through me. For as long as I can remember, it's been there. Not even the abhorrent depths of foster care awakened anything within me.

"No father listed, I see." Her watery-grey eyes flick over the scrawled notes. "Your last contact with your mother was at eight-years-old, correct?"

With a sigh, I cross my legs at the ankles then lean back.

"She made no attempts to contact you once social services intervened?" Doctor Chesterfield presses. "That must have been difficult to process as a child."

Little does she know, I've long since filed away the memories of my alcoholic mother. She's as good as dead. Abandonment is easier to accept when for all intents and purposes, the parent in question is deceased to you.

"I see there was an investigation after you were taken into care." She spares me a searching glance. "You refused to testify against her partner."

Waiting, she frowns at my continued lack of response. Bringing him into this isn't going to work. Worse people have tried. We never would've survived Priory Lane's program if we broke that easily.

"He was prosecuted though, wasn't he?" she asks in a gentler tone.

Jaw aching from grinding down on my molars so hard, I straighten in the armchair and speak for the first time. "I believe our sixty minutes are up."

"Xander—"

"Until next week, Doctor."

The weight of her eyes follows me out of the therapy room. I slam the door, perhaps a little harder than necessary, and glower at the wall for several seconds. Processing. Compartmentalising. Burying.

In the subterranean hellscape where we were held after everything with Ripley went down, memories were worth their weight in gold. The clinicians loved to pluck them free then parade them in front of us, desperate to elicit a response.

When we refused to crack, their determination increased. As did their torture techniques. The knowledge that our precious Ripley somehow arranged our admittance to that wasteland was a hateful twist they quickly used against us.

The innocent, vulnerable lamb.

But with a hell of a bite.

She's not the broken, unstable girl we last saw, screaming and sobbing as they took the body bag away, wheeled past her bedroom that was directly across the hall. The moment she turned and saw us admiring our success, she knew what we'd done.

I thought we'd scared her to silence. If the night she spent in my room didn't do the trick, then what Lennox did while I kept Ripley occupied should've sealed the deal. Instead, we set alight something I never knew lived within her.

A fighting spirit.

I was fascinated by her loneliness and vulnerability before, but the bloodstained creature I found mid-brawl in the quad intrigues me even more. Breaking her won't be easy this time around.

That thought excites me more than any small distraction I've found since I last tasted her. I'll need to do my due diligence. Study her. Discover who this new Ripley is—her proclivities, vulnerabilities, pressure points.

Broken out of my plotting by my phone demanding

attention, I fish it from my pocket. Like Priory Lane, we're allowed mobile phones here, but internet access is strictly limited.

That's how they do it—give you just enough freedom to feel grateful so you don't ask questions. If you give a death-row inmate a small length of rope, they'll make do and hang themselves without asking for an inch more.

"Yeah?" I snap.

"Xan. Code red."

My spine stiffens. "An OD?"

"No!" Lennox rushes out. "Fuck… I forgot the goddamn colours."

"You're useless," I mutter. "Where?"

"Music room. South wing."

Hanging up, I pocket my phone and move fast. The carpet-lined corridors are a blur around me. Harrowdean is small and easy enough to navigate, allowing me to quickly find the wing where the classrooms are located.

Classes are in progress, humming with voices as lessons take place. The educational aspect of these institutes is yet another tactic. Offer the sick or uneducated a nice, dangling carrot to keep them satisfied. All people want is a distraction from their misery.

Scanning the doors, I follow the signage to the music room. It's one of the less popular choices here from what I've heard. The instrument-filled space is cast in low light as thickly falling rain batters the bay window outside.

"Nox?"

"Down here," his voice echoes.

Picking through scattered chairs and sheet music stands, I search the polished hardwood floors for a body. Though we tried to avoid that by controlling his supply ourselves, it wouldn't be the first time we've found Raine passed out and incoherent.

"Here, Xan."

The broad set of Lennox's shoulders hunched over someone guides me to the farthest corner. He's kneeling down next to Raine, who rests against the wall with his glasses set aside and his blonde head lolling forwards.

Concern causes my pulse to spike as I join them on the floor. "What happened?"

"I'm fine," Raine mumbles.

"He's not," Lennox rebukes.

Resting the back of my hand against his forehead, he's blazing hot to the touch. Clammy sweat coats his face. He's breathing rapidly and shivering uncontrollably too. Sharing a glance with Lennox, we communicate silently.

I knew he'd run out soon enough, though he promised me he'd ration his stash until we could assess the situation. Ripley's presence in Harrowdean—as the clinicians' stooge, no less—has sent all our plans up in smoke.

"You guys know I hate it when you don't talk out loud." Raine winces at some invisible pain. "I'm f-fine. Just need another b-bump."

"So why haven't you?" I question as Raine weakly shoves my hand away from his face.

"He's run out," Lennox growls.

"Everything we brought with us?" I press the heels of my palms into my weary eyes. "Goddammit, Raine."

"I'll figure it out," Raine says in a frail voice. "Leave me alone."

This won't even be the worst of it. He's in for a world of misery if he doesn't re-up. Keeping him jacked enough to function but sober enough to avoid overdosing has occupied a lot of the last year.

Lennox usually handles him solo. He's the protective type, and ever the bleeding heart beneath his aggression, he took Raine under his wing last year when he arrived.

"What do we do?" Lennox worries his lip with his canine.

"We've got nothing and no supply routes in here." I watch

as Raine's teeth start chattering, his entire body still trembling. "You know who controls contraband in Harrowdean."

"Motherfuck!" Lennox slams a clenched fist against the floor. "I refuse to ask that whore for help."

"Then Raine will have to detox."

"Without medical supervision? He could fucking die!"

And knowing the shit that Raine's spent his life snorting, popping and once upon a time even injecting, that's a very real possibility. He ended up here for a good reason. Five failed stints in rehab and now this place.

"Can we buy from another patient?" Lennox suggests.

"Who? We don't know these people."

"You're not being very helpful, Xan." Lennox moves to grip Raine's shoulder. "Come on, let's move first."

Sliding a hand under his arm, I help Lennox manoeuvre Raine between us. He's limper than a strand of cooked spaghetti and groans in pain at even the slightest movements. This is going to be a nightmare.

"How do we do this?" Lennox mutters to himself.

"There's no discreet way to do it."

"We have to try. He can't stay here, anyone could walk in."

"Medical wing?"

Raine jerks in our arms. "B-Better leave m-me. No doctors."

"He's right," Lennox agrees unhappily. "I don't trust these assholes. Not after what they did to us."

"Let's just get somewhere private."

Half-carrying, half-dragging Raine across the room, even with our strength, we stumble several times. He's a dead weight between us.

We get close to the door before falling into a music stand, causing a loud clatter. Lennox trips and knocks over several chairs on the way down.

"Shit!" he groans.

Grasping Raine's waist, I hold him upright. "Good job."

"Fuck off, Xan."

Lennox makes even more noise, detangling his limbs and awkwardly lumbering to his feet. No one could ever accuse him of being graceful at his size. The lump of meat is deadly in his own right, but subtlety isn't his forte. It's why we make such an excellent team.

Just as he's brushing off his form-fitting sweats to retake his position, the door to the music room crashes open.

"Raine?"

Sweetheart-shaped face dappled with flecks of paint, Ripley's wild curls are pinned on top of her head by two paintbrushes. She's in her usual *I don't give a fuck* outfit, complete with a slashed black t-shirt depicting some obscure anime show I've never heard of.

"Did you fall?"

Stopping short when she sees us, I watch the concern melt from her lightly freckled features. It's quickly replaced by my new favourite look on her. Rage. Hatred emanates from her that is so palpable, I'd be surprised if she can even think straight in our presence. I know I certainly can't.

Hatred and obsession.

It's a fine line.

"What the fuck did you do to him?" she snarls, venom practically dripping from her words.

"What did we do?" Lennox hisses back. "What the fuck did *you* do?"

"He was fine!" Ripley defends angrily. "Raine's been practising in here while I paint every day this week."

"Has he now?" I clip out.

Lennox looks equally as surprised. I don't expect Raine to hate her the way we do; she didn't ruin his life. But some damn loyalty wouldn't go amiss after all we've done for him. My sick fascination aside, Ripley Bennet is bad news for us all.

Eyeing us warily, Ripley approaches then ducks to look at Raine's slumped form. "I thought his fever had broken."

"You knew he was like this?" Lennox glowers at her.

"You didn't know that your friend was going through withdrawal?" she hits back. "Maybe he'd be better off without you."

Moaning under his breath, I watch as Raine leans into her touch. She's cupping his cheek, brushing sweat aside as she inspects him.

Last I'd heard, Raine stood by while Ripley and Lennox beat the shit out of each other. Seems I'm working on outdated information.

"Take your filthy fucking hands off him," Lennox warns in a low voice.

Ripley straightens and steps back. "What has he been taking?"

"Raine isn't your concern."

"Because you're taking such good care of him?" she replies dryly.

"He never went through this shit when we were in charge!"

Lennox is a hair's breadth from choking her to death. I can see his palms twitching with the urge to close the kill while he has a chance. I'd enjoy seeing him try, but since he adopted Raine into our ranks, the kid is my responsibility.

"H," I answer. "That's his thing."

"He shoots up?" Surprise pulls at her features.

"Used to. Now just pills."

Rubbing her bottom lip, she seems to do some mental math. "Anything else?"

"How long have you got?" Lennox grumbles. "If it feels good, he'll pop it or snort it."

Enraged storm clouds invade her gaze. "You used to sell to him."

"We were just doing our jobs," Lennox combats. "I controlled his intake personally. We're the only reason he hasn't overdosed and killed himself already."

Ripley shakes her head, setting loose several tight curls. "One day, you're going to feel every ounce of pain you've inflicted. I'll damn well make sure of it."

"Who supplies Harrowdean's drug market?" I point out.

Her brown and green eyes dart up to me, narrowed defensively. "I haven't sold to Raine."

"But you have others. How much pain has precious, perfect Ripley inflicted, I wonder?"

From the gritting of her teeth, I know I've found a sore spot. How fascinating. Old Ripley never would've had the stomach for the role she now plays. That mousy, scared little thing was happy to hide behind her friend from the moment she arrived.

It gives me a pleasant thrill to imagine that we made her into this person—selfish, monstrous, capable of such cruel indifference. For every last drop of blood she's shed, our memories must have haunted her. The torture never ceased, no matter how far she ran.

"I can help him," she eventually announces. "But not here."

"He doesn't need your kind of help." Lennox puts a defensive hand on Raine's chest. "We need to get him clean, once and for all."

"The doctors are more likely to get rid of him than waste their time on a detox." Ripley quickly dismisses him. "He'll be discharged back to rehab."

"No!" Raine whimpers.

"Or end up somewhere worse." Her hazel eyes darken. "I've seen nuisance patients be admitted to the Z wing before."

Tales of the Z wing are told in whispers between the few who know about it. Even then, what happens there remains a myth. I don't know if Harrowdean works the same as Priory Lane, but from what I've heard, every institute under the care of Incendia Corporation has a Zimbardo wing.

Though few of us have actually seen it and lived to tell the tale. The Z wing program is a well-kept secret, hidden in the shadows that engulf the institute. Flashes of disjointed memories quickly overwhelm me.

The sharp bite of hypodermic needles. Chafing handcuffs. Ice-cold bathtubs of water. Padded cells. Scratch marks. Bloodstains. Screams and pleas for mercy. The Z wing is no place for humans. I suppose that's why none ever come out.

"P-Please," Raine begs, lifting his head long enough to look at her. "I'll take… anything."

Ignoring Lennox's violent cursing, Ripley locks eyes with me. Her visible anguish is so enticing, I'm actually hard at the sight of how much this decision is fucking with her head.

She doesn't want to hurt Raine, but in this fucked up world, all any of us know is pain. The suffering we inflict on others to lessen our own anguish. Love exchanged in droplets of spilt blood.

Jaw locked, I nod once.

She purses her lips and nods back.

"Let's get him to his room," I instruct, shifting his weight back onto me. "Take his other arm, Nox."

"We are not working with this cunt!" he seethes.

"Then go. I'll do it myself."

"Xan." Lennox drops his voice. "She cannot be trusted."

"You think I don't know that? You adopted the fucker. He's our responsibility. Right now, she's a temporary solution."

"She wants to punish us! For all we know, she'll poison Raine to do it."

"If it's any reassurance." Ripley's snarky voice chips in. "I did warn Raine that I'd kill him to get to you. But that doesn't mean I plan to do it like this. I have some tact."

Thick brows raising, Lennox stares at me as if to say *see?*

"Better the devil you know than the devil you don't." I pin

the devil in question with a long, hard stare. "Harm him and you'll join your pathetic friend in the afterlife."

With an eye roll, she gestures for us to follow her. Lennox winds Raine's arm around his shoulders. We move slowly, towing him out of the music room. Thankfully, classes are still in full swing. There's no one to witness our predicament.

As we approach the reception, other patients start to appear. Most avert their eyes when they see Ripley leading us, not daring to question the semi-conscious patient we're dragging along.

"Guard," Lennox warns under his breath.

Ripley doesn't even hesitate. "It's fine."

Aiming for the staircase that leads to the residential wing, we quickly gain the attention of the guard standing watch. His blue eyes widen as he takes in the scene, a hand moving to rest atop the baton strapped to his hip.

"Ripley? What's going on?"

She stops at the foot of the stairs, waving for us to pass. "It's fine, Langley."

"But—"

"Everything is under control."

Some silent message passes between them. Who the fuck is this guy? I don't like the way he's looking at Ripley like she's his to protect from us. I'll gladly rip out his spine and shove it down his throat.

Grumbling, Langley backs off and returns to his post. He refuses to take his eyes off Ripley though, even as she passes us and resumes leading the way upstairs. Definitely some spine ripping needed to wipe that puppy dog look off his face.

"Friend of yours?" I snark coldly.

She tosses a glower over her shoulder. "I don't have any of those."

"How much did he pay you to fuck him, then?" Lennox laughs.

"Not everyone is desperate like you."

"You little bi—"

His next word cut off by the sound of Raine groaning, Lennox settles for a death glare instead. We fall into stony silence until we reach the sixth floor.

"Where is your room?" I ask curtly.

Ripley scoffs. "Like I'd tell you that. I'll bring the goods to you."

"What do you think we're going to do? Break in and smother you in your sleep?" Lennox asks incredulously.

"I wouldn't put it past you. And frankly, it wouldn't be the first time you've eliminated the competition."

"Fine," I cut in. "Room forty-four."

She rushes off to head back down the stairs. Lennox turns his displeased stare on me as I watch her go, that tight ass shaking with each step, begging for the privilege of my handprint.

"You need to get a fucking grip, Xan. She isn't some little experiment for you to toy with and discard when you're done. That woman wants our heads on stakes, and she has the means to do it."

"I'm aware."

"You're aware? The fuck does that mean?"

Wrestling Raine towards his room, I huff out a breath. "Let me worry about Ripley."

"Let you fuck her into submission, right?" he snorts. "If that's what you call whatever you do with people."

"By the time I'm done with her, she will no longer be a concern. Let's leave it at that."

"Jesus. Sometimes you're legitimately insane."

Lennox fishes the keycard from Raine's jeans pocket then unlocks the door so we can escape inside. His room is neatly organised by necessity. Nothing is out of place or in disarray.

Raine has to know exactly where everything is, down to the precise steps it takes to reach furniture or doors. We deposit him on the bed then study our violently shaking friend.

This is the worst he's been in a long time. Supply issues are inevitable, but we've never let him get this far into the withdrawal process before.

"Here." Lennox returns from the bathroom with a wet washcloth. "Come on, Raine. Head up."

Grumbling unintelligibly, Raine doesn't even open his eyes. Lennox is forced to lift his chin for him to clean the sweat from his face. I watch on, lips pursed.

"You could help," Lennox mutters. "This is your idea."

"I warned you not to get attached to him. Look where it's brought you."

"Attached?" He shakes his head. "Raine is one of us."

"Which is why we're not leaving him to die on the floor. That doesn't mean we should care."

Balling up the washcloth, Lennox tosses it aside and rises. He gets in my face, every shred of rage that's bound tight at the core of his being on full display in those seafoam eyes.

"What they did to us in the Z wing broke something inside you, Xan. Something that I don't think can ever be fixed."

"What's your point?"

"You've always been a heartless bastard, but never cruel."

"Cruel?" I repeat flatly.

"This right here is fucking cruelty!" He gestures at me. "You used to care. You used to *feel*. Even if it was only a little bit."

Staring back into his eyes, I don't feel even a hint of remorse.

"I think you're confusing tolerance for caring."

Lennox recoils like I've punched him square in the teeth. Seeing his shock and confusion so viscerally carved into his expression almost summons an ounce of emotion. Almost. But the embers soon flicker out again.

"My best friend died in that dungeon," he accuses

acerbically. "I don't know who the fuck I escaped with, but I don't know him."

The sound of knocking on the door breaks our stare off. Lennox turns his back to me, returning to Raine's side. I exhale loudly and move to let Ripley inside.

"This is all I can spare." She pulls a clear bag of slightly off-white pills from her pocket. "Should last a few days."

I reach out to clasp the plastic baggie. "I've seen purer."

Her brows pull together into a frown. "How do you see anything from the high pedestal you've put yourself on?"

Ignoring her sass, I tear open the bag and tip a couple pills out into my palm. They have a slightly vinegary scent, the only sign that she isn't dealing tabs of paracetamol to migraine sufferers.

"I expect an extra ten percent," she blurts. "Rush fee."

Lennox barks a laugh. "You're un-fucking-believable."

"This isn't a charity." She briefly lifts one shoulder. "I wouldn't give this shit to a friend for free, and you guys sure as fuck aren't that. Be glad I'm helping at all."

"Why are you helping?" I can't help but ask.

Wringing her fingers together, Ripley can't hide the subtle glance she takes in Raine's direction. I spent months studying this woman. I know all her tells. The minute details that allowed me to create a profile as we plotted our moves.

I thought she was an easy target. Her fear called out to me like a siren's song that slipped beneath my skin and metastasised into something more. Something far more pervasive and deadly. But I never expected that night to come to mean something to me.

Once wasn't enough.

Not with her.

I want to tear apart the very fabric of her soul and keep the shredded remains for myself, like organs preserved in jars for the world to admire. Her carcass in my collection will be my finest achievement.

"My motivations are not your concern." She clears whatever strange glimmer was present in her gaze. "Tell him to pay up, or withdrawals will be the least of his concerns."

Keeping her eyes averted, she turns and leaves. Clasping Raine's pills in my hand, I stare after Ripley, wondering how the fuck my silent little lamb found the courage to make such threats.

And why it's so fucking hot.

CHAPTER 10
RIPLEY

THNKS FR TH MMRS – FALL
OUT BOY

"SO? HOW WAS IT?"

Munching on a carrot stick, I consider Holly's question. "What's there to discuss? It's therapy. Same shit, different doctor."

Her eyes twinkle with amusement. "I'm not sure that's the best attitude."

"You're telling me you seriously buy into their crap?"

Stabbing a limp French fry on her plastic tray, Holly sticks it in her mouth and chews as she thinks. I'm so glad she took a shine to me and hasn't let go in the months since I arrived. I was dreading lonely mealtimes in here like the new kid on the block.

"You're not getting out of here unless you get better," she explains with a shrug. "Not gonna do it on your own, are you?"

"Some of the world's greatest minds had bipolar." I gesture with my fork. "Van Gogh. Churchill. Hemingway. Maybe I don't need to be fixed. It's the rest of you norms who are the problem."

"Would your traumatised pizza delivery guy say the same thing?"

Wincing, I fight off a memory of screaming at the poor, terrified teenager. It made perfect sense in the moment—that he was a Martian attempting to invade my apartment. Like I hadn't ordered the pizza half an hour before and forgotten in my manic state.

He barely fled with his life after I attacked him with the baseball bat that any young woman living alone hides behind her front door. I'm not saying I would've cracked his skull open with it, but the broken bones he received got me arrested nonetheless.

The news story quickly broke when the kid started posting online about his ordeal. Uncle Jonathan's name, along with the company he works for, were splashed all over the press.

"Sure, he'd agree." I wave dismissively.

"Uh-huh. Nothing to do with the buttload of money your uncle paid him off with to shut up, right?"

"Bringing me that pizza was the luckiest day of his life. He can pay off the motorcycle he was riding and brag to all his friends about surviving the crazy chick with the baseball bat. I did him a favour."

"Is a broken collarbone a favour?"

"It is in my books."

Glancing up, we lock eyes then both burst out laughing. I've never told anyone about my complicated relationship with my uncle before, but I trust Holly not to judge me. She doesn't react like other people do when they hear my story.

Most people assume that money equals happiness, but for the orphaned girl in need of love, cash doesn't excuse the absence of a real parent. I would've taken a warm, loving uncle who took his role seriously over the shining gold credit card he offered up instead.

The sound of our laughter draws the attention of patients scattered around us. Like circling sharks, two rise from their seats and prowl over. I watch Holly's hand tense around the plastic cutlery she's holding.

"What exactly have you two got to laugh about?" Lennox slides into the seat next to Holly.

"Nox," Holly warns.

"You're running a sinking ship, Hol. We've heard all about your supply issues recently."

"Back off."

Running a hand over his messy chocolate locks, Lennox wears his signature, cruel smirk. "Why? Afraid that your new little friend will see you for what you really are?"

The bite of cold daggers piercing my skin forces me to look beyond

Holly's tormenter. Standing behind Lennox, I find the source of my discomfort. Xander is staring right at me, those bottomless pits of blue harshness burrowing into my flesh.

I stare back, transfixed by his attention. It's not the first time I've caught him watching me like I'm some fascinating scientific experiment. A curiosity to be dissected and documented. If I couldn't see his chest rising, I'd think he's a statue carved from ice.

"Final warning." Holly calmly places her plastic fork down. "I'm in no mood to take your shit today."

With malice sparkling in his eyes, Lennox leans close to whisper something in her ear. The chain around his neck gapes from his collar but doesn't quite slip out. I wonder, not for the first time, what he carries on that necklace.

Watching with bated breath as Holly's face sinks, she quickly smooths her business mask back into place. But for that brief moment, she looked so exhausted. Enough to give in.

Holly would never be defeated by a pair of bullies, right? She's the strongest person I know. A take-no-shit badass with a heart of gold beneath her steely exterior.

Lennox pulls back, his necklace disappearing. "Think about it."

"Not a chance in hell," Holly replies tersely.

"This doesn't have to get ugly."

"Then learn your fucking place, and back off," she snarls.

"Well… suit yourself. What happens next is on you."

Hands scrunching into fists, Lennox stares at her for another second, as if he can decapitate her with a mere glance. She doesn't deign to offer him another moment of her time, her complete lack of fear seeming to only piss him off more.

"Nox," Xander finally speaks. "We have somewhere to be."

His voice is a whip flaying every exposed nerve-ending, the flat tenor dragging down my spine like sharpened fingernails on a chalkboard. The man terrifies me. At least with Lennox, his rage is predictable. He hates Holly, and she hates him.

But with his best friend, it's different. Hatred would demand far too much of Xander's precious time and attention. He stalks around the *institute like we're all beneath him, only lowering himself to our level when he needs a new specimen to toy with.*

"You'll regret this," Lennox hisses.

Holly spares him the briefest of looks, utterly unfazed. "Threaten me again, and you'll regret it. Priory Lane is mine."

"For now." He storms off before she can respond.

Head cocked, Xander studies me for a moment longer. I'm flustered and sweat-slick beneath his rapt attention for reasons I don't want to analyse. When Holly lays a possessive hand on my arm, the corners of his mouth quirk.

"Challenge accepted," he murmurs, barely audible.

Vanishing after his friend, we're left in peace. The breath I didn't realise I was holding whooshes out of me.

"What the hell was that about?" I whisper furiously.

Holly's hand doesn't release my arm. "They want power and control. We're not going to give it to them."

"We?"

She meets my eyes. "We. You're in this with me now, kid. We're sticking together."

Her voice floats through my mind, accompanying the repetitive beat of my feet on the treadmill. Harrowdean's gym is deserted around me. No one would dare interrupt my private time for fear of the consequences.

Punching the buttons on the screen in front of me, I increase the speed, my legs pumping like firing pistons. I've been running for nearly two hours, and despite being drenched in sweat, the swarm of angry wasps eating at my insides refuse to abate.

You're in this with me now, kid.

"Get out of my head," I pant.

We're sticking together.

Head buzzing with dizziness, I urge my legs faster,

determined to exhaust myself. I should be dead on my feet after two sleepless nights, but when these manic episodes hit, not even sleep-deprivation can slow me down.

On a scheduled patrol, a female guard pokes her head inside the gym to scan the equipment-laden room. When she spots me glowering at her, she nods briefly then disappears again.

Not even Elon dared to comment or harass me when I rushed past him earlier, practically vibrating with the need to expel some energy before I incinerate like a supernova. He merely watched me go with that annoying-as-fuck smile.

They want power and control.

"You said we wouldn't give it to them," I hiss out between breaths. "You promised to fight."

She isn't real. I'm hearing nothing but mania-fuelled whispers of a long-dead ghost. I wish I could ignore the voices when they speak to me—it's been a while since I've had that symptom. My medication usually keeps the worst of it at bay.

We're not going to give it to them.

"Leave me alone!" I scream to the thin air.

The vows Holly once made didn't stop the inevitable. Their cruel taunts tore apart the woman who took me in, gave me a home in the most terrifying of places, and taught me how to survive. In the end, she couldn't save herself.

But that's what they wanted, right?

To slowly splinter the formidable badass who'd once opposed them. Rip her into breakable pieces then scatter the remains behind them as they strolled into their new notoriety. Taking her life wasn't hard—it was a convenience.

In the game of survival, it's dog eat dog. Holly was a mere speck on their non-existent moral landscape. An annoying fly buzzing around, forever eluding the hand of its swatter until that fateful moment arrives.

Splat.

You're left with an empty dorm room, a hurriedly cut

noose and a zipped body bag. Taking a life should be harder than that. It should leave a deeper scar. So where the fuck are their scars? Why did they get to walk away and forget, but I never could?

Lost in the unstable frenzy of my grief, I don't hear the soft *tap, tap, tap* of Raine's guide stick until it's too late. The golden-haired angel appears, leaning against the handlebars of the treadmill as he draws to a halt beside me.

"Really hoping no other girl in this shithole uses papaya body wash, or I've tracked down the wrong person."

I use my tattooed forearm to wipe sweat from my face. "Don't act like you just sniffed your way down here to find me."

"What? It sounds way more impressive than me asking Xander where you're hiding."

Honestly, I'm not even surprised that Xander's keeping an eye on me. I spotted him lingering outside my therapy session one morning too. This is how he prowls. Silently. From afar. Plotting and instigating until the right time to pounce presents itself.

"Tell your psycho buddy to stop fucking following me."

Swiping a hand over his sleek blonde mop, Raine braces an elbow on the treadmill. "Like he'd listen to me."

Inspecting him out the corner of my eye, I search for any signs of the wreck I left behind the other night. Dressed in jeans and ratty t-shirt, he seems loose, relaxed.

I can see past the act he puts on though. His grin is a tad too wide and voice a little high. I wasn't sure how long that bag would last him. He must be nearly out.

"Listen, Ripley. I need to say thank—"

"Don't mention it," I interrupt.

"Can't even accept a simple thank you?" His mouth curls into a grin.

"For enabling you to continue ruining your life? I'll pass."

He pauses for a beat, appearing surprised.

"Wow. Someone left their filter in bed this morning."

I want to bark out a laugh, but I'm too overwhelmed. Exhausted yet agitated. My body is buzzing like a live wire, and the brutal run has done little to abate the feeling. I've already scrubbed myself to the point of bleeding in the shower. This was my last resort to get the swarming energy out of my system.

I've learned the hard way that unless managed, manic episodes can turn bad. Fast. These days, I recognise my warning signs and act to stabilise myself. I don't want to ever get to the point where I lose control again. That's what landed me in here in the first place.

"Ripley?" Raine prompts. "You okay?"

Slamming a hand on the stop button, I wait for the track to slow. "Look, Raine. I'm glad you're alright. But me giving you those pills doesn't mean we're friends."

"Ouch." He chuckles.

"Leave me alone."

"I was hoping we could talk," Raine offers placatingly. "About you taking on a new customer."

A fresh burst of anger shoots through me. I'm here, battling tooth and nail to get control of myself, while he's sniffing around for more gear. The painful fizzing in my limbs only heightens my disgruntlement.

"Hey, Ripley," I mimic his deep, rattling voice. "You wanna take pity on me and help me continue to kill myself?" I return my voice to normal. "Sure, Raine. Why not? I have no morals and don't care. Give me your money."

Head tilting, it almost feels like his covered eyes are following me as I shakily climb off the treadmill. My entire body is drenched with sweat, and my legs can barely hold my weight. But still, it isn't enough.

I've pushed way past my comfort zone. I know this isn't a healthy way to cope with these emotional spikes, but it was this or do something truly destructive like hurl myself down the staircase, convinced that if I want it enough, I'll be able to fly. The intrusive thought did cross my mind.

"Did I hit a nerve?" Raine asks.

"You know, I used to be more than this." I scoff at my own bitterness. "I had a life. An apartment and studio. Friends. What the fuck would they think of the person I've become?"

Suddenly furious, I don't care that he's getting a front row seat to witness my unravelling. The cocky son of a bitch has never had much trouble reading me anyway. Maybe if he gets to know the real me, he'll stay away. We can forget this weird kinship ever happened.

"I'm so sick of being the person people call when they want to kill themselves. My survival isn't worth it."

Raine's head shifts as though his eyes are brushing over me. "Like it or not, you've survived. Haven't you?"

"What if I don't deserve to?" I counter.

He shrugs. "Few of us rarely get what we deserve. At some point, you have to stop caring, and just take what you're given."

Tears mix with the sweat still dripping down my face. The floodgates are down, and any scrap of self-preservation has deserted me. Right now, I want to give in to every last reckless thought racing through my mind at lightning speed.

"Is that what you do? Take what you're given?"

He gestures towards his eyes. "Like I've had any other choice."

Memories bubble to the surface. Being sat down by the social worker as a terrified child and told that my mum was dead, not even a year after we lost Dad. Leaving an empty house full of packed boxes behind. News reports. Sympathy cards. Bereavement therapy and child counsellors.

None of them ever cracked through the lake of ice I quickly erected around my heart. Losing people hurt less that way. Until Holly came along with her sharp tongue and possessive friendship, refusing to let me tread water alone for a moment longer. Somehow, she tunnelled through the trenches surrounding my heart and set up camp.

It changed nothing.

Death stole her from me too.

"Well, I refuse to live like that," I deadpan.

"Rip—"

"No! All I've done is take what I'm given! My parents left me. I have an uncle who incarcerated me the moment I embarrassed him. My best friend was bullied to death. And if I don't do as the warden says, I won't be far behind her."

Chest heaving, my feet carry me over to Raine of their own volition. I stop directly in front of him, shaking with fury, exhaustion and the fiery riptide of emotion that's loosened my tongue.

He's one of them. An enemy. So why does the sound of his heartbroken violin keep me awake at night? Why did I sacrifice my own supply to fund his addiction? Why the fuck do I care about this person?

Because despite all the shit I've seen, I still wasn't strong enough to plug the final cracks in my heart. Raine has managed to sneak in too with those damned smirks and snippets of vulnerability hidden behind a cocky demeanour. He found my weakness.

Well, *fuck him.*

I'll do the exact same bullshit to him.

"I don't want to take what I'm given." My voice drops lower as mania turns to blood-laced desire. "I want to take what I *want.*"

Raine hesitates, silently taking in the details he can sense beyond his non-existent line of sight. I wonder if the drugs in his veins feel like the poisonous sickness in mine. If we'd be here, together, without either of those things drawing us together.

"What do you want?" he asks breathily.

Salvation. Plain and simple. No matter the pain I must

inflict to reach that ethereal paradise, beyond the demons dragging me back to reality every goddamn time.

"The same as you." Hand trembling, I slide the glasses from his face to reveal his pinprick pupils. "To feel alive."

His throat undulates. "It's been a long time since I've felt that."

"Alive?"

Raine's habitual smirk reveals itself. "You're talking to a self-proclaimed junkie, babe. We shoot up to feel everything... Or nothing at all."

Tossing his glasses aside, I close the final gap between us. My heartbeat roars in my ears as I grab a handful of the loose grey t-shirt he wears over his ripped jeans and drag him closer, until our chests slam together with an audible *thwack*.

"Then feel something with me."

Raine's plump lips part on a sharp inhale. I could gaze into the molten caramel depths of his distant eyes all day long, not caring for a single second that he'll never be able to gaze back. I exist in his mind. That's a far greater privilege than many get.

Need overwhelms me. Need to be loved. To be wanted. To exist for someone in a far greater capacity than their dealer or destroyer. I want Raine to see me for the girl I used to be, not the girl I am now.

My mouth slants over his, sealing our twisted exchange with a hard, painful kiss. Eyes closing, I join him in the blackness. Our lips collide like two gamblers engaged in a ruthless battle of Russian roulette.

It doesn't take long for Raine to respond and move his mouth against mine. My breathing falters with the violent onslaught of his lips attacking mine. He's far too fucking good at this. One hand moves to clasp my hip as the other rises, searching blindly until he cups the back of my head.

The soft growl in the back of his throat causes warmth to flood my throbbing core. I thrust my tongue into his mouth, searching for a silent commitment to our shared need for an escape. I don't care if he's high and I'm on the verge of a manic meltdown.

I need his tongue.

His touch.

A reason to exist.

Dragging a hand over the rough scruff on his face, I clutch his chin and deepen the kiss. I want to suck the used oxygen from his lungs and let it poison my airways. Then he can offer his friends the victory of my death, and perhaps, I'll finally know peace.

His hips rock forward, revealing the hard press of his erection as it grinds against my centre. A moan rumbles from my chest with the movement, and Raine thrusts again, making his intentions crystal fucking clear.

I'm a second from letting him fuck me on the treadmill to give me the release I crave when an ear-shattering alarm breaks out, causing us to jump apart. It's excruciatingly loud, blaring relentlessly as the emergency lights begin to flash.

"What the hell is that noise?" Raine covers his ears.

"It's the panic alarm," I shout over the clamour, licking my now-swollen lips. "We're supposed to get on the floor."

"Screw that. We're not done here."

His hands find their way back to my head and hip. Fingers fisting in my sweat-drenched hair, he pulls hard until his lips meet mine with cataclysmic finality. Not even the painful shriek of the alarm can stop me from falling victim to his hot mouth on mine.

I know we only have a matter of minutes before a guard arrives to escort us to our rooms. That alarm signals the institute going into lockdown. An incident must be unfolding, but for the life of me, I couldn't care less.

Releasing my hip, Raine's fingertips search the stretchy material of my workout leggings. He's moving lower, feeling a path to the heat that's burning between my thighs. I gasp into his mouth as he cups my mound.

"Fuck, Rip. I can feel how soaking wet you are through your clothes."

"You gonna do something about it?" I challenge.

Lips equally swollen, he grins at my boldness. "Like I'd ever leave a girl wanting."

"We're going to have company very soon."

Finding my waistband, he eases his hand inside. "Then you'd better come all over my fingers fast, shouldn't you?"

Returning his lips to mine, he shoves his tongue back into my mouth at the same time his hand breaches the soaked cotton of my panties. I can't help rocking my hips, guiding him to exactly where I want his touch. The frenzy within me is begging for an outlet.

Even if this is a bad idea.

My unstable brain couldn't care less right now.

Raine's tongue is a bulldozing force of nature, claiming every available inch of my mouth and stealing it for himself. It feels like he's taking the time to catalogue every last corner, filing it away in his ever-expanding portfolio of information beyond his lack of sight.

I moan loudly when his fingers slip inside my panties and glide down towards my humming cunt. He easily parts my folds, his thumb circling my sensitive bud as he slides a digit through my heat.

"Fucking hell," he mutters into my ear. "I can't wait to feel this sweet cunt clenching around my cock."

Delivering his filthy words with a sharp thrust from his fingers, he pushes inside my slit. My back arches, a hot sizzle of need pulsating through me. I want nothing more than to feel him stretching my walls and filling every desperate inch of me.

"Are you always this wet, babe?" Raine murmurs.

I'm so not going to explain my hypersexual state when I'm

mid-episode. We may be using each other right now, but there's no need to underline the truth.

"I don't know," I gasp.

"Well, I'm looking forward to finding out."

A second finger pushes into me, stretching me even wider. I'm a panting mess of sensation, grinding against his palm as my legs begin to tremble. Raine finds a steady pace, finger-fucking me into a breathless wreck.

"That's it," he coos. "Ride my hand, Rip."

Each time I circle my hips, he thrusts back into me, pushing his fingers in and out of my entrance at a maddening tempo. I can feel how coarse his fingers are from a lifetime of violin playing. It gives me a twisted thrill to have them buried deep inside me.

Just as the cusp of my orgasm begins to rise, the sound of footsteps approaching registers. I grab a handful of Raine's t-shirt to stop him.

"Hear that?"

"Yeah," he grunts.

"We have to stop."

"Not yet, babe. I'm not done."

Curling his finger inside me, he touches a mind-blowing spot that swallows whatever protest I was about to muster next. Raine grins at my loud mewling, rubbing his finger up against my inner walls to tease more moans free.

"Raine," I groan.

"I want to hear those pretty sounds as you soak my fingers. Screw whoever's coming."

"We can't—"

"Shut the fuck up," he instructs.

Skating his hand up my body, he clamps his palm over my mouth. Well, that's hot. Each flick of his wrist causes his fingers to slam deeper into me, his speed gradually increasing as I moan and pant into his hand.

With my sounds muffled, the feeling of euphoria washes

over me. I'm so close. When Raine dares to slide a third finger into my sopping core, the coiled band of tension inside me explodes.

"That's it," he says triumphantly.

I scream into his palm, my eyes clenched shut as I detonate. Bolts of lightning crackles down my spine, and my knees weaken with the force of my climax. I'm suddenly adrift, but vaguely aware of the doors slamming open and boots stomping into the gym.

"You two!"

Aw, shit.

Not even the displeased boom of Langley's voice can shatter my post-orgasm high. I manage to peel an eyelid open to look over Raine's shoulder, finding Langley standing in the entrance, hands braced on his hips.

"What on earth are you doing?" he interrogates.

Not a single decent excuse manifests.

"Getting off?" I blurt instead.

His mouth drops open. "There's a brawl going on outside!"

"Well, shit." Raine grins lopsidedly at me. "Sounds like we're missing the fun."

"Both of you out!" Langley yells. "Right now."

Keeping his back to the displeased guard, Raine pulls his glistening hand from my leggings. I'm mesmerised and totally unembarrassed as he pops his fingers into his mouth and sucks enthusiastically.

"Now!" Langley adds.

Raine releases his now-clean digits then leans closer to speak into my ear. "Next time, I want you to spread these heavenly juices all over my face. Got it?"

Holy. Freaking. Shit.

"Got it."

His smirks deepens. "Good. Let's go before we get our asses kicked."

Quickly righting my clothes, I hand Raine his guide stick. We reluctantly walk over to where Langley waits. He turns and stalks out, muttering something I can't hear over the shrilling alarm. I bite my lip to hold in a laugh as Raine chuckles.

"Worth it," he declares.

"Eh. If you say so."

"Well, shit. Thanks for the glowing review, guava girl."

"We all have room to improve. I don't want to overinflate your ego."

"Something tells me that would be impossible in your company," Raine quips back.

When his spare hand connects with my arm and slides down to find my hand, our fingers somehow end up intertwined. I don't know if I'm exhilarated or terrified by how right it feels to be held by him.

CHAPTER 11
RIPLEY

BIPOLAR RHAPSODY – KID
BRUNSWICK

PATIENTS MARCH towards the cafeteria in regimented lines, trapped under the watchful gaze of stony-faced guards. Everyone's on edge. A sleepless night of shouting and constant alarms blaring has left us all haggard.

When we were escorted back to our rooms, no one on the fifth or sixth floor knew what had happened. Rumours circled, but I don't believe the ramblings of Joshua—our resident schizophrenic. He once claimed to have seen Santa Claus dancing naked in the quad.

Rae slips between several patients to sidle up to me. "What's the stink?"

"You didn't see what happened either?"

"Nah." She glances around at the heavier than usual security presence. "Just heard about it through the grapevine. Did someone get their ass kicked?"

"I guess so."

Fights in Harrowdean aren't uncommon, but most people lack the energy to start shit here. They're far too concerned with the messy business of surviving day to day. But when scuffles happen, they get violent fast.

"That's unlike you," Rae comments.

"Huh?" I shoot her a look.

Waggling her auburn brows, she grins at me. "You're usually the first to know everyone's business around here. What had you so busy that you missed a fight?"

Cheeks heating, I avert my eyes. The memory of Raine and his sordid whispers making me come so hard I saw stars fills my mind. Fuck, does he know how to get a girl off.

It was a shame that we were forced apart afterwards, or I would've happily returned the favour. I'm dying to get my hands on that man's body. I'd like to see if he'll live up to all his filthy promises.

"Oh," she says knowingly. "It's like that, is it?"

"I have no idea what you're talking about."

"Sure." Rae nudges my shoulder as she walks beside me. "I had no idea that you could blush. Must've been a hell of a show."

"We are so not discussing this."

Jogging to catch up to us despite the grumblings of disgruntled guards, Noah stands on my other side. I don't miss the way he scans over me, checking for any signs of harm.

"You both alright?"

"We didn't see anything," Rae answers.

His throat contracts as he skims a hand over his mouth. "Someone went berserk last night. Guards dragged 'em outside, and a bunch of others followed. A full-blown mob fight broke out."

Rae gawps at him. "Seriously?"

I know this place is a fair comparison to hell on earth, but seriously, what the fuck? The guards abuse their authority more often than not. The sedatives and restraints usually come out long before this kind of thing happens, though.

"You saw the fight?" I clarify.

He nods solemnly. "It was chaos with all these idiots joining in, but I saw who the three guards dragged outside. Carlos started it."

Well, double shit. Carlos is Rick's lapdog. If what Noah says is true, the resident asshole is going to be out for blood. No wonder several others joined in. No one messes with his friends and gets away with it.

"Where were you last night?" Noah frowns.

"The gym."

His eyes scan over me, cataloguing the bruise-like smudges beneath my eyes and the still-present trembling of my body on overdrive. The gruelling run and fooling around with Raine hasn't quite taken the edge off.

I only bother going to work out when I'm struggling to hold it together. I've also been known to seek Noah out for a quick fuck when those episodes hit. But not this time. I haven't even considered approaching him since my attention moved elsewhere.

"You didn't call."

"I didn't need to," I answer impassively.

Rae's gaze bounces between the two of us, caught somewhere between confusion and amusement. Great. It's painfully obvious that I wasn't with my usual go-to hook-up last night. I can see she's desperate for details about where I was.

"What about that... other thing?" Noah asks quietly.

"What other thing?" Rae looks between us.

"I need more time." I ignore her, pitching my voice low. "But be ready."

He nods in understanding. "I will be."

Before Rae can continue fishing for information, a harsh voice barks, startling us all.

"Silence!"

The guard, Kieran, is one of Elon's scowling sycophants. He pierces the three of us with a glare until we're forced to shut up. I catch Noah's gaze, and he shakes his head, warning me off talking back to this wanker.

"What crawled up your ass and forgot to die?" I snap, disregarding Noah.

Several nearby patients sneak us nervous looks, waiting to see Kieran's reaction. It's clear that even the guards are on edge this morning.

"You want to say that again?" Kieran returns, hands on his hips.

"Why? Are you deaf as well as stupid now?"

Laughing under her breath, Rae catches his attention next. His lips curl in a derisive sneer as he takes a step closer to her. She can't stop laughing at him.

"That's insubordination, inmate. Let's go."

"Go where?" Rae giggles.

"A night in solitary ought to shut you up."

The colour drains from her face as her laughter dies off. Rae hasn't experienced that delight yet, and I have no doubt a night in a cell with nothing but her own mind for company will truly end her.

"She's just laughing," I defend.

"Enough," he snaps at me. "You were told to be silent!"

"You're threatening my friend."

"Then she should've kept her goddamn mouth shut, shouldn't she?"

Seeing the visceral terror on Rae's face is the final straw. Regardless of the awful things I've enabled her to do to herself, I still care about her. I'll take this dick's wrath before letting her suffer.

"You can't talk to us like that," I chide. "We still have rights."

"Not that I noticed," Kieran sneers.

Consequences or not, I want to beat the shit-eating smile off this bastard's face. Whatever happened last night has nothing to do with us. He can take his bad attitude elsewhere.

"You all need to learn who is in charge around here!" he

rages loudly, his voice causing several patients to startle. "Disrespect will not be tolerated."

"I'm s-sorry." Rae is now trembling, her eyes filling with tears. "Please don't make me go to the hole."

"I don't give a shit, inmate. You're coming with me."

"No!"

"Enough! You're out of here!"

When Kieran reaches out to restrain her, I leap into action and step in front of Rae. She ducks behind my shoulder, her cheeks stained with tears.

"Leave her alone. She's done nothing wrong."

"You both wanna go down there instead?" His spit flies angrily.

"Gladly!" I shout back. "If it'll mean I don't have to look at your ugly mug for a second longer."

His narrowed eyes fill with discontent. "You little…"

Drawing his baton from the belt around his waist, he raises it high. I try to move to protect myself from the blow, but sandwiched between the tight press of patients, I'm too late to avoid it swinging towards me.

"Rip!" Noah bellows.

Pain blooms in my abdomen from the hard strike. I double over, coughing and wheezing as I fight to avoid hurling. I feel an arm wrap around me as I blink aside tears. I won't give him the satisfaction.

"That fucking hurt," I grit out.

"Now, now." Elon's smarmy voice nears. "What's going on here?"

With my head lowered, I can see his shining black boots approaching our huddle. He easily parts the crowd around us before stopping next to his dickhead colleague.

"Nothing to worry about," Kieran responds.

"Then let's not make a scene."

"But sir, she—"

"Move along, everyone," Elon commands. "Nothing to see here."

Surrounding patients begin to shuffle away, resuming their trudge into the cafeteria. I hear Elon move closer, his knees bending so he can lower himself to my level.

"When will you learn to keep that loud mouth of yours shut?" he hisses.

"Fuck off," I croak.

"Get your ass inside, Ripley. My patience for you is wearing very thin."

Returning to his full height, I hear Elon clap his pal on the shoulder before he saunters away. Kieran reluctantly follows him, still complaining to himself about tossing our asses in solitary.

"Jesus Christ," Noah grunts. "They've lost their minds."

"Can you stand?" Rae touches my shoulder.

Nodding, I straighten my spine, despite the fierce agony curling around my midsection. Rae backs off at my cursing, giving me some space to breathe.

My eyes catch a pair of seafoam orbs amidst the crowd. Lennox isn't even fighting to hold back his grin. He shifts to murmur something in Xander's ear, the pair of them watching me struggle. Raine is nowhere in sight.

Teeth bared, I flip them off.

Xander slips back into the crowd with his buddy. I've caught him silently following me several times recently, never once saying a word, but keeping me within his sights at all times. Stalking. Hunting. Studying.

I'd very much like to take that baton from Kieran and shove it up Xander's asshole. Perhaps he'd learn then that I'm not some scientific curiosity for him to tear apart. I don't even want to consider what he's planning.

"Come on." Rae grips my elbow. "Let's go before we get in more trouble."

"Yeah."

"Um, Rip?" A rush of breath shoots from between her lips. "Thanks for sticking up for me."

I study her tear-streaked cheeks and glassy, kohl-lined eyes. Emotion claws at my throat. Thick. Cloying. A bittersweet concoction that I usually shove down as deep as possible when I fulfil her regular orders.

"You deserve better, Rae."

"Than what?"

The backs of my eyes burn. "Than any of this."

Arm curled around my aching waist, I turn away and follow the moving flow of patients. Noah accompanies us through the packed reception and into the awaiting cafeteria where long tables are slowly filling up.

At the head of the room, Davis watches over us all with cold calculation. His salt-and-pepper hair is slicked back today, perfectly matching his impeccably tailored suit.

We approach an almost full table, the few patients spread across the seats quickly scattering when I cast an eye over them. A couple even mumble apologies without daring to look up at me.

Rae takes the seat opposite. "What does the warden want?"

I shrug, easing myself into the chair with a wince. Before Noah can sit down next to me, a huge, scarred hand clamps down on his shoulder. He's roughly shoved aside so someone else can take his place.

"Seat's taken," Lennox growls roughly.

I glower up at his smiling mug. "Like fuck it is."

Despite his smirk, the predatory gleam in Lennox's eyes is pure malice. He ignores Noah's put-out expression and slides in next to me, the overwhelming bulk of his shoulders brushing against mine.

"What are you doing?" I snarl under my breath.

Lennox fiddles with the silver chain tucked into his neckline. "That beating was a hell of a sight."

"Show's over, Nox."

He chuckles throatily, the sonorous sound rumbling from his chest. "I think it's just beginning."

Beneath the table, my fingers curl until I feel the sting of my nails piercing my palms. "I saved your friend. Leave me alone."

"You think that makes us even somehow?" he huffs. "We need to get a few things straight."

Determined to ignore him, I focus on the small scuffles and shows of aggression unfolding around us. Several patients are being shoved and manhandled. The tension is racketing up more with each second.

I don't recognise several of the additional guards that have been called in to beef up security. They seem even more overzealous, positioning their sheathed weapons clearly on display and barking at everyone who dares to scuttle past.

"Listen, bitch," Lennox demands.

"What?" I hiss back. "Get on with it, then fuck off."

He leans close, his tone frigid. "Raine was high this morning."

I don't respond at first. Wrestling with my decision to sell to him after what happened in the gym has relentlessly occupied my thoughts. But when the trembles returned, I had no choice but to cave.

"I won't watch you deal drugs to Raine and screw him up even more."

"You'd rather poison him yourself, huh?" I retort.

"We protected him," Lennox grinds out.

"And benefitted from every drop of goodwill, no doubt."

"You won't keep him safe." His shoulders hunch, lined with determination. "I refuse to watch someone I care about get hurt because you're too greedy to regulate his intake."

"Is it hard?" I peer deep into his pale-green irises. "Seeing someone you care about get hurt? I wouldn't know what that's like, would I?"

Ignoring my snark, his hard gaze cuts into me. "We will take control of Harrowdean, one way or another. Why don't you just give it up now?"

"Because, almighty Lennox, men like you are the reason why places like this exist."

At my words, he recoils like I've stabbed him in the gut. I can feel the rage and indignation pouring off him in waves. I almost laugh out loud at his visceral reaction. Drilling into Lennox's ceaseless vein of fury will never stop being entertaining.

Beneath the anger he wields as a deadly weapon, Lennox likes to think that he has this strict moral code. Some pathetic justification for the horrors he's inflicted in the name of keeping those he cares about safe.

Lennox isn't just an angry man; he's a broken one. And that particular brand of twisted love is the reason so many of us walk around with holes in our hearts through which our sanity escapes.

"If anything happens to Raine because of you—"

No longer able to stifle it, laughter tears free from my throat.

"What? You gonna kill me? Or perhaps another one of my friends?"

Casting a quick glance around the bustling room, Lennox moves fast for a man of his stature. I gasp as he seizes a handful of my short curls and slams my face down into the solid tabletop. Hard.

"Argh!"

Wrenching my hair in his grip, he lifts my head to inspect the blood that's exploded from my now-throbbing nose. I breathe raggedly, swallowing the river streaming down my throat.

Lennox's lips touch my ear. "I'll make what I did to Holly look like a walk in the park compared to your death."

"So you keep threatening," I choke wetly. "Yet... I'm still alive."

"Careful what you wish for, cunt."

Releasing my hair, he rises and quickly blends back into the crowd of patients. I straighten my septum piercing and pinch the bridge of my nose to staunch the blood. Today is not my fucking day.

"Here." With eyes the size of dinner plates, Noah pulls a crumpled tissue from his jeans pocket as he sits down. "Your face is covered in blood."

I quickly plug my nose. "Thanks."

"What the hell is his problem?" Rae gawps after the giant.

Watching Lennox's broad shadow part the crowd, I can't even answer her. If Holly were here, she wouldn't take this laying down. She'd know what to do. But with each passing day, I feel like I'm losing more control. Just like she did.

"Attention all." Davis's voice booms over the low conversation. "Be seated."

His authoritative tone matches the terrifying coldness in his gaze. The walls of the cafeteria are crawling with guards, shoulder to shoulder, all watching with the same frigid glares.

"Last night's violence was deeply unfortunate and will not be tolerated." Davis casts a look around the packed room. "A full investigation will be taking place to determine what unfolded."

"Where is Carlos?" someone shouts.

Glancing to my left, I spot Rick and his gaggle of buddies. They're all glaring and visibly bruised, like they spent the night plotting the institute's demise after getting their asses handed to them.

Davis clears his throat. "We have a zero-tolerance policy for violence here at Harrowdean."

"Violence?" Rick yells, breaking his silence. "What have you done to him?"

"Enough!" Davis shouts back with a rare flash of temper.

"Inciting group violence against our staff is unacceptable. We have rules that must be followed."

"Fuck the rules!" another person calls out.

"Where is Carlos?"

"You can't keep shoving us around!"

With each voice that adds to the melee, more and more patients are speaking up. Guards close in around us, pushing and shoving, but their intimidation isn't working. Not when we have strength in numbers.

Davis gestures for the guards to halt. "Our number one priority here at Harrowdean is your safety. Action was taken last night to preserve the peace."

"Bullshit!"

More enraged shouting ensues. Rick and his friends are at the heart of it, spitting and raging, despite the tight press of security attempting to contain them. Seeing their outburst sets off others until Davis's voice is no longer audible.

"This is going to turn bad, fast." I glance around at the advancing guards. "With all that extra muscle."

"We need to get out of here," Noah agrees.

Pulling the wad of wet tissue from my nose, I shove it in my pocket before offering Rae a bloodstained hand. She smiles gratefully then links our fingers so we can stand up together.

"Let's go."

"What if they stop us?" she worries.

"The guards are gonna have bigger things to worry about if this goes south." Scanning the crowd, I search for Langley. "Besides, I can get us out."

Seeing us rise, several other nervous patients begin to follow, seeking a safe route out of the increasingly unstable situation. How I became a symbol of safety, I'll never know. It's laughable, really.

Winding a path through the crowd, we're halfway to the doorway when there's a loud crackling noise. I glance over my

shoulder in time to see one of Rick's friends—Owen, I think
—thrashing on the cafeteria floor.

"Tasers?" Noah gasps. "Move!"

A cacophony of screams fuels the rising panic. There's
another loud crack. Thudding batons. Crying. Barked orders
to disperse. Now there's a tsunami of people trying to do
exactly the same as us—escape.

We're being half-carried by the shoving crowd. Sounds of
violence echo all around us, adding to the carnage. All it took
was a tiny spark to ignite.

"Ripley!"

Waving above his head, Langley motions for us to go to
him. Clenching Rae's hand tight, I tow her along, hoping that
whoever is behind me can fend for themselves. We have to
fight to get over to Langley as it is.

Snagging his shirt sleeve, I drag us the final steps. Langley
clears the rest of the path. He has a reputation for being one
of the good ones, so he doesn't seem to be attracting the
attention of those looking to fight.

"What happened to your face?" He winces.

"Just help us!"

Langley pushes open the exit doors then ushers us outside
into the welcome safety of the corridor. As soon as we're free,
I can drag in a full breath. It's short-lived, though. There's a
whole ass stampede hot on our heels.

"Get out of here," Langley instructs. "Go!"

Still holding Rae tight, I break into a run. Only this time,
it isn't a crazed fellow patient posing a threat. It's the very
forces hired to protect us who want to harm us.

My kingdom is crumbling.

Harrowdean isn't safe anymore.

CHAPTER 12
LENNOX

MONSTER – FIGHT THE FADE

ARMS FOLDED ACROSS MY CHEST, I lean against the corridor wall. My room is being thoroughly ripped apart by two guards, leaving no item of clothing or possession untouched. I don't know what they're hoping to find.

Down the entire hall, similar scenes of destruction are replicated. Why bother asserting their control when they know full well who supplies contraband in this place? Well, for exactly that reason.

It's all about control. Scare the herd enough, and they'll stay contained in their self-enclosed pen. The clinicians may be feeding this experiment to elicit the juicy results they desire, but the chaos must be strictly governed.

They want us to suffer. Self-destruct. Barter and bicker our way to dominance over each other. Those are the fascinating situations they want to see play out. But when the guinea pigs start to bite their masters? The chaos isn't so measurable then.

"Nox."

Tapping his way towards me with his stick outstretched, Raine whisper-shouts my name. I take a final glance at the guards ripping apart my mattress to check for stashed weapons and approach him.

"You alright?"

"I heard my room's next," he says in a panic. "I've got shit they can't find."

"Fuck, Raine!"

"I know. Help me, man."

Shaking my head, I snag his long shirt sleeve and frogmarch him towards his room. Raine hands me his keycard so I can unlock the door quickly. We step inside, hoping no one has spotted us.

"Where is it?" I sigh tiredly.

"Bottom drawer in the nightstand has a false bottom." He anxiously chews his lip. "And there's a loose floorboard behind the desk."

"Go stand near the door. If you hear them coming, shout."

Quickly nodding, he taps a path back towards the door then presses his ear against it. I set to work investigating the nightstand and quickly find a notch in the smooth, dark wood that I prise open.

He's been better since the night we begrudgingly enlisted Ripley's help. Regardless of my feelings about that soulless bitch, I know we couldn't let him stay like that. It was far too risky to let him detox there and then.

But the idea of her supplying him on the regular is making me want to demolish this whole damn room to ensure he has none of her pills to snort. I don't know how he convinced her to sell to him, but there's nowhere else he's getting this stuff from.

"Got it?" Raine asks.

I scoop up two baggies of pills in a variety of colours. "What is this shit, Raine?"

"Just get the rest. They're coming."

Slotting the false bottom back into place, I duck beneath the nearby desk next. It takes several seconds to locate the loose floorboard underneath. I have to dig my nails into the edges to wriggle it free.

More pills.

These ones are that weird, off-white shade and clearly the same as the ones in the baggie Ripley previously supplied. I gather his stash in a pile then shove it into the waistband of my sweatpants, tightening the drawstring to hold it all in place.

"We good?" Raine's voice is strained.

I slot the floorboard back. "All clear."

His shoulders sag with relief just as the lock on the door buzzes. It's flung open, narrowly missing him. The two assholes who were tearing apart my room order us outside before they begin obliterating Raine's neatly organised space.

"Fucking hell." He winces at the sounds of destruction. "There goes my system."

"We'll put it all back," I try to reassure him.

"The bastards aren't even pretending to be gentle." The sound of crashing punctuates his words. "Do they really think this tactic works?"

As I peer up and down the corridor full of terrified patients, seeing what Raine cannot, I hate to admit that it does work. Everyone knows where to get their illegal shit from in here, but few know the sinister secret behind the program's existence.

Most assume that Ripley has some pretty impressive connections to get her hands on anything that's requested. If the entire institute knew the clinicians are feeding this toxic machine of mental illness in the name of experimentation, they'd kill themselves or try to escape.

Few are doomed to know the truth.

Including us.

Those who remain clueless are petrified of raids like this. They scuttle around, obeying the rules and hoping their sentence will pass without incident. Forever ignorant to the fact that management wants the exact opposite.

Clasping Raine's elbow, I slowly guide him down the staircase and out into the windswept quad. Winter is rolling on, dousing the Victorian institute in frost and ice.

I have a maths class to get to before some anger management crap later on with my assigned therapist, but the surprise search threw everyone off. Even Harrowdean's precise routine seems to be breaking down.

"Pass me the stuff." Raine shrugs his elbow free.

"Not a chance. I'm holding this for you."

"Wait, what?" he splutters.

"You've got at least two weeks' worth here. I don't trust you not to take the whole lot at once."

"Nox!" Raine exclaims. "I don't want to kill myself."

"Yet you seem determined to try. Who needs to sit on this many pills at once?"

"I don't wanna run out again. That's all."

"Yeah, right," I scoff.

He tries to make a grab for me, but I easily duck out of the way, escaping his off-target hands. Raine growls in annoyance, unable to sense where I've moved out of reach with his stash.

"Lennox! This isn't funny!"

"Do you hear me laughing?" I fire back.

Giving up, he huffs, his lips pressed into a harsh line. "I think I preferred it when you didn't give a shit about me."

Jaw clenching, I battle the urge to grab him by the scruff of his t-shirt and punch the stupid out of him. I'm not a fucking idiot. I know I have some serious issues. But they've never included a lack of caring. Quite the opposite.

"If you think that's true, you don't know me at all."

"Stop pretending like I'm your problem to fix then!" Raine stomps his foot like a toddler. "I survived long enough on my own before I rocked up at Priory Lane."

"I'm trying to help you."

"Maybe I don't want your help!"

Staring at my stubborn as fuck friend, all I can see is the dark-green eyes of another staring back at me. My sister. She looked more like our mother, though. Daintier. Light-footed. Always dancing and practising her ballet.

Our coarse, often messy brown hair and big toothy grins were the same, despite the several years between us. She was always smiling too. I remember that detail.

Until... she stopped.

Breath seizing, I have to fight back the onslaught of memories that usually only visit me at night. I can't hold on to the cloak of my protective anger then. That's when she sneaks in to torment me about all the red flags I failed to see.

Even at her tiny height, she had the presence of a motherfucking giant when she yelled. It breaks my goddamn heart to hear these words from Raine now as much as it did hearing it from my sister then.

Just stop fussing over me, Nox!

I don't want your help.

Yet she needed it. Far more than I ever realised. I only knew just how much she needed her big brother to protect her when it was too fucking late.

By then, all I had left were ashes to scatter and belongings to pack. *He* wanted any memories of her existence scrubbed away. I'll never know if it was his guilty conscience or covering his tracks.

"Lennox?" Raine's voice drags me back. "Look, I'm sorry. I didn't mean that."

"Yeah," I say flatly. "Whatever."

Pulling the bags full of pills from my waistband, I don't care who sees us. Raine squeaks in shock as I grab his hands and deposit the stash there.

"Do what you want with these," I snarl. "Better than me trying to help, right?"

"Nox—"

"Just don't call me next time you're stuck."

For once, I don't have the desire to shout and rave. I've punched my way through life since Daisy died and fought off any threats against those I care about with fists and blood. But what has that left me with?

No living family.

Two messed-up friends.

And a whole lot of dysfunction.

I couldn't protect Xander from the fucked up shit they did to us in the Z wing. The deep freeze bathtubs that made him lose a toe. Electrocutions. Sensory overload. Sleep deprivation.

Every last medieval torture tactic designed to strip a person's soul away was tried at least once. After all that, they thought we were unbreakable. That we were in fact the perfect stooges to run their operation because we refused to crack.

But little did those sadistic doctors know, we did break. Just in ways we allowed our pain to escape undetected. Those moments happened when the machines were turned off and cell doors locked.

Breaking isn't always a loud, cataclysmic implosion of a person. Sometimes it's silent. Imperceptible. I took my hatred and stoked those righteous flames to keep myself warm at night. Xander wrapped his ice-cold detachment around himself for comfort instead.

"Later."

"Nox!" Raine shouts after me.

I'm already storming away, unable to look at him for a second longer. Seeing Daisy's sweet, teenage face superimposed over his is harrowing. I let her down. I couldn't save her from evil or even herself. Stopping Raine from slowly poisoning himself isn't going to bring her back.

The heavens open, sending silvery bullets of rain hammering to the ground. It doesn't stop me from storming into the thick tree line, needing an escape. I'm soaked through in seconds, but I keep walking into the underbrush.

I soon find the perimeter fence. Harrowdean is small and self-enclosed, a clandestine bubble of pure evil, tucked into the fringes of society. Grasping the slick chain-links that hold us all captive, I stare into the forest beyond.

If Daisy hadn't died, I never would've ended up here. That monster didn't just kill my sister, he killed us both in one fell swoop. I ruined my own life in a torrent of rage and grief, hoping that revenge would somehow ease the agony of finding my baby sister's corpse.

It didn't ease the guilt. The grief.

Instead, my anger only grew.

"You shouldn't be here," a familiar voice calls out.

Startled, I glance to the side. Ripley is blurry through the thick rainfall, but her mass of sopping wet curls is unmistakable. She sits at the base of a tall juniper tree, her knees pulled tight to her chest.

Even in the rain, I can see the purple bruising on her face where I slammed it into the table. Knowing I inflicted those bruises should be satisfying, but the usual fury that fills me at the sight of this bitch doesn't come.

All I can muster is sadness. If things had been different, perhaps I wouldn't have ruined her life. And she wouldn't have ruined mine. We're both caught in this ceaseless cycle of violence.

"Are you following me?" Ripley asks in her usual disinterested tone.

I bark out a bitter laugh. "Believe it or not, my life doesn't revolve around you."

"Well, shucks. Isn't that a disappointment."

I shouldn't enjoy the heavy sarcasm dripping from her tone. This short, curvy wisp of a woman is responsible for some of the bleakest months of my life. Unimaginable agony and desolation.

All in the name of some bullshit revenge. At least I can understand her motivations. The shit I've done all in the name of revenge would be newsworthy too. But what if she'd killed Raine? Or Xander?

Would I have done the same to her?

I don't know who the villain is anymore.

"It's raining," I point out the obvious.

Ripley hugs her knees tighter, keeping her eyes averted. "I'm aware."

"Then what are you doing here?"

Her gaze is stuck on the same impenetrable forest I was just studying. Yearning. Reaching. Perhaps even imagining a life beyond these chain-link fences. I hate how entrancing her big, hazel eyes are, brimming with so much grief right now, it's making me doubt myself.

I hate her.

I'm *supposed* to hate her.

But part of me still wonders what she'd be like out there— beyond the roles we've constructed for ourselves. Or rather, we've forced ourselves into, slicing apart and re-stitching our souls to fit into an unrecognisable caricature of our former selves.

"Having a fucking shower. Leave, Lennox."

With the rain pouring down on her, she looks lost and broken. I see the same gaping wound in her that I feel tugging at my insides. A black hole sucking in all light and hope. Neither can survive this place.

I despise the fact that the only one who could ever understand how I feel is the one person I hate more than anything. Ripley knows better than anyone the price we must pay to rule in this world.

She's sacrificed her own soul along the way too.

Are we so different?

"Go!" Her voice cracks a little.

I lick my dry lips, an alien sensation swarming in my gut.

"She didn't deserve what we did to her, you know."

Swiping dripping hair from her face, Ripley peers up at me. Chapped lips parted, those devilish eyes are blown wider than usual. She gapes at me like Bigfoot has just stomped through the woods to greet her.

"I know that," she cuts back.

"But we did it anyway."

"Yeah," Ripley deadpans. "You did."

"I'd be lying if I said I was sorry." My eyes bore into hers. "Holly had something I wanted. So I took it from her. That was a price I was willing to pay."

Her stare shimmering with unshed tears, she doesn't even flinch at my confession. I'm sure she already knows that I feel no remorse for our actions. Not anymore. It's a luxury I cannot afford.

"Why are you telling me this, Lennox?"

"It's just that we have good reason to hate each other."

"Too right. I've never hated anyone or anything as much as I hate you."

"Not even Xander?" I can't help but ask.

Ripley scoffs. "Xander is an animal wrapped in human skin. But only one of you walked out of that bedroom and left my best friend swinging from a noose."

Yeah. Me.

I'd never admit it to her, but I still think about that night. The cruel words of encouragement I whispered to Holly. Threats I made. Hell, even the sound of her choked, gurgling sounds. She didn't achieve a clean neck break.

The makeshift rope cinched around her throat instead. All while I stood there, chanting to myself that it had to be done. Only the powerful survive these institutes. She had the key to our survival.

I refused to lose the family I'd found in Xander—the second chance that caring for him, another victim just like Daisy, gave me. It didn't take much to see the same brokenness in him that I never spotted in Daisy. Not until it was too late.

"I did what I had to do to survive."

"Killing an innocent did that?" Ripley's nose wrinkles in disgust. "You make me sick."

"Tell me. Have the innocents you've hurt allowed you to survive?"

This time, my words find their mark and she recoils. Her mouth opens and shuts several times, but nothing comes out. Not a single line of defence.

"Are you sorry, Ripley?"

"Why do you care?"

"Answer the damn question."

Shuffling my feet, I have no clue why I'm doing this. I have the perfect opportunity to choke the stubborn bitch to death without a single person witnessing it.

But seeing the broken, pissed-off, beautiful fucking disaster I've created, I need to know the truth. Does she feel the same bottomless pit of despair where her heart used to be that I do? Does it drive her to the brink of insanity, knowing she's irredeemable?

Her face contorts, riddled with so much pain, I don't know whether to relish in it or take the question back. The latter option shocks the shit out of me. Since when do I give a fuck about her pain?

"Yes," she admits. "Every day."

"Then you're a better person than me."

"I know exactly what kind of person you are." Ripley slowly clambers to her feet, her sweats soaked and mud stained. "Holly was my friend. My *family*. You took that from me, and all for what? Power?"

"Power. Protection. Control." I shrug dismissively. "All the things you're looking for too."

Her small, paint-flecked hands scrunch into fists. "Then when I tie the noose around your neck and make it look like a suicide, you'll understand why I will never, ever be sorry either."

Stopping in front of me, she's a small but fearsome dot beneath my towering height. Raindrops cling to her eyelashes, framing tear-filled, mottled eyes that brim with such fury, it's formidable. I've never seen anger like it beyond my own.

I want her to hate me.

I want to feel every drop of her wrath.

The rage that found its home within me the day I lost Daisy has never found a fair competitor. Anger is a lonely road to madness, and staring at Ripley now, I know she's trodden that same path. We both have.

"What do you really want?" she deadpans. "Because if you think I'm going to break like Holly did, you're in for a long wait."

Head cocked, I consider her. Every steely, unterrified inch. She saw the very worst in us, the depths that we will sink to in order to achieve our goals, yet she's still standing. If Holly's death didn't kill her, nothing will.

"I know you won't break."

She rears her head back in surprise. "Why?"

"Because you're stronger than she ever was." I scan over her features, loathing the way I want to trace each dimple. "That's why I fucking hate you."

"I really don't understand you."

"Why aren't you broken like the rest of us? Why did you walk away unscathed when we didn't?"

"Unscathed?" Ripley repeats incredulously. "Do I look bloody *unscathed* to you?"

"I just had to confiscate a kilo of drugs from one of my best friends!" I explode. "I don't even recognise the other one these days, he's so far gone. Yet here you are, enjoying your luxurious life."

The more I speak, the more her outrage grows. Her face is practically shadowed with it—twisting, contorting, brows scrunched and gaze seething. I love it. So goddamn much. I want her to be as angry as I am.

"Nothing about Harrowdean is a luxury!" she shouts.

"Could've fooled me."

"You son of a…"

I see her clenched fist coming from a mile off and easily duck to avoid being punched. Ripley curses as I move to grip her balled hand, blocking another attempted blow.

Tugging on her arm, I drag her close enough for our wet chests to crash together. She slips through the grass and collides with me. I strangle the rush of appreciation that feeling her tight curves pressing into me provokes.

"Perfect Ripley, huh?" I taunt. "Can't even punch right."

"You're fucking dead!"

Relishing the acidic lash of her voice, I lean close. "Wrong again, little Miss Perfect. I already died a very long time ago."

Grabbing her other wrist, I hold them both, pinned against her chest. I know just how scrappy she can be, but I still have a couple hundred pounds of muscle on her.

"Struggle all you want. I may enjoy it."

"Sick bastard!" she screams.

"I never claimed to be anything else."

Twisting and writhing, she's a panting blur of rage. I narrowly dodge a swift knee in the balls, whirling us around so I can shove her into a nearby tree trunk. Ripley gasps in pain at the hard collision.

Sliding a knee between her thighs, I spread her legs wide. Our hips are glued together, and with her wrists still pinned to her chest, she doesn't have a single inch of space to move.

"Much better." I appraise her prone form.

Still, the fear I'm searching for refuses to enter her eyes. Nothing penetrates her hatred. It burns hotter than any other emotion I hoped to elicit, and as her lips poise, I can guess what's coming.

"Fuck you." She hawks a mouthful of saliva right in my face.

I let her spit trickle down my cheek, unflinching. "Is that all you've got?"

"You don't want to see the best I've got."

"Enlighten me, then."

Grimacing, she tries to twist her wrists to escape my bondage. It's futile. I've got her pinned too tightly. With a growl, Ripley slumps, giving the impression that she's given up.

"You're so weak an——"

Crack.

Her head suddenly snaps forward, slamming so hard into my nose, I see stars. My grip on her wrists slackens. I stumble back, cupping my nose as it pulses in time with the pain thrumming through me.

"Call me weak again," she seethes. "I'll skin you alive."

Spitting out the blood that's filled my throat, I cast her a glower. "Nice shot. Now we'll match."

"It's the least you deserve."

When she moves to strike again, I abandon my aching face and grab her. She grapples with me as we wrestle, both vying to gain control of the other until our knees give out, and we hit the forest floor.

Rolling and bucking, we're a rain-soaked tangle in the mud. Ripley snarls beneath me, semi-crushed by my weight. I grab a handful of her hair then yank hard, causing her to hiss in pain.

"Can't escape, Rip?"

"Don't call me that! You piece of shit!"

"Well, damn. Now you're hurting my precious feelings."

"You don't fucking have any."

Each shift of her writhing limbs beneath me sends blood pumping to my crotch. Apparently, my dick didn't get the memo that we're supposed to hate this whore. Not enjoy the feel of her battling to escape.

Antagonising her shouldn't be so goddamn hot. I have the perfect opportunity to choke the life from her lungs right here in the mud. There are no guards. And I don't give a fuck about the CCTV cameras positioned on the perimeter fence.

What can they do to me now?

I've already lost everything.

"Just stop," she cries angrily. "If you're going to kill me, do it. Fucking do it, Nox!"

"Why? Because you think that you deserve it?"

"Yes!"

With that confession, she stills. Her anger is fizzling out. I can see the despair I found her drowning in returning. Spreading with each second she spends trapped in the dirt.

No. I don't want her defeated.

Not anymore.

I want her so enraged, she can't breathe without thinking of her hatred for me. She wants to fade away? I won't fucking let her. She doesn't get to escape so easily. Her punishment is living with her own self-loathing.

Every bit of rational thought flies from my mind. With my pelvis pinning her to the slick ground, I shove her wrists above her head then trap them there. Utterly exposed, she can't stop my approach.

"Death would be too easy for you," I croon. "Torturing you will be far sweeter."

She blinks rapidly, a brief, fleeting whisper of delicious fear finally entering her gaze. Fanning those flames, I decide to hell with it. My lips slam against hers, swallowing her sounds of protest.

If this is the only way to truly hurt her, I'll cross the invisible line between us. But at the first touch, any thought of revenge flies out of my mind.

Fuck. Me.

I never expected her lips to be velvet soft and laced with such tantalising sweetness that I lose all sight of my plan. My need to destroy her by any means necessary is overtaken by the heat suddenly pumping through my veins.

She's rigid against my touch. That escaping fury comes roaring back as her teeth clamp down on my bottom lip, sinking in deep enough to break the skin. I rear back with a sharp hiss.

"Y-You…" Ripley splutters. "How dare you——"

"Shut the fuck up."

Crashing my mouth back on hers, I don't know if I'm punishing her or myself. This is just about hurting her, right? I know she hates me. I know my touch has to be damn repulsive to her. This is the only way to make her break.

So why the ever-loving fuck does her tiny, perfectly curved body feel so good against mine? Why do I want her to scream, shout, bite and kick? Why do I want her hatred and not her defeat?

Her sounds of protest die out. I'm not sure if I imagine the moan emanating from her throat. I'm not sure if I imagine the way it makes my heart pound, cock twitch, and skin prickle with arousal either.

Is the fucking bitch is enjoying this?

Am I enjoying this?

I'm not sure when her mouth begins to move against mine. Hard. Wet. Undeniably passionate. Lips sliding in a spiteful rhythm, she kisses me like she hopes to torture the truth out of me.

Hips grinding, I thrust into her core, seeking any amount of friction against the painful pressure gathering in my cock. Fuck, the way I want to fill her up and hear every last vindictive word spew from her lips as I do. I want her to despise how much she loves the feel of my cock inside her.

Shoving my tongue into her mouth, I relish in the way she responds. Enraged and thrashing. Invading my mouth with the same wrath that's fuelled the furious dance we've spent the last year locked in.

She's fighting it with every second our mouths are locked, but that doesn't stop her hips from lifting to press into mine. The woman is grinding against me. Pressing her core into my cock, silently pleading for more. That realisation shatters my lusty haze.

I abruptly break the kiss. "What are you doing?"

Her mouth is swollen and red. "What are *you* doing? Why are you kissing me?"

"Why are you kissing me back?"

Pupils dilated, she licks her inflamed lips. "You… This… What the fuck, Nox?"

I'm practically dizzy with the adrenaline and desire pumping through my system. Confusion only adds to the blur of emotions causing my control to falter. I wanted to provoke her. I didn't expect to want to fuck her too.

Scrambling for an excuse, I plaster on the smirk I know she detests. "I just wanted to see if you're as much of a whore as everyone says."

Before I can react, her knee collides with my still-hard cock. She knees me dead centre in the bollocks, easily shoving me off her body as I choke out a wheeze. I crumple onto the ground, panting through tightly gritted teeth.

"I will never be your whore, Lennox Nash." Ripley sits up and brushes herself off. "This changes absolutely nothing between us."

All I can do is lay here in the dirt while she stands up, casting me a final derisive look. Watching her stalk off, those devilish hips swaying and tight ass shaking with each step, I wonder when the fuck this parasite invaded my brain.

We're sworn enemies. She'll destroy me, my family, the life

I've tried to create since taking that plea deal to avoid prosecution. I thought I'd be safe in Priory Lane. Even in Harrowdean. Better than prison, right?

But nowhere is safe.

Not with Ripley Bennet around.

CHAPTER 13
RIPLEY

HERO – DAVID KUSHNER

PICKING at the dry flakes of paint on my hand, I cast a final look at my wet canvas. It's a pathetic effort. My mind is unfocused, agitated. With each swoop of the paintbrush, I get more and more frustrated

"Stupid fucking thing!" I hurl it across the art room.

Storming out of the room, the door slams shut behind me. I'm dead set on stomping back to my bedroom and scrubbing myself in the shower to remove the ghost of Lennox's touch. His hands. Lips. Roughened stubble. Hard length grinding into me.

But no amount of angrily showering multiple times a day has diminished the pure ecstasy that him pinning me down and forcibly inflicting his rage on me created. It's all I've been able to think about.

The anger. Mutual hatred. Battling for control. Power. The right to punish. Even admitting it in my head is fucking unbearable, but I was getting off to a literal monster paying me even an ounce of attention.

I'm a piece of shit.

Holly would be ashamed.

"Ripley? You good?"

The sound of Raine's gentle, melancholic violin halts. I'm tempted to rush past the half-open door to the adjacent music room, but I know he already heard me. He'd only follow. I asked him to practise in there today, needing some headspace.

"Yeah," I shout back.

"What's going on?"

Stopping in the doorway, I study his slim but well-honed frame. He's dressed in light-washed, grey jeans today with a loose, V-neck, black shirt that shows off his razor-like clavicles.

His soft blonde hair is smoothed back like usual, round glasses in place. He looks as tempting and mysterious as ever, but as I spot the empty plastic bag peeking from his jeans pocket, my inner contempt intensifies.

"Rip?"

I clear my throat. "Nothing. I'm fine."

His head cocks. "Are you staring at me?"

"No, jackass."

"Well, don't just stand there. It creeps me out."

"I'm done. I need some air."

Raine pulls the violin from beneath his chin. "Wait up."

"You're busy," I protest.

He shrugs, searching for his violin case. "Sure. My schedule is crammed. How will I ever spare a moment?"

Fighting a smile, I step into the room to help him. He'd never surrender his baby to me; that violin is practically his left arm. But I quickly locate the velvet-lined case then touch his wrist, guiding him to it.

"Why exactly are you still following me around?"

Raine lovingly packs his violin away. "This place is boring and lonely as fuck. I'm the only one taking music classes, so the teacher doesn't even turn up, meaning it's always deserted."

"You just want company? Is that it?" I laugh.

"I've had worse company than you."

"Oh, thanks. You do compliment me."

Clicking the case shut, he unfolds his guide stick next. "You told me off for flirting last week. This is me keeping myself in check."

If I'd known that fooling around with Raine would lead to him stalking me like a lovesick puppy, I wouldn't have given in to temptation. Well, maybe. Hell, who am I kidding? I was done for the moment I saw those warm, butterscotch eyes.

We haven't kissed since, though. Part of me is terrified the attraction I felt was just the mania talking. I needed an outlet. A quick fix. Raine was there to provide that.

But a bigger part of me is scared that the feelings I have for him are real and can't be excused as some semi-psychotic fluke. That would be bad. Deadly, in fact.

"You hungry?" he asks.

"Nope."

"Cool. I'd rather avoid the cafeteria."

Come to think of it, I haven't seen his two bodyguards lurking around like usual. Lennox has made himself scarce since our tangle in the mud, and Xander is still being invisible. But I know his eyes are always on me.

"Trouble in paradise?"

"Something like that," he mumbles.

"I'm shocked. You're friends with such good men."

"Don't start, Rip." His voice is oddly defensive. "Shit is complicated."

I blow out a frustrated breath. "Don't I know it."

Clasping his violin case, he stretches out his guide stick to begin tapping a path to the exit. I automatically take his elbow, helping steer the way. He's a little unsteady, but for a drug addict, I'd say he's high-functioning.

I'm not sure when we fell into such a familiar routine. Somehow, trying to keep my distance has had the opposite effect. Raine refuses to let me go.

Out in the corridor, classes are breaking for lunch. It's chaos. Patients make a beeline for food or therapy, wrapped up in their own little worlds. I have to manoeuvre Raine through the crowd so he doesn't get clattered.

"It's like they're pretending they can't even see the stick," I complain. "I'm gonna fucking deck one of these idiots in a minute."

"Chill out, guava girl."

"You could get hurt!"

Raine's chuckle is smooth like honeyed whiskey. "It wasn't so long ago that you were the one threatening to hurt me."

"I haven't taken it off the table."

The sound of his gravelly laughter is a soothing balm to the soul. Nothing is over-complicated with Raine, despite the disaster zone that surrounds us.

When we're alone, we don't discuss the drugs I've sold him. Xander and Lennox. Harrowdean... None of it. Instead, it's just my paint palette and his soft, crooning violin strokes keeping me company.

Silence and companionship. A mutual understanding for the art of escapism. I hadn't realised how lonely my own coping mechanisms had become.

When someone shoves my shoulder and doesn't bother to apologise, my patience snaps.

"Let's get out of here."

"You wanna catch a flight to Paris?" Raine suggests sultrily. "Or perhaps Venice? Little romantic getaway?"

"Sure, *darling.* Let me just pack my suitcase and call the driver, shall I?"

"Don't forget the bottle of champagne." He sighs in a wistful manner. "I remember those days. My manager used to bring me a glass of Dom Perignon after every show I performed."

I almost trip over my own feet. "Your manager?"

"You thought I just played violin for my own benefit?"

Mouth closing, I feel like an idiot. It never occurred to me that his talent went beyond mere passion. Being incarcerated in a place like this doesn't exactly line up with some luxurious celebrity lifestyle.

"I played professionally for several years. Four world tours. Things exploded after I recovered from losing my vision. Everyone wants to see the blind violinist play, right?"

"I guess. How did you end up here then?"

Raine rakes his teeth over his bottom lip. "Not a pretty story. I'm an open book, but let's talk somewhere else."

"Come on. I know a place."

Tightening my grip on his arm, I guide him through the reception and out into the quad. There are a few people filtering around, taking wrapped sandwiches and juice boxes outside to enjoy the rare blast of winter sun.

We walk towards the gym—a large, cinderblock building in the uppermost corner of the institute. Most don't bother to look behind it, though.

There are several abandoned buildings across Harrowdean with day-to-day operations now taking place in the manor itself. Tucked far behind the gym, a thick tangle of bushes almost entirely covers a second, smaller building.

This one is part of the original architecture with ornate, shuttered windows, moss-covered pillars and cracked entrance steps. We have to wrestle through the brambles to see any of that though, slicing our hands on sharp thorns.

Raine curses several times as he struggles to navigate the path, attempting not to trip. I do my best to hold the worst of the roughage out of his way. Eventually, we emerge through the building's sarcophagus.

"Watch your step," I advise. "There are five."

Raine nods gratefully. "Are you taking me to a quiet corner to kill me? I can't hear anyone out here."

"Well, I don't want any witnesses."

"Aw, shit. I wish you'd told me. I could've gotten high one last time."

"You've had enough."

He sniffs. "Not for my own funeral, I haven't."

There's a rusted combination lock on the door, preventing any unruly patients from escaping inside to fuck or shoot up in privacy. Though I doubt anyone could ever find this place without knowing where it is.

After quickly inputting the combination, the lock slides off in my hand.

"Is there anything you don't know about Harrowdean?" Raine asks.

"Doubt it. I make it my business to know everyone else's business."

"Sounds exhausting."

Surprised, I chuckle. "Yeah, it is."

Stepping inside the building, the scents of mould and disuse wash over us. Nobody comes here. Not even the guards. Harrowdean's dark dealings take place elsewhere, but I've kept this bolthole on my radar for those days when privacy is needed.

"Smells delightful." Raine scrunches up his nose.

"The original institute was built in 1843. I found some dusty, old documents in the library last summer. It was an asylum for decades, then a rich kids' boarding school."

"Smells like this place hasn't been used since 1843. What the hell is here?"

"You'll see."

Feet creaking over rotten floorboards and smashed tiles, we creep through the shadows. On the right side of the building, vintage changing rooms lie behind rusty shower curtains and clinking brass hooks.

The left side of the building contains a cavernous room marked by signage pointing towards what once was a huge swimming pool. Now it's merely an empty, mouldy basin filled with discarded trash.

Anything the previous owners deemed worthless ended up

in this concrete pit. Broken bed frames. Smashed chairs. Old, rotting books.

The first time I stumbled across this place, it was like discovering Atlantis. I felt more at home surrounded by destruction and decay than anywhere else.

Raine sniffs the air. "Chlorine?"

"You'd struggle to take a dip in this pool."

"Yeah, it's faint. How big was the pool?"

I steer him around a pile of collapsed bookshelves. "It's full size. No idea how long it's been empty for."

The ceiling is high and domed, peppered with small windows that have long since caved in or been smashed by extreme weather. Part of the roof is gone too. The wind whistles in, carrying a hint of winter sun into the murkiness.

On the other side of the empty swimming pool sit a couple of ripped, sagging armchairs I found while poking around. Sometimes, I escape here with my sketchbook and charcoals, needing the silence.

"Three steps in front of you," I direct him.

Poking the armchair with his guide stick, Raine strokes a hand over the ancient fabric. "Gotcha."

We both take seats facing the desolate pool house after Raine places his violin case and guide stick on the ground.

"What do you want to know?"

I twist in my armchair to face him. "How does a professional violinist end up somewhere like this?"

He snorts. "By being a total fuck-up?"

"Can't he get you out? Your... uh, manager?"

Mouth twisting into a grimace, his fingers tap out a staccato rhythm on the armrest. "He's the reason I'm here. The asshole sold it to me as a sweet deal."

"I mean... this is pretty sweet."

Raine's head moves on a swivel, his glasses-covered eyes casting around the swimming pool like he can actually see the opulence.

"Smells sweet to me."

"Don't complain about my choice of location for our first date."

"This is our first date?" He grins, waggling his eyebrows.

Smooth, Ripley.

"Back to the topic at hand." I shake my head, glad he can't see my embarrassment. "Why did your dickhead manager lock you up in a psych ward?"

He smothers his grin, straightening his posture. "Several trips through rehab failed. I kept messing up my shows, and my reputation was trashed. Calvin intervened. He sits on his ass and lives off my tidy salary now."

"Intervened... by getting you interred?"

"I mean, he acted like Priory Lane was some award-winning, state of the art shit. Far better than the hellish rehabs I'd spent years failing at. Stupid me thought this was my chance to get clean."

A beam of weak sunlight illuminates his face. The golden boy. Nimble fingers and perfect smiles. He's the full package, but beneath the act, Raine's just as broken as the rest of us. Perhaps even more so.

"When was your first trip to rehab?"

He smacks his lips together. "Fifteen, I think."

"Jesus. Really?"

"I grew up with addicts for parents. It wasn't hard to get curious about what they were snorting and shooting on a daily basis. The fear of drugs that most kids have was never instilled in me."

"They still alive? Your parents?"

"Apparently." Raine smooths back a loose strand of hair. "Haven't seen them since I lost my vision. They bailed real fast when I couldn't work and bring in money for them to snort anymore."

"Fucking hell."

"Yeah, they were shit. Tried to come crawling back when

my music became popular. I told them I never wanted to see them again."

Working up the courage to dig deeper, I try to keep my voice light. Even though he said he's an open book, it still feels rude to ask. I've wanted to know what happened to him since the moment we met.

"You were eighteen when you lost your vision, right? What happened?"

He nods. "Dirty needles."

"You used to shoot up?"

"Yeah, until I developed Endophthalmitis. Left the infection untreated for too long. By the time I got to the hospital, the doctors could only do damage control. My retinas were destroyed by scarring."

My heart squeezes, picturing a younger, terrified version of him curled up in a hospital bed. Alone and exploited. Paying the price of shitty parenting and a lifetime of bad decisions. He deserved so much better.

"Christ, Raine."

Curling lashes frame his caramel-hued eyes. I don't know how he can imbue his gaze with such emotion when he lives in perpetual blackness, but it's there. Fear embroiled in curiosity. A hint of challenge coiled around his pinprick pupils.

"If I'd never picked up a needle, I would still have my vision." He folds the glasses then places them on his violin case. "I wouldn't be trapped here. My life... it could've been so different."

"I'm sorry," I reply with empathy.

"It's not so bad, I guess." Raine smirks in his typically confident way. "I'm in an abandoned pool house with a beautiful girl. My life could definitely be worse."

"You still have no idea what I look like."

He wiggles his fingers. "I got a good feel."

I snort in amusement. "Uh-huh."

"Besides, I've already told you what I find attractive. And it has nothing to do with the way you look."

A hot blush races across my cheeks. Compliments don't usually mean a damn thing to me. But from him, it feels genuine. He sees beyond what everyone else does. There's no bullshit or games.

"Now I feel like an even bigger asshole for dealing to you," I groan.

"Yeah. You're the worst."

"Raine!"

Belting out a laugh, he shakes his head. "It's not a big deal. Just a business transaction, right? Nothing more."

"Is that what I am?" I retort. "A business transaction?"

"You're a damn sight more than that. But we can separate business and pleasure."

Can we?

"I don't know when I've ever been more than a business transaction." Even to my own ears, my voice is pained. "Not even my uncle saw me as more than that when my parents died."

Raine fixes his attention on me. It's a different kind of active listening to when others pay attention. His chin is tucked down, left ear tilted in my direction as he thoughtfully strokes the blonde scruff on his face.

"You said they left… but I didn't know you were orphaned. I'm sorry."

"It's fine." I brush him off. "Shit happens."

"How old were you?"

"Dad died just before I turned eight. Then my mum passed almost a year later."

I sound weirdly detached, even to my own ears. Anyone would think that I don't mourn my parents, though that couldn't be further from the truth. But if I allow myself to think of Mum's tight, floral-scented hugs or Dad's terrible jokes, I couldn't bear to live.

We were normal. Picturesque, even. A modest, working-class family living in the British countryside. Mum worked in a nursery, and my dad owned a butcher shop in the local village. Our lives were quiet but perfect.

But isn't that always the case?

Tragedy strikes without impunity or mercy. It takes whatever victims it desires, regardless of who deserves it. If we could collectively line up every bad person in the world to assign them to lives full of evil instead, don't you think we'd all do it?

I'd sacrifice a million souls if it bought my parents' lives. Hell, I probably belong in that queue of sinners now myself. Lining up to be fed to the devil's jaws to buy another innocent life back. My parents wouldn't recognise me now if they were alive.

"Your uncle adopted you?" Raine drags me back to the present.

"Yeah, my mum's younger brother. They weren't very close though, so he kinda got lumped with me as my last living relative. I moved to London and was basically raised by his housekeeper."

"He's rich, then?" he guesses.

"Investment banker. Unmarried, no kids."

Seeming thoughtful, Raine nods as he catalogues this new information. I haven't shared this much with anyone since I met Holly. She was the only one I trusted enough to share my life with. I don't know why I'm doing it now.

"I started painting at a young age. I was lonely and needed an outlet, I guess. Set up a business to sell my art, and after a few years, I bought my own flat. I moved out the first chance I got."

"That must've been hard," Raine muses. "Going out on your own like that."

I shrug, forgetting he can't see the gesture. "Like you, I grew up fast. Just in a different way."

"How so?" His head tilts.

It's not lost on me that we come from opposite worlds. I had wealth and comfort, while Raine struggled in poverty, turning over every penny he earned to fund his parents' addiction. Two polar opposites.

But we still turned out the same. Trapped in the same broken system. Equally forgotten by society and discarded by those who are supposed to love us. Left to pick up the pieces and find our own makeshift families.

"Uncle Jonathan didn't like having a bipolar niece. Bad for his reputation. It was easier to get far away from him and fend for myself than deal with his disgust when I had a bad episode."

Cursing, Raine shakes his head. "What an asshole. You didn't choose to have this illness."

I pick at my nail bed. "He didn't see it that way. The burden he got stuck with suddenly became a far bigger job to look after than he banked on."

"You still talk to him?"

"Nah. Only once since I started my three years. I was desperate when I called him. He got me out of Priory Lane and transferred here instead."

"Birthdays? Christmas?" Raine pushes expectantly.

"That would require too much effort."

He looks pissed off on my behalf, but honestly, I don't feel anything anymore. Not even disappointment. I already lost my parents, and when I realised that Jonathan wouldn't replace them, I lowered my expectations.

Being alone is far easier that way.

I rely on myself, no one else.

"Rip," Raine whispers. "Come here."

"Hmm?"

Crooking his finger, he gestures for me to approach. As vulnerable as I should feel after revealing all that, a broken part of me wants his comfort. I want to feel arms around me.

Warmth. Familiarity. It's been so long since anyone gave an actual shit about me.

Walking over to his armchair, I tentatively crawl onto his lap. Raine grips my hips, pulling me closer so I have to spread my legs either side of his waist to straddle him. My arms wind around his neck, bringing us flush together.

His freshly squeezed orange and sea salt scent infiltrates my nostrils. I greedily breathe it in. Everything about him is vibrant, fresh, alive. For someone who struggles to perceive the world and numbs himself to escape it, he burns so goddamn bright.

I rest my head on his firm chest, the sound of his steady heartbeat pounding in my ear. *Budum. Budum. Budum.* The sound is an anchor, holding me in the moment. I'm savouring the feel of being held so fucking tight, tears prickle my eyes.

"You act like nothing ever hurts you," he murmurs, tenderly brushing my cheek with his knuckles. "Being abandoned is easier to handle that way, right? When no one cares in the first place?"

Thick, bitter emotion clogs my throat. "I…"

"Don't pretend like it isn't true. I see you, Ripley Bennet. You're a fierce, terrifying spitfire, but beneath this untouchable act you've got going on, I know deep down there's someone who cares far too much."

"Only about those worthy of being cared about."

"So do I make the cut?" His chest vibrates beneath my ear.

"I'm scared, Raine," I admit in a tiny whisper. "I'm scared of caring about you. I'm scared of what that will mean. I'm scared of losing another person who matters to me."

"You wanna know what I'm scared of?"

I fist my fingers in the longer lengths of hair at the back of his head. "Yes."

"When I'm with you—listening to the flick of your paintbrush, mumbling to yourself, the way your breathing speeds up when you apply that last drop of paint—I feel so fucking alive."

His voice is so soft, it feels like a butterfly is dancing across my skin. I don't know whether to swat at the damn thing or cup it in my palms, keeping it safe and secure from a world determined to crush its wings.

"I've never found that feeling from a person before. That's what scares the shit out of me. But hell if I'm gonna let that fear take this chance away from me."

"Raine—"

"Don't tell me not to get attached, Rip, because it's already too late. I want to peel back these bullshit defences you've wrapped yourself in and get close enough to matter to you. I want that honour."

"Trust me, it isn't an honour. I'm nobody."

He moves me to sit upright, smoothing a hand over my loose curls. "You're somebody to me."

I lift my head, staring into his mesmerizing, sightless eyes. Letting the liquefied honey seep over me, thick and glutenous, until I'm trapped in a depthless pool and unable to tread water for a moment longer.

I'm drowning in Raine.

His confusingly fascinating contradictions.

His mutual search for meaning.

"I… feel alive around you too," I make myself admit. "More than I have in a long time. But I'm not ready for a commitment."

The corner of his mouth quirks, that goddamn confident smirk forever serving to drive me insane.

"I'm not asking for one. But does that mean we can't chase this feeling?"

"Of course not," I reply on a breath.

"Then run with it, Rip. I don't need a label."

Clumsily bringing his forehead to mine, his lips fumble. After he catches the corner of my mouth, I tilt my head enough to seal our lips together. Raine threads a hand in my hair to hold me still.

We kiss slowly, gently, meaningfully. A silent exchange. A promise. Both agreeing to drop the act around each other and run headfirst into the inevitable disaster that lies ahead of us.

He's chasing the high that no pill or needle could ever give him. I shouldn't want to be someone's drug, or even their escape, but I need this too. I want to be cared for. I want to fucking belong for once.

His tongue swipes against mine, velvet soft and exploratory. It's nothing like the violent lash of Lennox's kiss, attempting to punish me. I swiftly shove that psycho from my mind before I can contemplate the ethics of kissing Raine too.

Stroking the back of his head, I tease the strands of spun silk. The kiss intensifies. Growing deeper and more passionate, our teeth clash and lips smack together. He even tastes like sunshine.

The golden boy, but with a dark, fractured soul. Seeing past his playful pretence feels like a big deal. I shouldn't take it for granted.

Sliding a hand up my spine, he teases a path around my waist to find the swell of my left breast. Squeezing it over my oversized tee, his thumb strokes the hardened pebble pushing against my bra.

I press my chest into his hands, a whine crawling up my throat. Everything aches. I want him to relieve the need that's built within me with each whispered touch between us over several weeks.

"Rip," he says throatily.

"Yes?" I moan into his lips.

"I need you so fucking badly, it's driving me insane. I'm not asking for exclusivity or whatever, but I don't just want to be one of your regrets."

Peeling his hands off me, I quickly stand. He looks panicked for a moment as my weight disappears from his lap, but the rustle of me sliding my sweats over my hips seems to reach him.

"I'd never regret you, Raine."

Uncaring of our surroundings, I push my panties down and let them join the puddle of fabric on the ground. Cold air kisses my thighs. I rush to retake my place in Raine's lap where denim brushes against my bare pussy.

Searching out my naked ass, he grabs a handful. "That's so hot."

Retaking his lips, I grind against him. Each brush of his jeans on my core is a painful tease, the rough fabric feeling amazing against my throbbing clit. I'm practically trembling with my desire to feel him.

"I need you too," I whisper. "I haven't needed anyone for a long time."

Circling my hips, his lips peck mine in a fervent beat. "It's okay to be vulnerable around me. You're safe."

One hand splayed across my pelvis, his hand dips between my legs to reach for my pussy. I arch my back, sighing against his lips when he finds my sensitive bundle of nerves. His thumb bears down on my clit in small, teasing circles.

I move my hips in time to his rotations. Each flick of his thumb is a tiny firework display deep inside my core, setting alight nerves that beg for more. Reaching for his wrist, I take control, encouraging him to ease a finger inside me.

"So impatient," he mumbles.

"Yes."

With his finger sliding inside me, that impatience only grows. All of the anger and infuriation that prevented me from being able to paint earlier comes rushing back. I'm so sick of feeling like I'm losing control.

I reach beneath my careful perch on his lap to find his waistband. His jeans button pops open, allowing me to push the flaps of fabric down and expose his tight, black boxer shorts. His stomach is hard and flat, marked by a hint of abs.

Curling his finger, Raine smiles at the needy moan I release. My urgency to feel him around me causes me to fumble with his boxers, desperate to release the steel sheath trapped inside. He lifts his ass high so I can nudge them down low enough.

Finally, his long, hard cock is revealed. It's generous in my hand, studded with thick veins that beg to be licked. Wrapping a hand around his shaft, I work it over, familiarising myself with his proportions.

"Fuck, Rip," Raine hisses.

"Be quiet."

He fights back a grin. "You've got it, boss."

I'm soaked just imagining his long length pressing inside me. I want to feel every inch with nothing between us. Thank God for contraceptive implants.

Raine slides a second digit into my slit as I spread the bead of pre-come over his cock's velvet head. Our surroundings don't hold me back. We're alone here with no cameras, guards or prying eyes. Nothing but the lost. The broken. The abandoned. We fit right in.

Placing a steadying hand on Raine's shoulder, I can't wait any longer. I clasp his wrist to ease his fingers from between my legs then position his cock at my entrance.

Every muscle is shaking in anticipation of the sweet, euphoric relief I'm chasing. Fortunately, Raine doesn't offer a single complaint at my dominance.

Pinned beneath me, he lets me hold him in place as I slowly, torturously sink down on his length. We both groan at the same time, the feeling of being joined washing over us.

I wouldn't normally have the presence of mind to care in these situations, but knowing he can't even see me as we share this moment, I feel a burst of fear.

"This okay?" I check.

"Fuck yes, beautiful girl." His throat rumbles with a growl. "You feel incredible wrapped around me."

Vindicated, I lift my hips and rise on his lap. The next downward thrust takes him deep into my cunt, my pleasure increasing with each steely inch. Raine returns his hands to my hips, tracking each move as I rise and fall at a successive pace.

Riding him feels so good. Knowing that he's surrendering himself to me, giving me the gift of his control and pleasure, intensifies the hunger already consuming me. The trust is staggering. More than any meaningless hook-up.

Hand slotting beneath my t-shirt, he cruises a path over my stomach and to my bra line. Raine tugs the cup aside to free my breast, his fingers finding my nipple and gently rolling it. The brief pinch sends electricity sparking up my spinal cord.

"You feel alive now?" I laugh breathlessly.

Raine squeezes my breast playfully. "Do you?"

A sudden upward thrust of his hips causes him to surge into me at a deep angle. I mewl loudly, gripping his shoulders so tight, I'm sure he'll have fingertip-sized bruises tomorrow.

"God, yes," I admit.

"That feeling right there is what I'm chasing."

And I get it. Lord, do I get it. This place is designed to strip you down, remove your free will and leave you with nothing but rules and regimen. It's where souls are sent to die. But this right here is fucking nirvana.

He begins to move in time with me, surging upwards to seek out that aching spot. Each time he nudges it, my vision fuzzes over, unable to withstand the relentless waves of pleasure he's battering into me.

A morbid part of me wonders how intense this must feel to him with all his remaining senses dialled to ten. Each stroke must be overwhelming. Fuzz-covered jaw clenched, I can see that he's fighting to hold on.

Burying my face in his orange-scented neck, I work myself on him, hunting for the release I know will finally quiet my mind. Even if only temporarily. My lips pucker against his smooth skin, and I can't resist biting down to leave a mark.

No one would dare touch what's mine. Not in this place. And right now, I don't give a fuck who knows it. I want to trap his sunshine inside my chest and allow it to thaw my soul. Even if it sucks the life out of him.

That's what love is, right?

A mutual agreement to destroy each other.

I'll give him the gift of feeling alive in return.

Moving upward, Raine's fingertips dance over my clavicles before rising to clasp my jaw. It's a tight, bruising clamp that allows him to pull my mouth back to his. I surrender to the hot swipe of his tongue.

Suddenly, a loud clatter causes us to break apart. Raine bands a protective arm around me, still sheathed deep inside.

"What is that?" he urges.

I frantically look around the room, sucking in a relieved breath to see it's just a crow, entering through a broken window to find a perch.

"Rip?"

"Bird," I moan. "Don't stop."

"I wouldn't dare."

When he sucks my bottom lip into his mouth and bites down, the burst of pain throws me straight back into my upward climb. I'm getting closer to the edge. That tight, taut feeling inside me is getting stronger.

"Come on, babe," he coaxes into my ear, causing chills to stipple my skin. "I want to feel you come for me."

"Raine," I whimper.

"Let go. I promise I'll catch you."

Eyes squeezed shut, I follow that coiled thread. Deeper. Darker. It's a poised spring in my centre, waiting for the chance to snap. Mouth still locked on mine, Raine's thumb resumes its assault on my clit.

I'm done for.

I feel myself clamp tight around him. I'm exploding, thrown into the abyss and swallowed whole by ecstasy. He groans as he joins me in falling apart, his cock jerking inside me with each hot burst of his release.

Still moving on him, I drag out every second. I'm greedy. I don't want this moment to end. The raw satisfaction of warmth spreading between us is too damn good.

My limbs slowly turn to liquid. With a final sigh, I slump onto his chest. Raine braces me against him, stroking up and down my t-shirt clad back. His face buries in my hair, inhaling sharply.

Snuggled into him, we don't speak for a long time. Words would only burst our safe, temporary bubble. Even surrounded by junk, we're at peace. We can pretend like the rest of the institute doesn't exist.

I can't bring myself to consider the consequences of what we've done. The path to ruin I've set us upon. This man is best friends with the assholes I've vowed to destroy. And here I am, screwing him. A lot.

I'm fucked.

Utterly, utterly fucked.

My scalp prickles. Subtly looking around the room, I search for a pair of eyes. Nothing. But I know he's here, just like every other day I've felt him skulking. Xander's mastered the art of the silent prowl.

I'm surprised it took him this long to find us. He's never far away. While he doesn't feel the need to speak to me right now, he's made his presence known over the past couple of weeks. I want to ignore him, but I hate the thought of him seeing me exposed like this.

"Come on." I nudge Raine. "We need to go."

He groans in protest. "Don't wanna."

"Move it."

Before I can clamber off him and deal with our mess,

Raine tries to grab my arm. He narrowly misses and swears, seizing a handful of my t-shirt instead.

"Rip." The note of vulnerability in his voice is unmistakable. "I don't care if we're friends or whatever you want to call it, but don't shut me out like everyone else."

"You don't need me, Raine."

"I do. You make me feel less alone."

Any signs of his swagger and confidence are non-existent. Deep down, Raine is petrified of being left alone in his own head. He'll pop, snort or cling to anything that offers a reprieve from the loneliness.

But I can't be his life raft.

Not when I'm drowning too.

CHAPTER 14
XANDER
N/A – BRING ME THE HORIZON

BRIGHT, *clinical lights sear my eyeballs. The screech of incessant white noise rages on, hour after hour, never once offering a reprieve. The pain in my skull has dulled to a low ache. I wonder, distantly, if my brain has finally liquified.*

Cold water submersion didn't work. Beatings didn't work. Psychological torture didn't work. Isolation didn't work. Now the clinicians have resorted to over-stimulation on all fronts. It's impossible to rest with the ceaseless light and sound in the cell.

They want us to break.

Bend.

Reform.

It's rare that I see Lennox now. At first, we were held side by side. As if seeing the other in pain would somehow ignite the process. When that failed, they soon split us apart, each assigned to our own personal cell in the Z wing.

I've seen others. Ghosts. Skeletal and pale-skinned, their eyes stripped of all human awareness. That's the whole point. They don't want traumatised patients; they want mindless machines. The Z wing's true purpose is to create exactly that.

Vessels for the rich. Malleable and capable of inflicting whatever force is required to further their buyer's aims. Murder. Extortion. Torture. Anything deemed too dirty for the spotless hands of the powerful one percent.

But power isn't free.

Not in this world.

After months of wondering why the corporation that owns six private institutes across the country would risk everything by engaging in such horrific abuse, I understand. These aren't treatment facilities. That's just a cover story.

They're factories.

Manufacturers of machines.

We were always bought and paid for. The moment we signed ourselves over to the rehabilitative program, accepting a three-year sentence to avoid something worse, our souls were marked for exploitation.

Not everyone is admitted to the Z wing. Hell, most patients don't know it exists. Evil always lurks in the periphery. Formless and invisible until the secrets finally break open and the truth comes spilling out.

Will we live long enough to see that day?

I took this sentence with the same nonchalance I had while embezzling disgusting sums of money from the rich and stupid all from behind a computer screen. Child's play. I didn't even want their cash.

I just wanted to make them hurt for the entertainment value.

Own their cash, and I owned them.

The lawyers thought they were doing me a favour when they rolled out my so-called 'traumatic childhood' and personality disorder diagnosis to argue against decades of jail time. They offered up Priory Lane like some goddamn wonderland.

When the screeching white noise abruptly shuts off, it takes several moments for it to even register. My ears are ringing so violently. I don't bother shifting from my curled-up ball on the cold floor. They can drag me to whatever they have planned next for all I care.

The cell door swings open, emitting my favourite sadist, Doctor Farnsworth. He's an old, ugly son of a bitch. Only this time, he isn't alone. I don't recognise the other elderly, silver-haired man practically dripping with wealth and self-importance.

"This is one of our troublemakers." Doctor Farnsworth *gestures towards me like I'm a plant that refuses to grow. "No progress despite following our usual methods."*

The second old bastard casts a critical eye over me. "We haven't had one this stubborn since Patient Seven in Blackwood. He was a tough nut to crack."

"Unfortunately, sir, there are no signs of cracking here. I believe this subject has an extreme tolerance to our physical and psychological methods. His history is already extensive."

If I could move a muscle, I'd laugh. These assholes don't scare me. They haven't quite clocked the extent of my indifference yet. Their pain is no motivator. I cherish it. Lavish in it. The agony is a warm, soft blanket that will never compare to the horrors I've already survived.

Pain is my fascination. Other people's suffering. Fuck, even my own. For years, I carved pieces off myself, layering scar upon scar to see how much blood it would take for me to break. When that failed, my attention shifted to the agony of others instead.

"Cease all activities with this one."

"But, Sir Bancroft—"

"We've wasted enough resources." Old Bastard *looks thoughtful, his wrinkled mouth pulled taut.*

"Should we dispose of him?" Doctor Farnsworth *asks.*

"That would be wasteful. I can think of far better uses for such promising resilience. It is rare these days. Your last stooge met an unfortunate end, isn't that so?"

"Yes, sir. This one and his friend saw to it."

"Then allow them to clean up the mess they made. Make him your stooge along with the other one." Bancroft *approaches then crouches down to address me. "Do you want out of this cell, son?"*

I summon the energy to barely nod.

"You know the price for defying us now. Your freedom isn't free."

With a final lingering look, he straightens.

"You work for Incendia Corporation now."

―――――

I don't wake up screaming like most who suffer with night terrors. It's more like lucid dreaming. I'm often aware that the hell I'm trapped in isn't real, but that doesn't make the memories any less horrifying.

Sitting upright in the twin bed, soaked covers pool around my waist, letting cold air lash against my bare, sweat-slick chest. A shiver threatens to wrack over me as I cool down. Lennox is snoring his head off in the adjacent bed—unperturbed, as usual.

We had the luxury of separate rooms in Priory Lane. Being in close quarters isn't my favourite thing. I like silence. Invisibility. Some of my best work is done in the shadows, far from the distraction of those with more morals.

Your freedom isn't free.

I didn't give a fuck what price I had to pay. I would've done the damn job for free. Bargaining our release from the Z wing was a mere bonus.

Rising from the bed, my steps are light and barely audible. Lennox doesn't stir as I shut myself in the small, attached bathroom and set the shower to cold. Funny how the mind craves what once traumatised it.

Ice-cold water sluices over my body. Goosebumps dapple across scar-striped skin. Most of the marks are white and shiny, softened by time. It's been several years since I took a blade to my own skin.

The thin stripes of raised tissue cover both arms up to my biceps. When I ran out of room, I moved to my stomach, then thighs. Once every inch had been tested, I grew tired of my own pain and looked elsewhere.

Then the real fun began.

By the time I've imprisoned the dreams back in their mental confines, Lennox is sitting upright in bed. I tuck a towel around my hips and comb a hand through my wet, snow-white hair.

"Another dream?" he asks.

I hum noncommittally.

"What was it this time?"

Ignoring him, I rifle through the cupboard tucked into the corner of the room that houses my selection of polo shirts and jeans.

"Xan. Don't shut me out."

"There's nothing to discuss."

"Has it been like this every night since we got out?" Lennox presses despite my clipped tone. "If I had known—"

"What, Nox?" I whirl to face him. "What could you have possibly done?"

Lennox dealt with what we went through differently. His survival was out of sheer stubborn will and rage. Nothing can break a man who has already lost his whole world. He quickly bounced back once we were released.

He sighs, though it lacks his usual anger. "I should've burned that goddamn place to the ground when I had the chance."

"That's your solution to everything," I point out.

"Do you have to be such an asshole?"

Admittedly, that was a low blow. Lennox's history is a matter of public record. First-degree murder has a way of making the news, especially the cases involving petrol and a well-aimed match.

It's what impressed me so much in the first place. His vengeance wasn't quiet or dignified. He didn't even care that he got caught. All Lennox wanted was to snuff out the life that killed his sister.

"Whatever." He lays back down then angrily stuffs his pillow. "Go skulk around somewhere and leave me alone."

Quickly getting dressed, I don't spare him another look, let alone an apology. He should know better than to expect that from me. Grabbing my ID, I slip out of the bedroom and head downstairs.

It's early enough to beat the morning rush. We've been

taking mathematics classes together, much like we did during our last incarceration. Numbers were an easy choice for me. Simple and mind-numbing, allowing me to continue plotting in the background.

When I met Lennox, he didn't give a fuck about anyone or anything. It was sheer chance that landed us in the same class together in Priory Lane. I'm not sure what he saw in me that made him latch on so tight.

I'm queuing for a breakfast tray when I catch the first rumblings. The handful of early risers in the line are whispering amongst themselves, and it's easy to tune in to their low conversation.

"You hear about some riot over the weekend?"

"I heard there were fatalities."

"Where?" someone replies.

"Blackwood, apparently. The patients escaped then practically destroyed the place on the way out. I've got a friend on the outside. He said it's all over the news."

"Are they on the run now?" another voice chimes in. "The people who escaped."

"I guess so. This fancy private security company is investigating. Not the patients—the institute."

"Blackwood is under investigation?"

"That's what I hear. They've been doing messed-up shit to their patients."

Sounds like Priory Lane was only the first to fall. Investigations come and go, but usually, nothing ever sticks. That's what money can buy. Complete and utter impunity. But a riot is far harder to cover up, and it seems to have loosened a few tongues too.

"You think that's why they've stepped up security here?" a female patient wonders. "If a breakout happened at Blackwood, it could happen here."

"Yeah, dream on."

"I'm serious!"

Tuning them back out, I stifle an eye roll. They're all so desperate to escape. And for what? Like the outside world will offer them anything more than rejection and disgust. None of us can ever go back to our former lives.

Especially me. I don't even have a life to return to. My existence was a solitary one, and at least in here, there's plenty of fresh meat for my machinations. Endless targets. Curiosities. And the one victim I can't seem to take my eyes off.

Ripley's routine is loosely set. Her moods rise and fall like the tide, and with it, her day-to-day activities. It's taken me a few weeks of careful observation to familiarise myself with her habits.

One of those habits was an eyebrow raiser. I doubt Lennox has clocked that his adopted stray is fucking the girl he loathes. Raine has been a little distant, but given his new Velcro-attachment to Ripley, it isn't surprising.

Right on time, she stalks into the cafeteria. Today, her loose, tawny curls are pinned back by a crisscrossed pair of paintbrushes, leaving those fierce, mottled brown and green eyes to take centre stage.

They'd look better filled with tears.

I can still remember the magnificent sight.

Absently fiddling with the silver ring slotted into her septum, she pauses to snag an apple and shove it into her pocket. The sweats she wears are ripped and paint stained. Apparently, she couldn't care less about her appearance or what anyone thinks.

It's one of the things that makes her so enticing. Previously, I would've gone for the weak, insecure ones. Their fear always tasted the sweetest. But getting Ripley to break with her newfound backbone is a far sweeter challenge.

I follow her out, my breakfast long abandoned. Rather

than heading for her scheduled therapy session, she stops outside, where the early signs of spring are beginning to reveal themselves.

Ripley pauses at a picnic bench occupied by that sullen, auburn-haired girl she's often with. Something exchanges between them. The glint of blades, I think. Leaning against the exterior wall, I can just hear them.

"Make these last a bit longer this time?"

The girl shrugs. "You know I'm good for it."

"That's not the point, Rae."

"You going soft on me? What's with the sour face?"

I watch Ripley's hands fist. How interesting. She usually wields her authority with complete detachment. It's enough to make me proud. But right there is a hint, a mere snippet of a different reality within.

The prospect is intriguing. I can work with that. The more I watch her, the more I uncover the chinks in her armour. It's why I'm doing my due diligence. This time, when I ensnare my little toy, I have no intention of her walking away after.

"Just… Fuck, Rae. Whatever. Forget it."

"Rip!"

But Ripley is already storming away, her lips clenched tight. Fascinating. I could stay and torment her frowning friend—she seems practically begging for an excuse to splinter apart—but Ripley has my sole attention.

I follow her, tucked out of sight as she scales a small staircase in the west wing, above the therapy rooms. She's detouring from her schedule. My intrigue spirals. With her all-access pass, obstacles like the locked, staff-only doors are no issue.

Lunging through each door before it can click shut, I follow her ascension to the top floor then prop a shoulder against the wall, hanging back in an empty corridor.

Ripley punches in a short, six-digit code on the door's keypad. I let her go ahead, the numbers already committed to memory. Though it will be disappointing if she's resolved to toss her pretty ass off the building before the fun has begun.

When enough time has passed, I tap in the code, finding a narrow service staircase on the other side. Cool morning air beckons me upwards, a silent footstep at a time, until I emerge on the manor's rooftop.

"Took you long enough."

Ripley's voice is flat, resigned.

I step out of the shadows. "Secret hiding place?"

"More like testing how far you'd be willing to follow me. How many more weeks are you going to keep up the stalking for?"

"I prefer the term enthusiastic observation."

The rooftop is slanted on either side with a flat strip down the centre. She's tiptoed her way down that platform to find a safe perch, her legs hanging over the edge to rest against slatted roof tiles.

"I prefer the term fucking sociopath." She flashes me a cold look.

I click my tongue, sensing that I should be offended, if I were capable of feeling such emotion. Enough psychiatrists have explained the difference to me.

"Sociopaths are violent, impulsive creatures with no self-control," I point out, leaning against the wall before shoving my hands in my pockets. "I'd prefer not to be compared to such recklessness."

Ripley's lips purse. "Are you giving me a psychology lesson?"

"If you're going to insult me, then at least use the accurate term."

"You're right," she scoffs. "You are a fucking psychopath."

"Much better."

Her shoulders stiffen at my slow approach. From up here, we have a limitless view of the surrounding woodland.

Nothing but trees, rolling hills and the winding road that services the institute.

"Now that we've cleared that up." I crouch down next to her, my head tilted. "Let's discuss your little excursion with our friend, Raine."

"You're real sick for watching, you know?"

"There's an argument to be made for you continuing despite knowing I was there."

"I only realised afterwards," she spits back. "Why are you following me?"

I summon a loose shrug.

"This isn't like before, Xander. Whatever you're hoping to achieve with these mind games, it isn't going to work."

My, what a sharp tongue.

"There was a time when you quivered at the sight of me," I muse aloud. "Whatever happened to that scared little mouse?"

"She grew teeth and learned how to bite back."

Smiling, I slowly reach out to trail a single fingertip down her cheek. I'd forgotten the fascinating pattern of light freckles that blemish her skin. Each mark detailing its own tale. Ripley's jaw clenches tight.

"Do. Not. Touch. Me."

"Or?"

Her head turns, pinning two livid eyes on me. "Or this time, I really will kill you."

"Oh, dearest Ripley." I lean close to breathe her familiar, oil paint scent in. "I'd like to see you try."

Brushing the back of my knuckles along her silky-soft cheek, I watch each micro-expression. Nostrils flaring. Muscles locking. Eyes narrowing. Although her mind repels me, her body remembers our time together.

The sad, abandoned child. Desperate for love and attention, even as she cuts the world off with walls thrown so high, she thinks no one will ever dare climb them.

But I did.

She willingly shredded herself for the pleasure of my touch. The relief I drove her to the edge of insanity to achieve did not come easily. Only once I'd conditioned her body to the extremes of ecstasy earned through pain.

"Xander," she breathes out.

"Hmm?"

Fingers sliding down to her lips, I stroke the chapped swell. She's been biting her bottom lip again. I've seen her do it when she's anxious or overwhelmed. How very telling. The infallible image displays a few more cracks.

"Get the fuck away from me." Her voice is strained, telling me she's forcing this attempt at showing strength.

If only her cowering clique could see her now. The way she trembles with each minuscule touch, her breathing becoming shallow, knuckles slowly turning white. I've seen her bravado around Lennox.

But not with me.

My scared little toy is still in there.

"There's nowhere in this world you can hide from me," I warn in a low tone. "Not even your little party trick in Priory Lane got rid of me."

Pushing my thumb past her open lips, I brush the pad against her soft, wet tongue. She shudders, her eyes smouldering, caught somewhere between defeat and hatred. I don't mind either. But her fight is what I really want.

"Did you think all this power would protect you?" I push my thumb deeper into her mouth. "That I wouldn't come back for what I'm owed?"

The shift is instantaneous. Her gaze sharpens as her teeth suddenly clamp down on my thumb. Biting hard, she waits for the yelp that never comes. Instead, I force her teeth apart again by shoving my index finger into her mouth for good measure.

"Nice try."

With droplets of saliva trailing down her chin, I push deeper into her mouth until my index finger is touching her throat. She gags a little, those smouldering eyes now covered in a wet sheen.

My other hand circles her neck, finding a loose grip. I squeeze incrementally, feeling for the erratic pulse of her jugular vein, pumping fear in the form of spillable blood. All it would take is one precise slash.

But what would be the fun in that?

We have plenty of time.

"Tell me, did you fuck him to prove a point?"

Her eyes widen, followed by an almost imperceptible shake of her head.

"Has the self-proclaimed Queen of Harrowdean gone and caught *feelings?*" I speak the word distastefully. "How predictable."

I can only imagine how much she'll plead when my cock's in her throat instead. Nothing compares to the thrill of tasting her inner conflict. Desiring humiliation when she demands compliance from the rest of the world.

Tightening my grip, I can almost feel the struggling flow of oxygen attempting to penetrate her trachea. What I wouldn't give to have her limbs tied and spreadeagled for me right now so that I can do as I please.

I'd tarnish each inch of her body. She bruises so beautifully. Perhaps bloody the rest. Carve my mark into her delicate flesh in case she ever forgets her place again. When the pain becomes unbearable, I'd make that sweet cunt sing.

Sliding my fingers from her mouth, I smear her own saliva over her lips. A single, defiant tear has escaped and rolls down her cheek to join the silvery smear. Capturing it, I bring the salty droplet to my tongue. I'd bottle it if I could.

"I don't want your throne anymore." I shake my head. "Instead I want the satisfaction of breaking this body and owning every single move you make while you sit atop your empire."

She'll own the world.

And I'll own her.

My hand loosens enough to grant her several deep gulps. She sucks in air, frenzied and desperate. When she speaks, her voice is a raw rasp.

"You will never, ever control me."

Vision going red, I release her throat to roughly grab the swell of her right breast. Her tits are as pert and shapely as I remember, the soft mound filling my palm.

"Then what is this if not control?" I counter. "Look at these hard buds threatening to break free."

I seize the sharp nipple poking my palm through the thin material of her t-shirt. Generous without being too big, her breasts can get away with no support beneath the baggy shirts she insists on wearing.

She whimpers when I twist, her tongue sneaking out to swipe her lips. "Please…"

"Yes, little toy? Please?"

Waiting for the next words to pass her lips, I'm hanging on a deadly precipice.

"Please… tell me." Her lips curl into a small, defiant smile. "Who hurt you so badly that you have to harm the rest of us to feel even remotely in control?"

It's a sharp slap to the senses. A bucket of frigid water. I feel my lips thin, the mental bars slamming into place and concrete walls hastily rising to hold back any weakness she may sense.

"Better yet… was his name Daddy?" Ripley gibes.

My mouth goes desert dry.

Her smile expands. "Gotcha."

Before I can attack, she seizes her advantage. Ripley throws her arms around my neck and flings her entire body to one side. I'm carried with her, rolling and twisting, down the side of the roof.

Jagged tiles slice into my back and sides, but I can't find purchase to break our tumble. She doesn't care that she's risking her own life to end mine. Ripley's arms remain resolutely locked around my neck.

The world is a blur. Trees, sky, an approaching ledge. It's all a dizzying muddle. Crying out, Ripley abruptly releases me and throws out her limbs. We reach the industrial-strength gutter at the same time.

Falling.

Thin air.

Biting panic.

Pain slices into my fingers as I catch the edge of the gutter before it's too late. My hold breaks, but I quickly recapture the thick metal and hold on for dear life. My entire body is hanging on the verge of a fifty-foot drop.

Is this what fear tastes like?

Head whipping from side to side, it takes a moment to register that Ripley isn't hanging with me. The image of her splattered brains several stories beneath me is a mental assault. Then her voice reaches me.

"What is this if not control?" she taunts.

The bitch is sprawled a few feet above me, her fall halted by an upturned roof tile. Panting and wild-eyed, she shifts to a safer position, preventing herself from slipping towards me.

Ripley eyes my precarious hold from her safe perch. "Falling from that height... you'd be dead on impact, I'd imagine."

"Help me!" I shout.

She huffs out a cold laugh. "Help? Oh, Xander. I didn't know you had a sense of humour."

Arms burning fiercely, I have to watch as she finds her feet then starts a slow crab-crawl back up the sloped roof. Never once looking back to see if I'm still fucking dangling.

"Get back here!"

Her laughter echoes. "The almighty Xander Beck doesn't need my help."

"Ripley!" I bellow.

It doesn't stop her from leapfrogging back onto the central platform and strolling away like she just deposited a parcel at the damn post office. The sound of the exterior door slamming matches my ragged breathing.

Fucking perfect.

CHAPTER 15
RIPLEY

.INTOODEEP. – DEAD POET
SOCIETY

I CAST an apprehensive eye around the deserted loading bay. I'm in my usual spot behind the back of an abandoned storage building, one of many scattered across Harrowdean's estate. All off-limits, of course.

Elon is late. Every Wednesday morning, we have a standing appointment. He delivers the shit I've ordered, then I peddle it to the poor fucks paying top dollar for their personal vices. It's clockwork. He's never late.

Sighing, I study the rough gravel surrounding the dock. Sleep has been rough going. Given recent disturbances, the guards have taken to performing hourly checks. Our doors are thrown open, lights blazing and covers ripped back.

It's just another psychological game. Another tactic. Any way they can dehumanise us further. The ones brave enough to oppose the recent crackdown are being singled out and targeted. Pull a stick out of a bundle, and it's easier to break, right?

Rumours have been swirling for days about what's happening beyond Harrowdean's walls. Our internet access is meagre, but they can't silence word of mouth. And everyone's abuzz about Blackwood.

The escaped patients haven't been caught. More and more fatalities are being confirmed with each passing day too. I heard from someone that bodies are being pulled out of the institute's ruins by authorities every hour.

Some shit definitely went down. No one knows exactly what, but we will all feel the repercussions if the situation escalates. Secrecy and subterfuge have kept this program intact for decades, and Harrowdean is no friend to the spotlight.

Finally, the crunch of footsteps approaches. I look over my shoulder in time to see Elon arrive, his backpack slung over his shoulder. He glances at the CCTV camera—switched off, naturally—before pinning his sour gaze on me.

"You're late," I call out.

He scowls. "You adhere to my schedule, inmate. I'm not your fucking lapdog."

"Sure. I have nothing better to do than sit here and wait for you."

Stopping at the edge of the dock, he dumps the backpack. "I am in no mood for your lip today."

Tempted to poke the bear a little more, I decide to relent. The last thing I want is to pack myself off to solitary again. With the mood management's been in of late, I doubt it'll be a fun experience.

After surrendering this week's cash, I unzip the backpack and take a cursory glance. It's half-empty. Only a few baggies of the usuals, but none of this week's special requests. Glancing up, I find Elon even more stony-faced than usual, his grey eyes lit with frustration.

"You're also light."

"Deal with it," he snaps.

"Letting customers down is bad for business. I have orders to fulfil."

"You think I give a shit?"

Biting my tongue, I rifle through everything, mentally

taking stock. This is barely half of the list. I'm going to have a lot of pissed-off patients on my case if I rock up with this load to sell.

"What gives?" I glance at him.

Elon rubs a hand over his cropped hair. "We're being closely monitored. I have to be cautious."

"This got something to do with Blackwood?"

Shutters immediately fall over his expression. "Why do you ask?"

"Come on. Everyone knows what's happening."

"You don't know shit, inmate."

"Who the hell died?" I gesture towards the backpack. "Because this haul is pathetic."

"The fucking warden did!" he erupts.

Not expecting an honest answer, I reel back. The gossip I've heard made it sound like unsuspecting patients lost their lives in whatever chaos engulfed Harrowdean's sister branch. Not the bloody warden.

"You're… serious?"

"The entire corporation is under investigation by some fancy assholes from London. All our asses are on the line."

Holy. Freaking. Shit.

Mind spinning, I try to pin down the ramifications, but I can't wrap my head around them. How does the perfect business model go so horribly wrong? What kind of courage did it take for patients to take down Blackwood?

"I still need the rest of the items on my list. I have requests to fulfil."

Towering over me, Elon's face is a stormy landscape. "Just go out there, do your job and keep your mouth shut. This place is a powder keg. You really wanna be striking that match?"

"Maybe," I retort without thinking.

He grimaces. "If this shit explodes, we're all going down

with it. You think everyone will just forgive and forget what you've done here?"

"I… I haven't—"

"Sold drugs? Needles? Knives?" Elon laughs coldly. "How about you tell me why a patient was spotted dangling off the goddamn roof the other morning?"

I duck my gaze. "Not a clue."

"Your pass was used to unlock the doors. I checked."

"Nothing to do with me."

He snorts derisively. "I hear the bastard hauled himself up. Did you even care to check he hadn't crashed to the ground below?"

I didn't care to or need to. If Xander had fallen to his death and splatted like a broken egg, it would've been big news. And let's face it, I'm not that fucking lucky. The son of a bitch isn't that easy to kill.

"You were warned," Elon continues. "One more slip-up, and it's night-night for Ripley. You're on thin ice."

"Then it's a good thing he's alive, isn't it?"

Done with this pointless conversation, I occupy myself by picking up the backpack and slinging it over my shoulder. The rooftop showdown was reckless, but the psychopath needed a warning. These silent mind games have to stop.

"It doesn't matter who you're related to." Elon turns, calling over his shoulder. "You're evidence. They'll dispose of you like the rest of the problems that disappear in here."

I watch him swagger off with a lead weight curling in my stomach. Less than a year. That's all I've got left. I'll soon be free to return to my life. I have to survive that long.

But what if it's true?

What if this crumbling system is going to bury me too?

One hand gripping the strap, I suddenly feel like I'm being crushed by the insubstantial weight of drugs slung over my shoulder. A few handfuls feels like several kilos. I couldn't begin to guess how much I've sold since transferring.

How many overdoses is that?

How many deaths?

All written off as the price of business. Justified. Filed away in the jam-packed drawers I keep in the darkest recesses of my mind. I locked those drawers then set them alight for good measure.

Looking over my shoulder, I check the loading bay one last time. Still empty. Yet it feels like something is snapping at my heels. And I'm not talking about Xander. This is something invisible. Perhaps it's not even real. But it's catching up to me nonetheless.

I walk fast, a painfully tight grip on the backpack. It's still early for deliveries, but the sooner I can offload this shit and hide from the inevitable disgruntlement of those who will go without, the better.

Finding my usual CCTV blind spot, I rest against the tree's thick trunk and place the backpack at my feet after removing what I need to add to Noah's stock. It's taken several weeks to build a decent pile.

I'm deep in thought and attempting to calm myself when the *tap, tap, tap* of Raine's approach startles me. He's wearing different jeans today, these ones boasting a rip in the left knee that adds to his edgy vibe.

"Different shampoo?" he offers in greeting.

Weirdo.

"It's Rae's. I'm out."

Nodding, he continues towards me. "Just don't change the papaya body wash. I'll never be able to find you."

"Good to know. I may need to disappear sometime soon."

I try for a joke, but the words come out all wrong. Raine's blonde brows knit together as he reaches for me, snagging my t-shirt's hem then moving higher to touch my arm.

"What's wrong?"

"Shit's going down." I drop my voice. "I'm missing half

my stock, and all the rumours that have been circulating are true."

"About that riot?"

"Yeah. People are dead."

Raine curses softly. "That's fucked up."

"It's gonna blow back on Harrowdean soon. Sounds like authorities are involved."

Humming, he releases me then rolls his guide stick between his hands. "Isn't that a good thing? The world may actually pay attention to the bullshit that's under the radar for once."

How do I tell him that my neck is on the chopping block too? Raine knows what I do. Hell, he buys from me on a weekly basis now. But that doesn't mean I want to spell it out for him.

"It'll be alright, Rip." He tries to comfort me. "No matter what happens."

"You don't know that."

"Worst case scenario, all the institutes are shut down. We can get the fuck out of here."

"And go where? Somewhere worse?"

"I was thinking somewhere far away from any psych ward or rehab centre. Hell, the fucking wilderness if that's what it takes."

Just the thought of him managing in the damn wilderness causes laughter to burst out of me. Raine quickly catches on to my line of thought and joins in.

"Okay, perhaps not a jungle. I need good ground clearance. There's nothing to trip over on a beach though, right?"

"You're ridiculous. We're not going anywhere."

His shoulders slump. "You are. I've got two more years of this."

My chest spasms at his palpable defeat. His assumption that me getting out first would be an issue is both heart-warming and petrifying. Criminal or not, everyone signs up for the same three years just to get accepted into Harrowdean's rehabilitative program.

Raine must sense my unease because he quickly drops the subject. "What are you gonna do with this lot, then? You can't fulfil half their orders and half not."

"Shift what I can, then haul ass. People will be mad."

"It's not your fault everything's going to shit."

"But I can't exactly tell them that, can I? I have appearances to maintain."

Catching sight of Luka lingering nearby, early like normal, I beckon him over. Raine remains silent as we exchange pills and payment. He shuffles off to gobble his laxatives, and I quickly re-zip the backpack.

"What will you do once you get out?"

Raine fiddles with the nylon strap attached to his stick. "Not a clue."

"You have a career waiting for you."

"Pretty sure I drove it off a cliff long before I wound up here. I honestly don't know what's waiting for me now."

I bite back what I want to say. *I will be.* I've known him for little more than a few months and spoken to him for less than that. I don't know what's waiting for me either, and I won't make promises I can't keep.

"Maybe you'll need some kind of musician in residence at your studio," he suggests with a smirk. "Free performances for the lady."

"If I go back."

"Where else would you go?" he asks.

I close my eyes, giving myself a brief moment to dream. "Somewhere no one knows my name."

"You want a fresh start."

"I want to forget."

He tilts his head back to rest on the tree. "Does this

forgetting plan include erasing me? Your maybe platonic, maybe not, casual hook-up?"

Hesitating, I weigh my response. We haven't discussed what this is. There's no formal label and no need to assign one. But I've long since discovered that Raine's confidence conceals bone-deep insecurities. I won't hurt him with a lie.

"I doubt I could if I tried."

"I can't figure out if you're happy or mad about that," he admits. "But I'll take it."

"Things aren't so black and white, Raine. You know that. I'm glad you're here. Isn't that enough?"

"It'll always be enough, guava girl. I just…" He trails off with a sigh. "I just wanna know if this means something to you too."

Turning to face him, I ball the fabric of his shirt in my hand and pull him close. The cool surface of his blacked-out lenses touches my face as my lips peck his.

I'm shitty at this emotional stuff. Any ability I had to be vulnerable was long ago wiped out. But with Raine, when the jokes fall flat and we both turn serious, I want to try. I know he needs that reassurance.

Maybe I do too.

We're both just afraid.

"This means something to me," I murmur.

"Entertainment?"

"Well, I wouldn't want to blow smoke up your ass. But you were pretty good."

He guffaws. "You weren't so bad yourself."

The tension broken, I toy with this t-shirt.

"So… round two?"

"Aren't you working?"

"Self-employed," I joke.

"Well, fuck. Little Miss Entrepreneur. Anyone ever tell you how sexy that is?"

"Surprisingly not."

Several raised voices interrupt our banter. I cast a subtle glance over my shoulder and groan. Rick and a handful of his friends are wandering closer, exchanging heated, angry whispers. Yeah, no thanks.

"Come on." I release Raine and grab the backpack. "We've got company."

He cocks his head slightly. "Is it that asshole?"

"Rick. Five others too."

His hand clenches tight around mine as soon as I seize it. Raine's stick swings from side to side, but he lets me steer our path away from my delivery point and deeper into the institute's grounds.

At this hour, most patients are in classes, therapy or sleeping. Guards are peppered around, though. I try to ignore the prickle of unease I feel as Rick and his entourage remain on our tail.

"They're following," Raine mumbles.

"I know. Keep walking."

"Oi! Freaks!" One heckles.

Fingers tightening on Raine's hand, I attempt to slow down to clap back at the son of a bitch, but he tugs me onwards to keep walking.

"Don't bite back."

"But—"

"Rip," Raine warns. "There are six of them."

"So? What do you think they'll do?"

"I don't fancy finding out. Do you?"

Relenting, we continue walking. Our pace slowly increases, passing the red-brick exterior of the west wing. Shit. It's quieter at this end of the grounds. No guards to stop Rick if he decides to pounce. The library isn't far from here, but it's often deserted.

"Where are we?" Raine asks.

"Near the library."

"Is there a door leading inside?"

"Yeah." I pull Raine to the right. "But it's around the other side."

Their footsteps are still following. I hate giving the impression that we're afraid, but if Raine doesn't want drama, I'll attempt to keep myself leashed. If I were alone, I wouldn't be so restrained.

"We want to fucking talk to you!"

I recognise Owen's voice. He's a bulky, obsessive compulsive from the fifth floor. A recent addition to Rick's little gang and desperate to prove his worth. I'm sure he'd benefit from a good punching.

With the rear door to the library in sight, we're almost there when the first hands reach us. Raine is ripped away from me as someone's arms band around my middle, causing me to drop the backpack.

"Get off!" I shout.

"Voice down, Ripley."

Fucking Rick.

Owen and some other sneering dickhead whose name I haven't cared to memorise have hold of Raine. They kick his guide stick aside then hold an arm each, keeping him trapped in place. All while he curses and fights against them to no avail.

Rick's strong arms around my waist hold me against his chest. "It's rude to ignore people."

His breath is hot in my ear, making my skin crawl. I haven't sold cigarettes to him for a while now. His breath has certainly benefited from the detox.

"You think I give a shit about hurt feelings?"

"Come on, Rip. I wanna have a little chat with you."

Two of his friends go ahead, holding the doors to the library open so they can wrestle us inside. My heart sinks when I see that Linda, the on-site librarian, isn't at her desk like usual. Must be her lunch break.

"Get out!" Rick roars.

The handful of patients browsing the towering rows of books scatter.

"Go watch the doors," he barks at his two pals. "Don't let anyone in."

They dispatch to follow his command. Raine thrashes, trying to peel Owen's hands off, but his arms are wrenched backwards to hold him prone.

"Here's how this is going to work." Rick's hips press into me from behind. "Tell us a lie, and we'll fuck with your new boyfriend. Got it?"

Oh, hell no.

Desperately wishing that Raine could see the pointed look I want to give him, I force a nonchalant voice. I can't let them have this leverage over me.

"Do what you want to him. He's worthless to me."

"Is that so?" Rick chuckles in amusement. "You won't mind if we test that theory, then."

Drawing back a cocked first, Owen slams it into Raine's midsection. Air whooshes out his mouth as he doubles over, coughing and spluttering.

I grit my teeth. "Test away."

"Damn, bitch. You're cold. Hit him again."

This time, the other dickhead punches him square in the face. I wince at the sound of Raine's glasses cracking and flying off his face. Blood spills from the corner of his mouth as his eyes are unveiled.

Owen leans closer to get a good look. "Huh. Figured you'd have some ugly, gaping holes beneath those things."

"Fuck you," Raine spits.

Punching him in the gut again, a thick globule of blood flies from Raine's mouth. His breathing is laboured through the pain, teeth bared and spine curved to absorb each hit.

"Still nothing?" Rick taunts. "Alright then. Again."

It's the brief flash of fear on Raine's face that breaks my resolve. Before Owen's fist can crush his nose, I scream out.

"Wait!"

Chuckling again, Rick squeezes my waist. "There we go. That wasn't so hard, was it?"

"Leave him alone, for fuck's sake. What do you want from me?"

"I want to know where Carlos is."

Laughter rips free. "Seriously? All this for that idiot?"

"Hit him," Rick instructs.

Owen slams his fist into Raine's face again. Blood explodes from his nose and mouth, the crimson splatter staining his golden hair red. I battle harder against Rick's restraint.

"You asshole!"

"Watch your damn mouth, then. Where is Carlos?"

"How the hell should I know?" I yell in panic.

"You're Harrowdean's whore. Don't pretend like you don't know."

"I have no idea!"

"Another lie. Again."

This time, it's a throat punch. Owen releases Raine's arm as his friend does the deed, leaving Raine to crumple, his knees hitting the polished parquet floor. The strangled gasp coming from his throat makes me see red.

"I'll rip you apart for hurting him!" I scream.

"Where is Carlos?" Rick asks calmly.

"I told you that I don't know!"

He sighs, the stickiness of his breath stirring my hair. "Perhaps you need a different motivation. Selfish cunts can't be controlled by hurting others, right?"

Raine tries to sit up at that, but Owen draws back his foot and boots him firmly in the kidney. He lands flat on his back, unable to contain his heart-rending howl. There's blood splattered all over him.

"Ease off," Rick drones. "Come hold the bitch down. Watch him, Ant."

Stomping and kicking, I do my best to break free as I'm forced to the floor. Owen positions himself over me, seizing my wrists then stretching them high so I'm pinned with my arms above my head.

Taking the lower half of my body, Rick casts an eye over my predicament. He looks far too fucking smug. When he gets close enough, I quickly snap out my leg and kick him right in the face.

"Ow!" he screeches.

Removing his hand from his face, I'm awarded with the sight of blood trickling from the corner of his mouth. Damn, I got him good. He moves to sit on my legs, his disgusting weight bearing down on me.

"That wasn't very nice, Rip."

"I don't know where Carlos is!"

Rick shakes his head, now straddling my thighs. "He steps one foot out of line, and he's gone. No parents or siblings to worry about him. Just us. Convenient, huh?"

"He was probably transferred or some shit!"

"You think I'm fucking stupid?"

Striking me hard, the hit causes my head to snap to the side. I feel my lip split and blood begin to ooze from the stinging cut.

"Where is he?"

When I don't respond, he repeats the same move. My neck and head ache as I blink back tears. Doesn't mean I'm gonna give him shit, though. His friend is probably dead.

"How do you live with yourself, huh?" he seethes. "Selling for the goddamn enemy?"

"Wait—"

"You make me sick."

Raine's distant shouting doesn't stop Rick from striking again. Again. Again. Each hit harder than the last. Slaps turn to punches until I can feel the blood drenching my battered face. Everything is spinning and ticking.

"Stop it!" Raine yells. "She doesn't know!"

"Bullshit," Rick rages.

Boneless, I cough up blood. "Probably dead."

His next blow halts. "What was that?"

"They just... remove troublemakers. He'd be easy to erase."

The festering fury in Rick's eyes amplifies. Owen holds my wrists tight as he grabs my jaw, his grip bruising, causing teeth and bone to creak like old wooden beams. I'm surprised nothing has broken yet.

"Where do they take them? The people they want to erase?"

It isn't worth my life to reveal that information. Of the tiny minority who know about the Z wing, no one knows its location. Only me. If I reveal it, I'll face a far worse fate than this.

"Don't know."

"Liar!" He squeezes my jaw hard enough to grind. "Where?"

"Don't... know!"

"You're lying!"

Releasing my jaw, he takes my wrist from Owen. I try to scratch him, but Rick slams it on the floor to hold me still. His spare hand grasps my index finger tight.

"I've spent the last year watching you swan around this place like you own it. Hurting people. Mouthing off. Throwing your weight around. I know you're a lying piece of shit."

My gut boils with anger. Everything he hates about me is everything I fucking hate about me. And I don't care how mad it'll make him, I want him to pay for voicing my biggest shames out loud.

"Even if I knew where he is... I wouldn't tell you." I lick warm blood from my mouth. "Imagine what they're doing to him right now."

"Rip," Raine hisses.

"You wanna know what they do to disposable patients?" I continue regardless of the possible consequences. "Your stupid friend won't even know his own name by the time they're done."

I know I'm in for a world of pain when Rick begins to overextend my finger joint. He forcefully pulls until I feel something pop, followed by a sharp, intense burning that sets my whole left hand alight.

"You will tell me," he orders through gritted teeth. "Or I'll dislocate every single finger you have."

"Do it! I don't care!"

Moving on to the next finger, he wrenches it from the socket with a low growl. The pain is even more intense. This time, I can't hold back a wail. It feels like my fingers are being dipped in acid and corroded down to the bone.

"Shut her up," Rick barks at his friend. "We don't need company."

Clamping his sweaty palm over my mouth, Owen silences my cries. I continue to shriek into his damp skin as Rick dislocates two more fingers, each wrenching motion as merciless as the last.

Raine's yelling and frantic battling to escape barely register. He's still being held down, unable to throw his captor off in his weakened state. All I can feel is the steady pounding in my burning hand.

"Well?" Rick prompts.

Owen lifts his hand from my mouth long enough for me to respond. I pant roughly, my entire body slick with sweat and trembling all over.

"I h-hope you never find him."

"You stupid, stupid cunt."

Smiling through the pain, I scream myself hoarse when he moves to the last victim—my thumb. It's snapped out of place with a sick clicking sound. But Rick doesn't seem in the least bit satisfied by my escaping sobs.

"Maybe we should do him again?" Owen nods to Raine.

"I want the little bitch to hurt, not him!"

"Just an idea, man."

"Well I have a better one."

Reaching around the back of his waist, Rick tugs something free from his jeans. A switchblade, not unlike the one I stabbed him with, reveals itself with a distinctive flicking sound.

"It took eight stitches to patch me up after our last tangle." Rick studies the glinting blade. "So I owe you at least double that, right?"

Raine must clock the soft flick of the blade unlatching because he goes wild. Bucking. Bellowing. Promising death. Ant—the other dickhead—grabs a handful of his sandy locks and slams his skull into the floor with a crack.

He goes limp, limbs splayed and mouth lolling open. With that distraction taken care of, Rick kneels on my wrist and shoves the sleeve of my long t-shirt up past my elbow, despite my vicious cursing.

He holds the blade poised between his fingers. The curved tip almost resembles the bristles of my paintbrush, I think distantly. But I'm not the manipulator behind it this time. Pain is going to be inflicted on the canvas of my body instead.

"Hold her. I need to get close."

Owen places his hand on my mouth again then clamps the other one on my shoulder to stop me from struggling. I shout behind his gag as Rick leans closer, inspecting the intricate ribbons of inked vines wrapped around my forearm.

"Damn. These are good." He runs a finger over the painstakingly realistic tattoo. "Almost a shame to ruin it."

When the tip of the blade presses into my elbow crease, I feel a piece of me shatter. Something internal. Irreversible. A part of me I never thought I'd have to lose. Confirming that nothing stays safe forever.

The blade slices in deep, precise slashes. I can feel letters being carved into my skin. Each scrawled letter is a white-hot poker on my skin. When he curves the blade to cut each swoop and twist, my frantic cries die out.

"Fucking hell," Owen mutters in disgust. "That's sick."

"Shut up," Rick snaps. "She deserves this!"

"I dunno, dude. This is fucked up."

Frowning hard in concentration, Rick curses when his hand slips. My throat is too raw to wail at the sudden stabbing sensation of the switchblade sliding in too deep. He blanches when he realises his mistake.

Owen leans down to look. "Is it meant to bleed that much?"

"I fucking slipped."

"I didn't sign up for this shit!"

"She isn't gonna die, asshole! Shut up already."

Warmth trickles down my arm. I can feel a pool gathering. A twisted part of me wants to drag this out for as long as possible—without medical attention soon, I'll bleed out. That's freedom, right?

No.

I didn't come this far just to die at the hands of some power-tripping son of a bitch. If nothing else, the horror show I've created here must amount to more than that.

I won't die on the library floor. Even if this brings the wrath of Harrowdean's management raining down on me, at least I can accept that fate and go down swinging. Letting Rick bleed me out will be far more pathetic.

Mumbling weakly behind Owen's hand, it takes him a moment to notice. When he does, he grumbles for Rick's attention and releases my mouth once more.

"Yes?" Rick cocks a brow.

"K-Kingsman."

"What?"

"The disused dorms… B-Behind the storage buildings. Go to the basement."

"Carlos is there?"

"If… he's alive."

Triumphant, he nods at Owen. "Go get the others."

I'm quickly released. Relief is a misty cloud sinking into my pores, but it's short-lived. With Raine beginning to stir, Rick pinches his chin, considering me for a moment longer.

"You should've started with that."

Returning his blade to my flesh, he resumes carving, this time careless and hurried. There must be a final reservoir of adrenaline left inside me because I manage a choked screech as he completes his work.

The sound of my agony rouses Raine from his semi-awake daze. Lifting a hand to his head, he groans in pain. Ant doesn't bother knocking him out again. They already got what they wanted.

Owen returns with the two others. "Let's move!"

"Almost done," Rick murmurs.

With a final, few flicks, his artwork is complete. He wipes the blade off on my t-shirt then closes it, staring down at my arm with a weird look of pride.

"You'll never forget this place now, Ripley. No matter how far you run. I hope the memory of the evil you've inflicted follows you to your deathbed."

With that parting shot, he stands and follows his grunts out. None of them spare us a second glance. I don't bother to warn them about the impenetrable layers of security they'll face. No one enters the Z wing. Not successfully. But more importantly, no one gets out. If their asshole friend is down there, it's a suicide mission to even attempt to find him.

"Ripley?" Raine grunts.

I can't move my lips or tongue to respond. Everything is heavy. Numb. Powering down. All I can feel is the expanding puddle of blood growing around me from whatever the fuck Rick's nicked.

"Jesus… I can smell your blood. Where are you?"

Manoeuvring himself up, he resorts to haphazard crawl. His head collides with several bookcases before he touches the slick, warm trail of blood leading back to me. All I can summon is a whimper.

"Fuck! Rip, stay with me."

Raine collapses next to me, desperately feeling his way over my limbs.

"Where are you bleeding?"

It takes all my energy to prise my lips apart. "Arm."

Still cursing, he locates the mess that Rick's made and applies pressure. The weight of him pressing down on my shredded skin feels like live electrodes have been wired into my nerve cells and set to fucking vibrate.

"I'm sorry… I'm sorry…" he chants. "Forgive me, babe."

"S-Stop…"

"I can't, Rip. You've lost too much blood. Did he hit a damn vein?"

I'm so cold. Exhausted. My eyes feel far too weighty to bother trying to hold them open. When I don't respond, Raine presses down harder on my wounds, causing my spine to arch as I screech hoarsely.

"Stay awake! Please!"

Eyes blurred with coursing tears, I watch him fumble to pull off his shirt. I get a glance of my arm before he quickly wraps it up and ties the shirt as tight as possible, freeing up his hands to locate his phone.

It's a slightly chunkier smartphone with a tinny voice that speaks to him each time he presses the screen. I remember the laughter we shared the first time I saw him use it. The voice's faux-British accent is ridiculous.

Scrolling through his contacts, the limited list of names are read aloud. I want to scream *no* at the name he lands on. I don't want him to see me like this. Let alone someone far, far worse.

The line quickly connects.

"What, Raine?"

"Library. Bring medical help."

"Code red?"

"Just hurry."

There's a growling curse.

"We're coming."

Dropping the phone, Raine quickly shifts his attention back to me. Even through my fuzzy vision, I can see those limitless, maple pools darting around. His face is already swelling beneath the fresh blood and bruises.

"I d-didn't mean it," I struggle out.

"Mean what?"

"What I told them... You're not worthless."

He looks stricken, his frown lines pronounced and toffee eyes watering. "I couldn't protect you. If I could see—"

"No. Not your fault."

"But—"

"No."

The sound of incoming shouting reaches us. Thudding footsteps. Several guards, no doubt. Raine doesn't stop holding pressure on my arm, though he looks ready to keel over himself.

Everything fades out in the flurry of noise. I feel Raine being pulled away from me and replaced by someone else. Questions are barked. That familiar, sonorous voice sounds even angrier than usual. Now there's an achievement.

"Who the fuck did this?"

"I'm fine, Nox. I need to help Ripley!"

"Forget her! She deserves this."

"She's bleeding!" Raine shouts loudly. "You can't—"

There's a scuffle. More pained moaning. Through slitted eyes, I can see Raine clutching his head, like he tried to struggle but couldn't escape the muscled boulder pulling him from my side.

Lennox actually spares me an uncertain glance. Our eyes meet, hazel on seafoam. Hatred on disdain. Only neither of us can muster either emotion in the midst of such destructive violence.

The evil bastard should be enjoying the satisfaction right now. But instead, he looks physically sick as he studies my bruises, swelling and finally, my haphazardly bandaged forearm that's steadily leaking blood.

"Fuck," he splutters. "Xan?"

"Yeah. I've got her."

Kneeling in my blood, I can just about distinguish Xander's spearmint scent in the copper-laced air. A pair of scarred arms slide beneath me and lift, half-pulling me against his body.

My head is cradled in his lap. I have no choice but to stare straight up into those midnight globes, filled with endless nothingness. The dark-blue hue is a mere breath away from murderous black right now.

"Who did this to you?" he whispers in a dangerously low voice.

"Why… do you… care?"

Those terrifying, onyx eyes catch on my dislocated fingers. I watch his throat bob up and down. Jaw muscles tightening. So many silent tells told in the smallest of reactions. Xander can't strangle all his emotions.

"Hold still," he orders.

Picking up my hand, Xander studies each traumatised joint in a clinical way. Cataloguing and assessing. I don't have time to wonder how he knows what to do with them.

"Breathe in."

He swiftly clicks the first finger back into place. The pain is intense but short-lived. Numbness resurfaces, filling me instead. It seems I've reached my threshold for the time being.

Xander is unperturbed by each swollen, misshapen finger he finds. Not even blinking, he deftly shifts them back into place, working efficiently despite my continued whimpers. Only experience can teach that perfect motion.

"This must make you h-happy."

His eyebrows knit together as he works. "Do I look happy?"

No. He doesn't.

Not even a little bit.

With more voices arriving all around us, I break eye contact with the devil watching over me. I don't need him to see my humiliation as the final chunk in the dam holding my emotions at bay breaks.

Xander's grip tautens when a sob bursts from my chest, though it sounds weak and lacklustre. He's holding me so tight; it feels like he's trying to stop me from slipping from his grasp and drowning.

I know what mess now decorates my body. I caught that brief glimpse. The scribbled craftsmanship inked in my own blood. Disfiguring my tattoos with the path of his blade. Rick left me a message.

Harrowdean's whore.

CHAPTER 16
RIPLEY
START A WAR – KLERGY & VALERIE BROUSSARD

Present Day

DROPPING my eyes from the camera lens, I look down at the lace-detailed cuffs of my off-white blouse. The beautiful foliage on my right arm is still intact, swirling upwards from my wrist to cover my whole forearm.

The left tattoo sleeve used to be an identical match. I got them done on my nineteenth birthday after spending months saving up from every piece of artwork I sold. I thoroughly researched the artist and even illustrated my own design.

Now the design is distorted by old, jagged scarring. It's faded a little over the last decade, but the skin is still puckered and shiny against dark spirals of ink, making the words easy enough to read. I should know. I trace them every day.

Harrowdean's whore.

"You never considered tattooing back over it?" Elliot asks me.

"Why? So I could forget? Pretend like Harrowdean never happened?"

Wisely, he keeps quiet. I've long hated journalists and their impertinent questions. Every single one of them who's attempted to buy my story has been out for one thing—blame.

They see me as an easy target, a place to put the world's rage, now that Incendia is gone. Even all these years later, unanswered questions remain. The scars left by our psychiatric sentences have never truly faded.

"Everything changed after Rick's attack." I look back up at Elliot. "Things were already shifting at Harrowdean, but that was the turning point."

"How so?"

"Wars often start silently. Pieces were sliding into place to precipitate what happened next, but even if we'd known... we couldn't have stopped it."

Flicking through his notebook, he studies lines of scrawled handwriting. "You've mentioned the rumours circling about what was also happening at Blackwood Institute."

"News travelled fast. Even when management didn't want us to hear it."

Elliot nods thoughtfully. "It was a national scandal at the time. We've attempted to interview several Blackwood inmates, including Brooklyn West, on a few occasions. But no such luck."

I suppress a snort. Brooklyn wouldn't waste a single second of her time on something like this. She's never played well with the media and doesn't care to revisit her past.

For a long time, I felt the same way. Like talking about what happened inside Harrowdean Manor would somehow drag me back there, into the clutches of evil beyond comparison.

"Incendia left many victims, Miss Bennet. I'm sure you know that better than most."

Because they're my victims too.

Feeling flushed all of a sudden, I tug at the collar of my blouse. All of the air in the room has vanished. It's like I've stepped into an airlock. I take a sip from the glass of water on the table, but it does little to calm me.

This is precisely why I never leave my safe bubble. When the panic attacks hit, they're intense and ugly. Old Ripley would laugh at the mess of a person I am now. Traumatised and haunted by all she's seen.

She'd eye me with disdain and keep walking, unwilling to spare a drop of empathy. I cared less back then. All I cared about was survival; nothing else mattered to me.

"I... need a moment," I choke out.

"Of course." Elliot gestures for his cameraman to stop rolling. "Would you like some more water?"

"Just... air. I need air."

Tugging the clip-on microphone from my lapel, I toss the handful of wires onto my chair then flee. The doors to the soundproof studio slam shut behind me.

Several startled employees working for the production company look up as I run past, though none look surprised. I bet I'm not the only interviewee who's ran from that damn camera.

The elevator ride is a painfully long wait that only adds to the pressure squeezing my throat tight. Finally breaking outside, the hustle and bustle of Central London is an unwelcome slap in the face.

I'm almost mowed over by a distracted commuter when a strong hand clamps around my bicep. Dragged out of the way, I'm propped against the wall of the huge glass skyscraper.

"You promised to let me do this alone," I pant raggedly. "I don't need a private security team."

"No, we promised not to follow you inside."

Tall, muscled and coated head to toe in tattoos, Hudson Knight is an intimidating force of nature. He's never caught out of black clothing, and there's an earpiece tucked beneath his chaotic mop of raven hair.

A few paces behind him, two others stand at ease. I stare into Warner's familiar baby blues. Along with Hyland, his number two, they're both members of Sabre Security's ruthless Anaconda Team.

"Ripley?" Hudson prompts.

When I turn back to him, his gaze is boring into me, a pierced eyebrow quirked in challenge. I should've known Kade would send his brother to hold the perimeter. He got all uptight and stressed when I mentioned that I'd accepted this interview request.

"I don't need the head of Sabre Security here to keep me safe."

"Technically, I'm only one half." He smirks at me. "Nobody would put me in charge of the company on my own."

"You're right about that. The place would crumble."

"Precisely," Hudson drawls. "So where's the fire?"

Pulling a pack of cigarettes from his pocket, he lights up and takes a long drag. I eye the tempting little death stick. Never been much of a smoker, but right now, I'd take a stiff shot of vodka and a fucking sedative.

Hudson rolls his eyes and surrenders the cigarette to me. "You don't smoke."

"I don't do a lot of things."

My hands tremble violently as I hold it between my lips and inhale deeply. Smoke fills my struggling lungs, causing me to splutter. The amused look on Hudson's face is gonna get him punched in a moment.

"Not sure smoking is the answer," he comments.

"Please leave the therapy shit to Jude. You're no good at it."

Hudson snorts. "Fair enough."

With Hyland and Warner keeping a close eye on us, we

stand in silence. It's a welcome reprieve after hours of relentless questioning and reliving the past. I tune the hustle and bustle of England's capital city out.

Although I feel less trapped outside the confines of the blacked-out TV studio, it takes time for me to calm down. We've been talking non-stop. I'm exhausted and we've still barely scratched the surface of the story.

"I don't know why you're even doing this interview." Hudson lights his own cigarette. "These producers have been trying to pin us all down for years. It isn't worth the hassle."

"Not all of us have been able to move on, Hud."

"You think we're not still haunted by the shit that went down?" He shakes his head, pulling in a long draw of nicotine. "You're not the only one who can't forget. But that doesn't mean I'd entertain some clickbait interview."

Shrugging, I take another drag. I'm not going to judge how he's chosen to cope—how any of them have. We've all managed in our own ways. But this is my decision, and I made it for a reason.

"My point is, you don't have to do this."

"No." Feeling steadier, I drop the cigarette and stomp on it. "I don't have to do it. I *need* to do it."

"What about the backlash? You ready for that?"

"Well, it's a good thing I know the country's top private security company then, isn't it?"

Hudson drops a strong hand on my shoulder. "We can handle threats to your safety. I'm more worried about the impact the shit people will say about what we all did to survive will have."

"I don't care what people think."

"Then why put yourself through this?"

Placing my hand on top of his, I lightly squeeze. "I'm not looking for their forgiveness, Hud. I'm looking for my own."

He sighs, blowing out a cloud of smoke. "Then I'm not letting you do this alone."

"I can take care of myself."

"It's not for your benefit." Hudson puts out his cigarette then gestures for me to head back inside. "If Brooke heard that I'd sent you back up there alone, she'd serve my fucking balls for breakfast."

With a nod to Hyland and Warner, remaining on guard outside, we head back inside the building. Hudson's scruffy jaw is set in a hard line as he follows me into the elevator and back upstairs.

"You know the interviewer is going to shit himself when he sees you're with me. He's been fishing for the scoop on Blackwood for hours."

Hudson chuckles. "He can dream on."

"Just play nice, alright?"

"I'm always nice."

"Sure. You're a fluffy fucking teddy bear."

"Damn straight," he echoes.

Walking back into the studio, several assistants do a comical double take at the wall of glowering, inked muscle escorting me. Sabre Security has had many high-profile cases in recent years. Hudson's scowl is well known, much to his chagrin.

"Ripley." Elliot stands as I walk back into the interview room. "Is everything okay?"

"Fine. I just needed a moment."

"Of cou…"

He trails off as Hudson stalks in behind me, his trademark intimidating glower in place. This was a fucking terrible idea. The man is incapable of playing nice, and I don't trust him to keep a cool head if he sticks around to listen.

"My security detail wishes to be present," I try to explain.

Elliot sticks out a hand to be shaken. "Perhaps your security detail would care for a microphone too? I've been following your story for a long time, Mr Knight."

Lip curled, Hudson eyes Elliot's hand with disgust and doesn't take it. "No doubt."

Clearing his throat, Elliot drops his hand.

"I'll be right over here, Rip." Hudson takes his position in the corner of the room.

I pick up the microphone and reclip it to my lapel. Warily eyeing Hudson, Elliot sits back down and picks his notebook up. Once I'm comfortable, he instructs the cameraman to resume rolling.

"Where were we?" I sigh.

"What happened after the attack?"

I wring my fingers together, letting the past drag me back.

"I thought all I wanted was revenge. But what do you do when you're led to slaughter with no chance of escape? When your enemies are in fact your only allies?"

Heart pounding, I touch the scars on my arm again. They aren't the only marks I left Harrowdean with. Some scars I hate less than others. Some were made by force, and others I took willingly. My hand lifts to my throat, absently tracing the thin knife line there.

Hatred breeds insanity.

And all we had in hell was each other.

CHAPTER 17
RIPLEY

STREET SPIRIT (FADE OUT) – RADIOHEAD

Ten Years Earlier

I DON'T REMEMBER MUCH about my mother. Even the memory of her scent is vague—a generic, floral fingerprint, but I couldn't say what perfume she wore or her preferred bouquet for Valentine's day.

Over time, those details faded. Whether by choice or design, it's hard to say. Eight-year-old Ripley wanted to lock her pain in a box and bury it at the bottom of the ocean. To do that, she scrubbed her memories too.

I tried painting Mum once. My uncle never kept photos of his sister around. All my parents' belongings were either sold or put into storage after I moved, so I had to use nothing but memory alone.

Reaching for the image of my mother, I found an empty cavern instead. I'm not sure I could even tell you the colour of her eyes. Brown? Green? Blue? Grey? Whatever hue, they still turned to mulch beneath the ground she was buried in.

But I do remember one thing.

A few months before Dad's heart attack, I had to have my tonsils removed. I was always getting throat infections, spending whole months living off ice cream. My dad kept the freezer well-stocked.

When I woke up in hospital after the surgery, Mum was there. Curled up in the bed next to me, her body lined up against mine, that nameless flowery scent wrapped all around me. I remember how safe I felt. How loved.

She never let me go through the scary stuff alone. Splinters stuck in fingers. Grazed knees. Failed spellings tests. Dad's funeral. Mum was always there. Until the day she didn't come home.

I have no one left now.

Not for the hard stuff.

A tickle in my nostrils rouses me. The scent of hospital-grade bleach is an unpleasant stench. It sneaks into my awareness and pulls me from the hazy shroud of my mother's perfume, still floating in my mind.

"Come on. You've been discharged."

"No! I'm not leaving her."

"Who is she to you, Raine? What's going on here?"

"I care about her! Back off."

An incredulous scoff. "You know what she's done! This is where she belongs."

"I don't give a fuck about this feud between you two. It has nothing to do with me. I'm not leaving her."

This time, there's an irritated groan.

"She'll break your heart then walk all over the broken pieces. Don't come crawling back to me the moment she does. I'm not gonna be the one to fix it."

Imposing footsteps thump away. Each whack of the heavy soles on what sounds like tile or linoleum is a thunderclap. I want to cover my ears, but moving doesn't seem like a possibility. Not even my eyelids will lift.

"Your friend's an asshole."

Huh. Rae.

"Yeah," Raine responds tiredly. "That he is."

"You can go. I've got her."

"No, I want to be here."

"At least sit down. You look half-dead."

Chair legs scrape across the floor. Plastic cushions creak. I think I hear Rae sigh. They don't talk, their silence allowing me to hear the sounds of the medical wing. I'm certain that's where I am. It's a tiny corner of the institute.

I don't know how long it is before Rae speaks again.

"The guards track those bastards down?"

"I don't know." Raine sounds so exhausted, his voice raspier than usual. "I'm not sure what wild goose chase Ripley sent them on."

"We'll hear soon enough. I hope they're all transferred or sent to prison."

"That seem likely to you?"

Rae definitely sighs this time. "Nothing does anymore."

Lapsing back into silence, it's a long time before I hear Raine's rough voice again. It's thick with emotion now.

"I let her down."

"Come on," Rae sympathises. "That isn't true."

"I was passed out while that lunatic carved her up like a piece of meat. Ripley needed me. I'm fucking useless."

"Ripley would never admit to needing anyone, even if it meant life or death. She doesn't let anyone get close."

"What about you?" Raine asks.

Her pained chuckle hurts my soul. "Not for a lack of trying. I think she needs a friend. But after a year of back and forth, she still holds me at arm's length."

"I thought you were her friend."

"I'm not sure she has any of those. That would give her too much to lose."

Their murmurs are interrupted by a door creaking open. Shoes squeak across the floor, and from the swish of hospital scrubs, I'd guess it's a member of staff.

"Alright. Time to go."

"We're staying," Raine replies firmly.

I hear Rae hum in agreement.

"She's on strong pain medication. The blood transfusion will go on for a few more hours. Go get cleaned up."

"But—"

"Go on. Scram."

At the sounds of their reluctant retreat, I feel the warmth embrace me again, darkness creeping back in. With whatever magical drugs they're pumping into me, I can't say that I even want to wake up.

I float on a pharmaceutical cloud until the tug of someone pulling a needle from my arm drags me back to the surface. This time, the soft warmth of drugs has faded, pain exploding from every cell in my body.

My entire body pulses in time with each fresh wave of agony. Ribs burning, fingers aching, nose stuffy and sore. Excruciating pain emanates from my entire left arm. I'm convinced it's on fire.

"Here she is, Warden. We're easing her off the pain medication."

What sounds like dress shoes tap closer.

"What have you done this time, Miss Bennet?" There's a weary sigh. "Alright, lead him in."

A door clicks then more footsteps approach. I must still be high. I'm imagining talking, dismembered legs hovering around my bedside with no bodies attached to them. Until another voice forces me to discard that hairbrained theory.

"Christ."

"Jonathan," Davis greets politely. "I hope we didn't disturb you. How was the helicopter ride?"

"Fine. I was in a board meeting when you called. What's the situation?"

"Your niece will recover with time. She took a severe beating."

"Obviously," he quips. "Unprovoked?"

"Unclear. Though as far as Miss Bennet is concerned, she would not struggle to provoke someone. It's unlikely this was a motiveless attack."

"Sounds about right."

Yeah, definitely high. There isn't a chance in hell that my uncle is here having a nice little chat with the goddamn warden. I haven't seen Uncle Jonathan in years. He wouldn't trouble himself.

"This role was supposed to keep her safe from further trouble." Jonathan's voice is matter-of-fact. "That was the agreement when her transfer was arranged."

"Indeed it was."

"Then what's the issue here? Was my donation not sufficient?"

"Your niece has proven to be a difficult beast to tame. She steps beyond the bounds of her role on a daily basis. We can't risk our operations with such a loose cannon anymore."

Another longer, wearier sigh comes from my uncle. "These are precarious times for all of us."

"Then you understand our predicament."

"Of course, Abbott. I'll deal with my niece. I'd appreciate your discretion in removing the threat against her while I do so."

"On this occasion," Davis agrees. "Any further conflict or disruption, and I'm afraid not even your investment in the corporation will keep her safe."

"Naturally. You have a business to run."

My uncle's voice drips with detachment as he casually discusses my fate. Not even a moment's hesitation before so quickly washing his hands of me all in the name of fucking *business*.

Betrayal is a silent knife in the gut, tearing past intestines and kidneys to reach something deeper. Something that was broken to begin with, but I hadn't wanted to admit that sad reality.

He isn't my family.

He doesn't love me.

Maybe he never did.

I think I hear a shoulder being clapped before a set of footsteps fade away. Someone sits down close by. Tapping loudly on a phone screen, their breathing is even. Calm. I know it's him. He isn't leaving.

There's no avoiding this shitty conversation. With a lot of willpower, I wrench my eyes open. I have to blink rapidly to get the cubicle to settle. I am indeed in Harrowdean's small but functional medical wing. Curtains are drawn to offer my bay some privacy.

With white sheets pulled up to my chin, my right arm is resting on a pillow off to the side, a thin rubber tube leading into the crook of my elbow. I watch the dark, gloopy droplets of borrowed blood feed into me.

Thick swathes of bandages are twined around my other arm from elbow to wrist. Lower still, each finger has been splinted with black Velcro, holding the throbbing digits in place.

"Ripley."

Jonathan has what my mum called a *business meeting* voice on the rare occasion that she mentioned her baby brother. I remember that detail clearly. It's one of the first things I noticed when I was forced down to London as a kid.

He's ten years younger, now in his mid-forties, but he wears his age with well-pampered youthfulness. His dark-brown hair is an expensive dye job that covers the silver wisps he was developing when I last saw him.

With smooth, tanned skin, a well-trimmed beard and clear eyes that both captivate and terrify, it's no wonder he's a formidable opponent in the boardroom. Capable of negotiating even the trickiest of business deals or investments.

Elbows braced on his knees, his broad shoulders strain against his perfectly fitted, pinstripe suit. It probably costs more than the yearly salary of his multiple personal assistants. He has a whole walk-in wardrobe full of designer clothes.

"What are you doing here?" I manage to croak out.

He casts an eye over me. "Perhaps you'd like to answer that question. What am I doing here, Ripley?"

"You didn't have to come."

"When I get a phone call saying my niece has been half-beaten to death and sliced up by some punk, I'm forced to find out what she's gotten herself into."

Wincing, I try to sit up to see him better. He doesn't bother to help or offer to fluff my pillow. The needle feeding into my arm tugs, forcing me to give up and slump back on the lumpy mattress.

"It was a misunderstanding."

"A misunderstanding?" he echoes coolly.

"This idiot has it out for me. Thought I knew where his friend got shipped off to. People assume I know stuff... for obvious reasons."

Jonathan exhales through his nose. "The whole point of this role was to offer you protection. Do you have any idea what strings I had to pull to sort this safe haven for you?"

Safe haven?

For a man who's used his intelligence to amass a multimillion-pound fortune, he can be so fucking obtuse. Harrowdean isn't safe for anyone—patient, stooge or otherwise.

"You asked to be transferred from Priory Lane," he continues smoothly. "I made all the arrangements and ensured you'd have a comfortable life here. Perks included."

In my exhausted state, I can't hold my tongue.

"Do you think it's comfortable to be management's bitch?"

"You asked for this position!"

"I asked to be saved! Not sacrificed!"

Folding his arms, he leans back in the chair. "And what about the sacrifices I've made for you?"

My eyes prickle with furious tears. I've dealt with too much today to hold them back or plaster on a brave face. My mum isn't tucked into this hospital bed with me, holding me tight. In fact, no one is.

I'm alone.

Eternally.

Years of frustration and pain come rushing out. All the times I've wanted to scream and rave at him, but have managed to hold it back with a shoestring of control. I hate the pathetic tremble in my voice.

"The only thing you sacrificed was another dusty, unused room in your mansion. You never wanted to get stuck with me. If we had any other living family, you soon would've shirked the responsibility."

He shakes his head. "You're so ungrateful."

"Tell me what I should be grateful for, then. The missed birthdays? Weeks left in the care of your staff? Being stuffed with medication? Or packed off to the first place you could find to keep your batshit-crazy niece quiet?"

"I've taken care of you for all these years."

"No. You've tolerated me. Sometimes even that was too much to expect. I'm another business transaction to you like everything else in your life."

I wonder if I see a flicker of regret. Or even sadness. But his clear grey eyes don't reveal any such weakness, and the perfect poker face he's used on me for my entire life never once falters.

I wish I cared as little as he does. I've spent a year trying to emulate that same business-minded detachment. And where has it got me? To this goddamn hospital bed.

"I don't know why Mum left me in your care. Perhaps she thought the day she wouldn't be around anymore would never come. You were nothing more than a last resort to her."

Not even a flinch. It's like my words bounce right off him and roll back into the ocean without pulling him under. He straightens his cuffs before sweeping his gaze around the clinical room.

"Do you even care?" I feel more tears spill over.

"About what?" He sighs.

"Me!"

Jonathan clicks his tongue. "I care about the investment you've squandered by getting into pointless fights with your peers. Your place here is hanging by a thread."

"And it would be so inconvenient if I wasn't quiet and off your radar, right? Do you even want me to go home?"

His lips purse. Not even a nod. He can't muster the smallest amount of energy it would take to make me feel the slightest bit better. Is it any wonder that I've turned out like this? I learned from the best.

My cheeks sting with the lash of salty tears over deep bruises and swelling. But it still doesn't compare to the pain writhing in my chest, right about where my heart should be. Where nothing but a black hole resides.

"You've tied my hands, Ripley. There is nothing more I can do for you."

"What does that mean?"

Jonathan shrugs. "I can't risk myself any further."

"We're supposed to be family." My vision blurs with torrential tears.

He spares me another detached glance.

"Why couldn't you have been normal?"

His words are the final kick in the gut. Years of abandonment slam down on me. The unwanted niece who became the disastrous situation. That's all he sees me as. That's all I will ever be.

"Next time you find yourself in a mess, don't call my office. I can't help you anymore. I suggest you tread very carefully from here on out."

My hospital gown soaked from fierce sobs, I watch him

stand up. Jonathan brushes off his tailored suit and turns away without another glance.

Tears gather in a pool at the base of my throat as I watch him walk away. My last remaining relative abandons me without any pomp or circumstance. It's a quiet retreat. The pinnacle of his slow withdrawal from my life—as limited as his presence has been.

And once again, I'm left alone.

It's been a long time since I allowed myself to completely fall apart without holding anything back. I've done everything in my power to hold that inevitable, cataclysmic breakdown at bay.

Hundreds of long, scrubbing showers. Hours spent on the treadmill. Countless splattered canvases. Brawls. Threats. Mask after mask, slotting my bravado in place. Avoiding friendship and intimacy at all costs. These things kept me safe.

Safe from caring.

Safe from getting hurt.

Safe from being abandoned again.

Hurting other people, supplying them with the means to hurt themselves, it's all allowed me to maintain a cobbled-together image of self-control. Broken shards duct taped together in a haphazard puzzle.

I hate the words that sneak out.

"Please come back," I whisper brokenly.

But he doesn't.

Nor does the person I always wished he'd be. The illusion I've clung to. Now both versions are gone. All that's left is an empty hospital room and the steady drip of someone else's blood feeding into me.

Not even the sound of the partition curtain scraping back halts my sobbing. It's peeled aside to reveal the unlikeliest of alabaster faces studying me. The midnight-blue in his eyes has returned to the surface.

Circling the bed, seeming as uncertain to his presence in

my room as I am, Xander sinks into the vacated chair. He doesn't utter a word. But my dry blood still staining his polo shirt is telling enough.

He hasn't left me once.

Just remained tucked out of sight.

Face blank, his gaze slides down to my splinted fingers. The same ones he snapped back into place like he's been doing it since before he could talk. His eyes remain there.

It shouldn't be funny. None of this is. But the despairing laughter comes anyway. All I have left in the world is the man who hates me more than life itself. The iceman with his secret obsession.

"Go!" I shriek.

But he doesn't.

So I fall apart some more.

What feels like hours later, I stare back up at the popcorn ceiling. There's nothing left inside me. Not even defeat. My swollen, gritty eyes screw shut, too painful to hold open for a second longer. Oblivion is beckoning.

I must imagine it before I drop off.

But I swear, Xander takes my hand and squeezes.

CHAPTER 18
RAINE

PRETTY LITTLE DEVIL – SHAYA
ZAMORA

I WAIT against the smooth trunk of a tree in our usual spot. After resting for as long as my limited patience would allow, I dragged my bruised and aching body down here for our usual weekly deal.

I don't want drugs right now, though.

Just Ripley.

Ears straining and senses dialled to ten, I listen for her approach. Ripley's footsteps are always soft and light, in total contrast to her fierce spirit and wickedly sharp tongue. She seems too small to hold such spunk.

Inhaling deeply, I can't smell her body wash. The scents of juniper and birch trees linger in the air instead. Spring is in full-swing, and the world is thawing, bringing with it a new miasma of stimuli to paint my internal world.

The scents I'd usually spend hours dissecting hold no interest today. She has to come. I was turned away from the medical wing at every opportunity, forced to wait for her discharge to smell her again.

But that was three days ago now and still nothing. She isn't at mealtimes. Not in the corridors nor the art room. Not so much as a passing encounter. I'm not going another bloody day without catching her.

So I wait.

Foot tapping and nose twitching.

I don't know how long I stand here, looking like a total fucking idiot. I feel completely exposed without the comforting weight of my glasses resting on my nose, but until I can locate a replacement pair, I have no choice.

Right now, it's probably a good thing I can't see the likely pitying stares of all who shuffle past. God knows what I look like, but I don't give a shit what anyone thinks.

What're a few bruises and a nice egg on the back of my head after what they did to her? I don't give a shit what Ripley's weird non-friend says. I did fail her. When she needed me, I couldn't stop them from hurting her.

"What are you doing?"

I stifle a groan. "Go away, Nox."

Ignoring me, his heavy weight thuds closer. "You're waiting for her, aren't you?"

"I don't see how it's any of your business."

"Anything involving Ripley Bennet is my business."

A morbid smile tugs at my mouth. He really doesn't hear it. The way his anger and disdain sound a whole lot like something else. No one can feel that amount of hatred without passion too.

"Do I detect a hint of jealousy?"

Lennox's laughter is a rumbling earthquake. "I wouldn't touch that whore with a fucking ten-foot pole."

"Then we don't have a problem. Do we?"

I sense him stopping in front of me, his enraged teeth grinding audible. Even when she isn't around, Ripley still manages to get under his skin like nothing else. His hatred for her is borderline obsessive.

"Look what happened to you because of her!" he booms.

"You're lucky those bastards didn't kill you to get whatever the hell they wanted."

I've kept tight-lipped about what went down. The last thing Ripley needs is for me to give Lennox or Xander more ammunition to use against her. Sure, those thugs beat the shit out of me to provoke her. But it wasn't her fault.

With the overnight disappearance of Rick and his trigger-happy posse, no one but myself and Ripley knows what happened in the library. I need to ask her where she sent them.

Part of me is afraid to know. I blacked out the moment my head cracked against the floor and woke up to them hauling ass. They didn't leave us without good reason. She sent them on a hunt.

"Raine." Lennox's voice softens, almost sounding like a plea. "Don't let her get in your head. You don't know what she's capable of."

"Like you're any better?" I scoff.

"What's that supposed to mean?"

"Come on, Nox. We all know why you're in here. What about the shit you're capable of?"

He gulps hard, the gurgling sound painting a mental picture of his throat bobbing up and down. With darkness all around, I have to piece together countless jigsaw puzzles. Thankfully, he's never hard to read.

"If I have to remove her from your life to keep you safe, I will," he redirects.

"Stay away from Ripley. I mean it, Nox."

"Listen to me! She's bad news!"

"Go." My voice is steady despite the ire seizing my muscles. "Don't talk to me again until you've learned to respect my fucking privacy. What I do with her is none of your concern."

He hisses out a loud breath. I can already sense the cogs in his mind whirling. Plotting. Scheming some great, heroic gesture to save the poor charity case he took pity on. The problem is, Lennox only knows how to use violence to achieve his aims.

Fuck that.

He isn't my damn bodyguard.

"Have it your way," Lennox declares.

Sighing, I rub the back of my neck as his stomping feet disappear. I just hope to God I haven't painted an even bigger target on Ripley's back by defending whatever the hell we are to each other.

When I feel my cheeks and nose starting to burn from sitting in the sun for too long, I know she's far past late. Ripley isn't coming. If she thinks she can scare me off with this hiding act, she's in for a shock.

I didn't want to resort to this.

But she's left me no choice.

Moving slowly and deliberately is the first step to getting around when I'm not being escorted. I struggled to use my guide stick for a long time—terrified of walking face-first into an obstacle despite swinging it around.

Now that instinctual fear has faded. Collisions still happen, but I have a deeper sense of spatial awareness than most people. Even on the days I'm high as a kite or blissfully numbed. Survival instincts kick in.

Climbing the stairs is another matter. It takes precise concentration. Mentally measuring each incline, feeling for the perfect height to place my foot down. After a couple of months here, I've sussed it out.

Regardless, it still takes longer than I'd care to admit to reach the sixth floor. I have to count each time the staircase curves around another corner, taking me farther upward.

Dragging my spare hand down the corridor's papered wall, I bear left and check every door. Metal numbers are screwed into each one, allowing me to fumble my way to my destination.

"Xan?" I rap on door thirty-seven.

It's a long moment before he swings it open. "Lennox went looking for you."

"Yeah, he found me. Listen, I need that favour."

He's silent for a moment. "What for?"

"I just want to borrow it quickly."

I briefly worry that Xander has developed a conscience. But when he mutters for me to wait, I know he's not going to ask any questions. I'm relieved to have at least one semi-uncomplicated friend.

Returning, Xander tugs my wrist then slaps the cool, plastic keycard into it. "Don't get caught with that. It's an all-access one."

"How did you manage to steal it anyway?"

"Probably best that you don't know."

With that, he slams the door in my face. Ever the charmer. I slide the keycard into my back pocket and painstakingly make my way back down to the fifth floor, searching for room seventeen next.

I want to respect Ripley's privacy, but what we just went through together is all kinds of fucked up. She must've gotten it in her head that it's changed something between us. But I won't let that stand.

With a cursory listen for any guards lingering nearby, I double check the metal numbers on her door before knocking twice. Tapping my foot, I wait. Then I knock again. When there's still nothing, I pull out the keycard and scan it.

Her door clicks open with a buzz. Stepping inside feels like a gross violation, but I quickly crush the feeling. I don't have time for ethics right now. Though I do call out her name.

"Ripley? It's me."

Silence.

"You in here? We need to talk."

Not a single whisper.

I'm about to curse up a storm and step outside to

formulate a new plan when I hear it. The faint sound of breathing floating from deeper in the bedroom. Tuning everything else out, I can smell the fruity richness of papaya lingering in the air beneath the scents of human hibernation.

She's in here.

"Come on, Rip. You can't hide forever."

Her breathing changes—seizing on an inhale, like words are begging to be set free, but she's biting her tongue. Stick extended and one hand out, I tentatively step farther into the unknown space.

"If you think this hiding crap is going to work, we need to have a serious conversation. I'm shit at hide and seek."

Not even my terrible joke rouses a response. I curse when I stub my toe on something that feels a lot like a dresser. Bloody thing was jutting out from around the corner. I must be getting closer.

"Talk to me, guava girl. Tell me you're okay."

The tip of my stick meets something that isn't solid wood nor wall. I bend to feel what it is, my fingers depressing into fabric. Her mattress. I've located her bed. Her breathing sounds close too.

"You having a pity party without me?" I try again.

A sigh whistles from her. "Go, Raine."

"Ah, she speaks. I was starting to worry that I'm invading some random girl's bedroom."

Stopping next to the bed, I place a hand on the stiff cotton sheets. Warmth radiates from her curled-up form beneath the duvet, tucked into the top corner of the small twin bed. She's cocooned in a tiny ball and doesn't react to my touch.

"Thanks for making room for me. Did you hear me coming?"

"Please," she whispers. "I want to be alone."

"What you want and what you need are two different things. I know what this is. And I'm not going to leave you in here all alone."

"Why not? Everyone else does."

My stomach twists. "Because I'm not everyone else, alright?"

Propping my guide stick against the wall, I easily kick off my shoes. The laces are never tightly fastened to avoid struggling when I dress. Ripley doesn't protest as I slide back the covers and lower myself into her bed.

With her tiny body tucked against the cold wall, there's enough room for me to stretch out next to her. But I don't touch her. Not yet. It's like those early days after I lost my vision and couldn't lift myself from the despair I'd sunk into.

Like a terrified animal trapped in a cage, she has to be coaxed out of this state. Nothing but words will work. Ripley thinks she has my number, but I also have hers. She's always expecting abandonment.

As hot as I find her violent sass and strong headed will, I can see what pain lies beneath it. The way she holds the entire world at arm's length, so it doesn't get close enough to matter. She avoids any opportunity for vulnerability.

Until me.

What she gave me was precious.

I'm selfish enough to admit that I chased her for the thrill of it. The way her attitude made my endorphins spike better than any other drug. She makes me feel alive in a world determined to lock me in the darkness.

But more than that, I like her. More than I've ever liked anyone. This isn't just about feeling alive, it's about feeling whole. And when I'm with her, I don't feel lacking. I'm complete and present in the world just like everyone else.

"Are you asleep?" I murmur.

"No."

"Then you can listen." I moisten my suddenly dry lips. "I'm so, so sorry."

"I told you it wasn't your fault."

"They almost killed you."

She exhales loudly. "I wish they had."

Her broken admission is another brick on the heavy pile I'm being crushed beneath.

"Don't say that, Rip."

"Why not? There would be no one left to mourn me. No parents. No uncle. Not a single family member."

"You have friends," I argue.

"No. I don't."

The pressure in my chest expands. "You have me."

She's silent for several agonising seconds.

"You got hurt because of me, Raine. Because of what I know. They used you to get to me. How can I ever risk letting that happen again?"

"Rick and those shitheads are gone. No one has seen them for days."

"You think that matters? There's a long list of people who hate this place and hate me by extension. I can't say I blame them for wanting a pop at *Harrowdean's whore*."

Ripley spits the last words out with such hate-filled emotion, I can almost hear a flicker of the spitfire I've come to adore. When I overheard the onsite medic, Doctor Hall, discussing what Rick carved into her, I wanted to punch a fucking wall.

"He didn't even say goodbye," she mutters.

"Who?"

In the stillness, I can practically hear her chest seize. "My uncle came to visit me in the hospital."

"Shit. What did he say?"

"Nothing I didn't already know." Her voice wobbles. "I'm on my own now."

Oh, fuck this. She doesn't need coaxing. She needs someone to pick her up, wrap her in love and tell her that she's worthy of receiving it. I don't care if she has to hurt me in the process of accepting that.

Reaching across the bed, I band my arms around her

tightly-balled form. She complains at first, but as I drag her into the shell of my body, her whispers die out.

I hold her against my chest, tucking her head beneath my chin and stroking my hand along the ridges of her spine. I can tell that she hasn't showered for a few days, but it doesn't bother me. We've all been there.

Holding her tight, I give her the safe space to break apart. Wet warmth soaks into my skin as she hides her face. I wonder if anyone has held her and given her permission to be weak since she lost her parents.

"Just leave me alone, Raine," she cries.

"Not a chance, guava girl."

"I'm tired of being the bad guy." She hiccups into my throat. "I don't want to be the reason anyone else gets hurt."

"That isn't your choice," I say gently.

"Why not?"

"Because we all get hurt in life. The trick is to find the person you care about enough to let them hurt you."

"I've never had that," she confesses after a long pause.

In the darkness that has long represented fear to me but now feels like home, I can admit the truth.

"Me neither. I guess we both just want to belong somewhere."

Ripley's lips brush against my pulse point. "Or to someone."

With her tears soaking into me and our breath mingling, I can feel our essences dancing hand in hand. There's something intimate about seeing someone at their lowest point. It's not just a milestone, it's a privilege.

I didn't have anyone to hold me when I needed it the most. I was alone. Afraid. Abandoned. Everything she's feeling right now. I won't let her go through it alone.

No one held me.

But I can hold her.

"Your uncle didn't deserve you as a niece."

I can practically hear the gears in her head grinding. It's a long time before she responds mournfully.

"He set this whole thing up for me. Gave me the fucking keys to the kingdom. But if I wasn't this awful person, perhaps I wouldn't be alone. Instead, I have nothing."

My hand moves higher to slide into her hair, gently massaging. "You're not a bad person, Rip. You're just a survivor."

"And a monster."

"This place has a way of making even the best people into monsters."

"Then why are you here?" She lifts her head, and I can imagine her staring down at me. "Why are you still humouring whatever this is?"

"Because I don't judge people on their worst mistakes. We've all made enough of them. And I'm not going to let you ruin this based on some whacked opinion of what you think you deserve."

"Damn. Say it how it is, huh?" An invisible smile peppers her words.

"Always, babe." I dramatically sniff the air. "On that topic… You're cute as fuck, but when was the last time you stopped moping around and showered?"

"Raine!"

"I don't have to be blind to smell that ripeness."

Her laughter fading, Ripley sighs. "It's hard for me to do basic stuff when these episodes hit. Even moving is difficult."

"In the future, we need a signal."

"Huh?"

"I've been sitting around like a chump for days waiting for you to show up. I just need to know you're safe, even if functioning is too much."

"What kind of signal?" she asks.

"A code word. A hand squeeze. Hell, I'll take anything. But on those days when your limbs are too heavy to move and everything is unbearable, I need to know so I can come hold you close."

Her legs slowly uncurl, like she's preparing for the long, tiresome walk to the attached bathroom. It's invasive that I can also hear the empty gurgling of her stomach, but my dialled-up senses didn't get that message.

"I guess I'm just used to dealing with my illness alone."

"That changes today. I'm making the decision for both of us."

Ripley snickers. "Then I guess a code word will do. Aren't they usually reserved for sex, though?"

"You wanna have one for that too? This friends with benefits arrangement just got interesting."

The bed springs creak with her standing up. "You're incorrigible."

"Like you'd want me any other way."

"I guess not." Her hand snags my arm then tugs. "Come and wash my back."

Letting her pull me out of the bed, I'm guided through the bedroom. The sound of the light clicking on and the shower starting are my first clues that we've reached the bathroom.

Ripley hisses in pain as she peels off whatever clothes she's wearing. My hands hover mid-air, looking to help, but she doesn't ask. So I work on unfastening my jeans and pulling off my t-shirt instead.

My body feels awkward and stiff. They did a real number on me. Nothing permanent, but I was lucky to avoid a concussion. The pain will fade soon enough.

"Christ," she gasps.

"How's it looking?"

"Well, your ribs and stomach look like an elephant stomped all over them. Matches your pretty purple face, though."

"You think I'm pretty?" I cup my own cheeks.

"Get in the fucking shower, Raine."

"You know that you have the advantage here. I've got no idea how rough you're looking right now."

I hear her step into the shower. Feeling for the entrance, I join her beneath the spray, the door sliding shut behind me. It's a tight squeeze, forcing her bare frame to press up against me in the steam.

"Shit." Ripley's body leaves mine. "I'm not supposed to get my stitches wet."

"Hold your arm above me and away from the spray."

Shifting, her breasts push into my chest as she finds the right position. My hands locate her hips, perfectly curved and slippery with warm water. Anyone would think that I'm dead inside not to be turned-on right now.

But this isn't about fooling around. As tempting as the slick heat of her body moving against mine is, I just want to take care of her. Beyond anything physical, I need her to know that she's going to be okay.

We both will be.

I'll make sure of it.

"Looks like I'm on cleaning duty. Pass the body wash?"

After twisting away from me again, Ripley curls my hand to place a plastic bottle in it. "I'm an arm down. Sorry."

"It is a hardship, having to lather you up."

The familiar, heady scent of papaya fills the shower as I spread body wash between my palms. Ripley holds still, letting me slowly run my hands all over her generous curves, ensuring every inch I locate is thoroughly lathered.

What feels like her forehead rests on my chest, just below my clavicles. I can tell by the wet tickle of her hair on my pectorals. My cock twitches, suddenly paying attention. She lets me massage every part of her before I begin to sluice the bubbles off.

"Feel good?"

"Mmm," she groans unintelligibly.

"Don't fall asleep on me. Where's your shampoo?"

Her head briefly lifts. "Here."

Once she's slumped back onto my chest, I move my attention to her hair. Washing someone else without a visual frame of reference takes a lot of trial and error. Ripley doesn't complain when I attempt to shampoo her face twice before eventually finding her hair.

The wet curls slide between my fingertips like reams of fine silk. I've been a scents and textures kinda guy since losing my vision. The details that are insignificant to everyone else can hold all of my attention.

Without any distractions, I can take my time memorising every inch of Ripley's topography. The small, rounded peaks of her ears. How her curls spring back even when wet. Her slim shoulders and the pronounced divots in her spine.

She lets me drink my fill, content to rest against me and enjoy the attention I'm lavishing her body with. Proportionally, she's everything I find attractive in a woman. But it's her spirit that makes her stunning.

Once she's thoroughly washed, I hold her close beneath the spray. I'm debating how I'll wrestle her sleepy body out of the shower without us both faceplanting when she sighs, her lips puckering against my throat.

Small, open-mouthed kisses spread across my collarbones. Exploring and leaving a static charge in their wake, her lips retreat before pushing against mine. I return the kiss, magnetised by the draw of her skin against mine, holding me steady in the world.

"Rip," I murmur. "You're hurt."

Breaking the kiss, she touches the back of my hand then guides it down to cup her tight ass. Well, shit.

"Please," she whispers. "I... need to feel you, Raine."

"I can't... we're not—"

"I don't want to feel their fists anymore," she insists, cutting me off. "I've spent days reliving the feeling of his body weighing me down, his breath on my face, his knife slicing me up. Please make it go away."

"They won't hurt you again. I promise. No one will."

"Doesn't erase the memories." Her whispered voice catches.

My other hand clasping the back of her head, I plant kisses across her mouth. "I know you're feeling alone and scared right now. But you're going to get past this."

"How?"

"Because falling down is a part of life, Rip. Getting back up? That's living."

Mouth crushing against mine, she replies with a hard, almost frantic kiss. Like she's desperately kicking her legs, trying to tread water, and I'm her last source of oxygen.

Screw this.

Needing reassurance of my own, I kiss her back with every ounce of fear that's been eating away at me since I blacked out. The terror of not being able to defend myself or help. Then the silence of the past few days, all the while wondering if she's ever coming back to me.

This isn't the time or place. Sex was the last thing on my mind as I marched here, determined to find the woman I was told to hate, but I'm learning to… *Fuck.* Learning to what?

Like?

Maybe even love?

The realisation that she's wormed her way far deeper than I ever thought possible only spurs me on to seize this moment before it's ripped away from me like everything else.

Nothing good ever lasts, but I'm not ready to let go of this feeling yet.

Releasing her hair, I find the dripping swell of her breast and squeeze. She moans into my mouth, hips shifting with each kiss, pressing her centre up against my growing hardness.

When she abruptly pulls her lips from mine, I panic.

"Shit. Did I hurt you?"

"No."

Skimming her hand down my abdominals, she makes her intentions clear. Now unbandaged fingers wrap around my swollen cock, sliding up and down the shaft with a delicious application of pressure.

I grit my teeth, feeling a surge of heat deep within. Her hand feels far too fucking good wrapped around my dick. I hear her shift, feet squeaking against the shower floor, before the feeling of pleasure intensifies.

"Fuck, Rip!"

Her lips have found their way to my cock, taking it into the warm, welcome prison of her mouth. She must've kneeled down. I quickly locate her lowered head then retake a handful of her hair.

Beginning to suck, she bobs up and down on my length, her tongue sliding against my shaft with each movement. The loud shower and absence of sight forces me to focus on nothing but her mouth fucking me.

Lips tighten. Teeth graze. Her hands move to cup my balls and lightly play, causing me to jerk inside her mouth. Holding her hair, I let my hips thrust, working in time to her sucking.

She lets me slide deeper and deeper each time, until I can feel her throat nudging against my tip. Despite the quiet gagging sounds, Ripley doesn't stop sucking. I'm soon riding her mouth and battling to hold on.

"You're so perfect," I hum.

Her mouth cinches around me in response, teasing another surge of pleasure free. Those devilish lips know just how to imprison a guy and demand ransom in return.

What began as a small collection of embers is now a raging blaze inside me. I need to be balls deep inside her right now. She's turning me into some kind of primitive caveman.

Pulling her head back, I slide out before I can spill my load down her throat. As tempting as that is, my girl deserves a thorough fucking, and I'm not the kind of man to disappoint.

"Turn around and bend over," I instruct roughly. "Spread yourself open for me, babe."

Reaching behind me, I fumble to turn off the shower. The last thing I want is to soak her stitches. By the time I've twisted the knob, I can sense that she's moved. Her tight rear butting up against my erection confirms it.

Placing a hand on her lower back, I push down to make her bend even farther. I want to slide deep into her in one brisk thrust and feel her contract around me. She's breathing hard in anticipation, waiting for relief to come.

What I wouldn't give to have a view of her perfect cunt glistening with desire right now. Even a fucking glimpse. Instead, I have to slide two fingers over her ass then lower to locate my target.

Her moans intensify as I find her entrance and breach it, too impatient to tease her with featherlight touches. Her pussy responds immediately, pulling my fingers into its heat. She's so damn tight.

"Raine," she whimpers.

"I've got you, babe."

Working her over several times, I know she's good and ready. Her moans have dissolved into needy wails, and I can feel the silkiness of her juices on my fingertips.

Holding a thumb just above her cunt, I fist my cock and line it up with her slit. The euphoric cry that spills out of her as I piston inside is music to my ears. She cries out so loud, it reverberates around us.

I'm already buried deep in her, but shifting my hips back, I drive into her once more. She stretches around me, her walls hugging my dick in a vice. I already want to fill her up.

"This is going to be hard and fast," I warn her.

"Yes," she moans. "Please... Yes."

Gripping her waist, I pull out again only to surge back in. Faster with each pump. Harder with each slam. She takes me so well, I don't care how long this is going to last.

Taking her like this feels better than mainlining fucking heroine.

Her escalating cries spur me on. Each time I advance into her, Ripley makes the most incredible sounds. The woman who stripped off and rode me like a goddamn pro in an abandoned building is roaring back to life.

Each plunge reignites the sore bruises that I can feel littering me, but the pain is inconsequential. It sharpens my senses until I can practically taste her sweet arousal dancing in the lingering steam.

"Raine," she pants. "I'm so close."

"Let go then, babe."

Driving into her hard and fast, I feel her clench tight. The increased pressure is pushing me to the finish line too quickly. I'm happy to go fast, but I still need to satisfy her first.

Ripley cries out again, her moans reaching a fever-pitch. I can feel her climaxing as every muscle tightens, holding her on the verge of a steep plummet before letting her freefall.

She isn't allowed to come down from that high. Not yet. I want her limp and boneless by the time she leaves this shower. Maybe then she'll think twice before hiding from me again.

Collecting moisture by gliding my thumb over her clit, I search for the tight ring of muscle I used as a compass earlier. She's a gasping wreck, but the moment my thumb locates her asshole, Ripley jerks back to life.

"Oh God!"

"Hold still. You're okay."

Her voice takes a hot as fuck, guttural note as my thumb pushes into her backside. I'm still sheathed inside her, and with both holes now filled, she's trembling so hard it feels like vibrations.

"Do you like it when I play with your asshole, dirty girl?"

"Yes," she whines.

"Are you going to come all over my cock again?"

"I can't… I'm…"

"That's the wrong answer."

Pushing deeper into her rear, I resume thrusting at the same time, adopting a brutal pace. My own climax is threatening. I'm tight with tension, and my balls feel ready to explode.

She's so wet and spent, it doesn't take much to push her to the edge again. Folded over, Ripley lets me fuck her raw like a man possessed. I have no idea how we're both still standing as my release finally crests.

Ripley calls out my name, her second orgasm milking me of every last drop. I spill into her with an uncharacteristic roar, letting pure instinct take over. My body is calling the shots.

When she wobbles against me, I move fast, sliding an arm beneath her folded-over body before she can crumple. Ripley lets me pull her upright, and her back meets my chest, our pants for breath filling the shower.

"Well." I suck in a lungful of air. "Next time you're in this state, my plan is to fuck the sadness out of you. Seems like it works pretty well."

Her breathless laugh is all the agreement I need.

CHAPTER 19
RIPLEY

HARDER TO BREATHE –
LETDOWN

I STARE out the window at the storm clouds. Thick, pyroclastic swarms of dark-grey cover the sky, swallowing the sunlight and bathing the institute's grounds in melancholy. There's an almighty storm brewing.

Attending therapy like usual was the last thing on my list of priorities this morning. It covered taking medication, having a check-up and figuring out how the fuck I'm going to stay alive. But then Langley intervened.

I've never been escorted to a therapy session before. The clinicians don't usually pay that much attention to my so-called rehabilitation. So being marched to the north wing after he finished fussing was a new experience.

"Ripley. Please answer the question."

I cast Doctor Galloway a half-hearted glance. "I don't know what happened."

"This is a safe space."

"Really?" I drawl.

"Of course. You can tell me what's going on."

If I had the energy, I'd laugh in her face. I doubt my lies will make any difference now. If Rick and his friends found the Z wing, it'll be obvious who sent them searching. I'm surprised I haven't been cuffed already.

She exhales, studying me over her notes. I'd usually stare back. Defiant and unfazed. But the fight that once drove me forward hasn't reappeared. So I return my gaze to the billowing storm clouds instead.

"You don't have much time left in this program," she attempts again. "I understand that recent events have been difficult, but don't allow them to set you back."

"Why do you care?" I quip.

"You're my patient, Ripley."

"And what about your other patients? What about the people in here with no one to vouch for them? Or the ones who will never complete their sentence and go home? Do you care about them?"

"We're getting off topic."

Indignation sprints through me. "How much do they pay you to keep your mouth shut? To sign off falsified medical notes and turn the other cheek?"

Looking back at her, I wait for a response. An ugly flush is spreading up her throat like a bad allergic reaction. Slowly, she stacks her paperwork then caps her fountain pen.

"Perhaps we should leave it here."

"Do you think about the people you've hurt when your head hits the pillow at night like I do?" I finger the edge of the bandage covering my arm. "Or does the promise of your next payday soothe the sting?"

She doesn't go as far as to call me a hypocrite, but I can see the accusation boiling in her eyes. That's precisely how I know she's full of shit. When my head hits the pillow, it's all I can think about. She has to feel the same torment.

I may be equally as guilty, but I didn't take an oath to do no harm like her. Though it makes me no less culpable, it sure damns her alongside me. She's supposed to be a doctor, yet she's in on the big lie too.

"You want to know what happened?" I lean forward in the armchair. "All the shitty decisions I've made finally caught up to me. And I hope the day comes when the same thing happens to you."

I stand and head for the door. I'm not going to sit here and be lectured about the benefits of opening up and sharing my pain. Not from a power-hungry opportunist who wants to package it with a fancy label and sell my sickness to the highest bidder.

When I open the door, it isn't Langley waiting outside. Although he surely thought that he was being helpful by bringing me to therapy today, it infuriated me to no end. I'd gladly take his meddling ways over the displeased mug staring back at me now.

"Ah, Ripley." Elon's thin lips pull into a grin as he looks me over. "Good to see you back on your feet."

"Is it?" I respond blandly.

"Nice bruises. You look like a punching bag."

"Spare me the small talk. What do you want?"

Flashing teeth, he beckons me into the corridor. "Let's take a walk."

The command feels like being offered a steep cliff to hurl myself off. I don't trust the sadistic gleam in his eyes. Between more of Doctor Galloway's torture fest or whatever trap Elon's sprung for me, I should've just stayed in bed.

"No cuffs?"

"Will they be necessary?" He cocks an overgrown brow. "I can assure you that declining or running isn't advisable. I'll simply return with a friend or two."

"You'll need more than that to drag me anywhere."

"I'm aware. But they will be able to carry you after I've jammed a sedative in your thigh. So, care to take that walk?"

Considering my options, I see no alternative. He nods in satisfaction when I fall into step beside him, keeping a safe gap between us. I don't fancy getting stabbed with a hypodermic needle.

When he doesn't lead me to the warden's office or the solitary floor, the first flickers of panic set in. I look around the reception, fruitlessly searching for a means of escape.

"Don't even think about it," he warns.

"Think about what?"

Elon looms over me. "Starting any shit. This place is locked down tighter than Fort Knox right now. You'll only get your ass kicked."

Now that he mentions it, there's an array of blank-faced guards manning every wall, corner and doorway. At least triple the usual fanfare. Their weapons are no longer carefully concealed—batons, tasers and glinting cuffs hang on every belt loop.

Biting my lip, I watch the show over my shoulder as Taylor, a loud-mouthed girl whose room is a few doors down from mine, gets pulled aside for a random pat down.

"Are you serious? I was just walking!" she shouts.

"Up against the wall, inmate."

"No! This is such horseshit."

When she doesn't comply, Kieran, the wanker who struck me with his baton, shoves her hard. She slams into the wall with a pained squeak, her hands forced to flatten and legs spread apart by his foot.

"You asshole!" she screeches.

Tension is at an all-time high. Some patients don't raise their heads as they scuttle past. Whatever fire filled Harrowdean's population before, recent displays of force seem to have tamped a lot of it down.

But others like Taylor? They're openly defiant. Bickering and shouting. Fists swinging and arms getting pinned. It doesn't take much to provoke a guard into getting handsy. They seem determined to prove their point.

We're still their puppets to control.

And puppets don't have any rights.

Her head turned to the side and cheek smashed up against the wall, Taylor's gaze connects with mine. I'm unnerved by the venom directed towards me churning there.

This overzealous shithead is running his hands all over her, but she's staring at me like it's my goddamn fault. Maybe she's right. I didn't make this world, but I sure as hell benefited from it.

Thinking no one's looking, Kieran skates a hand over her ass. She hisses a selection of insults, but it doesn't deter him from grabbing between her legs next. I watch the horrified tears stream down her cheeks.

"You're clean," he declares.

Taylor pushes off from the wall, her wagging tongue now silenced. I look away as she leaves, her arms wrapped tight around midsection. The guard saunters off, smirking to himself like he hasn't just committed a crime.

"Ripley," Elon snaps.

I catch up to him with a sickening weight curling in my stomach. It's never been hard to find examples of abuse in Harrowdean. But never has it been so blatant and relished in. Something has shifted.

"Did you see what he did?" I demand.

Elon rolls his eyes. "Just move it, inmate."

He grabs my bicep and tows me across the quad. My scalp prickles when I spot a familiar headful of ash-white hair. At least his vantage points are getting more creative.

Xander sits on the grass, back against a tree trunk. He's pretending to be occupied by the thickly bound maths textbook in his lap, but instead, his narrowed eyes follow me across the quad.

We stare at each other for a brief, tension-laden second. Just the sight of him causes my heart to speed up to a traitorous gallop. Whether in fear or some twisted sense of anticipation, I don't even want to know.

The memory of him sitting at my bedside in his bloodstained clothing rushes to the forefront along with the ghost of his hand grasping mine. As my world fell apart, he ensured I wasn't suffering alone.

Was it real?

Does the infamous iceman… care?

That can't be right.

Xander doesn't know how to care. That would require far too much emotional range. I don't know what he feels for me —hatred, fascination, a desire to torture and maim—but caring isn't a remote possibility.

His perched form disappears as we descend farther into the institute's grounds. The stirrings in my chest morph into a nausea-inducing pitter-patter of anxiety. Blood pounds in my ears with each step towards what I know is coming.

It's unassuming. Nondescript. An abandoned façade coated in ivy, cracked brick and signs of disuse. Even the once sparkling stained glass windows have been boarded over and eaten alive by overgrown shrubbery.

To the untrained eye, it's another relic of Harrowdean's colourful past as an asylum in the nineteenth century. Most of the unrestored buildings scattered across the grounds hail back to that sombre period of time.

"Wait—"

"Shut it," Elon snips.

"Please. I can't go in there."

"I said shut it, inmate. That sedative can still be arranged."

Tucked out of sight in a cluster of glossy ivy leaves, I recognise the blinking eyes of several CCTV cameras. Why protect an empty husk? It can't be for the cobwebs and ghosts of inmates long past that live inside.

The most sinister of evils always hide in plain sight. Hidden behind politicians' smiles and their empty promises.

Glossy brochures with photos of therapy rooms, green forests and happy, smiling patients.

As I stare up at the disused exterior of Kingsman dorms, I understand how this place and so many like it have operated under the radar for all this time. Even those who pay attention fail to see the truth that's right in front of them.

Harrowdean isn't real.

It's just a well-crafted disguise.

"You don't have to do this." My voice trembles pathetically.

"Scared, Ripley?" Elon laughs. "Come and see where you sent your little friends."

I send a silent prayer into the unknown as Elon tugs me up the crumbling stone steps, his head swivelling to ensure no one has followed us.

There isn't even a padlock on the door. They want it to look inconspicuous and blend in with the other worthless ruins. These people are truly shameless.

"We've had plenty of curious inmates wander in here over the years," he explains conversationally. "Most get bored though. There isn't much to see upstairs."

The interior of Kingsman dorms, once a lavish oasis for upper-class, privileged kids packed off by their parents to receive an extortionate education, is now an abandoned wreck.

Sagging wallpaper lines the corridor, yellowing and water-damaged. Bare, cobweb-covered bulbs hang from the ceiling, though they aren't lit right now. The early afternoon sunlight illuminates the dusty old signage denoting the different floors.

Elon heads in the direction of the basement, causing more dread to bubble inside me. It takes several twists and turns to reach a wrought-iron door protected by a security system. He scans a black keycard, unlike any I've seen before.

"Down we go," he announces jubilantly.

I stare down at the aged, concrete staircase. No fucking

chance. People who go down there do not come back up. The fine hairs on the back of my neck stand up, while my skin suddenly feels too tight for my body.

"Please, Elon. Let's talk about this."

"Now she wants to talk." He snickers to himself. "The time for cooperation has passed."

"No! I'm not going down there!"

"I was hoping you'd make this difficult."

With a sinister grin fixed in place, he bends his knees and wraps his arms around my legs. I squawk as I'm lifted off my feet and slung over his shoulder like a sack of potatoes.

"Get off me!" I howl.

"Make as much noise as you want."

Battering my fists against his back, I thrash and shout, trying anything to break his hold. The bruising across my ribcage and stomach screams in protest at his shoulder digging into me.

After slamming the heavy-set door shut behind him, Elon begins to descend. The temperature plummets as we're devoured by darkness. It's like all the warmth has been sucked from the world and spat back out as clear, freezing fog.

Thick concrete swallows all sound and light until it feels like we're following Dante on his quest deeper into the seven circles of hell. I start to shiver violently, trapped by his arm banded across my legs.

"No! Stop!"

"Come now, Ripley," Elon croons. "You don't want to see what all your hard work is for?"

The terrain levels out, and I'm yanked back over his shoulder. My joints ache with the force of being dropped back on my feet. All around me, locked cells line a seemingly endless, subterranean hallway.

"Welcome to the Zimbardo wing."

I spin to face him. "Let me go. I'll keep my mouth shut, I swear."

He smothers a chuckle. "When has that ever happened?"

"I don't belong here!"

"Just walk."

Shivering, I take a tentative step into the corridor. The floors, walls and ceiling are all made of polished concrete. Thick sheets of steel carve each cell door, fitted with sliding hatches so guards can peer inside.

I've barely taken a step when the first yells ring out. Unlike the wails of whoever occupied the adjoining cell to mine in the solitary wing, this sound is guttural, inhuman. Like someone has pulled the very life from the poor bastard's soul and set it alight.

"While you're out there, pushing our product and creating a steady supply of material for the team to examine, the real work happens down here." Elon shoves me forward. "The rest is just an added bonus."

Half of the cells boast an occupied sign. The sound of someone punching or kicking a metal door reverberates with the continued shrieks. The farther we walk, the louder the cacophony of sounds becomes.

"What is that noise?" I ask fearfully.

"Sounds like Patient Three has been causing trouble again."

Elon stops outside one of the cells where a different thudding sound is leaking through the reinforced steel. He slides back the hatch to give me a clear view inside of the brutal beating taking place.

The woman being pummelled to a meaty pulp barely resembles a human. More like a misshapen, bruised bag of organs, slick beneath a curtain of fresh blood. She doesn't even grunt in pain at the blows being rained down.

"Afternoon, Professor," Elon calls jovially.

Beyond the man delivering the beating, another stands, watching on. I don't recognise him from the clinical staff. With silver-streaked, gelled hair, a thin but strong nose and square-framed glasses, the professor wears a pressed white lab coat over his suit.

Seemingly enraptured by the show being put on for him, it takes him a moment to look up at Elon. The moment he does, his curious smile blossoms, creasing weathered lines and wrinkled skin.

"Elon! What a surprise."

"Just making a delivery. Ripley, this is Professor Craven. Lead researcher of the Z wing here in Harrowdean."

Craven turns his attention to me. "My, my, she is a fine specimen."

Disgust crawls over me. He's looking at me like I'm some five-course tasting menu to be savoured and dissected, dish by dish. I tear my gaze from his ebony eyes and look at his thug, dressed in all black.

"Harrison." Elon nods in acknowledgement.

The man delivering the beating pauses, his vacant gaze briefly flickering up. "Elon."

Harrison uses the back of his black glove to swipe sweat from his brow. He leaves a thick smear of blood across his face, his gnarly features resting beneath a sharp military buzz cut. He seems unfazed as he looks me over.

"Got some fresh meat for us?"

Elon jabs a thumb over his shoulder at me. "Just giving our stooge a little tour of headquarters."

"She still causin' trouble?"

"Not if she'd like to avoid the same fate as Patient Three."

To illustrate his point, Elon flashes me a sick leer. My blood freezes in my veins as his friend nods, casting a critical eye over me again. With a glance at Professor Craven, he ducks out of sight to retrieve something.

"Bring her closer, Elon. This'll teach her not to bite her master."

I'm dragged close to the door before I can think about fleeing. Elon pins me against the steel slab, forcing me to look directly through the hatch and into the dank, padded cell, lined with bloody handprints and deep scratch marks.

I can now see a table of instruments tucked in the corner. Harrison inspects the selection, humming lightly under his breath. When he picks up a medieval looking pair of shackles, the inner circles lined with wickedly sharp spikes, I recoil.

"Fancy those cuffs, Rip?" Elon breathes in my ear.

I gulp hard. "What are you doing to her?"

"Reconditioning."

Harrison nods agreeingly. "The human mind can only endure so much pain before it splinters apart to cope. We reform those shattered pieces and create something new. Something useful."

Booting the semiconscious woman in the stomach, he kneels down and grabs her wrists. She's still conscious despite looking like she got shredded by a violent woodchipper. Something tells me this isn't her first beating.

But when Harrison clamps the torture cuffs around her wrists, the scream it elicits makes me fear for the integrity of my eardrums. The spikes inside the cuffs sink deep into her flesh, causing blood to ooze down her arms.

"Why are you h-hurting her?" I ask despite the boulder in my throat.

Craven produces an amused chuckle. "Ah, it's been so long since we had a new recruit. I forgot how entertaining their naïvety can be."

They all share a laugh.

Fuck you, Professor, I respond mentally.

"Patient Three failed to complete a recent assignment for the corporation." Harrison snaps the cuffs into place. "We don't tolerate such failure in Harrowdean."

A hand slapped over my mouth, I watch in horror as he drags her around the filthy cell by the chains connecting the two halves of the cuffs together. She howls in agony until eventually, she passes out.

Harrison drops her unconscious body like she's trash to be discarded. He then proceeds to boot her in the stomach for good measure, verifying that she's unconscious.

"How dull."

"Should've paced yourself," Elon snickers.

"She's proven to be a resilient one. But no matter." Harrison shrugs indifferently. "They break all the same."

A throat clears. "Gentlemen. You're keeping us waiting."

Still holding me prone, Elon spins us both to face the scowl I know awaits. I'd recognise the warden's voice anywhere. Here I was, thinking he kept his hands clean and didn't get involved in this side of the business.

"Ah, Miss Bennet." He flashes a PR-perfect smile. "So good of you to join us."

Frozen by terror, I can't make my tongue move to form a response. All I can see is the patient being dragged around her cell, leaving a trail of blood.

Davis tuts like I'm a mannerless schoolchild. "So quiet now, eh? Let's take this elsewhere. The professor has work to be getting on with. Harrison, Patient Five is prepped and ready for you both."

"Sir." Harrison bobs his head.

Moving his hands to my shoulders, Elon pushes me away from the two men watching me like I'm some delicious delicacy to be consumed. With wobbly legs, we follow Davis to the bottom of the corridor.

I don't dare look over my shoulder at whatever Harrison does to that poor woman next. I can hear him talking to Craven, the pair exchanging light-hearted conversation as they continue to inflict a brutal atrocity.

Through another door, we enter a hallway housing several different offshoots. A glimpse into the first room is enough to turn my mouth into sandpaper. I quickly look away and focus on the warden's footsteps.

"Don't fancy a trip in there?" Elon goads. "The

submersion tanks aren't so bad once you learn to function on ten percent oxygen. The lungs quickly adjust."

Fear like I've never felt before coils around my lungs. Those huge, two-metre glass tanks were full of murky water and sealed tight with barred lids. It doesn't take a genius to imagine what floats inside. I doubt they've ever been emptied or cleaned.

The next room, to my relief, is an office. But instead of Davis's name on the door, it boasts the initials *SJB*. I'm led inside and roughly deposited in a dark-brown leather, wingback chair.

"No funny business," Elon warns, a deliberate hand on the taser attached to his belt. "I'll happily fry you."

"Now, now." A regal voice emanates from the chair behind the desk. "There will be no need for such unpleasantries. Will there, Ripley?"

With Davis settling in the corner of the office, I'm left to face the elderly figure who turns in the office chair. It takes a moment for me to place his coiffed, silvery hair, wrinkle-lined jowls and lizard-like eyes.

When I transferred to Harrowdean, I made it my mission to understand the truth behind the world I'd entered. It wasn't hard to find the face behind the program. Sir Joseph Bancroft II has a spotless reputation.

Richer than God and arguably more powerful, Bancroft owns a portfolio of companies across the globe. His pride and joy, the infamous Incendia Corporation, has its finger in many pies.

Psychiatric institutes. Private schools.

International conglomerates.

Even… investment firms.

I knew I recognised him when the first news articles popped up detailing his philanthropic work and various charitable endeavours. On the rare occasions when my uncle remembered my existence, he did play the orphaned niece card to his advantage.

As a result, I attended a handful of events put on by his firm over the years. Smile and wave, right? I even met his boss. Not the guy running the daily board meetings and doling out redundancies, but the real boss. The one behind the board of directors.

"Nice to see you again." The same man smiles at me now. "It's been... dear me, ten or twelve years? You're all grown up now."

Play this smart. Stay alive.

"Sir," I return stiffly.

"Always such a polite, well-mannered little thing." Bancroft eyes me. "It's a pity, what happened to you. So much wasted potential. Jonathan was most disappointed by your... predisposition."

Of course, he'd label a chronic, enduring mental illness as an inconvenient waste of potential. Eight-year-old Ripley was already an inconvenience. But bipolar Ripley? She was a problem to be erased.

"Naturally, I offered you a place in our rehabilitative program." Bancroft actually sounds proud. "It's a shame that Priory Lane didn't prove conducive. Though your transfer here was an easy request to grant."

I peel my tongue from the roof of my mouth. "Why am I here?"

"Because, dear Ripley, you were given an opportunity. A chance to be a part of something bigger. But the reports I've been receiving of recent disturbances here are yet another disappointment."

"Perhaps if your men didn't beat us at any available opportunity, the patient population would be more content," I reply without thinking.

He chortles in amusement. "It is unfavourable to resort to

such measures. But your control is slipping. Defiance cannot go unpunished."

"I've done my job here."

"Then do better!"

His voice raises several octaves as spit flies across the desk. Behind Bancroft's well-versed speeches and charming smiles, it's clear a predator lies coiled at his centre. I've seen that threat brimming in his eyes before.

"Your job is to keep your peers dependent," he continues briskly. "Those who are dependent are compliant. Those who are compliant… don't ask questions."

The air flowing into my lungs halts. I cast a nervous glance around, but there are no escape routes. Not even a small basement window. This place is a concrete box designed to trap its prey.

"Our recent visitors to this wing asked many questions." Bancroft rests back in his office chair. "I wonder if they knew they were being sent to their deaths. Did you think to warn them?"

"I don't know what you're talking about."

"Cut the shit, Ripley," Davis interjects.

Feeling the weight of their collective gazes searing into me, sweat trickles down my spine. "I had to give them something."

"That wasn't the question." Bancroft smiles again in that creepy, all-seeing way. "Did you think twice before sending those boys to their deaths? Did it even cross your mind?"

Is there any point in lying? I don't need to pretend to be something I'm not here. These three men know the lows I've sank to in order to preserve my own existence.

"No. I wanted to hurt them. Just like they were hurting me."

While Davis looks furious at my admission, Bancroft seems positively thrilled. Like I've somehow ticked a box only he can see. It makes me want to scrub a year's worth of invisible bloodstains from my skin.

"Interesting," he muses, fingers tapping his lips. "Perhaps we still have use for you after all."

"Sir." Davis steps forward to address his superior. "Our program here is compromised enough."

"Which is precisely why it's a bad time to be training a new stooge," Bancroft responds. "I will not add another unstable element into an already difficult situation. We have enough to contend with."

Picking up a stack of folded newspapers from the corner of his desk, he slides them across the gleaming surface for me to take. I reluctantly accept them and begin flipping through the papers.

"Our future is compromised, Ripley." Bancroft rests his chin on his folded hands. "Therefore, your future is compromised too."

The blazing headlines catch my attention, one after another. All of the papers are dated within the last few weeks.

Deadly riot at Blackwood Institute.

Incendia Corporation under investigation by Sabre Security.

Allegations of abuse and malpractice across Britain's six institutes.

"I see a problem for you." I shrug. "Not me."

Bancroft swipes a hand over his silvery coiffure. "Do you think the authorities would agree with that assessment when they hear what you've done on our payroll?"

"I don't get paid. You're the ones profiting."

"Your continued survival is not payment?" he challenges. "You could have been disposed of long ago. But we maintained Jonathan's request to keep your situation quiet and... controlled."

The newspaper judders in my hands. I lay it down, attempting to disguise the fine tremble.

"Ah, now you get it." Bancroft observes my obvious nerves. "Uncle's protection has expired, hasn't it? I am surprised that his patience for your continued disruptions has lasted this long."

"Disruptions?" I repeat.

"If only his colleagues and investors knew that his very own niece was confined to the institute he endorses. Rather embarrassing, isn't it?"

I want to shrivel up and disappear. But I won't give him the satisfaction of humiliating me. So I decide to parrot the disgruntled warden watching our exchange.

"Cut the shit. If you're going to threaten me, get on with it."

"I have no need to threaten you, Ripley. Look around at where you are. If Harrowdean falls, don't doubt that we will all fall with it."

The broken part of me that's endured the cost of surviving the past two years wants to throw open the fucking gates and let the authorities march in here. For the lives I've exploited, I owe them that much.

He's right, though.

The world needs a scapegoat. As humans, we assign an outlet for our rage long before we think of compassion. It'll come down to blame. Incendia won't protect me from the wolves. We will burn together.

I've come too far to let their crumbling empire take me down. Sacrificed too much. I didn't care that a different Ripley would be leaving those gates, as long as I walked out at all. So I wilfully destroyed the person I was to become the person they needed.

The stooge.

The instigator.

The *blame*.

"What do you want me to do?" I grit out.

"Sir, I really must insist—"

"Enough," Bancroft cuts the warden off. "Ripley has proven herself to be an asset despite recent transgressions. These are dangerous times. We cannot squander loyalty."

Gaze catching on the nearest newspaper, I study the mugshot of an escaped detainee from Blackwood Institute. Another chess piece in this eternal game of moves and counter moves.

Staring into the dead-eyed stare of Brooklyn West, the so-called instigator of the riot that engulfed Harrowdean's sister branch, I wonder what this stranger would do in my position. If she'd tell me to let it all burn, even if that included myself.

"Help us weather this storm, Ripley. Control the patient population. Manipulate. Instill fear. Exploit. If Harrowdean survives, you will have your freedom."

"And if I refuse to play my part?"

His wrinkled mouth pulls taut. "You will make an excellent addition to the professor's Z wing program. I do hate wasted potential. But repurposing? Now that's just good business."

I look into Bancroft's eyes. Full of challenge and determination. He isn't afraid—monsters with power and money never are. This world will always be institutionally weighted in their favour. People like us are the foundation of their empires.

I'll be his weapon.

I'll even make it look real.

But the moment his house of cards begins to fall, I don't intend to stick around to bear the consequences. Even if that means shedding the person I am and the life I've fought so hard to resume.

Instead, I'll run.

And leave my soul behind.

CHAPTER 20
RIPLEY
LOVE ABUSER (SAVE ME) – ROYAL & THE SERPENT

"THE NEWS IS SAYING it's a once in a lifetime storm. Half the country is underwater."

Pierced nose pressed against the glass, I study the violent sheets of rain hammering into the ground like machine gun fire. The deep, almost purple clouds that have been looming over several days finally burst open a few hours ago.

"You read the news?" I laugh.

"No," Rae snorts. "I listen to gossip. Other people read the news."

We're standing on the grand staircase, gathered around one of the huge stained glass windows. Several other patients hang nearby to watch the apocalyptic light show of thunder and lightning. Crackles illuminate the night sky, tearing apart the heavens.

Already, the ground is saturated and overflowing with murky rainwater. The quad is slowly turning into a quagmire. We've all been confined to the main building until further notice.

"You think it'll wash this shit hole away?" she asks hopefully. "We can all swim to safety."

"Where's safe, Rae?" I sigh.

"Literally anywhere but here. I saw that dickhead guard, Elon, break someone's nose with that kinky baton thing he loves so much the other day. He fucking laughed."

"Believe me, there's nothing kinky about that baton." I shudder at the thought.

"You're missing the point. He broke her nose!"

I wish that was shocking to me. In any normal hospital or secure facility, it would be big news. A disciplinary matter for sure, maybe even a public scandal. But not here. Not in the shadows.

Remembering Bancroft's words, I force myself to respond. "She should've followed instructions, then."

Rae turns her attention from the storm to gape at me. "You're kidding? No one deserves that."

"I don't know what else to tell you. It's her own fault."

Several of the other patients clustered nearby are listening but keeping their gazes averted. Like if somehow they displease me, I'll arrange a personal nose-breaking of their own.

"Seriously, Rip?"

"Follow the rules, and you won't get hurt. It's simple."

"What the hell is wrong with you?" Rae's head rears back, her brows drawn.

"I'm just saying that we all need to comply."

"They shouldn't be using violence in the first place! You're sick for condoning it."

"Do we have a problem here?" I clip out.

Whatever she sees in my expression causes her eyes to bug out. Rae takes a step back and shakes her head.

"No. Not at all."

"Good. I'd hate to run into a supply issue with your weekly deliveries."

With a blank mask and flat tone that would make my uncle proud, I cast a quick look around at the others listening.

Ensuring they all get the message. This isn't the first spectacle I've put on this week.

I push off from the windowsill. "That goes for *all* weekly deliveries."

Rae just stares at me like I'm some alien creature. Ignoring her and the soft murmurings I leave behind, I head downstairs. Exhaustion doesn't begin to describe the extent of my current downward spiral.

But I have a role to play. Expectations to fulfil. No one is paying me to be the hero. Martyrs are romantic in theory, but people forget they have to die in order to make a fucking difference. And I intend to survive.

Like a cockroach.

Holly would be so damn proud.

In the reception, chaos is unfolding. Several members of staff are attempting to block the entrances and exits with all manner of towels, rags and even boxes of paper. Filthy rainwater is spilling inside from the rapidly rising water levels.

Fitting, I suppose. Perhaps we'll luck out, and Harrowdean will be washed away, taking all its evil and evidence with it. We'll be left with nothing but our stories. And no one will ever be interested in those, right?

"Warden?" one of the therapists calls out.

Davis is standing farther back in the safe zone, watching his staff try to keep the place afloat. He eyes the impending disaster, his shirt sleeves rolled up and arms folded.

"What, Doctor Chesterfield?"

"The water, sir."

"Fetch more towels then!"

A sudden rush of water heads towards him and engulfs his expensive leather shoes. He curses and lifts a sodden foot, water now dripping from his trouser leg. I cover my mouth before he catches me laughing.

"Towels! Now!" he screeches.

The sound of his indignation is engulfed by a sudden, ear-splitting crash. Everyone instinctively ducks at the loud smashing sound. Shards of coloured glass slice through the air, catapulted by wind and rain.

Ducked down, I peer out from beneath my arms wrapped around my head protectively. The arched, stained glass window high above the exit doors has been destroyed. One of the rubbish bins from the quad now lies inside the reception.

"Christ!" Davis exclaims.

"Sir, we need to call an emergency lockdown."

"Yes! Now!"

Watching them deliberate, I squeak when a hand circles my wrist and yanks. I'm hauled backwards into the adjacent corridor then slammed up against the wall.

"Where is he?" Lennox hisses in my face.

I shove him away from me. "What are you talking about?"

He pushes my shoulders, causing my spine to slam against the wall again. "Raine! I can't find him anywhere. He's being a stubborn shit, and it's all because of you."

It hasn't escaped my notice that Raine's been sticking to me like glue since he tracked me down. He turns up at my bedroom door most nights and has made a point of ignoring Lennox in particular.

"Raine's decisions are his own," I defend. "It's not my fault you're a shit friend."

"Because I don't support him sleeping with a psycho slut like you?" Lennox seethes. "I've tried to warn him. The son of a bitch is determined to be your next victim."

This hot-headed moron is genuinely deluded. But he makes a good point—I haven't seen Raine all day. He was notably absent from lunch, and with the storm battering us, I need to know he's safe.

"Did you check his room?"

Lennox narrows his eyes. "Great idea. Why didn't I think of that?"

"Ease off, asshole. You haven't got two brain cells to rub together. I have to ask."

"You know what? Forget it. I'll find him myself."

With a final shove, he storms back off into the reception. I hate myself for appreciating the way his tight, white t-shirt bulges over his biceps and the fit of his sweatpants accentuates his perfectly curved rear.

I don't have to like the guy to admit that he's sexy as sin in a rugged, no fucks given kind of way. It's a shame he has to open his damn mouth and ruin that attraction.

That's when the real Lennox emerges. No amount of muscle or delicious stubble can fix that disaster. He's a cruel soul hidden behind a pretty exterior.

Concerned for Raine, I head for the music room. It's outside his usual practise hours, but the list of spaces he feels comfortable and safe in is limited. If something is wrong, he'd seek refuge there first.

In the south wing, it's deserted. Classes have finished for the day, and everyone is taking refuge while the storm rages. I stop outside the pitch-black music room to take a quick glance inside.

"Raine? You in here?"

There's no response, but I step into the darkness regardless, flicking on lights as I go. When I see his ajar violin case, I know the voice screaming in my head is on to something. The case is empty and haphazardly discarded.

"Raine?"

Nothing.

"Where are you? Raine?"

After searching the room from top to bottom, I find nothing. Just an empty case and no answers. Heading down the hall, I slam on the lights in the art room. My canvases and supplies are still in the top corner of the room.

With thunder exploding outside the bay windows, I make my way to the back of the room. Bingo. Raine's sitting on the floor, surrounded by stacks of dry canvases and boxes of oil paint. His violin rests in his lap.

"Why are you hiding in here? You scared the shit out of me!"

Inching closer, I realise his head is lolling to the side. I drop next to him, quickly seizing his hand. It doesn't tighten around mine. His fingernails are blue, matching the strange purplish tint of his lips.

Fuck!

That's when I notice the empty plastic coin bag resting in his limp hand. I haven't seen one of these since I used to help out at my dad's butcher shop as a kid. He'd sometimes let me count the change at the end of a shift.

There's a pale, powdery residue left in the bag from whatever pills were stashed inside. But the more horrifying realisation is that whatever he's taken, I didn't supply it. These aren't the bags we use.

I've been carefully controlling Raine's intake ever since he started coming to me. I never oversell and often reject some of his requests. Plus, the product is safe. Well, as safe as drugs can be. But this bag… it's not mine.

He bought from someone else.

Who the fuck sold this to him?

Shoving the baggie into my pocket to figure out later, I look back at Raine.

"Come on," I plead urgently. "Wake up, Raine."

Withdrawal looks different than this. He's completely out cold. Peeling back his eyelids, I find his pupils smaller than pinpricks. His healed, bruise-free skin is cold and clammy, but he's breathing, albeit in a worryingly shallow manner.

Shaking him several times, I repeat his name, my voice taking on a frantic edge. Not even a twitching of the eye. All I've got is the rapid rise and fall of his chest to reassure me that he's still alive.

I can't leave him. Not like this. If he stops breathing, I'll have to perform CPR. The mere thought is terrifying. Accident or not, I'm certain this is an overdose.

Patting down his pockets, I search for the lump of his smartphone. It's in his jeans and chirps back to me as I stab the buttons, searching his contacts. I have to swallow my pride to press the ring button on Lennox's name.

"Where the fuck are you?" he barks in greeting after two rings.

"It's Ripley."

Lennox pauses. "Where is Raine?"

"Out cold. Looks like an OD. You need to raise the alarm."

"This isn't a funny joke. Where is he?"

"Stop wasting time, Nox! Get fucking help!"

After a beat, there's a loud thud like he's punching whatever available surface is nearby.

"Where?"

"Art room. Next to where he was last time."

"Stay with him!"

When the line disconnects, I toss his phone aside. Raine still hasn't stirred. Pulling him away from the wall, I cradle his head in my lap and wrap my arms around him, attempting to transfer some warmth into his frozen body.

"Why?" I whisper through pooling tears. "I know we're in a world of shit, but you didn't have to do this."

Smoothing sweaty hair from his face, I focus on the whistling of his nose, indicating each breath. Inhale. Exhale. Inhale. Exhale. My world narrows to those two functions, offering me the faintest sliver of hope.

"Please, Raine."

Keeping a hand on his chest, I feel for the thrum of his heartbeat against his breastbone. Seconds pass sluggishly, turning into agonising minutes marked only by the beat of his continued existence.

"You deserve better than this place. I'll let you go if I have to, but I need you to get help and be okay. You'll never heal in Harrowdean."

Holding his hand in a deathly tight grip, I feel the faintest twitching of his fingers. Just a whisper. Enough to convince me that he's heard my voice in whatever drug-trapped hole he's stuck in.

"You had to make me go and give a shit about you, huh?" I laugh wetly. "You couldn't just take no for an answer."

Ducking down, I press a kiss against his clammy, blue lips. My tears drip on his face, absorbed by golden stubble. I hold him close, trying hard not to sob, until the sound of company approaches.

"In here!" I shout.

The door cracks against the wall, mirroring the violence of the storm still raging outside. Lennox is at the head of the group, followed closely by Doctor Hall from the medical wing and Nina, the smart-mouthed nurse who cared for me.

"How long has Raine been unconscious?" Doctor Hall asks calmly.

"I don't know... Ten minutes? He was like this when I found him."

He crouches down, taking the medical bag from the nurse. "What has he taken?"

"I don't know!"

He sighs. "Move aside please."

"No, I'm not leaving him."

Hands slide underneath my arms, and I'm yanked away from Raine. The doctor gently takes his head and rests it on the floor before he begins his examination. I hiss and curse as Lennox drags me backwards, his fingers digging deep into me.

"What did you sell him?" he growls in my ear.

"This wasn't me."

"Where'd he get it from, then? The tooth fairy?"

"It's not my shit. I've been monitoring him."

Lennox keeps me pinned against his front, unable to

wriggle free. "I warned you, Ripley. You just crossed the fucking line."

"We've got loss of consciousness and signs of respiratory depression." Doctor Hall straightens. "Likely opioid intoxication. It'll have to be an intramuscular injection."

Nina roots around in the medical bag. After checking the labels, she pulls out two wrapped syringes and begins to prep them. Doctor Hall quickly radios to whoever is listening to request additional help.

We're both transfixed as the nurse lifts Raine's right leg to give the doctor a good angle to approach his thigh from. Doctor Hall holds the first needle at a right angle then inserts it into Raine's thigh through his clothing.

"Naloxone administered at 19:04." He checks his wristwatch. "100 micrograms."

"What are they doing to him?" Lennox snarls.

I struggle against his grip. "It'll reverse the OD."

After waiting two minutes, they check his breathing again before administering another dose. My heart is ready to tear free from my chest, and I can feel how hard Lennox is shaking. He still hasn't released me from his muscled prison.

After several minutes, Raine's breathing is a little less shallow. He still hasn't woken up, but I can see his chest rising and falling with deeper breaths. Nina keeps two fingers clamped tight on his wrist, measuring his pulse rate.

"Is he going to be okay?" Lennox's voice is rough.

"I'm familiar with Raine's file." Doctor Hall disposes of the used needles. "There's a higher risk of acute withdrawal following this treatment in cases of chronic drug abuse."

"Meaning?" Lennox snaps.

"He'll need to be admitted and monitored."

Barely able to see through my tears, I'm not sure when my body stopped fighting to escape and started leaning into the warm embrace of its captor. Feeling Lennox's firm chest at my back keeps me upright as I watch another nurse and two extra guards roll a mobile stretcher in.

"On three. Okay, one... two... three."

It takes two of them to lift Raine's limp body up and onto the stretcher. He's still deathly pale and clammy, those molten eyes sealed shut. Lennox's tight grip on me finally slackens, but I don't leap away yet.

"Please," I whisper. "I want to—"

Disregarding me, they wheel him away. I'm left staring after them, unspoken words hanging on my lips, regret holding me captive now. I can't move. Can't blink. All I can see is Raine's blue lips and slack face. Just like Holly.

She was still hanging when I found her. Tiptoes barely scraping the bedroom carpet. Jeans soaked with urine. Throat crushed. Lips blue. Eyes wide. She was as still as stone and cold as ice.

Worlds coalesce and become one. I'm staring down the barrel of another potential loss while being held by the person who instigated the last. I'm not sure when fate decided to become such a cruel bitch, but I'm sick of the irony.

"Let go!" I erupt.

Seeming to snap back to his senses at the same time, Lennox abruptly releases me like I burned him. "With pleasure."

"We need to get to the medical wing."

"You're going nowhere," he deadpans.

Spinning around, I meet his hard, seafoam glare. "Raine needs me!"

"Raine needs you to leave him the fuck alone!" Neck muscles corded, rage pours from Lennox. "Which you seem incapable of doing. I won't let you sell another fucking pill to him."

"I didn't do this!" I throw out my arms in frustration. "They weren't my pills!"

"You're such a manipulative cunt. I don't believe a self-serving word that leaves your mouth."

"What about the words that leave your mouth?" I shout back. "He deserves better than a *murderer* for a friend."

"Shut the fuck up, Ripley."

But I'm not done.

"Holly wasn't even the first person you killed, was she?"

Lennox recoils like I've slapped him. "Choose your next words carefully."

If I have any hope of getting to Raine, I need to remove this stubborn obstacle. I'll rip out his heart and grind it to a paste without feeling a speck of remorse.

"It wasn't hard to dig in to you. Plenty of news articles out there. The angry, grieving teenager left all alone to piece together what happened to his baby sister."

"Enough," he warns, nostrils flaring.

"What was her name, huh?"

"I said enough!"

It isn't enough. Nothing will ever be enough when it comes to Lennox. For a man who has experienced the deepest depths of grief and despair, he has no concept of the evil he's inflicted in the name of love.

And he expects me to abandon Raine because he says so? Raine is the one who needs protection from him. Lennox is a fucking disease. One that needs to be eradicated, once and for all.

"Rose... Or Iris? No, that's not right."

His chest vibrates with a growl. "Stop."

I snap my fingers. "Ah, Daisy."

Lennox's pale-green eyes swim with intense pain.

"Beautiful kid," I continue spitefully. "It's hard to believe that you didn't know what dear old Grandad was doing to her every night. Not until she killed herself anyway."

The colour has drained from his face. Pulling his innards out for inspection and splattering them all around us has never felt so sweet. His pain is my pleasure. I'll never get enough of this sweet satisfaction for as long as he's still breathing.

I raise a hand, and after years of wondering, lift the silver necklace that hangs around his neck. I've never been close enough to pull it free from his t-shirt before. It's always hidden with the chain peeking out of his collar.

At the end of the silver chain are two military dog tags. My thumb smooths over the inscribed surface. *Alfred Nash.* I recognise the name from the news reports. That doesn't explain why Lennox still wears the insignia of his first victim and sister's abuser, though.

"Did you care for Daisy so little that you'll happily wear *his* name around your neck?"

Grabbing my wrist, Lennox prises the dog tags from my hand. "I wear that monster's name as a reminder to always do what's necessary to protect those I love."

"Like murder?"

Spittle flying, his next words come through clenched teeth.

"I don't care if the world hates me for what I've done, I'll do it all over again. Alfred deserved to die. And Holly was a threat. Now... you."

"And what am I? Another threat to be removed?"

For a flash, I swear I see a hint of remorse in his eyes. The briefest whisper of something akin to enjoyment of our toxic back and forth. However, it's soon crushed and replaced with his signature brand of hatred.

"Yes."

His fist snaps out then slams into my stomach. My bruises have only just healed and faded from Rick's attack. Winded, I double over, gasping for air.

Lennox moves fast, wrapping a burly arm around my neck to trap me in a headlock. I hit him repeatedly, but it doesn't stop him from choking me out.

"By the time Raine wakes up, you'll be gone." Lennox

tightens his arm to crush my windpipe. "And there will be no one left to fuck up his life. He'll be safe."

Dragging my nails down his exposed arms, I desperately search for an opening. Even the tiniest weakness. He doesn't flinch at the blood welling beneath my fingers to paint his skin. The tight, strangling pressure of his headlock is constant. I'm going to pass out. What will he do to me? Panic sets in along with cold, hard survival instinct.

I'm kicking. Writhing. Scratching. Anything to secure the oxygen that my lungs are begging for. But Lennox won't let me escape. Not this time. He's found his moment and won't surrender me again.

"That's it," he encourages. "Shut your eyes."

Everything is growing heavy. Limbs filling with lead and blood flow decreasing. My head feels like a balloon set to burst. I can't stop my eyes from falling shut as nothingness permeates my vision.

His voice is the last thing I hear.

"I'm sorry, Rip."

CHAPTER 21
RIPLEY

CHOKEHOLD – SLEEP TOKEN

WITH THE SOUND of Xander's shower running, I finally wriggle out of the wrist restraints that have rubbed my skin raw. I can reach down my body to my ankles now. I'm tied with some kind of thin, flexible nylon rope. Fuck knows how he sourced it in here.

My limbs are like liquified jelly. I'm not sure how they're even still attached after the past few hours. Fumbling with the rope, I'm trembling too hard to even attempt unfastening the expertly tied knots. Xander left nothing to chance.

The glint of black steel catches my eye. He discarded the folding pocketknife once he'd licked my blood from its blade, his tongue an inch away from being sliced open. I was fascinated, watching that twisted display. And fucking soaked too.

Straining as hard as I can, my fingertips brush against its curved handle. I manage to seize the knife then quickly set to work slashing the rope from my ankles. It's tough and doesn't cut easily.

Once the restraints have given way, I try to stand up but crumple instead. I'm weaker than a newborn baby. The ordeal he put my body through, equal parts pain and pleasure, has left me exhausted beyond measure.

Wincing at the sting of bruises across my skin, I can't find the clothes I wore when I nervously tiptoed over here, too curious for my own good. I *wanted to know if he would live up to his threats. If I could survive a night in Xander Beck's bed.*

Snagging a t-shirt that smells like him—spearmint and something darker, somehow more primal—I quickly dress. My panties are peeking out from beneath the bed. That'll have to do.

I flee before his shower is finished. My mind needs time to process what we just did together. The lines we crossed. His confusing blend of sick fascination for pain and attentiveness for my pleasure. The scarred iceman hides many perplexing secrets.

Those scars weigh on my mind as I creep back to my room. They were everywhere. Littered all over his arms, biceps, stomach, thighs. Not an inch of skin was untouched. And neat, regimented lines too. Some deeper than others. But so clearly self-inflicted.

What internal pain does Xander have that's so great, he has to expel it on to himself? And at what point did that blade stop serving its purpose, and he switched to hurting others instead?

Reaching my door, I realise I don't have a keycard to unlock it. I left it tucked inside my sweats, still lost somewhere in Xander's room. I'm not brave enough to return yet.

Instead, I head for Holly's door. She has a fancy, all-access pass, courtesy of her perks. I can't tell her where I've been. I'll have to find an excuse.

If she knew I'd slept with Xander, she would blow a gasket. But as I lift my arm to knock on her door, my silent plotting halts. Realising that it's ajar, unease swarms in my chest.

For the year that I've known her, Holly has always been paranoid about her privacy. She would never leave her door unlocked. Licking my lips, I gently knock on the door frame.

"Hol? You in here?"

Silence answers me.

"I'm coming in."

My state of undress long forgotten, I creep inside. Light emanates from a lamp deeper in the room. It's as neat and organised as ever. She's particular about her space. But then the broken light on the ceiling with knotted bed sheets looped through the exposed fixture draws my attention.

I look lower.

Squeeze my eyes shut.

Reopen.

Still there.

I'm not sure how long I stand here. At some point, I must start screaming. But I can't feel or hear it. People arrive, and hands usher me outside where I collapse against the wall. Vision unfocused, all I can see is my best friend. Or rather, the remains of her.

Guards arrive. Staff arrive. Medics arrive. Footsteps. Shouts. Barked orders to clear the floor. None of it registers beyond the basic observations of a detached mind. I'm left here, huddled in a ball and gasping for each breath as they take a body bag out.

That's when I look away. Only for a moment. My head turns, allowing me to catch sight of the two patients who haven't been escorted to another floor. They stand at the end of the corridor, shoulder to shoulder. United in their success.

Seafoam rage.

Midnight detachment.

Something fractures inside me. It's almost a visceral thing—the breaking of my sanity. Like an overstretched rubber band that snaps and recoils but never reverts back to its original shape. I watch Lennox's lips lift into a grim smile. Like he's performed a hard but necessary task.

Xander's expression doesn't change a bit.

He just stares.

Transfixed by the sight of my life falling apart at the seams as my best friend's corpse is removed. That's when I start screaming again. I don't stop until the sedatives are administered.

Thunder rumbles.

Deep. Sonorous.

Enraged.

My mum used to say that thunderstorms are just God moving furniture. She was religious in the way that most

Brits are—made to endure weekly Sunday school as a kid but never truly committing themselves to the idea of faith. Being force-fed the notion of religion kinda destroys that possibility.

The rumbles continue, each louder than the last. I wonder if the reception is flooded now? I really should go check on Raine. I wouldn't want him to get stuck or hurt.

Raine.

With the distant memories of Holly's death still swimming in my mind, awareness slams back into me. Finding Raine unconscious. Blue and lifeless. The medics taking him away. Lennox's threats. Passing out.

With each mental flashback, my senses trickle back in. The frigid cold hits first, then searing heat in my wrists and arms. Groaning in pain, I force my eyes to open.

It makes no difference. I'm in total darkness. My body is shivering, it's so cold. I can feel that something tight and painful binds my wrists together.

It feels like I'm tied to some kind of metal pipe. The pain in my arms must be from hanging all my body's unconscious weight on whatever binds restrain me.

Attempting to move, I feel water slosh around my legs. The sound of torrential rain echoes all around me in what sounds like a cavernous space. It collides with whatever water I'm submerged in. I'm soaked to the bone.

"Hello?" I call out hoarsely.

The emptiness answers me.

Thick, desolate silence.

"Hello!"

Echoes tell me I'm somewhere spacious. It feels empty. Still. The smell of old chlorine burns my nose, shoving out the last dregs of drowsiness. Kicking around in the water, my foot collides with an unknown object, causing me to yelp in fear.

A sudden burst of lightning cracks above me, illuminating my surroundings for a few seconds. I look around as quickly as possible, ignoring my sinking sense of dread. Then everything falls back into blackness.

Lennox. Fucking Nash.

I'm in the swimming pool.

My rapid look around revealed the zip ties securing my wrists to the bottom rung of the pool's steps. I'm surrounded by discarded furniture and rainwater that pours from the broken windows and ceiling.

Rapidly rising rainwater.

It's fucking flooding.

That twisted, vindictive man couldn't just kill me. Oh, no. That would've been too easy for the bitch who supposedly threatens his precious family, right? Instead, he's left me to slowly drown as the pool floods.

Hysteria quickly sets in. It's human instinct. Inescapable. I scream myself raw and contort my body at every available angle to escape bondage. Muscles burn and protest, but I don't stop.

Nothing breaks the layers of zip ties fastened around my wrists to form an unbreakable plastic chain. He's done his homework. I'm completely immobile.

"Fuck you, Nox!" I yell to the emptiness.

Part of me wishes he'd respond. Even to laugh or bait me. Revel in his victory. Anything but the lonely silence he's condemned me to die in. The lack of humanity is cold, even for Lennox.

By the time my voice gives out, the water has risen a few inches, now up to my thighs. Each flash of lightning reveals its progress. The storm shows no signs of letting up and halting the flood.

Working my wrists back and forth, I'm taken back to that night. The excitement and anticipation I felt as Xander sprawled me out, pinned me down and fastened each limb to his bed frame. All with that predatory gleam in his eye.

It sounds fucked up beyond words. I can admit that in the

safety of my own thoughts. But that night, I found a sense of freedom that I'd never had before.

All the money in the world can't buy the ecstasy of handing your autonomy to someone else. Someone who will leverage it to torture you in the most exquisite way. The pleasure he found through hurting me only intensified the satisfaction.

I shove Xander from my thoughts as I battle against the layers of zip ties. My skin splits and bleeds, but I can't stop crying. Not when the freezing cold water is slowly creeping up to my waist.

"Please!" I wheeze uselessly. "Someone help me!"

Rumble. Crash.

All I have is God moving furniture and the ghosts of everyone who has damned me to die like this. Even if I didn't supply the pills swimming in Raine's system right now, I might as well have.

It didn't stop me from doing exactly that to so many others and with the same outcome. Harrowdean's list of victims is lengthy. I've contributed my fair share. Perhaps this is what I deserve. I shouldn't be allowed to go home when they never will.

Villains don't get happy endings for a reason.

How would the good guys cope if they did?

The tears come thick and fast. Tears for Raine. Rae. Everyone I've hurt in order to survive. The other version of Ripley who walked into Priory Lane, deluded enough to think it was her chance to get better. She died like so many others.

Wrists throbbing with each rivulet of blood flowing down my arms, I give up and hang here. Dead weight. Defeated. Powerful Ripley, reduced to a sobbing wreck in an abandoned pool. Without a single soul to miss her.

No one will find me in time.

Not when there's nothing to miss.

Water tickles my ribcage. The shivering has stopped. I'm

numb now. Slowly sinking into the abyss. I won't even fight it, there's no point. Maybe Lennox was right. Raine deserves a better friend than me.

He will be better off without me.

Everyone will.

Letting my head loll, I listen to the violent slam of the torrential rain. It becomes rhythmic. Trance-like. Lulling me into a state of detached calm as my body is engulfed by water, inch by inch.

It feels like an eternity has passed when the crunch of broken glass rouses me. Water laps at my clavicles and forearms as I peer around sightlessly, wondering if I've finally lost it. I'm probably hearing ghosts now.

Lightning flashes again, illuminating the outline of someone at the pool's edge. I blink through my crusted, swollen eyes, trying to discern if I'm imagining things in my desperation.

Another strobe of lightning. Reflections dance off platinum hair and alabaster skin. I've definitely lost it. There's no way he'd be here to save me, not when he's obsessed with bringing about my end.

A beam of light breaks through the obscurity. It's pointed in my direction and moving closer. Squinting, I realise that I'm seeing a phone's flashlight heading towards me.

"Found yourself in a spot of bother?" he utters in a cool voice.

Light shines in my face, making my eyes water. I blink through the haze, waiting as the image of Xander settles. Hair rain-soaked and plastered to his face, his polo shirt is soaked through and jeans mud-streaked.

"You're not really here."

He stops at the pool's edge. "Hearing whispers, little toy?"

Another loud clap of thunder rumbles overhead. The water is tickling the base of my throat now. Even if I crane my neck, I don't have much time left. It'll be in my mouth and nose soon.

"You disappeared." In his phone's weak light, I see him frown. "I dislike losing track of my own property."

"You're normally more focused than that," I rasp.

"I was searching for Raine. Only to find him passed out in the medical wing and you gone. Is this some kind of elaborate suicide plan?"

"I didn't tie myself up!"

His forehead puckers in concentration. "Ah. Lennox was rather cagey about how he discovered Raine in such a state. But it wasn't him, was it?"

Half-drowned and gasping for each breath, icy water kisses my throat and chin. I tilt my neck at a painful angle, hoping to preserve my air supply for as long as possible. Perhaps long enough for someone to follow Xander and find us both.

Watching my predicament, he takes a seat on the tiled edge. Xander studies me unhurriedly, disregarding the rapidly rising water. His eyebrows are pulled together like he can't decipher his own thoughts.

"I suppose he's making a point," he muses. "Drowning his problems instead of burning them alive this time around."

"X-Xander."

"Yes, little toy?"

I can't bring myself to beg. Not to him. Not again. So instead, I suck in each precious mouthful of air left, battling to keep the water level beneath my chin. The rain has to stop sometime. I can still make it.

Xander watches me bob, his head cocked to one side. "I've dreamed of watching your corpse turn blue so many times. In the Z wing, I played out different scenarios in my head while they tortured me."

Funny that.

I've done the same thing for him.

"Then I came here. I started watching you. Following you

each day to observe your new routine and patterns. Learning about the person we created, rather than the obsession I once had."

He watches me spit up a mouthful of water that crashes into me in a miniature wave. His stare has hardened from one of intrigue to something akin to concern. If soulless psychopaths can display such emotion.

"I've watched you beat and threaten. Sob when no one is watching. Eat, sleep and take medication. Fuck for the thrill of it. Fall for the one person you never intended to. Hurt those you so clearly care about."

The water sloshes over my mouth and touches my nostrils.

Xander just watches me struggle. "I stopped seeing an object."

Whatever epiphany he's having, I don't want to hear it. Not with my last gasps of oxygen. Water laps at my nose, rising those final few centimetres faster than ever. The panic has come swarming back with a vengeance.

"I want you broken." Xander gracefully draws to his feet. "But I don't want to watch others break you."

Reaching into his pocket, he pulls out a familiar black pocketknife. The same one I used to free myself once before. Taking a final breath before I'm taken under the surface, I see him frown at the blade.

Then… nothing.

Xander is gone.

I keep my eyes screwed shut as the cold water covers them. That way I can pretend I'm floating out to sea on a blissful wave, content to let the current carry me back to shore when it's time to return.

Chest burning with each passing second, the pressure is a slow build. Lungs seeking to expand once all the air has escaped as dying bubbles. But there's no air underwater. No reprieve from the inevitable conclusion.

Just nothingness.

The watery grave of Harrowdean's whore.

I hear a crash ringing all around me as something collides with the water. When the first bit of water pushes into my mouth and lungs, causing me to gag, I feel hands grasping at my wrists.

Snap.

The plastic zip ties give way. More water spills into my mouth, filling my lungs with each new iteration of panic. Something sharp nicks my wrist as the bindings release, tie by tie.

I feel the last bubble escape my mouth. My throat, chest cavity… everything feels like it's on fire. The snipping of my wrists being set free feels faraway, lost in the expanse of the pool's inky depths.

I hope Lennox is satisfied.

I hope Raine is safe.

I hope Xander learns to feel again.

One wrist suddenly breaks free, floating at my side. I'm too weak to even move it. Sharp nicks from a blade pierce my other wrist, working its way through the plastic trapping me in place.

On the verge of fading out, I feel the last piece of plastic leave my skin. I'm left afloat, sinking deeper into the welcoming nothingness. Until arms wrap around my waist. I'm propelled upwards, through layer after layer of umbra.

Rain showers down on my head as we break the surface. I frantically try to suck in a breath, but the oxygen can't seem to find its way into my airway. Nothing penetrates the blockade of swallowed water.

"Breathe, goddammit."

The voice offers what should be a cold command, but it comes out sounding more like a plea. The desperate call of salvation from the unlikeliest of sources. I wish I could appease that voice. I want to breathe.

Wet clothing slaps against hard ground. Pain radiates up

my spine. Hands slip and slide all over me, searching for signs of life. I feel his arms band around my ribcage before I'm jerked—once, twice, three times.

On the third painful manoeuvre, water comes spewing up. It pours from my mouth and nose, burning so fiercely, I may as well have swallowed fire. When the heaving stops, I'm laid back down, and a mouth seals over mine.

Short, sharp bursts of air are pushed past my lips. The five rapid rescue breaths force my airways to reopen and accept sustenance once more. Lips disappearing from mine, I'm free to drag in my first excruciating breath.

In.

Out.

In.

Out.

Each ragged gasp brings life back to my soul. I can feel my limbs twitching and wrists throbbing. I'm flat on my back, still being hammered by rain. But something must be braced above me, protecting my face from most of the downpour.

Fingertips smooth wet curls back from my face. Gentle. Almost tender. The same hand that clasped mine in the medical wing despite thinking I wouldn't remember his momentary compassion.

My eyes flutter open. His face is shadowed but visible. Water drips from his hair and clothing, the continued flashes of lightning revealing what I'd never believe without seeing it myself.

Emotion.

His almost-black eyes are full of it.

"Y-You... saved me."

Xander's features seem to cave, overcome with sudden exhaustion. "You're worth more to me alive."

"But... you h-hate me."

His lids close, as though bracing for impact.

"I thought I did too."

CHAPTER 22
XANDER

DO YOU REALLY WANT TO HURT ME – NESSA BARRETT

KICKING Ripley's door open after scanning my stolen all-access pass, I heave her inside and let it slam shut. Carrying a semi-conscious woman through the quad would've been impossible on any day but this.

I heard the alarms ringing as I resolved to check the swimming pool earlier on, taking a lesser-known guards' exit to avoid being seen. Harrowdean has gone into lockdown. Everyone is confined to their rooms for safety.

It took some stealthy wading through flooded grounds to get back to the manor in the dead of night. And some even stealthier tactics to get upstairs without being spotted. No one can know about this.

Ripley doesn't need the heat.

I'm sure she's already on thin ice.

Telling myself a few months ago that I'd one day worry about her would've been entertaining. That Xander would have revelled in the notion that she'd lose her protection and suffer the same fate that we did.

Her tactics don't work on me. The public displays of solidarity for management and their aggressors. Using threats and manipulations to control an increasingly disenchanted client base. She's playing it well, for sure.

I've studied her enough. Theorised the best ways to break her down and reclaim those pieces for myself. Plotted and waited then plotted some more. While I may feel nothing, Ripley feels the world all too acutely.

But that isn't true, is it?

Did I feel nothing while watching her drown?

Brushing those peculiar thoughts aside, I mentally debate what the fuck I'm doing here, and more importantly, what the fuck I'm going to do with her. We're both drenched, shivering and near-hypothermic.

With the storm still battering against her barred windows, I locate the bathroom and hit the lights. She's breathing normally but still waxy and ashen. Heat. We need warmth. I quickly turn on the walk-in shower.

"Raine," she murmurs groggily.

If the motherfucker wasn't already half-dead in a hospital bed, I'd quickly send him to one for being the name on her tongue right now. She's *my* Ripley. My toy. I've let him have his fun, but I won't be observing from the sidelines anymore.

I carry her into the shower fully clothed then hold her up beneath the warm spray. When she doesn't respond, I inch the temperature higher, watching the steam billow around us.

"Come on."

Ripley jerks in my arms, crying out at the lash of hot water on her frozen skin. Now that she's beginning to respond, I prop her against my front and slowly peel the sopping clothes from her body.

"Easy," I whisper when she struggles.

I'm not certain she knows where she is or who holds her. There's no other explanation for the way she curls into me, seeking some kind of protection from the pain of warming back up. Like I'd ever be the one to protect her.

Turning my attention to her wrists, I rinse off the blood.

She's rubbed them raw in an attempt to escape. I even cut her a few times while fumbling in the pitch-black water. My cock unashamedly stirs at the sight of blood drawn by my hand.

A once-white bandage covers her forearm. The adhesive edges are peeling from water damage, with all manner of detritus and filth stuck to the fabric. I pinch a loose edge and begin to peel it off.

When her still-healing stitches are revealed, I try not to get distracted by the sight of her skin held together by synthetic fibres. Only the deeper cuts required treatment. The others have scabbed over in precise carvings.

A risk of infection joins my list of concerns. It was far simpler when I was content to let her suffer. I never anticipated the jealousy that watching others torment my toy would inspire.

Only I'm allowed to hurt her.

Now I have the responsibility of helping her too.

Thoroughly rinsing the wounds, I settle for getting them as clean as possible. I'm woefully unprepared for this task. Lennox is the bleeding heart; he would know what to do here. If only he weren't the one who attempted to kill her in the first place.

"Warmed up?"

Her teeth chatter together. "B-Better."

Sagging against me, I'm forced to pick Ripley up bridal-style to exit the shower.

"Raine... okay?" she asks.

I strip her down to her underwear, wrapping her in a towel to carry her through to the bedroom to be deposited. "Last I checked."

"M-Medical wing?"

I study her steady breathing until I'm satisfied she isn't dry-drowning. At least for the time being. She isn't out of the danger zone yet.

"With Nox."

Gasping, she fists the bed sheets beneath her in an attempt to leverage herself upright. I place a hand on her shoulder and easily push her back down.

"Stay."

"Len-n-nox... I... he..."

"Isn't going to drown Raine in an abandoned pool," I finish her rambling. "If that sets your mind at ease for now."

Her eyes are swollen slits, landing on me. "Why?"

Sighing hard, I perch beside her on the bed. "Why what?"

"Why help?"

Staring into blood-lined hazel orbs, I don't have an explanation for her. Not even a deflection or lie. My reasons for diving into that pool to save her life are as unfathomable as the way she makes my senses come alive.

It's been a long time since I felt the stirrings of a normal human existence. Switching those parts of myself off became a necessity. A means of survival. I endured my childhood that way. Not to mention the years of foster care afterwards.

But I could never turn it back on again. Not with a blade. Not with the cries or pleas of others. Not even as Priory Lane's doctors beat, whipped and tortured me to their heart's content. Cracks formed but failed to split my defences open.

"Lennox wants me dead," she whispers. "You do too."

Her raspy voice wraps around my heartstrings and tugs. Those ancient cracks that I thought I'd plastered over have become deep crevasses that I'm at risk of falling into. The same bleak crevasses that I spent years hiding in to escape what was happening to me.

Whatever darkness Ripley sees brewing in my gaze makes her flinch. She pulls the towel tighter across her chest and swallows hard.

"You should go."

"Is that any way to treat your saviour?"

Her reddened eyes shine with tears. "Thank you for helping me. Now go."

Standing up, I leave a sodden patch behind on her bed. I'm not sure what prompts me to look over my shoulder at her, a single question hanging on my tongue. Seeking an answer I didn't realise I needed.

"Do I scare you that badly?"

Ripley watches me closely. "Versions of you do."

"There is only one version of me."

She swipes escaped tears from her cheeks. "Does that version feel? Or is he still in denial that he's human at all?"

Those words detonate whatever internal defences remain inside me. The ice in my veins solidifies, expands then shatters. Deadly shards rip me apart from the inside out until it feels like I'm bleeding in front of her.

I don't need to be told to leave again. I'm already running as far from this devil woman as possible. Far from her questions and pain-laced stares tugging something free from my soul that I have no intention of giving.

Her door crashes shut behind me. I slump against the solid wood, sliding down until I'm crouched, my knees pressed to my chest. Luckily, the corridor is deserted with no one to witness my ragged breathing.

How dare she?

I dragged her from that pool because only I get the privilege of deciding when it's her time to die. I'm the one who gets to claim that reward after all she's done. No one else. Not even Lennox.

But the even more disturbing realisation is that I don't know if I want that privilege. Seeing her ruthlessness and will to survive firsthand has ignited an obsession too strong for petty revenge to get in the way.

Still breathing hard, I can feel myself vibrating. What the hell is happening to me? My chest is tight. Jaw clenched. Brain whirling. Too many foreign sensations from a time long past are returning.

That conniving bitch is making me fucking *feel* again. I will not go back to being that person. I took the victim I once was and crushed that little kid into a tight corner in my mind. He's been chained there since.

I don't care about others.

I don't care about myself.

I only care about the next target.

Head resting against the door, I know I should leave. She doesn't deserve my concern. If she's found dead by morning, it will be one less concern for all of us. We'll go back to our original plan—taking Harrowdean for ourselves.

Even if she's not in it.

That thought is unbearable.

Banging the back of my head against the door, I savour the dull ache. Pain has always been a means of control to me. A way to check that my bulletproof shields are still intact. Only now, the pain has wormed its way back inside me.

I need to expel it. Purge this spreading poison from my veins and reset my operating system. I can go back to my last safe backup. The uncompromised version of Xander.

Before I ever met Ripley Bennet. Before she sunk her claws into me. Before seeing her in pain made me revert back to that wounded child who endured so much.

The storm rages outside and my own inner tempest grows with it. A battleground has opened up in my mind. The cold logic of removing the malware attempting to corrupt me versus embracing the bug and letting it tear my system apart.

Taking the pocketknife from my still-wet jeans, I spin it in my hands. Considering. Analysing. Reaching the only logical conclusion to end this madness. I've humoured my obsession for too long.

Pulling her from that pool was a mistake. Becoming infatuated in the first place... I never should've been so weak. Allowing hatred and fascination to become so inextricably entwined was only ever going to lead to ruin.

Scanning the keycard, I slip back into her room. The knife

is cold in my grip. I follow the path to her bed, lit by lightning flashes. In the time I've spent deliberating, Ripley has passed out in her towel.

I stop a metre or so away, statue still and frozen. She's breathing deeply, sticking it out at this fickle thing we call living. Nothing seems to kill this girl. She's survived far more than I'd ever thought she would.

It would be so easy to sink the knife into her, removing any further temptation. She couldn't survive that, right? Not if I stayed to watch the life fade from her eyes. I'm longing to hear her dying breath.

But my body doesn't respond. Not to move an inch closer, not to lift the knife and not to sink it deep into any available organ. Instead, I'm fixated on the continued evidence of her breathing.

What is she doing to me?

Not even hatred can offer me comfort as she whimpers in her sleep. My stomach lurches, filling with the most unwelcome sense of anxiety. She's afraid. Not in the pleasurable way I want her to be—in actual fear.

I don't want her fearful of the world's monsters. I want her to fear *me*. The real monster. No one else has earned the right to haunt her nightmares. I deserve to be the object of her hatred and revulsion.

If she hates me, this feeling will stop.

I'll regain control.

But still… my body doesn't comply. Not even the slightest twitch of my finger. I'm left staring at the rise and fall of her chest, the scrunch of her dark-brown brows, each vulnerable whimper sliding past her lips.

The cracks are deepening.

I'm being dragged down.

It's several hours before the storm breaks, and clouds disperse enough for a weak beam of sunlight to break through the barred window. I distantly realise there've been no overnight checks from the guards—the situation downstairs must be disastrous.

The faint morning light makes the air sparkle through drizzling rain. I've watched her sleep for hours. Fingers clenching and unclenching around the knife. The morning dawn reveals my predicament. She could open her eyes at any moment and catch me. But doing what?

Watching her?

Or watching over her?

I may be obsessed with her, but in the sickest way possible, it's learned behaviour. I've been the subject of fascination before. If that's even the right word. Stitching the haphazard quilt of my identity back together when I escaped took years. She's going to rip those unhealed stitches apart with her bare hands.

My muscles protest as I finally move. I crawl onto the bed and hang over her, eyes tracing the edge of the towel barely being held in place. Her arms are curled up to her chest protectively, but her throat is exposed.

The moment my blade touches her skin, she inhales sharply. Ripley's eyes flutter open, revealing still bloodshot whites surrounding her greenish-brown irises. It takes a moment for recognition to filter in, her nostrils flaring with a panicked breath.

"I won't let you destroy me, Ripley."

Her throat bobs beneath the sharp kiss of steel. "Please—"

"Begging for your life won't change the outcome. I should've left you in that pool. It would've been simpler."

"Then why didn't you?"

"Human weakness. But I won't be weak anymore."

She blinks, her expanding pupils betraying well-kept secrets. "Is it weak to care?"

"It's weak to feel." I press the knife in deeper. "It's even weaker to want something."

A fat tear escapes the corner of her eye and rolls down her cheek. I watch its path down to her chin.

"Then get on with it. Kill me." Ripley sucks in another short breath.

"Why?"

"Because I hate you, and I hate myself for also wanting something more."

Thin dribbles of blood paint her neck. They coat the blade that could so easily end this for the both of us. All it would take is one swipe. An easy slash.

Her skin would cut like butter, and I could watch her choke on her own blood. My mouth moistens at the thought. I could own her final moments.

"You've fought so hard to survive." I frown in confusion.

She offers a bleak smile in return. "Maybe I'm tired of being the survivor. Look what it's cost me."

Blood speckling the sheets beneath her, Ripley wraps a hand around my arm. But she doesn't attempt to prise the pocketknife away. Her fingers glide over rigid lumps and gnarly scar tissue, tracing each individual scar like she wants to spend hours memorising the exact details.

"What did being the survivor cost you, Xander?"

I hold her life in my hands as I answer. "Everything."

"What would you do to get it all back?"

"Anything." The unexpected admission breaks free.

With the pocketknife still slicing into her neck, I lower my mouth to hers then slam our lips together. I don't care if it hurts. I don't care if she wants me to kiss her or not. I want to taste her fear and see if she's as terrified of this as I am.

Perhaps we're not so different after all. I'm holding her at knife point and taking exactly what I want, regardless of whether she wants to give it. In many ways, she's doing the exact same thing to me.

Hatred and desire collide hard enough to split the fucking atom.

I shove my tongue into her mouth with the necessary force to prise her lips apart. I don't know if she grants me access or simply accepts defeat, but her mouth opens up to me.

Teeth clinking, our kiss is a violent duel. I'm determined to find the answer to my inner turmoil. Even if it means tunnelling my way inside her soul to find those elusive secrets. I have to know why.

Why now?

Why here?

Why her?

Old Ripley was a pleasurable thrill. An intense fuck. Spanking her until she bruised satisfied me. Dragging my blade across her skin and smearing the resultant blood spill enthralled me. Holding her on the cusp of an orgasm made her irrevocably mine.

I broke her.

Claimed her.

Kept a piece of her soul as a souvenir.

Little did I know that she did the same thing to me. All this time, she's been waltzing around with a twisted part of me living and breathing depravity into her too. The girl I broke became the ruthless woman I created.

Perhaps I've broken her enough.

Perhaps now I should worship what I created.

My mouth rips from hers, nipping and sucking from her chin to her throat. Her tiny whimpers make my cock twitch as I slide the knife free and admire the uneven slash it leaves behind. All that glistening blood. Perfectly formed droplets of pleasure.

I lick the crimson beads up. Copper ripples across my tastebuds, far sweeter than any other nectar. Her essence is inside me now. I'll be able to find the control I'm looking for in the metallic tang of her blood.

"Xander," she pants. "I... we can't... Raine. I have to see him."

My temper burns white-hot. "He can wait. You were mine first."

"Please… No. I can't do this!"

Her fresh blood still slicked across my mouth, I grab the edges of her towel and rip them apart. Her now semi-dry panties and bra are revealed beneath the rough, hospital-grade cotton.

Ripley recoils and tries to hide herself, but I prevent her from covering up. She's hidden from me for long enough.

"I don't care what you want," I state fiercely. "I care what you need. What we both need."

Her eyes are gaping saucers. Not even I recognise the raw possession in my own voice. The sheer breadth of emotion and passion colouring each syllable instead of a thick coating of frost.

Blood smears over her collarbones and chest as I trace a path to her breasts. She's struggling to escape, still protesting like I believe a word she says. But as my bloodstained lips clamp around her left nipple, those protests morph into high-pitched moans.

I bite down, sucking the pert bud into my mouth. Hardness rolls between my lips and grazes against my teeth, each suck serving to heighten her arousal, evidenced by panting moans. I grab her right breast and squeeze, adding enough pressure to elicit just a hint of pain.

"Xander!" she mewls. "Please… stop."

Still massaging her breast, I release her now reddened nipple and skate lower still. My lips coast a path down to the apex of her thighs. She whines those pathetic little complaints all while lifting her hips to seek out what her body craves.

I kiss the soft curve of her belly before moving lower. Despite soaked cotton covering the desire she's so frantically trying to hide, I can smell the promise of her wet cunt. All mine. I bring the knife to the elastic holding her panties in place.

"Hold still. I wouldn't want to slip."

"No," she moans.

"No?" I tap her clit through the fabric.

Her hips buck, pushing her clit against my thumb again. She smashes her eyes shut while grinding against my hand. Always so needy. That much hasn't changed.

Sliding a finger beneath her panties, I push it between her awaiting, slick folds. Ripley cries out as I find her molten core and slip inside, burying my finger deep in her enticing heat.

"Still saying no, little toy?"

She clenches tight around the single digit, her pussy spasming in response to the intrusion. Unwanted or not, she's practically dripping on my hand, she's so wet. That's why I'll never believe the lies she tells herself.

"No," she repeats.

"Wetter than a bitch in heat," I observe plainly. "And still telling me no."

Stretching her with a second finger, I love watching her squirm. She wants to hate my touch so badly. Let's see if she feels the same way when my tongue is buried in her cunt instead.

Sliding the knife's edge across her public bone, I watch the gooseflesh that rises. My dick swells at the sight. Her writhing abruptly halts when she realises I have a knife so close to her most vulnerable place. Keeping one hand at her pussy, I twist the knife and begin to slice her panties free.

Elastic pings, then the fabric falls away, revealing her swollen nub. I easily sever the strap on the other side, still pushing two fingers in and out of her entrance. Her inner-thighs are already slick.

"Why does your body tell a different story?" I croon.

She gasps as I curl a finger inside her. "I... I... fuck! I hate you so much."

"If that's what you need to tell yourself, then go right ahead."

Pulling my fingers free, I suck them dry. Ripley stares down at me, wide-eyed and trembling. When I bury my face between her thighs, she immediately responds.

Hips bucking, her pussy opens for me so perfectly. I push my tongue inside and lap at her core, sucking up every drop of moisture she's fighting so hard to hide.

Stopping for a short breath, I turn my attention back to her clit as I insert my fingers inside her again. She moans at the pressure of my lips on her tight bundle of nerves.

Licking and teasing with the lightest graze of teeth, I steadily fuck her with my hand, reading her body like it's my favourite playbook. She's clenched around me and panting so loudly, I know she's close to climaxing.

"Does my little toy want to come?" I whisper against her clit.

Ripley huffs in response.

Such a stubborn brat.

Sucking her clit between my teeth, I apply enough pressure to take her to the edge. Then I cruelly rip my fingers from her cunt and sit back up. Her subsequent whine is music to my fucking ears.

"No!" she wails.

"No again, hmm?"

Only this time, she isn't protesting but mourning the loss of what I could give her. What she's too chicken shit to ask for. Smirking, I bring my hand down on her glistening cunt. Hard. The wet slap echoes around us.

"You have to ask for it," I command. "No. You have to *beg me* for it."

"Fuck you!"

I slap her wet pussy again. Ripley's back arches, her lips parting in the perfect O shape. I wonder if I could make her come from doing this alone. She's always had a masochistic need for punishment.

My jeans have become painfully restrictive. I want to strip

off and prowl over her so she can see all that she's denying herself. Contemplating the pocketknife, I flip it to hold the blade portion then raise the smooth handle to her lips.

"Suck."

"Go to hell," she seethes.

"Already there, sweetheart. Suck or I'll find another use for this knife."

Gulping hard, she opens wide to accept the slightly curved black handle. I move it in and out of her mouth, letting her saliva coat the surface. Strings of spit stretch from her lips when I pull it free.

"Now, I can't leave this greedy cunt empty. Can I?" Pinning her legs completely open, I run the lubricated handle over her folds. "Keep those legs open for me."

"Xander?" Her voice trembles.

"I told you how this works before, Rip. You're mine to do with as I please. That much hasn't changed."

I push the pocketknife inside her like any other sex toy. Even when I lift my hand from her thigh, she keeps her legs spreadeagled, exposing every last inch of herself to my perusal. Her pelvis must be aching.

"Perfectly safe," I murmur. "As long as you don't move a muscle."

She can't see it from her position, but the blade is a safe distance away. Her fear is delicious, though. I keep an eye on the blade impaling her as I stand and peel off my rain-crusted clothing. Her eyes drink in every pale inch that's revealed.

I've never had trouble baring myself. I'm not ashamed of my scars. Only the secrets behind them. From the feverish gleam in her eyes, she's as dedicated to unearthing them as I am to forgetting.

Standing over her, I wrap a hand around the hard length of my cock. That smart mouth remains clamped shut as I begin to pump my shaft, imagining the glistening heat that will soon be around it.

"Are you ready to tell the truth?"

Her locked jaw tightens.

"I see. We can play this game all day if that's what you desire."

Settling between her legs, I slowly slide the pocketknife from her cunt. It's glazed with her juices. Such a tantalising sight. I raise it back to her mouth then cock a brow expectantly.

"Clean up your mess. This is my favourite knife."

Her rosy lips remain tightly sealed.

"Ripley."

Still being a brat.

"Fine."

I keep the blade pinched but drag the razor-sharp tip across her lips as if I intend to carve her up. She quickly follows my command, letting her mouth open. I push the handle inside and watch her lick it clean.

"Good," I hum. "Not so hard to obey, is it?"

Once the knife's clean, I flip the blade to retake the handle. She can't suppress a terrified squeak when I suddenly stab it into her bed, mere centimetres from the side of her head. Her breaths are sharp and rapid.

"Give me attitude again, and I'll sink it into your heart instead."

Ripley gulps in response.

Perfect.

Kneeling between her legs, I have a great vantage point to study every trembling inch of her. Disfigured ink. Stitched wounds. Trails of dried blood. Odd fading bruises. Every imperfection is its own siren's call.

I don't want her perfect and unblemished. Some of us are brave enough to admit that we find beauty in the twisted and depraved instead. I only wish someone else hadn't touched what's mine to tarnish.

"Poor Ripley. So desperate for relief, yet so willing to deny herself too."

Her tattooed arms are limp at her sides. That won't do. I seize her wrists, above raw abrasions inflicted by zip ties and hand-carved letters, to pin her arms above her. My body knows where to go without needing a map.

Already, my cock is pressed up against her entrance. I nudge it inside a small amount before withdrawing and swirling the head around her moisture again. Each rotation causes her to thrust upwards, a silent beg for more.

"Please," she whines.

"Not until you say it."

"Say what?" Her temper explodes. "That you're a cruel bastard for making me want this?"

There she is.

My furious hellhound.

"No. Say that you want me, the man you claim to hate so fucking much, to fill this sweet cunt up to the brim."

Ripley hisses in frustration as I push inside her again, a tiny bit farther, then withdraw. Such exquisite torture. I'm feeling the pressure already, but I won't relent. Not until she does.

"I told you to beg me, Ripley. Do it now."

When she curses under her breath, I move one hand lower to press against her wounded wrist. The lash of pain soon loosens her tongue, but I squeeze hard for good measure.

"Please!" Ripley gasps.

"Yes?"

"Please… fuck me, Xander. I'm begging you to fuck me. I need you."

How odd it is to be needed.

Satisfied, I surge into her in one fast pump. She takes my full length, but it's a snug fit. Her yelp takes me back to the first night I forced her to beg. Oh, how she wailed when I finally let her fall apart.

I retreat fast then thrust back inside, not giving her even a moment to catch her breath. Watching her blood-streaked tits bounce with each movement is close to godliness. There's no better sight than her submission.

Each time my hips surge and I slam back into her, Ripley moans in such agonising ecstasy. The animalistic sounds burst free, unable to be suppressed for a second longer. She can no longer deny that she wants this.

Wants me. Wants us.

Do I want the same?

CHAPTER 23
RIPLEY

LOVE YOU BETTER – THE HAUNT

I'M NOT sure where my pleasure ends and my hatred for the man gifting it to me begins. All I know is that if he dares to stop right now, I'll surely lose my mind. Analysing what a mistake this is can come after he's fucked me senseless.

I'm restrained tightly by his iron-clad grip and can feel the protest of my wounded wrists. It hasn't entered Xander's awareness. Or perhaps it has, and he simply doesn't care enough to ease up. It's hard to tell with the iceman.

Right now, he isn't that man at all.

This creature is all fury and flames.

My body is nothing more to him than the scorched earth beneath his feet. He'll trample me underfoot to get what he wants. In this frenzied state, I'd probably thank him for it. I'm all sensation, blindly grasping for any opportunity for relief.

His midnight-blue eyes have descended into inky blackness. Each stroke he inflicts makes his jaw tense and wiry muscles spasm. He's built similarly to Raine, lean and agile, but still hiding significant strength. Strength that is marred by scars and pain.

I want to feel guilty. I want to stop this. Walk away. Never look back. Take my rightful place in Raine's hospital room.

But selfishness is a powerful motivator, and after what Lennox did, I need this.

I need the safety and control of surrendering to someone else. Someone evil. But I don't know if I can even call Xander that anymore. His icy nonchalance hides a far more horrifying reality that I've yet to unearth. I don't know who he really is.

The enemy?

The man who saved me?

Both paradoxes wrapped up in one?

Seizing the pain that's setting my mind alight, I focus on my throbbing wrists. It's a wonderful juxtaposition to the way my limbs are turning to mush.

Xander is slamming into me, his tempo inching ever higher. But his attention doesn't waver. After all these months, he's still studying me. Searching for whatever answers he's so willing to sacrifice everything for.

I know I antagonise him. His icy façade can't withstand whatever the fuck this twisted sickness burgeoning between us is. I don't understand it and wouldn't expect anyone else to either.

We're as toxic as all good tragedies are, and that only makes me want him more. Finally accepting that feels like a defeat. This man has brought nothing but grief and misery into my life, but in this moment, that doesn't change a thing.

I want Xander.

I want every emotion he has left.

I want to hurt him back.

Releasing one wrist, he moves his grip to my chin. His short fingernails dig into my skin as he drags my mouth to his. Our lips clash. There's no hesitation on my part this time. I want to bruise him just as badly.

Tongues meeting, his spearmint taste fills my mouth. I bite down on his bottom lip, luxuriating in the blood that wells up to meet me. A deep, satisfied groan rolls up from his throat as I suck the bloodied lip dry.

Taking that tiny bit of control back and hearing his reaction fires me up. I'm already a sweaty mess, clawing ever closer to the edge of a welcoming oblivion. He's tortured me enough. I want to spiral and explode now.

With my freed-up hand, I stroke over Xander's neatly-packed abdominals. The tight lines of muscle are visible beneath layers of scar tissue. Seeing those marks again only reignites the questions I'm too scared to ask.

Years have softened each light-pink laceration but failed to obscure them entirely. He must've been so young when he started cutting himself. Young enough for the marks to bear witness to all he's done to avoid feeling ever since.

My broken boy.

My twisted, damaged man.

"Eyes on me," he grinds out. "Now."

I drag my attention from his scars. Xander is glowering at me, unable to stand being ignored for even a second. Like somehow I could forget he's making it his mission to command my every thought.

Seemingly appeased, he lowers his face to my breasts. I cry out at the sudden onslaught of his lips. He lavishes each nipple, alternating between kissing, sucking and biting down hard enough to sting. Each sensation makes my nerve endings sizzle.

My legs clench around him, holding his waist in a vice. When he rolls one nipple between his fingers while sucking on the other, I feel an orgasm begging to take over. My nails dig deep into his mottled skin.

"Please," I beg for a release.

"I don't think so," he clips out.

When his lips disappear from my breast, the steely warmth of his cock within me vanishes. I hit a brick wall and ricochet, an unbearable pressure threatening to rip me apart. My orgasm is cruelly snatched away before I can gasp.

Xander holds himself over me, observing each iteration of

disappointment. I cry out in shock at the sudden loss, my thighs clenching tight around him, like I can force the clock to rewind and give me the release I need.

"No... Please!"

His grip on my chin loosens. "Hurting, little toy?"

"God-fucking-damn you, Xander!"

"That's more like it." His grin is full of sinister satisfaction. "You haven't begged enough."

Moving to grasp my hips with both hands, he roughly flips me over. I land back on the mattress in a faceful of bedsheets. Fingertips glide down my spine, tracing each curvature as another hand circles my hips and ass.

I brace for the hit I know is coming. His soft touches never last long. When the first spank cracks against my rear, it jolts my whole body. Pain flashes up my spine in time to the exploration of his fingertips.

"You still mark so exquisitely."

Fisting the bedsheets, I swallow a cry. It'll only satisfy the son of a bitch. If he isn't going to give me what I want, then I sure as fuck won't return the favour. He'll have to hit me until I bleed.

Xander strikes my other ass cheek, the force of his smack making my skin tighten and prickle. I can feel blood rushing to the area. My back arches, absorbing the force, still enduring the tease of his featherlight fingers.

Those dancing fingers traverse upwards to wind into my tangled hair. Though it's unkempt and matted from my brush with death, that doesn't stop Xander from fisting the coarse strands.

He wrenches hard, forcing my head to tilt up. I'm suspended, half-upright at a vulnerable angle, breasts jutting out and knees wobbling.

"Is this what you wanted?" He nudges back between my soaked thighs from behind. "Someone to fuck you like the object you desire to be?"

"I'm not your object," I gasp in delicious pain.

"I forgot. You're not mine." He yanks sharply on my curls. "You're Harrowdean's whore, right?"

Before I can snatch the knife from my bed and stick it in his fucking eyeball, he slides back into me. From this angle, his strokes are shallow and fast. A constant drilling that takes me right back to the brink.

I want to wail and rave. Batter my fists against his bare chest and throw him out of this room. But each stroke of his cock inside me silences whatever hatred I'm ready to spew. He owes me this much.

Xander pulls my hair with each pump, merging fierce pain with toe-curling pleasure until tears are pooling in my eyes. I'm too overwhelmed. Overstimulated from every angle. His other hand clasps my hip in a bruising grip.

When that grip slackens, I prepare for the next slap. It's a hard, fast strike against my right ass cheek. Bracing for it doesn't decrease the way my skin burns. With each spank, the fire spreads.

"Still pretending to hate me?" Xander groans.

"Yes!"

His pounding continues, relentless and battering. It's like he's trying to beat the truth out of me. The reason why I sacrificed their lives to get my revenge. He still doesn't get it.

"You... ruined... me," I pant.

"Oh, I know." His breathing is almost as laboured as mine. "And truthfully, I don't blame you for feeding us to the wolves. In fact, I was impressed."

"Why? I wanted you dead!"

"Exactly." His breath teases my ear as he pushes my hair aside. "Look at how formidable we made you."

When his teeth sink into the shell of my ear, I moan again, sparks flying with each sensation. It's all building to the grand finale, but I know he'll make me work for it. Nothing is easy with Xander.

"I hate the person you made me."

"Do you?" he grunts. "Because I find that hard to believe."

I'm climbing a steep cliff, dragging myself up inch by agonising inch. His cock worshipping me shoves me higher up that slope until I can see the tempting fall once more. The edge I need him to throw me off.

This is what he's reduced me to. A submissive, needy wreck, willing to sacrifice my integrity and secrets just to earn his surrender. Just when I thought I couldn't stoop any lower.

"You want the truth?" I grit out.

Xander drags his nails over my skin, leaving scratches behind. "Yes. Admit it."

"Admit that if it wasn't for you... I wouldn't be here at all." My legs quiver as my climax nears.

"More, little toy."

Releasing my hair, he abruptly pushes me down so I'm bent over with my ass high. I turn my head to the side to suck in ragged breaths as his thrusts deepen, finding an angle that pushes me past my breaking point.

"You made me ruthless. You made me cruel." I moan through another punishing spank against my sore ass. "You made me into a monster fit to walk beside you."

"Where." He pumps into me. "You." His cock jerks as I spasm around him. "Belong."

My muscles spasm with the force of my hard-won orgasm. After all the baiting, he finally yields. Xander's roar is a fucking triumph that makes me shatter. I steal his remaining control and plummet with it into the unknown.

My name rolls off his tongue like a lamentation. He's grieving the loss of whatever flimsy protections remained in place between us. The hate that once kept us apart now binds us together in a far more intimate way.

The iceman has finally thawed, and it feels so fucking good to relinquish the fight. That realisation makes my release even more intense. I feel my extremities turn to mulch as Xander pours himself into me.

His body becomes a dead weight above mine. At some point, he collapses next to me on the bed, and we end up entwined. Our limbs are a sweaty tangle as we both search for air, neither able to form a coherent word.

Don't do it, Ripley.

But the voice of reason can fuck off right now. I snuggle up against my enemy's chest and rest my head over his out of control heartbeat. At first, it's like embracing stone. Then a scarred arm curls around me. I feel his nose bury in my hair.

I'm where I belong.

Sleeping with the devil.

"What happens now?" I eventually break the silence.

His buried face doesn't lift from my hair.

"I have no fucking idea."

CHAPTER 24
RIPLEY

DROWNING. – EDEN PROJECT

MY PALMS ARE slippery with anxious sweat as I'm escorted into the medical wing by the on-duty nurse, Nina. This quiet corner hasn't been touched by the water damage that's causing carnage elsewhere in Harrowdean. Half the institute is flooded or trashed after the storm.

Cleanup was unfolding as I picked my way through the rubble earlier to get here—tree branches, waterlogged leaves and all manner of unnamed detritus coating every surface. Patients are being confined to the unaffected areas, but a quiet word with Langley, who was luckily working, allowed me to pass the guards' blockade.

"Is he awake?"

She holds open the door for me. "Yes. He's under observation."

"For how long?"

"Until his blood pressure stabilises. He was in a bad way last night."

Breathing deeply, I follow her to Raine's cubicle. The curtains are drawn. I have a moment to grapple my nerves, letting her walk ahead to pull back the thin blue fabric.

"Raine," she chirps. "Visitor for you."

Propped upright in the bed, Raine rests on several plumped-up pillows. His sandy-blonde locks are uncombed and pointing haphazardly in all directions, while a blanket covers his patterned hospital gown.

Those rich toffee eyes seem to gleam brighter when he breathes in, his lips quirking into a smile. I showered using his favourite body wash before coming. Seeing that grin makes my throat tighten.

His gaze swings around the cubicle. "Hey, Rip."

"Anyone could smell like papaya, you know."

"But no one could smell quite like you."

"I'm never going to be able to sneak up on you. Am I?"

"I wouldn't count on it. Besides, I don't see many other girls queuing up to sob at my bedside. Do you?"

"I don't know. I had to fight my way in here to get past your fans."

He swats a hand through the air. "Feel free to let them in. I'm bored as fuck laying here."

"Perhaps think of that next time, mister." Nina bustles around him, fiddling with his multiple IV lines and frowns at various machines monitoring his vitals. "Ain't nothing fun or interesting about drugs. You worried your girl here."

"Alright, Nina." Raine sighs tiredly like this isn't the first time she's scolded him. "Enough of the lecturing already. Isn't your shift over yet?"

"Behave. I'll be back." With an eye roll, she scurries from the cubicle.

Even with her gone, I can't bring myself to walk over to him. He looks so small and ashen in the hospital bed, an array of needles poking into his arms and the low, steady beep of a monitor measuring each heartbeat.

Part of me wonders if he'd be laying here had we never met. I know this isn't Raine's first rodeo. He's been playing this game for far longer than I know. But I thought things were under control. I thought he was being safe.

"Rip." He pats the bed. "Come here."

I shake my head before realising he can't see it. "I can't do that."

"I need to explain."

"Well, I don't need you to. This... It's my fault."

"Don't do that to yourself. Please."

"It's true. I never should've sold to you in the first place. If you'd gone through withdrawal and maybe gotten clean back then, none of this would've happened."

"Because I'd be dead," Raine deadpans.

"You don't know that."

He fiddles with a clear plastic tube wrapped around him. "I'm here because I was reckless. That's all."

My chest constricts. "Why'd you do it?"

"It was just a dumb mistake." He exhales loudly through his nose. "Something else must've been cut into the pills I took. I wasn't trying to overdose or do anything stupid."

"It was an accident? Really?"

"I swear, I didn't do this on purpose."

That loosens the pressure on my panic-strapped lungs a small amount. Outrage floods into me instead. I'm in no position to lecture or judge, not after what I've done, but it doesn't stop me from feeling hurt.

"Where did you get those pills? I know they weren't mine. You've been buying from someone else."

His lips pucker then twist. "It doesn't matter."

"No one else is supposed to be selling in here!" My voice raises. "So it does matter. They sold you a bad batch, and it almost killed you. I want a name."

Unseeing eyes gazing over my shoulder, he seems perfectly calm. Like swallowing God knows what chemicals and almost dying as a result is just an average weekday. I don't know whether to kiss him or kill him, I'm so furiously confused.

"Just leave it." He cringes in pain as he shifts his position. "I'm fine."

"Nothing about this is fine. You were blue, Raine! Fucking blue!"

Exhaustion is catching up to me after everything that's happened. Part of me wants to run far away from Harrowdean and all its complications. Three in particular.

Raine.

Xander.

Lennox.

Everything has been spiralling out of control since they arrived. Before then, I had a plan. Less than a year left and I could've walked away. Now I'm in deep waters.

"If you won't tell me who, then tell me why." I stop at the end of the bed. "Why not come to me?"

"Does it matter?" he sighs.

"Yes! I thought you trusted me!"

Raine scrubs a hand over his face and the roughened stubble on his chin. "Please just sit down, okay?"

Still trembling all over, I perch on the end of the bed. Raine moves his covered legs to make space for me. His head is tilted down, eyes unfocused on the hospital sheets.

"You said you're tired of being the bad guy."

I blink several times, certain I've misheard him before the memories of admitting that float back to me. I felt so broken in that moment, tired of being the source of so much pain.

"So?"

Raine shrugs. "I didn't want to be another thing for you to feel guilty about. I figured if I bought elsewhere, it might ease some of that burden."

"So you bought shit heroin from some random to spare my feelings?" I gape at him.

"Erm..." He fights a smile by biting his lip. "Something like that?"

All I can do is stare, stunned to speechlessness by this complicated, enigmatic man with so much damage wrapped up in his pure soul. He really is incredibly stupid but in the most thoughtful way.

"Turns out, you're the only good dealer in this place." He laughs at the irony. "I don't even want to know where those pills were from."

"I really, really want to punch you right now."

"I'm blind and bedridden, babe. That's foul play."

"You want to schedule in a better time for me to kick your ass?" I quip back. "I'll clear my diary."

"It's a date."

Brain still whirling, I'm trying to filter through possible options of who could be smuggling pills in from the outside. It's hard, but not impossible. Some patients have regular visitation.

Raine releases the tube wrapped in his fingers, tentatively stretching out his hand palm up. "So can you forgive me for... uh, almost dying?"

"No! You're so... so..." I slam my eyes shut to try to hold the tears at bay. "I can't do this again. I've lost everyone I have ever cared about."

"I know, Rip. I'm sorry."

The tears escape anyway, trickling down my cheeks with a harsh sting. "Just don't make me lose you too."

"You're not going to. I'm still here."

"For how long?"

"As long as you need me to be," he says confidently.

I open my watering eyes and snatch up his hand, needing the comfort. Our fingers thread together. We hold each other tight, neither of us speaking for a few moments before he chuckles under his breath.

"What?"

"Nothing," he mutters.

That goddamn smirk.

"Spit it out, Raine."

"Just wondering what happened to the whole no commitment thing?" He laughs. "You've changed your tune."

Wiping off my tears, I scoff. "It's complicated."

"No doubt. You know I don't care about labels either way." His playful tone turns serious. "It's nice to be needed by someone."

Chin tucked down, it almost like he's staring at the place where our hands are joined. This situationship is quickly turning into a clusterfuck with two very clear obstacles.

"I thought you'd be here when I woke up." He seems to read my mind. "Where were you last night?"

Shuddering, I hope he can't hear the way my breath catches. Stupidly optimistic, right? Raine immediately sits a little straighter and lifts his head to follow the sharp sound.

"Rip? What is it?"

"I... had a run in with Lennox," I say vaguely.

"A run in?" His brows knit.

"He thought those pills you took were mine and wouldn't listen to me." My voice wavers a little. "Things got physical."

"Jesus." His grasp on my hand tightens. "Are you okay? What did he do?"

Memories of inky rainwater swallowing me whole threaten to take over. I'm just glad he can't see the raw, scabbed-over marks that line my wrists. Nor the slice at my throat from the... well, aftermath.

"I'm alive. It was... uh, Xander bailed me out."

"Xander," he tests the word.

"Yeah. He found me."

"Where, exactly?"

I don't trust myself to speak. Not yet. Not when the memory of Xander is so fresh. So vivid in my mind. That near-death experience was petrifying, but what unfolded with him after scared me even more.

"Bailed you out of what?" he demands.

"It doesn't matter, Raine. Xander helped me."

"It *does* matter. Did Lennox hurt you?"

Gripping his fingers tight, I grimace. "Yes."

"That son of a bitch! I warned him. I told him to stay away!" He breathes heavily.

"If it wasn't for Xander…" I trail off.

"You know he has feelings for you."

Studying his face, there's no hint of anger or jealousy. Raine wears a look of weary acceptance, like he's known this all along. It's startling.

"He hates me," I correct him.

Fucking liar.

"You can want the very thing you hate," Raine states knowingly. "Sometimes, that makes you want it even more."

The unspoken question lingers between us. Since the moment we met, I've made my intentions clear to Raine. I want his friends dead. For a while, that included him too. Until I saw past his affiliations.

But everything is upside down now.

I've lost sight of why this all began.

"So… Xander." He keeps his voice light. "I guess things are complicated."

"This is such a mess. But I still need you in my life, Raine. I know I'm asking for a lot. You didn't sign up for this disaster."

"Not exactly low maintenance over here either, guava girl." He raises my hand to his lips so he can kiss my knuckles. "Besides, I quite like your mess."

"What if it isn't just my mess?"

He hesitates, nibbling on the inside of his cheek. "Then we figure it out."

"How?"

"I'm not willing to give this up because you have a psychopathic… Well, whatever Xander is. That's for him to figure out. But don't expect it to scare me off."

"Maybe it should," I reply jokingly.

"Maybe." Raine relaxes and sinks into the pillows. "But I clearly have no regard for self-preservation anyway."

"Clearly."

Giving a soft cough, I reach into the pocket of my sweats. "Got something for you."

"A hospital gift, huh? I must've been a good patient."

"Call it a loan."

Cupping the back of his hand, I place the folded sunglasses into his palm. They're not the same as his special, blacked-out lenses, but I know he misses the security blanket they provided.

He takes them and begins his inspection, tracing the curved glass lenses and wire arms to map out the shape. I watch him work.

"Sunglasses?" he guesses.

"From my personal collection. Aviators are unisex, right?"

"I've always wanted to look like a fighter pilot."

"Figured it's my fault your real ones got trashed. Will these do as a temporary fix?"

Unfolding the old sunglasses, he fumbles to slide them into place.

"Thank you." His blossoming grin is enough to make my heart flip. "They're perfect."

"Scoot over, would you?"

Shifting in the hospital bed, he shifts over to make a small sliver of space next to him. I crawl into the gap then burrow into his side, my head resting on his shoulder. Raine's head slumps to rest on top of mine.

I bathe in his warmth and citrusy, sea salt scent. Just feeling the steady weight of his body pressing into mine helps to alleviate the terror that's taken root since I found him passed out.

"So what happens now?"

"They've got me on methadone for when the withdrawals start," he murmurs. "But it's temporary. The doctor said I can either detox here or be sent back to rehab. They won't let me out without a plan."

I've never been able to quite pin him down, but I've long suspected that Doctor Hall is one of the good ones. Though few and far between, they're scattered throughout the staff. Anyone else would be releasing Raine without question.

I chew over this for a moment before whispering back. "Do you want to leave?"

"Of course not. If I'm gonna detox, I'll do it here."

"You'd put yourself through that? Detox?"

A short breath sighs out of him. "I've been fucked up for so long, I don't know any different. I'm scared to live any other way. But it's this or go back to square one in some other shit hole… alone again."

The thought of him detoxing alone in some hellish rehab facility hundreds of miles away makes me want to implode. He can't leave. But I also can't ask him to stay and put himself through this.

"Don't freak out on me, but it's different now." He seems to choose his words carefully. "Back then, I didn't have anyone to disappoint when I failed."

My chest warms with emotion. It feels so good to be wanted by someone. But it isn't long before fear slips back in, ever the silent assassin to hope.

"This place… It isn't good, Raine. If you want to get clean, I'll support your decision. But people don't get better in Harrowdean. You deserve the chance to give this a real shot."

"What are you saying?"

"That I don't trust these doctors to keep you safe. None of us are safe. Not here."

His head rubs against mine. "It's this or leave Harrowdean."

"I know."

"I'm not going back to rehab. It's never worked before.

But here, I don't know... Maybe I can clean my act up...
Ready to make a go of life again when I get out."

The giggle that bubbles up is totally inappropriate. "Raine
Starling talking about cleaning his act up."

His chest rumbles with a chuckle. "Shocking, I know.
Think the world ended in that storm."

"Mine almost did," I croak.

We both sober, still huddled together in the tiny hospital
bed. His breathing is evening out, in time to the drip of the IV
feeding into him. I continue to breathe in his clinical hospital
scent, savouring those faint notes of summer and seaside.

"Stay?" Raine whispers. "I'm gonna be in for a while yet."

"Rest. I'll be right here."

Within seconds, the light snores coming from his mouth
tell me he's fast asleep. Nina returns to check his vitals again,
grumbling about our sleeping arrangement before she
vanishes.

Listening to the rhythmic beeping of the heart rate
monitor, my eyes slide shut. I'm drowsing on the edge of sleep
when someone thumps into the cubicle. There's a startled
inhale followed by a deep growl.

"You."

Recognising his sonorous bark, my eyes fly open. Lennox
stands near the curtain, his chocolate-brown hair tousled and
face a lurid shade of red. I quickly slide out from Raine's
embrace, my eyes locked on him.

"Come to finish the job?" I goad.

"I should've done it myself in the first place instead of
messing around," he spits furiously. "How did you get out?"

"That's the thing about cockroaches, Nox. We always
survive."

Stepping forward, Lennox moves towards me. I stand but
hover a hand over Raine's shoulder to shake him if needed.

"You want me to wake him up so he can hear you
apologise for trying to drown me?"

"I wasn't going to apologise." He stops and crosses his arms. "Raine told me about the pills. Someone else is supplying him."

"You believe me now? Awesome. Thanks for taking my word for it before trying to drown me alive."

"Because your track record is so spotless," he gibes, palming the back of his neck. "Are we going to stand around talking about our feelings, or do you want in?"

"On... what?"

His mouth hooks up at the corner. "I got the name of his dealer."

"Well don't hold me in suspense."

That hint of a smile disappears. "I'll tell you when I have your word that you'll cut Raine off. Stay the fuck away from him. Don't even look at him. You're never going to sell him another pill."

"I told you what they do to nuisances in this place." Tampering my immediate desire to hurl abuse and threats, I summon a sense of calm. "You really think he should detox under Harrowdean's supervision?"

"No, but I don't want to see my friend half-dead again!"

"That's exactly what he'll be if management decides to intervene."

"What's the alternative, huh? Let him kill himself?"

A snore emanates from the bed, prompting us to lower our voices. Lennox spares Raine a glance, my gut twisting when his gaze briefly softens. His protection isn't love. It's control.

"And what about the day he crosses you?" I rebuke. "What about when he displeases you? Will you be the one to throw him in a pool then?"

"I would never hurt Raine."

"You don't know how to do anything but hurt people."

Any hint of softness dissipates the moment I finish my sentence. "Move away from him. You're done."

"I have every right to be here. You're the one who isn't welcome."

"Like I give a fuck where I'm welcome." Lennox scoffs. "I go where I'm needed."

The curtain twitches, silently parting to add another complication. Xander's in a fresh pair of jeans and his usual smart polo shirt, though his hair is still slightly damp. He halts to look between us both.

"I see I'm interrupting."

"Ripley is just leaving," Lennox chides.

"You think I'd leave Raine with you when he's vulnerable?" I laugh at him. "He'll find himself zip tied and underwater the moment he steps a foot out of line."

"That little dunking was just a taster—"

"No," Xander interrupts.

Lennox swivels to stare at his best friend, mouth hanging open slightly. Seeing him gawp in shock is so fucking satisfying.

"Stay away from Ripley," Xander orders unequivocally.

"Xan?" Lennox scowls. "She… What? You know what she's done."

"I know." His voice is ice-cool.

"What the fuck, man?"

"You didn't hear me? Stay away from Ripley."

Lennox looks between us several times. It's almost comical. He's stubborn as a mule but not stupid. Xander's jaw muscles clench, his almost-black eyes glittering like a knife's edge.

"You've spent every single day plotting how to get rid of her." Lennox steps into his friend's space.

"Yes." Xander's voice drips with disdain. "Far cleaner methods than leaving a dead body floating in a pool. That was sloppy, Nox."

"You… helped her escape?"

"I did. She isn't your problem to eliminate."

"Then whose problem is she?" Lennox chuffs

incredulously. "Fuck, Xan. Has the bitch made you go fucking soft? Are you deluded enough to think she's *yours*?"

His deliberately impassive expression not wavering, Xander seizes a handful of Lennox's shirt. He drags him close enough for their noses to touch.

"No, she isn't mine. Ripley belongs to herself. But dare to even look at her for another goddamn second, and I'll have your tongue."

"Who the hell are you?" Lennox seethes, his voice rising. "We only have each other, Xan! She's trying to tear our family apart!"

"What family?" Xander claps back.

"How can you even say that to me?"

A third voice interrupts their fight.

"What on earth is going on in here?"

Nina storms into the cubicle with her clipboard in hand. She takes one look at the three of us then jabs her finger towards the door.

"This is a hospital, not a boxing ring!" she adds.

Xander releases Lennox's shirt and steps back. "He was just leaving."

"I want you all out. Right now." She points towards the curtain's opening.

Brushing his wrinkled shirt, Lennox spares a final look at Raine's hospital bed. He escapes the cubicle without another uttered word then vanishes. I suck in a breath, but I still don't look at Xander.

Truthfully, I don't trust him enough not to stop me from what I have to do next. My plan was faulty all along. It isn't enough to break their family. I know Lennox has lost everything before. Ripping his world apart will take far more finesse.

Killing him won't cut it.

I'll feed him to Harrowdean's monsters instead.

CHAPTER 25
RIPLEY

PLAY DEAD (JUST FOR TONIGHT)
– THE MESSENGER BIRDS

WALKING SLOWLY with my arms clasped loosely around my waist, I hold the bulge of contraband inside my sweatpants. With my usual, oversized t-shirt on top, the large bag of pills is well-concealed anyway. I'm just on edge and paranoid.

It's taken me months to build up Noah's stash. Sneaking small quantities from batches here and there, I've had to carefully count each pill, ensuring the plan will work. He's still sure about the desired outcome, and despite the way it makes me internally flinch, I won't let him down.

He's made his choice.

I'm just a means to an end.

Detaching from the reality of my actions has gotten me this far in life. What's one more scratch on the scorecard? No one ever likes to admit that in order to get what we want, or even protect the ones we love, there's always a price to be paid.

I wonder if that's what Lennox told himself before he entered Holly's bedroom that night. Was she simply just another scratch on his scorecard? A price he was willing to pay? I guess that's all we ever are to each other in the end. Pawns to be manipulated and wiped out of the game.

This is my best move.

I'm removing Lennox from the chess board.

The loading bay is deserted. No one else knows it, but the CCTV cameras are always kept on a loop here. Maintaining pretences for the sake of posterity. If anyone was ever to check the feed, they'd see old footage peppered in to reflect normal comings and goings.

But I'm not here to meet Elon today. Instead, I hop down from the dock then head for the collection of wooden pallets clustered in the far corner. Tucked behind them is a small gap in the dock's concrete base. I noticed it while ignoring Elon's scowl during one of our exchanges.

The collection of pills weigh heavy in my hand as I stash them in the gap. After locating a discarded brick to wedge in front of it, they're completely concealed.

I don't know how long it'll be before he can retrieve his pharmaceutical payment, and I can't be caught delivering the drugs. When Noah attacks Lennox, it has to look like any other fight. No one can know I've bribed him to do it.

Brushing my hands off, I quickly glance around before slipping away. The walk back to the quad is quiet. It's been a few days since the flood, but normal business hasn't resumed. The manor itself is suffering from the acquired damage, and we've even had intermittent power outages.

Hired help bustle about the destroyed grounds, loading trucks with broken trees and smashed picnic tables. Several of the institute's stained glass windows have been boarded over, awaiting repair.

The destruction seems to have awakened something wild in the patient population. Violence has been erupting constantly between patients and guards. But now, I see two people creating faux snow angels in the still-wet mud. Their clothing is slowly turning brown, the thick mud covering their hair and faces.

It's a welcome reprieve.

I can't look away from their bright smiles. The sound of laughter sinks into me and thaws something. Even somewhere like this, there's still joy to be found. What I wouldn't give to find some joy of my own.

"Seriously?" a familiar voice gripes. "Come on, guys. Not cool."

The two patients ignore Langley's approach. He stops at the edge of the quagmire and braces his hands on his hips. His round baby blues are filled with aggravation as he contemplates what to do with them.

"You ever consider a career change?" I call out.

His head snaps in my direction. "Got any suggestions?"

"I went to school with this guy, a real entrepreneur type. He used to buy these knock off t-shirts online then sell them for a profit. Last I heard, he's living in a townhouse in Surrey now."

"By selling dodgy t-shirts?"

"Nah. Pretty sure he's a drug dealer now."

With an eye roll, he briefly looks back at the two troublesome patients before crossing the few short steps to join me. I dodge a puddle to meet him in the middle.

"How is Raine today?"

"Still laid up." I shrug absently.

My anxiety for Raine couldn't be more acute. The medical team has kept him in for monitoring. He's on a controlled regimen of drugs and fluids to give him the best shot at making this work.

Each morning that I return to see him, I'm convinced it'll be the day I find his bed empty. I don't trust Harrowdean to do something good for once. They prefer their patients dependent in every sense.

When management hears about his situation, I don't know what they'll do. With the chaos of the storm and subsequent cleanup, no one seems to have realised they have a surplus patient who's ripe for the taking yet.

"Listen, Rip." Langley lowers his voice. "I know you're worried about Raine. Maybe I can help, but it'll require your cooperation."

I blink up at him. "Cooperation?"

"People are paying attention now. Things are changing."

"What are you saying?"

His eyes dart around, checking that we're not being overheard. "Cooperating is your best chance to get him out of here unharmed. You have inside knowledge. We can use that."

My feet inch backwards. "We?"

Langley grabs my shoulder to stop me from leaving. I flinch, my hackles immediately rising.

"All it would take is one phone call, Rip." His voice is low and urgent.

"Take your hands off me. You're not making any sense."

In my periphery, I see Noah's gangly height step into the quad. He glances around, catching sight of me then nodding once. We're on a strict schedule to make this work. I don't have time for riddles.

"We can offer you protection," Langley explains hastily. "But we need your help."

"Who are you talking about?" A hint of suspicion sneaks in. "Wait… Who do you really work for?"

"Just think about it." Releasing my shoulder, he captures my hand and presses something into it. Langley stares into my eyes for a prolonged second before taking off to deal with the mud-soaked patients.

I slowly look down at the glossy business card he's passed me with a single contact number on it. The organ trapped behind my breastbone does somersaults.

Hunter Rodriguez.
Director of Sabre Security.

Quickly shoving it into my bra before anyone can spot what we've just exchanged, I barely have a second to reel in my shock before Noah jogs over to me.

"Classes let out in a couple minutes."

I shake my head from side to side, trying to focus. "Right. The plan."

"You with me, Rip?"

"Yeah, of course. Payment has been stashed."

"Sure this shit can't be traced back to you?" He scans my facial expression.

My heart is pounding so hard, it feels like it could shatter my ribcage into tiny flakes. Why the hell do those people want to talk to me? Aren't they the same investigators who want my head on a stake? Bancroft warned me what would happen if Harrowdean falls.

I'm culpable too.

I can't trust anyone.

"Ripley!" Noah nudges me. "It's now or never. Are we good?"

"Y-Yes." I rub my eyes.

"So? The pills?"

"There's… uh, someone else pushing product. I put your shit in one of their plastic money bags. Leave it in sight, and it'll lead right back to them."

"Okay." He blows out a heavy breath. "I guess this is it."

Indecision tears at my psyche as I wrestle with the sudden urge to call the whole thing off. I want Lennox gone, but that phone number and all it represents has thrown everything into disarray.

Someone out there wants to help.

Will they still want to if I do this?

Before I can utter a word, Noah tugs me into a hard, fast

hug that makes my teeth clack together. I squeak in shock. He quickly releases me then steps away with a small, sad smile.

"Watch your back, Rip." His eyes shine with a weird look of resolution. "You deserve a life outside this place. I hope you find it."

"Noah, wait…"

He's already striding towards the door that attaches to the south wing where classes are about to finish. It wasn't hard to pin down Lennox's routine. Whenever he's done with the maths class he got roped into attending, he always needs to step outside. I suspect it's a habit leftover from his smoking days.

Noah props himself against the brick wall. Right on time, the door bursts open, and patients flood outside. The corridors are being cleaned and repaired after the flood, so there's more footfall heading outside than usual.

Panic takes hold as I scan the crowd, recognising a few familiar faces. The invisible hand at my lungs tightens its grip as I spot his pile of chocolate-brown hair. Lennox's bulky height towers over everyone else.

He's stony-faced as usual in his standard white t-shirt and fitted sweatpants. Walking with big strides, he escapes the throng to stand in the middle of the lawn. The puddles don't seem to bother him.

I watch in morbid fascination as he tilts his head upwards and sighs heavily. His toned shoulders are drooping, reflecting the slump of his posture.

Lennox looks defeated.

Abandoned like the rest of us.

So why doesn't that satisfy me?

Pushing off from the wall, Noah squares his shoulders. I'm carried forward several steps to intercept him before the devil on my shoulder wins out. He's choosing this. I'm just a facilitator. This is the price of war.

If I tell myself that enough times, perhaps I'll be able to

sleep at night. But excuses haven't eased the guilt that haunts my nightmares from every other incident I've justified this way. And deep down, I know it won't now.

Noah approaches him then shoves his shoulder. Seeing him facing off against Lennox and his poundage brings home the reality of what I've arranged. Noah's going to get himself killed—by Lennox's rage or the drugs I'm paying him with to provoke it.

If I do this, I'm no better than the monster I've condemned. Lennox hurts people to further his own gains. This right here is me doing exactly the same thing to get what I want.

Holly wouldn't be proud of this. She'd be fucking ashamed. This is wrong. Revenge isn't worth this price. I've been caught up in this twisted game for so long, I've lost my humanity along the way.

It isn't too late.

You can stop this.

As Lennox whirls around and begins to shout, I move. Noah's too far away for me to make out what he's saying, but it doesn't take much to provoke Lennox. Especially since I gave Noah a few pointers. He knows all the pressure points to hit.

Having dragged the patients out of their muddy playground, Langley is occupied by escorting them inside. He hasn't noticed the disaster about to unfold. I have no backup to break apart the impending brawl I've instigated.

Noah shoves Lennox again, hollering something in his face. I watch Lennox slowly turn red, grabbing Noah's shirt and wrenching him forward so fast, he stumbles. His face sails straight into Lennox's fist.

"No!" I screech.

Spitting out a mouthful of blood, Noah laughs as he says something else to Lennox. My yelling doesn't stop the next punch from flying. Only this time, Noah hits back, causing Lennox's head to snap to the side.

Several patients have gathered to watch. I slam into someone's shoulder, desperate to reach Noah and drag him away from Lennox's onslaught. He's still baiting him despite the blood smeared around his mouth.

"Right this way, ladies and gentlemen." A voice rings out across the quad as several pairs of footsteps echo behind me. "You know, we were so delighted to be contacted for this interview opportunity."

Bancroft's gloating is unmistakable. I'd recognise his smug, regal tenor even in a pitch-black room. The old man speaks like we're living in a period drama.

"As you can see, we're pouring every resource into the cleanup effort this week. Here at Harrowdean, we care for our patients."

Horrified, I look over my shoulder. Bancroft is here, with Davis and several guards in tow, Elon included. There's also a leggy blonde with three cameramen. Her bright pantsuit screams journalist.

She points a microphone towards him. "We're here to talk about the investigation."

"There's plenty more for me to show you!" Bancroft quickly deflects. "We have lots of exciting initiatives here."

"Sir, would you care to respond to recent rumours of medical malpractice and violence in your institutes?"

"Violence?" Bancroft shakes his head, a charming smile in place. "No, never. This is a place of healing. We're helping to rehabilitate those in need."

There's a series of bellows before the shouting catches their attention. Surrounded by a gaggle of onlookers, Lennox has Noah on his back, two hands wrapped around his throat as he slams him repeatedly into the ground.

The blonde reporter perks up, instructing her cameramen to begin recording. Bancroft's smile morphs into a look of outrage. To add insult to injury, patients have started cheering the pair on, each body slam eliciting another excited roar.

"You seem to have a security issue," the reporter comments.

Bancroft's enraged gaze bounces over me, his eyes narrowing as he takes in the fracas. I'm running before I can hear whatever crap he's going to spew next. Lennox is going to break Noah's spine on national fucking television at this rate.

This was a mistake.

I've crossed a line.

I should turn around and disappear before I'm incriminated too, but I have to stop this before it's too late. Throwing myself into the mix is probably the stupidest thing I've ever done.

Yet the weight of that damned business card burns against my skin. There's still a world out there, watching this unfold from the outside. A world that would be disgusted by me.

I'm disgusted by me.

"Get out of the way!" I barge past leering onlookers. "Move!"

Close enough to the fight, I can see that Noah's limp but conscious, laying crumpled on the ground. He's given a good defence—Lennox has a split eyebrow that's spilling blood down his face, and his nose is gushing like a waterfall.

"Stop!" I shriek at Lennox.

He glowers over his shoulder at me. "You again. Come to watch the show?"

"Leave him alone, Nox. This was all a mistake."

"Mistake?" Lennox swipes blood from his eyeline. "Did you set this up, huh? Is this some kind of game?"

"Just get away from him!"

"The son of a bitch started it."

Launching myself at Lennox before he can resume pounding Noah into a pulp, I land on his back. My legs cinch around him as I squeeze his neck, attempting to throw him off balance.

He hisses a curse and easily tosses me into the air, causing me to slam to the ground. My bones creak in protest at the hard landing. Teeth gritted, I roll onto my knees and crawl my way back to them.

Lennox and Noah are grappling again, a sea of angry voices spurring them on. But it's the fear in Noah's eyes that hits me like a tonne of bricks. So I throw myself at Lennox again.

This time, he hits the ground from our collision. We twist and roll, sliding through a wet mudslide caused by the flooding. I get in a decent hit before he starts to choke me.

"You have ruined everything," Lennox growls. "Taking my sanity wasn't enough, was it? You had to take my family from me too."

I buck up and down, attempting to throw him off. There's a blur of movement before something crashes into him. Lennox is torn from my body, now tangled up in Noah's long limbs.

Noah's caught him off guard and regained the upper hand. The pair resume beating each other to death as I try to gain enough purchase to intervene.

"Break it up!" Elon's voice booms.

Several guards swarm all at once. Two are holding the reporter and her cameras far back, the combined brawn of Bancroft's remaining men circling the three of us.

When Elon raises his baton, I quickly lift my hands in surrender. He spins around, turning his attention to the two brawling men.

"Enough! Stop!" he bellows.

Noah doesn't seem to get the message. He makes it on top of Lennox, slamming a bloody fist into his jaw. Two guards have to seize his arms to drag him off, but he keeps struggling.

When he manages to punch one of them, a black taser is pulled free.

"Stop!" I shout frantically.

The taser connects with Noah's midsection first. He jerks midair, his knees crumpling as he lands on the muddy lawn with a grunt.

Elon spins to yell at his subordinate. "Stand down! We have reporters here."

I recognise the asshole he's admonishing. It's Kieran, the same one who hit me and groped Taylor without a care in the world.

The red-faced brute completely disregards Elon's order. Kieran hits Noah with the taser again, this time directly in the chest. I watch in horror as his limbs convulse and spit trickles from the corners of his mouth. Teeth bared, Kieran targets him for several painstaking seconds.

Hands clutching his chest, Noah struggles to stand back up before falling backwards onto the ground again. He's bug-eyed and breathless. That's when a vague memory of him mentioning his weak heart slams into me.

"Noah!" I screech.

Elon reprimands Kieran as onlooking patients begin to scream. Eventually, two other guards have to drag Kieran backwards, the taser torn from his hands. In all the commotion, it falls to the ground.

"What are you thinking?" Elon clamours.

"Insubordination, sir!" Kieran splutters, shoving off his co-workers.

Still cowering on the ground, I watch Elon fling his arms around, gesturing wildly in anger. I've never seen him so enraged before.

"He was down!"

"Patient was out of control," Kieran insists.

"You damn knucklehead. We're being filmed!"

Between their arguing and the patients crowded around in

every direction, no one is paying attention to Noah. He's clawing at his chest like an elephant is sitting on it, a hiss coming from his throat.

"Hey!" I fume at the bickering guards. "Help him!"

When I try to move closer, Elon reacts. I'm shoved down and pinned with a foot in the centre of my back. My lungs heave, compressed against the wet ground by his bodyweight.

Any sounds I was able to make dry up. Lennox is slumped over while Elon shouts at his men, gesturing around at the chaos. Still, no one pays any attention to Noah. His grip on his chest slackens, and he eventually goes limp.

"You think a good time to get that out is in front of a film crew?" Elon rages on. "You're supposed to be discreet!"

When Kieran spots Noah's limp form, the red flush on his face pales. "Uh, sir?"

"I don't want to hear another word from you!"

"Sir, the patient…"

All eyes finally turn to Noah. Through the sheen of tears bubbling in my eyes, I can see he's now still and lifeless. Elon growls a curse, his foot lifting from my back. He quickly kneels down beside Noah to check his pulse.

"Dammit," he mutters. "Radio the medical wing for support."

I drag myself upright as Elon begins to deliver chest compressions. The other guards are trying to herd patients away from the show, but there's resistance. Everyone wants to see the drama.

Determination fuelling my sore body, I claw my way through gelatinous mud. Noah isn't breathing, curled up at an awkward angle on his side, head twisted and legs splayed. Horror is pouring into me in a relentless wave.

"Come on," I plead.

The panic around us is intensifying. All noise fades into the background as I wait for Noah to take a breath. Elon's grunting with each deep compression, his subordinates anxiously watching.

"Get them out of here," he barks over his shoulder.

All eyes turn to us.

"No!" I protest.

Shuffling away from the armed guards approaching, I'm split between watching them and Noah's still-lifeless pile on the ground. Sweat drips from Elon's face as he continues to administer CPR.

Desperately searching around, my gaze lands on the taser that was dropped in the hubbub. Kieran attempts to block my lunge, trying to retake his weapon, but I slide across the lawn to reach it first.

My hand grasps the black and yellow handle. Kieran stands over me, trying to snatch it from my hands. Teeth bared, I slam it into his cargo-clad thigh and deploy a shock.

"Shit!" he squalls.

Seeing him jerk and thrash before hitting the ground only spurs me on. The other guards react in shock, cursing and trying to reach their colleague. I'm about to hit him again when someone hoists me up from behind, prising the taser from my hands.

"Miss Bennet. Causing trouble yet again."

The warden himself has appeared to grab hold of me, eyeing my dousing of mud with distaste. I struggle, attempting to lash out at him. He swiftly hands me off to his guards.

"Control her!"

I turn feral. Kicking, screaming, throwing out every insult under the sun. Noah still isn't moving. Elon stops trying to resuscitate him to check his pulse again. Sweat dripping down his temples, he swears quietly and resumes compressions.

Kieran is still flopped across the ground, twitching all over as a fellow guard tries to help him sit up. He's keeping a keen eye on Noah.

"Elon?" Davis asks.

He pauses briefly to recheck Noah's pulse. "Nothing, sir."

"Keep going. We have eyes on us."

In the distance, I can hear Bancroft's best imitation of a politician's voice, trying to distract the journalist and her team. They're trapped behind a wall of muscle holding them out of sight.

When the medical team arrives, Elon steps aside, Doctor Hall and his team quickly surrounding Noah to intervene. I get one last look before he vanishes behind them.

His mouth is hanging open, but it's his bloodshot eyes that drag me into a living nightmare. Wide but empty. There's no brimming sadness anymore.

Lifeless.

Gone.

Joining his men in a huddle, Elon looks contrite as Davis turns his hard stare on them all.

"How on earth did this happen?"

Elon wipes sweat from his brow. "Just... a little hiccup, sir."

"A hiccup?" I howl like a banshee. "He's fucking dead!"

"Shut it, Ripley." Elon flashes me a grimace.

"Or what? Are you going to kill me too?"

"Don't tempt me!"

Davis casts a disbelieving look around the scene we've created. "Clean this shit up. The cameras can't see."

His callous tone pushes me to my breaking point. I stomp down on the foot of the guard still holding me then elbow him sharply in the gut. There's a satisfying grunt before the arms banded around me slacken.

I take advantage of the opening and lunge forward. Davis can't duck in time to avoid me. I clutch him by his suit jacket, determined to inflict any amount of damage. But he looks more disgruntled by the mud I'm covering him in than anything else.

"He killed Noah!"

"Enough," Davis replies tersely.

"No! It's not!"

"This is the final straw, Miss Bennet."

Rage consumes me like flesh-eating bacteria finding a tasty new host. I don't care. He can do what he wants. Playing their game hasn't saved me, it's damned me. Along with everyone I've thrown into the line of fire along the way.

"You know what?" I lose all sense of self-preservation as I rant in his face. "The world is going to know what happened here. What's *been* happening here. I'll make sure of it."

"Is that so?" Davis smiles snootily.

"You think I'm scared?"

"Perhaps you should be."

"Well I'm not!"

He dismisses me with a head shake. "Take her away."

Releasing him, I try to duck from the unknown hands attempting to grab me once more, but my wrists are yanked backwards then swiftly cuffed in place. Davis watches on, a seed of a smile playing on his lips.

"Consequences, Miss Bennet." He leans in to gloat. "You've run that loud mouth of yours for the last time. There will be no one to listen where you're going."

I won't let him see even a crack of fear. He'd enjoy the satisfaction far too much. Keeping my head held high, I hold eye contact. Davis clicks his tongue in disappointment.

"Foolish child."

"What about this one?" Elon calls.

Looking away from me, Davis turns his attention to Lennox. He's now been forced to his knees, trails of blood still tracking down his face. Elon forcibly twists his arms behind his back to restrain him.

"Mr Nash." Davis sighs in a distinctly disappointed way. "I should've known when I signed your transfer papers that you'd be nothing but trouble."

Lennox curls his lip in disgust. "You're running a sinking ship, Warden."

"Then I'd better start plugging those holes, hadn't I?" Davis gestures between us. "Take them both down."

"Where?" Elon asks with a slowly blossoming grin.

I can feel the thud of the final nail being hammered into my coffin. It isn't audible, though. The sound boomerangs around in my mind, bouncing from each dark corner, collecting every last scrap of evidence to doom me to this fate.

"There's a cell in the Z wing with their names on it."

CHAPTER 26
LENNOX
ADHD – TWO FEET

THUD. *Thud. Thud.*

The metallic banging repeats on an endless loop. It feels like someone is chipping away at my brain with a jackhammer. Grimacing, I reach for my pillow to hide beneath it. I don't even want to know what Xander's doing to make that horrific noise.

Thud. Thud. Thud.

When I search for my pillow, all I find is cold cement. The aches and pains in my body soon flare to life with that realisation. It feels like I've been violently fucked by a bulldozer. More solid concrete lies beneath me, leaching any remaining warmth from my bones.

Thud. Thud. Thud.

"Don't leave me in here with him!"

I have no desire to peel open my eyes to verify if this is some fucked up, lucid dream or not. I'm no stranger to nightmares, but would my brain be cruel enough to lock me up with that bitch? I'm not that masochistic.

"The feeling's mutual," I mumble groggily.

My muscles relax when her ceaseless banging on the door stops. Colourful cursing precedes the sound of footsteps. I'm unprepared to be kicked in the shin so hard, it makes me grunt. My eyes slam open, and bright lights sears my eyeballs.

"And here I was, hoping you were dead," Ripley complains.

Squinting through my hazy vision, I can make out her silhouette. She's looming over me, handcuffed wrists curled up to her chest, two furious mossy-brown eyes watching me with revulsion.

Definitely real.

Fucking perfect.

We're in what appears to be a hybrid cell. The floor is made of pocked concrete, boasting too many dark stains that don't bear thinking about, while the walls are lined with scratched, padded material.

Artificial light emanates from a panel built into the ceiling with several air events. This place is ancient. Every surface is scarred and dirty, unlike Priory Lane's more modern facilities.

By contrast, Harrowdean's Z wing feels like a final frontier for the doomed. Not even Incendia can be bothered to maintain this place. I'm sure far too many have died here for them to ever get it clean again.

"What happened?"

Ripley rubs a spot between her brows. "You don't remember them drugging us?"

"Clearly not." I wrestle myself up to rest against the padded wall. "How long have you been making a racket?"

"A while." She shrugs. "You were out cold."

Watching her shuffle to the other side of the cell and sink down against the wall, I try to sort through my fuzzy memories. It's all a blur after some dickhead restrained me.

A quick search of my neck reveals a swollen bump from being needle stabbed. Ripley does her best to ignore me as I silently take stock of my injuries.

Her stupid friend put up a good fight for such a skinny bastard. He sure was determined to get his ass beat. Idiot that

I am, I just had to take the bait. Now he's likely dead, and I'm stuck here.

"Was this part of your plan?"

"Winding up in here with you?" Ripley snorts acerbically. "Far from it."

"Either way, it was a pretty stupid plan."

"Almost as genius as drowning someone in an abandoned pool? That sure looked accidental and non-suspicious. You really covered your tracks there, Nox."

Head crashing against the wall, I let my gritty eyes sink shut again. "You have a point."

"Please don't agree with me. It's unnerving."

The last thing I anticipate doing is laughing. But still, the chuckle spills out of me. All these months of threats and counter moves, just for us both to end up buried in an inescapable hellscape. Together. Life's irony really is a son of a bitch.

"Not much need for pretences in here, is there?" I sigh.

"I guess not." She examines her arm, the carved letters pink and shiny with new scar tissue. "Do you think Noah's alive?"

"It sure didn't look good."

I don't have the energy to get up and hammer on the door, but even if I did, it would be a mistake. I made that mistake last time I woke up in a cell. Pissing off the overlords only worsened the next visit they paid.

It took several rounds of near-death beatings to get the message. Resistance is a deadly temptation. You don't survive the Z wing that way. The clinicians and guards only see that as a challenge.

They'll work harder to break your spirit just to grind out any speck of defiance to their regime. The trick is to switch off... To pain. To humiliation. To loss. Everything.

"Fuck."

I crack open an eye. "What?"

Ripley hides her mud-streaked face in her hands. "Fuck!"

"Can you have a mental breakdown quietly?"

"This isn't a game, Nox. Raine is upstairs all alone right now. I haven't seen Xander either. Who is going to keep Raine safe?"

"Maybe you should've thought of that before setting me up!"

Yanking on her cuffs, she tries unsuccessfully to break the chains several times. Even going as far as to wedge her foot between the two halves and attempt to break them apart that way. It's entertaining to watch her struggle.

Ripley winces at the sight of blood oozing down her tattooed arms. Her wrists are a raw mess, still healing from our last altercation. The cuffs are digging deep into the scabbed-over wounds.

"Goddammit," she hisses. "You know what? You're right. I shouldn't have set you up. I'm not a piece of shit like you."

"Debatable. What was the price?"

Ripley glowers at me, lips sealed.

"Come on."

"I don't know what you're talking about."

"He didn't agree to get himself beaten to hell for free. I get it… You provoke me, get me thrown in some dank hole and out the picture. Skip off into the sunset, right?"

"Something like that."

"So. What was the price?"

Licking her lips, she ducks her gaze. "Enough pills to off himself with no questions asked."

I whistle under my breath. "Now we're talking. I guess he kinda got his wish. Still think you're not a piece of shit?"

Eyes squeezing shut, Ripley tilts her head back against the wall. Stray tears break through the thick coating of mud on her face and leave winding trails.

"I wanted you dead… more than I wanted him alive."

"Trading lives, huh?"

"You're one to talk." She sucks in an uneven breath. "I wanted to call it off. Now he's dead anyway. His body will disappear along with his records. There will be no one left to ask any questions."

Her broken hush causes some strange feeling to bloom in my chest. It isn't pity. I could never pity someone like Ripley; she isn't deserving of it. Neither of us are.

I understand what it's like to commit evil in order to survive. To become the villain to keep others safe. It's precisely why I tried to kill her. And why she did the exact same thing back.

"You know..." she trails off.

"What?"

"It's just that... If we'd stopped trying to kill each other and focused on everyone else who poses a threat, we would've had a far better chance of survival."

The bitch just read my mind.

But I won't tell her that.

"Yeah, I prefer taking my chances."

"Stubborn bastard," Ripley chuffs.

"You know me."

"Do you think I want to be locked in here with you? I'd much rather be facing whatever shit they have planned alone. You're a liability."

"Me a liability? You're the reason we're in here!"

"Because you're still not sorry!" she snaps, like the words are a weapon she can wield.

I stare at her. "Sorry for what?"

"Holly was all I had. She became family." Her voice splinters, leaking with despair. "And you took my family away from me to save yours."

For all the sorrow and heartache we've inflicted on each other, I can look at my nemesis and admit to myself that it wasn't worth it. I didn't know what kind of monster my actions would breed.

She has become the threat I never could have anticipated. In many ways, I can see now that I masterminded my own downfall. It was always meant to be her.

Mouth clicking open, I'm not sure what words are forming. Nothing feels quite adequate to summarise the undeniably toxic importance we've come to mean to each other. At least hatred was simple.

But understanding?

Maybe even empathy?

I can't possibly have those things for Ripley. Not for the woman who orchestrated our incarceration and torture. We ruined her life, but she perpetuated the cycle of violence the day she offered us up for slaughter.

Even here, she's continued to destroy our lives from afar—ensnaring Raine in her web then somehow penetrating my best friend's icy shell. We've tried our best to ruin each other without stopping to consider the greater threat.

Before I can figure out what to even say to her, the hatch in the door slides back. Eyes peer in, finding us both awake, before the hatch slams shut. The steel door clanks as it's unlocked.

Shoulders set, a bastard with regimented military hair saunters in, his fingers hooked into his belt hoops. Cruel eyes scan over us.

"Always nice to have new arrivals."

"You," Ripley breathes in fear. "Harrison."

"Nice to see you again, stooge. Or should I say, ex-stooge. Is the accommodation to your liking?"

His voice is lilting and playful in an entirely unhinged way. I've met his likes before. We're in for a rough time if he's in charge of our reconditioning.

"No?" He pulls his lips down in a dramatic pout. "Such a shame. Perhaps we should clean it up in here a bit before the fun begins."

Stepping out of the cell, he huffs loudly while dragging a

covered machine in with the help of another guard. This one wears a cap over his short hair, shading slightly effeminate features.

"Bath time!" Harrison exclaims.

Yet another guard enters the padded cell, this one bald and dead-eyed, joining the other one wearing a cap. Harrison leans against the machine, still smiling to himself.

"Strip them."

"Not a chance." Ripley gingerly draws to her feet.

I wobble, trying to stand. "Seconded."

"I wasn't giving either of you a choice."

Each with an approaching guard to contend with, we both find protective stances. I'm still dizzy and can't seem to get my legs to work. Ripley, on the other hand, is ready for a scrap with her knees bent and fists cocked.

I lose sight of her as baldie stalks towards me. He grabs my ankles then heaves, splaying me out on the concrete. Pain reverberates through me. I move to boot him in the leg, but when he pulls out a taser, trepidation causes me to tense.

I'm too weak to stop him from hitting me in the side. Electric slams into me, frying any sense from my struggling limbs. Pausing for a moment, he studies me before doling out another hit.

Jerking violently, spit bubbles spill from my mouth. My eyeballs feel like two overinflated balloons. When the tasing stops, I can't even lift a finger to fight back.

The guard makes quick work of stripping off my sweatpants and boxers. Eyeing my cuffed hands, he reaches for a blade attached to his belt, using it to slice my t-shirt away.

"Excellent." Harrison claps his hands together. "Let's begin."

I get a clear view of Ripley being slammed into the concrete hard enough to split her forehead open. She slumps, the fight draining out of her in time for the guard to strip her too.

We're both left completely bare. It's humiliating. With the help of his two sadists, Harrison uncovers his machine. Dismay unfurls within me as I recognise it instantly. It's a huge water pump on wheels with industrial hoses attached.

Casting Ripley a look, I watch her moan and writhe. Blood is a thick curtain spilling from her forehead to cover her face. She swipes it from her eyes long enough to spot the horror that awaits.

"W-Wait," she pleads.

Harrison waggles a finger at her. "No complaints now. Consider it a welcome spa treatment for our latest projects."

The whirring of the pump's engine fills the cell. Just as feeling re-enters my still-twitching extremities, I'm hit by the first blast of water. It's an immense force, catapulting me back into the wall.

Another hose is unspooled and pointed at Ripley. She cries out at the impact. We're both lashed with icy whips, our bodies battered and frozen by the water's bruising power.

This isn't my first time, so I know not to fight it. Slipping and sliding holds no benefit. It's better to preserve strength for the hours this can go on for. But in typical Ripley fashion, she's struggling.

"That's it," Harrison jeers. "Get nice and clean for your luxury vacation."

Retaining any awareness soon becomes impossible. The constant onslaught is too much for anyone to bear. Pain combined with the cold temperature saps any defiance from me far faster than I anticipated.

I lose track of Ripley and the passing of time. All that exists is the violent hammering of water into my body, leaving bruises that feel bone-deep. A chill has settled in my bones, the only indication that I'm not dead already.

At some point, a familiar sense of delirium sets in. My eyes are squeezed shut to avoid the powerful spray, and behind my shut lids, images start to form. Flashes here and there, forming mental snapshots.

My grandfather resting in his armchair, surrounded by framed medals and family photographs. Daisy proudly handing him her grade three ballet exam certificate to be added to the collection. The way he kissed her head so proudly.

The years speed up.

This time, I see a teenaged Daisy, now stick-thin and sullen. Her pointe shoes buried in the bottom of a drawer. The way she made herself small and invisible in our grandfather's presence. Her certificates disappeared.

I'm not sure when the onslaught of water ceases and a beating begins. Fists pummelling into me feel a lot like the beat of water anyway. Each painful blow fires more disjointed flashes at me as my mind contracts.

Things were blurry after Daisy's death. Glazed-over by grief and shock. It wasn't until I discovered her diary while clearing out her bedroom that I realised why she did it. The note made it clear enough. It's all disjointed from there.

Handcuffs.

Psych evals.

An empty jail cell.

"Lennox. Snap out of it."

Daisy's rosy cheeks.

Seeing my childhood home burn.

Court cases and signed plea deals.

"Get it together, Nox."

Fire.

Screams.

Salvation.

I gradually float back down to reality. It's the same practised routine. A coping mechanism I perfected during months of this same treatment. I'd always come back once the reprieve came.

But Xander?

He never returned.

I open my eyes to Ripley crouched over me, something akin to a look of concern on her bloodied face. Wet hair is plastered to her head, the cut in her forehead still trickling.

She's trembling from exertion, like it took all of her remaining energy to slide over to this corner of the cell. Fresh scrapes and bruises are scattered all over her.

An arm crossed over her bare breasts, she seems to be favouring her left side. My own body aches even more fiercely than before, promising fresh bruises to evidence the onslaught of kicking and punching.

A quick glance around reveals that we're now alone, the machine vanished with Harrison and his grunts. Our tormentors have delivered their welcome gift and left. I really did check out.

"You back?"

I heave a breath. "Yeah."

"Don't die on me yet," she jokes hoarsely.

"You wouldn't like that?"

Ripley sighs, her weight braced on one cuffed hand. "No need for pretence, right?"

Hissing in pain, I breathe through the fire in my ribcage. "Do I look capable of that right now?"

"I guess not. Truthfully, I don't want to die alone in here." She summons a weak smile. "How's that for honesty?"

Coughing wetly, she shuffles her back against the padded wall. I remain curled up in a puddle of water, too limp to lift a finger. There's no concept of time in here. I don't know how long the torture went on for, but we're both drained.

"You kept saying your sister's name." Her voice is a needle in the heart. "And Xander's too."

"It's nothing."

"You can't let them get in your head like that. It's exactly what they want."

"Who survived this shit before?" I wince on an inhale. "Don't lecture me."

"Fine. Be like that."

From the corner of my eye, I can't help but watch her. It's the same sick desire that's brought me into her orbit for months now. A drive I wasn't willing to acknowledge before. Look where that got me.

Disaster follows Ripley at every turn, and I've followed along like a storm chaser on the heels of a promising tornado. In all the plots and schemes, a part of me hoped I wouldn't succeed in destroying her.

Then the chase would end.

And I'd be left with a heavier conscience.

"You need to put pressure on your head," I point out.

"Worried about me?"

"Hardly. Just don't fancy being stuck here with a dead body."

There's an odd rattling sound before a sudden blast of cold air spews from the vents in the ceiling. More is pumped out, over and over, until the cell's temperature has dramatically dropped.

Both sopping wet and exhausted, it doesn't take long for shivers to set in. Ripley hugs her naked body, shaking like a leaf from head to toe. She's curvy but small without a whole lot of meat on her bones to keep her warm.

"What is th-this?" She sits against the wall, her hands wrapped around her knees, appearing to be curled up as small as possible.

"They break you down first, exhaust you mentally and physically." My limbs quiver with each word. "Then they roll out the big guns."

Air vents whistling, there's another quiet click before the lights suddenly cut, and we're plunged into darkness. I focus on preserving any small amount of warmth I have left, but the sound of Ripley's panicked gasps soon filters in.

"Ripley?" I whisper into the dark.

"I c-can't… We're n-never… getting out of h-h-here."

"You need to calm down. They're messing with our heads."

"So c-c-cold," she whimpers.

That fucking sound. I swear, she does it on purpose. Like she knows it makes me feel all kinds of fucked up and confused.

"Focus on something else," I mutter.

"Like w-what?"

"I don't know. The incredible scenery?"

"It's pitch black, dick."

"You still have the pleasure of my voice."

"You know what? F-Fuck you."

"You wish, Rip."

"Are you s-seriously flirting with m-me while we're being t-tortured?" Her teeth chattering is audible.

If it keeps her talking and that goddamn whimpering to a minimum, I'll tell the bitch I love her. Anything to keep those sounds from breaking my fucking heart all over again. Though I'd never admit she has that power.

"Don't tell anyone." I sigh shallowly.

"It isn't necessary t-to be an asshole all your l-life, Nox."

"Really? That's news to me. Thanks for the head's up."

"I hate you s-so much."

"The feeling's mutual."

Unable to hold it back any longer, my teeth begin to clatter too. Anything to maintain what little heat remains in my core. Frigid air is still being pumped into the cell, glaciating our soaked, bare bodies.

It won't be long before hypothermia sets in. If their intention is to make us as weak and vulnerable as possible, it'll be an easy win. We've been tortured, beaten, and now damn near frozen to death.

Lost in thought, I realise Ripley has gone quiet. I can't hear her teeth crashing together or even her snivelling anymore. Just the whistling of more ice-cold air being injected into our cell.

"R-Ripley?"

I strain my ears for any signs of life.

"Come on, Rip. T-Talk to me." I silently pray for a response. "Tell me you h-hate me again."

There's still nothing. I despise the burst of fear that settles in my gut. When did this evil woman come to mean something to me? Or have I just learned to enjoy the sick torture of her presence? I can't tell anymore.

Jaw locked, I fight through the pain as I wrench myself upright. It takes a lot of fumbling in the darkness for my fingertips to catch skin. My cuffed hands skate over her, blindly searching for some identifiable body part.

When I've found what feels like an arm, I tug with my remaining strength. Ripley grunts at the force of being dislodged from her perch against the wall and pulled across wet concrete.

"S-Stop," she moans in pain.

"Don't g-go quiet on me, then."

"No..."

"I'm not dying a-alone in here."

With some awkward manoeuvring, I get her close enough to tuck her into my chest. It takes some serious mental gymnastics to justify cradling her naked body against my chest. It's just self-preservation, right? I can steal her body heat.

Lifting my cuffed wrists over her head, I hold her in a tight embrace. My hands rub up and down her knobbly back to stimulate some warmth. I'm acutely aware of every naked inch pressed up so close to me, it's like we share the same skin.

Any personal space or privacy has deserted us. I can feel each quiet inhale and exhale that tells me she hasn't curled up and died in the dark. Her lungs expanding pushes her soft breasts into my chest each time.

Despite her quivering, body heat is soaking into me due to our extremely close proximity. My teeth stop chattering, allowing me to speak.

"Talk to me," I plead in a painfully neutral voice.

"T-Tired. Cold."

"I know. Me too." I keep rubbing her back, desperately fighting her shudders. "How did we end up like this, Rip?"

"Karma," she jokes feebly.

"I guess we've earned it."

Ripley sniffles in my arms. "I have."

"You've survived."

"So h-have you."

A wave of tiredness washes over me. "I never cared about me. Just them."

"Your family?" she whispers.

"The one I chose."

"Tell me how. P-Please."

I don't know why I comply.

"Xander was an accident. He'd never admit it, but I knew he needed a friend. Then Raine came along. They both just... snuck in. Became important. I'm not sure how."

Silence is a heavy blanket in this freezer, but not a warm one. Instead, it sucks us deeper into the barren emptiness. A place that lives within us, born of guilt and desperation, used to justify all manner of evils.

"W-Why Xander?" Ripley asks.

"What do you mean?"

"Why d-did he need a friend?"

"The clinicians were always interested in him. I guess I was too. It wasn't hard to break into the office one night and read his file. I wanted to disprove what I suspected so I wouldn't care anymore."

Ripley drags in a shaky breath. "You... know?"

Surprise sparks in me. Xander hasn't even confirmed it to me. Not when I witnessed him thrashing in his sleep for the first time. Not when I questioned his diagnosis. Not even when the Z wing clinicians weaponised his past to break him.

He refused to break.

Or even acknowledge his trauma.

"Do you?"

"Just a th-theory. Someone hurt h-him." She continues to tremble in my arms. "Like y-your sister was hurt."

"Yeah. They did." I swallow thickly. "When I saw his scars, I had a hunch. No one becomes fascinated by pain without experiencing it."

"So y-you wanted to h-help him?" Ripley guesses, her teeth-clacking gradually easing. "To p-protect him."

"Yes, like I couldn't protect Daisy. It's fucked. I know."

"No." She shakes her head in a quick, curt jerk. "It's not. Y-You just wanted to do right."

With nothing but her breath and cold skin to hold me in reality, I can't find the heart to lie. The likelihood of us ever leaving here is non-existent. She may as well know what kind of monster she's dying with.

"I had no idea what was happening to Daisy. It went on under my nose for years." My voice catches. "I didn't protect her. I didn't even see her pain until it was too late. She needed someone to keep her safe."

"It w-wasn't your fault."

"Perhaps not. But failing her was my fault. In a twisted way... I figured that if I could help Xander, if I could be his friend and keep him safe... maybe Daisy would forgive me for letting her down."

"Nox." Her tone enters dangerous territory.

"I know how stupid it sounds. But when I realised that

management was interested in Xander's mind... I resolved to do anything to protect him."

She's quiet, no doubt aware of what comes next.

"He has no family, no life or career. It would be so easy for him to disappear into their program. And with that much damage? Xander was an easy target. I needed a way to make him untouchable."

"Like by making h-him a stooge," Ripley finishes.

"Yeah. If we worked for them, then maybe they'd leave him alone. That couldn't happen while someone else held the role. I needed to remove the obstacle first."

It feels so wrong to be justifying why I killed someone she cared about while holding her in my arms. Like I'm giving her no choice but to listen. But the speck of light left inside me wants her to know. *Needs her to know.* This was never about hurting her for fun.

"Holly didn't deserve what I did to her," I admit before I can change my mind. "She was a means to an end. I didn't care that her death would hurt others. I was selfish and single-minded."

"For someone you l-loved," she surmises.

"You don't have to pretend to understand."

"I w-wish I was pretending." Her face is damp with tears against my chest. "When I g-got you and Xander s-sent to the Z wing... I did it for h-her. The person I loved and didn't protect. You were my m-means to an end."

And there we are.

We've been waging a war for the exact same fucking reason all along.

Hatred. Love. Family.

"You know, I can't even say I blame you for doing that to us. I've spent too long consumed by hatred and revenge not to understand the madness it pushes you into."

"The same m-madness that l-love creates, right?"

A short laugh lights my chest. "Right."

The two aren't so unlike after all. We love to hate and hate that which we love. Whoever said humans can't be made of extremes clearly had the privilege of a life without trauma or heartache. The rest of us know that it's a careful tightrope walk between the two.

"I still want to h-hate you so b-badly," Ripley says into my icy skin. "And I d-don't want to understand why you murdered my b-best friend. But... part of me d-does."

"I didn't tell you any of this to change your mind, Rip. I'm not asking for forgiveness... some of us don't deserve it."

"No. S-Some of us don't."

You know what? Fuck it.

I'm tired of the charade. I'm tired of justifying my hatred and looking for the next opportunity to inflict it. I'm tired of being Ripley's nemesis when all along, we were both just collateral damage. The price of surviving Incendia's abuse.

They've taken so much from us.

I want to die with a shred of humanity left.

"But for the record, I am sorry," I say slowly, deliberately. "For all of it."

After a brief pause, she sucks in sharply. "I'm sorry t-too. For all of it."

There's no puff of smoke or sparkling golden gate appearing above us. Redemption isn't a tick box to be checked and filed away. Though we wish it would be, right? Forgiveness would come easier that way.

Hatred doesn't disappear with a few words.

But it does soften and contextualise.

It does *relent.*

"Then I guess... At least we're dying on the same side?" I suggest uncertainly.

"What s-side is that?"

Stroking her wet curls, I let myself savour a split-second of satisfaction. She's in my arms. For tonight, I can pretend she's mine.

"The side of the villains."

CHAPTER 27
RIPLEY

MY NAME IS HUMAN – HIGHLY SUSPECT

I STARTLE AWAKE to the sound of a man screaming. Deep, blood-curdling screams. The kind that only a few are unlucky enough to ever hear. It's a barbaric sound.

My cheek is pressed up against something warm and hard. The earthy smell of burning wood lingers beneath blood and mildew lacing the air. It emanates from the sculpted chest I quickly realise I'm cuddled up to.

Our hips are aligned, legs tangled together and bodies conjoined. Not a scrap of fabric to keep us apart. The fact we survived the night pales in comparison to our current sleeping arrangement. Lennox's face is spooned in the crook of my neck.

Lennox.

Fucking Lennox!

He didn't release me for even a second as we drifted, shivering and near-hypothermic, through hours of misery. When the lights slammed on and the air conditioning stopped, he didn't move to let go, and I didn't ask him to.

We slept like this.

Entwined as one.

Bathing in the body heat of the man who should be my

enemy, I let my thoughts stray. Raine is never far from my mind. I'm plagued by the image of him being dragged in here and tortured alongside us.

Xander's almost-black gaze soon sneaks in too. Hardened diamonds of hatred and fascination. For once, he can't follow me. I'm far beyond his reach now. He'll never get the chance to break me—not before the clinicians do.

"Fuck." It sounds like Lennox's throat is coated in gravel. "That hurts."

"No shit, Sherlock."

At the sound of my laughter, he tenses up. "Hey."

"Hi. Comfortable?"

It seems to take him a moment to remember our conversation. The sordid truths we told in the dead of night. Even now, it feels like an immaterial dream. Lennox would never apologise for any wrongdoing.

Only, he did.

Perhaps I don't know Lennox at all.

"Five-star luxury," he grumbles. "I can't feel my legs."

"Be thankful for that."

Every limb feels like it has been dipped in gasoline and set alight. A combination of hydrotherapy, beatings and sub-zero temperatures has left me feeling like a pack of wolves ripped me apart at the seams.

When he shifts, hissing in pain, I expect to be shoved away. Talk of redemption never holds up in the cold light of day—even when day constitutes fluorescent lighting and waking from agony-induced unconsciousness.

Yet the inevitable rejection and return to status quo never comes. Lennox stills, his handcuffed arms remaining curled around me, chiselled muscles contracting as he crushes me closer. I can hear his heart beneath his breastbone.

"We won't be left alone for long," he advises. "Better prepare yourself."

"Why don't they just kill us? It's quicker. Cleaner too."

"While we're alive, we still have our uses. The Z wing repurposes every piece of discarded trash."

I'd rather die than be treated like a lab rat. I don't want to become another one of their creations. An experimental prototype rolled out to the highest bidder.

"What if they hurt Raine?" I whisper in horror. "Or Xander?"

"That's why we have to keep them entertained," Lennox replies like he's given this some thought. "As long as we're here, we have their attention. Our family will be safe."

"Our?"

Breath stalling, Lennox's head lifts from my neck. He looks down at me through vicious bruises. One seafoam eye is swollen shut, while dried clumps of blood are soaked into his thick stubble.

The necklace around his neck is still intact, stark against burnished skin. I'm surprised they haven't taken it. Anything to dehumanise and antagonise. Perhaps that stage is yet to come.

"You care about Raine." His eyes ping-pong between mine

"Yes."

"Do you care about Xander?"

When I don't immediately answer, he lifts a thick brow. Right. No pretences. We have nothing in here but our truth. Last night, Lennox gave me his.

"I... Yes. No." I close my eyes for a moment, drawing in a deep breath. "Look, it's complicated."

It takes him a moment to find the words to respond.

"Family isn't who you're born to. It isn't blood or birth lines or adoption papers. It isn't even a legality."

"Then what is it?"

Licking his plump lips, Lennox's stare bores into me. "It's the people you choose to give a fuck about, through thick and thin."

"You think it's that simple?"

"I do."

Considering this, I study the swell of his inflated cupid's bow. "Then what does that make us?"

Lennox furrows his brow. "I don't know. Probably not enemies."

Don't do it, Ripley.

But not even Holly's whispered warning can stop me.

"How about allies?"

"Allies," he repeats.

"What do you think?"

"I guess… I can work with that."

The corner of his mouth twitches, not quite manifesting into a smile. We're still staring at each other. Suspended in this flux-like state between life and death, our worlds torn apart, and futures gone. There's nothing left to fight for. We both lost.

"Do we have to like each other to do this?" Lennox murmurs.

My breathing halts as his lips near. Lennox holds my gaze until his mouth captures mine, then nothing else matters but the feel of his skin on mine. Only this time, he isn't trying to hurt me. This isn't a punishment.

It's a surrender.

A white flag.

An abdication.

My mouth responds to his without being told. I don't know when hatred transformed into the most acute sense of need, but I couldn't care less. We're facing the unknown together now. At the end of this road, I can accept Lennox Nash for the monster he is.

He pauses to let me answer.

"No," I breathe. "We don't have to like each other."

"Then I guess… allies it is."

His mouth returns to mine, hard and insistent. The man

who tried his damndest to kill me is breathing life into my lungs, one kiss at a time. I'm trapped in hell with an enemy, and disaster has never felt so fucking good.

Lips parting, I let his tongue seek passage. He tastes like blood and rage. Hope and fear. The perplexing tale of a man capable of inflicting so much horror in the name of love. But to Lennox, that is love.

Not the half-baked version of love that normal people proclaim. Nothing quite so ordinary or pedestrian. This is a man who will maim and kill to protect those he's deemed worthy of his care. Those lucky enough to be loved in the fiercest of ways.

Not even the intensifying shrieks around us disrupt the moment. While some anguished soul loses his mind, I hand mine over to the devil himself. Yet even the devil once danced with angels. Lennox's evil matches mine.

For we were both forged in the same hell.

And we'll both die here too.

Our kiss breaks at the sound of the cell door being unlocked. Lennox pulls me in close, going on high alert. Footsteps enter before Harrison's sneering voice shatters the morning's relative peace.

"Well, isn't this cosy. Survived the night, I see."

"Afraid so," Lennox retorts.

"Dress, Ripley. We're going for a walk."

When Harrison stomps over to us, I catch a flash of a black weapon before it presses into the back of my head. It takes a moment for the metallic coldness to register.

"Now," Harrisons says tersely. "I have permission to paint your brains across this cell if you disobey."

There's a gun nudging my skull. Not a baton. Nor a taser. It seems that not even Harrowdean's false pretence of being a safe, law-abiding facility can survive the evil of the Z wing. We've all been stripped to our bare selves, guard and patient alike.

"Move, Ripley."

"It's okay," I whisper to Lennox. "Let me go."

"No," he clips out.

"He'll only shoot us both, Nox. Let go."

His jaw set in an unyielding line, Lennox eventually surrenders me. My cuffed wrists held to my chest, I slither towards my discarded clothing, utterly humiliated by the show I'm putting on. Harrison doesn't have the decency to look away as I locate the wet pile across the cell.

"What about me?" Lennox asks.

"You're staying right here, lover boy. Professor Craven will be along shortly."

My blood freezes solid as fear takes root.

"The professor doesn't want to see me?"

"Oh, no. Sir Bancroft would prefer to deal with you himself."

Something tells me I shouldn't be relieved.

With Harrison's leer still locked on me, I pick through the wet clothing. Panties first. He rolls his eyes while watching me struggle with my bra, stepping forward to unlock my handcuffs. The metal chafes my raw skin and rips scabs open as it moves.

"Ouchie." Harrison grins.

I blink away tears. "Had worse."

"We'll see how long that bravery lasts."

Gingerly putting on my bra, I pick up the mud-stained t-shirt to pull on next. Something dislodges from the sodden fabric and hits the floor. The flash of white card captures Harrison's gaze.

"What is that?" he demands.

Terror lashes against my insides. "Nothing!"

"Up against the goddamn wall."

With the gun trained on me, cocked and waiting to be unloaded, I have no choice but to slip the t-shirt on and inch away. Harrison keeps his weapon pointed at me as he squats down to retrieve the business card.

Amidst all the carnage, I forgot about stashing it in my bra yesterday. The guard didn't notice when he stripped me off, far too preoccupied with being a sadistic overlord. That goddamn card has just stamped my death warrant.

"Sabre Security?" Harrison reads in disbelief.

"I d-don't know... how that got there."

Lennox looks between us, as shocked by the presence of the business card as Harrison is. I may as well have walked myself in front of a firing squad.

Stomping over to me, Harrison grabs my bicep. I struggle against him until he smashes the butt of his gun into my head. Excruciating pain flares through my skull, reigniting the wound from my last act of defiance.

The handcuffs are quickly snapped back in place while I'm still reeling. It's taking all my self-control not to hurl on his freshly cleaned steel-capped weapons of mass destruction.

"Ripley!" Lennox shouts, still bare and bloodied as he finds his feet. "Don't tell them shit."

"Silence!" Harrison barks.

"Rip!"

The bleak acceptance in his pale-green gaze offers the most twisted form of comfort. Lennox knows what's to come. I suppose I do as well. Those two words inscribed on the luxurious card have ensured my suffering.

Lennox shakes his head. A clear message.

Don't let them win.

Harrison tows me from the cell, tugging on the metal chain connecting my cuffed wrists. Each yank causes lava to shoot through my veins. My mutilated skin is now bleeding again, pulsating with heat and pain.

I'm barely able to stand, let alone march down the seemingly endless corridor of cells. He drags me beyond the rooms I last saw, including Bancroft's office, stopping outside another door.

"Good morning," a cheerful voice greets.

Harrison glances over his shoulder. "Professor. Your new recruit is waiting for you in cell seven."

Dressed in a pale-grey suit and white lab coat, Professor Craven nods in acknowledgement. His ebony eyes are lasered on me behind square-framed glasses.

"Pleasant sleep, Ripley?"

I glower at him. "Toasty."

With a barked laugh, he sidles away. "I'll pay your cellmate a visit, then. Please do join us later."

I don't have time to let my dread for Lennox spiral. With a quick scan, the door's lock disengages, and Harrison unceremoniously shoves me inside the unfamiliar room.

"I just have to share your little misdemeanour with the boss. Please do enjoy the facilities in the meantime."

"Wait, please…"

The steel door clanks shut, sealing me in yet another cell, though the walls are white-washed brick this time. It's the sloshing of water and rasping laughter that causes me to tense up.

"Ain't this a sight."

I have the displeasure of knowing who that voice belongs to. Slowly turning around to face the room reveals the deathly pale, almost-blue face of a ghost.

Rick's once olive-toned face is gaunt, his skin sagging and cheeks shallow. He looks half-dead. Starved, bruised and broken.

"You're alive."

"Am I?" He coughs.

The set-up causes my stomach to bottom out. It's a room filled with rusted bathtubs, the four metal shells evenly spaced out and each equipped with shackles at the edges. Rick occupies the nearest one.

He's restrained inside the tub, a black plastic sheet buttoned up to his neck so only his head is visible. From the freezing temperature in the room, I can quickly connect the dots.

Cold water immersion.

An old asylum favourite.

"Christ." A wave of nausea has my mouth filling with saliva. "This is insane."

"Tip of the iceberg." His voice is weak and flimsy. "Didn't think I'd see you down here. Your luck ran out, then."

"Something like that."

Rick's eyes scan over me, taking in the multi-coloured bruises, swelling, deep lacerations and more. His attention catches on the portion of my scarred arm visible through the blood pouring from my wrists.

"How's the brand?" he jokes lamely.

"Sitting pretty. How's the friend?"

"Carlos is dead."

"I hate to say I told you so, but look around you... No one survives this place."

Rick's eyes sink shut. "Then I'm glad you're here."

I'm tempted to dunk him beneath the water and hold him there for old time's sake, but Harrison's return scuppers that plan. His smile seems even wider than before. I cringe as I stand against the wall.

"Change of plan," he singsongs. "We're going to have a little chat while the boss gives your *friend* a call."

"I don't know anything about Sabre or that number," I blurt out. "I never called them!"

"I couldn't care less. Now, Rick here has been cooling down after his last bout of defiance. Shall we reward him with a show?"

I try to run, hoping to somehow duck past him, but I'm easily captured and plucked off my feet. Harrison tosses me like I'm little more than a trash bag to be discarded. My tailbone screams as I hit the floor and roll.

Striding after me, his playful expression evaporates. I hate knowing that Rick is watching as Harrison begins a violent campaign of kicks, punches and slaps to punctuate each deafening question.

"Who gave you the business card, Ripley?"

Kick.

"Answer me!"

Punch.

"Where did you get it from?"

Slap.

The pain is relentless. Blow after blow. Strike after strike. There isn't a part of my body left untouched. Already bruised and battered skin feels like it's ready to rupture and spill organs across the floor.

Harrison's hand grips my chin to wrench me upright. His eyes are a curious blend of amber and chocolate-brown, like volcanic magma trapped beneath the earth's crust. Rage sealed in nerve tissue and skin.

"Did you contact them? Promise to give those nosy bastards all the juicy details?"

"No," I cry out.

"Lies."

With a swift backhand, he drops me again. I collapse, too feeble to even spare our audience a glance.

"Not so loyal after all." Harrison chuckles to himself. "Are you?"

"I'm l-loyal... to myself." I spit out blood.

"So ungrateful. It's a pity, all that wasted potential. But your loss is our gain."

When he boots me in the face, the pain is too unbearable. Finally, my consciousness snaps as I black out. Eventually I come to again, finding Harrison now talking to a suit-clad pair of legs, visible through my unsteady vision.

My mind has turned to soup, but I can make out a few words. Enough to tell me that something is afoot. They sound tense, on-edge. Like troops perched on a hillside, preparing for enemy fire.

"Sabre… video sent… retaliation."

"Phoenix?" a voice responds.

I recognise Bancroft's regal tone.

"Tank," Harrison answers.

"Fine." Their footsteps are muffled. "And her?"

"Nothing, sir."

I hear the shuffle of clothing before a hand strokes over my tangled hair. Peeking through tear-logged eyes, I look up at Bancroft. He's crouched beside me, darkness filtered across his aged features.

"All empires fall, Ripley," he croons softly. "But not this one."

"I d-didn't… The number…."

"Hush, dearest." I want to recoil when he pets me like a dog, but I'm too weak. "It's no matter. They're coming for us regardless now." Bancroft smiles shrewdly. "We have their plaything."

Their… plaything?

"I'm still mightily disappointed in you, Ripley." He sighs dramatically. "After all I've done for you. But it's no matter, your uncle already issued his consent. You're ours to repurpose now."

Desperation barely registers.

"Please." My whisper comes out frail and paltry.

"It's a little late to plead for your life, isn't it?" He tuts under his breath. "You should've thought of that before you betrayed us. I do hate disloyalty."

Straightening to his full height, Bancroft smooths a hand down his front. He casts a critical eye around the room, taking each iteration of horror in.

"Your friend Rick here is learning his own lesson about

not sticking his nose where it doesn't belong. But I think we have something more suitable for your level of transgression."

"Sir?" Harrison prompts.

"I believe Professor Craven requested both Ripley and Lennox. Let him have his fun. I am sure she'll be returned as a clean slate, ready for sale."

I groggily watch Harrison unleash a grin. "As you wish, sir."

Bancroft casts me a final look of disappointment. "Goodbye, Ripley."

This time, I'm a lifeless flop in Harrison's arms. I don't even have the energy to acknowledge Rick as we exit. My head lolls, the steady patter of blood dripping from multiple lacerations leaving a trail behind us.

Flashing in and out of consciousness, I startle when the clank of a metal door opening permeates my mind fog. We're in yet another cell. The scent of spilled blood rushes up to meet me, so thick and cloying it makes me gag.

"Ah." Craven's voice is a featherlight tenor. "Right on time."

CHAPTER 28
XANDER
V.A.N – BAD OMENS & POPPY

SPINNING the all-access keycard between my fingers, I study the unfolding scene. A female guard is beating the shit out of a screaming patient, wearing them down while her backup prepares to deliver a sedative. They don't seem to care that we're watching.

It's funny how quickly a façade crumbles once the damage is done. Those spiderweb cracks soon lengthen and multiply. No one can stop the progression of an avalanche once that first clap rings out and the snowfall breaks.

Destruction is imminent.

Who will emerge remains to be seen.

"Take them to solitary!"

The patient bucks and writhes. "No! You did this! We know the truth now!"

It all began when the patient started running from group to group, shoving his phone in every available face. Everyone was sitting outside for lunch, silently stewing after whispers of what happened to Noah spread overnight.

Everyone is furious.

Sick of the injustice.

Ready to revolt.

I didn't bother to collect food, preferring to observe instead. Fury is a necrotic wound eating away at me. Lennox would be proud if he were here. Instead, I had to hear through the fucking grapevine that he was drugged and hauled off.

But not alone.

They took my toy too.

I have no idea where they are. The Z wing seems like a fair guess. But until I figure out where it's located, I can't do shit for them. Powerlessness is a feeling I hoped to never revisit.

As the patient is towed away, I spot Ripley's red-haired friend whispering with a gaggle of others. They were shown whatever played on his phone before security intervened. As they stand up to leave, I also rise.

"You," I shout.

She startles, sparing me a meek look. "Me?"

I search my memory for her name. "Rae. Come here."

Scampering over, Rae stops next to me. She's pale and shaken beneath her auburn hair. Like she's looked evil in the eyes and lived to tell the tale. I loom over her, my voice low.

"What was on the phone?"

"N-Nothing." She avoids my gaze.

"If they want to beat you, the guards will. If they want to kill you, they will. Pretending like you didn't see it won't protect you."

Her throat bobs, working up and down. "It was a video."

"A video?" I frown at her when she finally looks up at me.

"Some grainy phone footage. It's splashed all over social media and the news; not even the internet filters can block it. Looks like it was deliberately leaked from Blackwood Institute."

My mind churns. "What kind of footage?"

"I don't know." Rae raises a slim shoulder, her nose scrunched like she bit into a lemon. "Some kind of basement place. Full of cells and some weird-ass torture stuff. Blood everywhere. I think it's from the riot."

Well, I'll be damned.

"Do you know what that place is?"

"Few do," I reply absently.

If evidence of another Z wing has leaked to the press, this tinder box is about to blow. Rumours are one thing. Video evidence is another, whether or not Incendia plays it off as doctored or part of some smear campaign.

Looking around, I can see all the warning signs. Patients conspiring in small groups. Furtive glances and death glares shot at overzealous guards. A real-life plot is unfolding before my eyes.

"Where is Ripley?" Rae pulls my attention back to her.

"She was taken."

She licks her lips while rocking from foot to foot, clearly uneasy. "Do you think she'll come back?"

Staring down at the wraithlike creature, I study her tell signs. Glistening eyes. Twitching fingers. Lips puckering and red from being chewed. She's battling concern or fear, but I don't know which. Ripley should've never allowed a customer to get so attached.

I shrug her off. "Not a clue."

Rae watches me leave, her tears spilling over. I don't care to offer any shred of comfort. Tension is growing fast. Like an invisible storm, there's an electrical charge in the air and madness in each and every mind. Something is going to erupt.

I stride past gathered patients, trading gossip faster than even management can suppress. Walking inside the reception, several guards are gathered too, nervously glancing from side to side. Snippets of conversation float over me.

"Media shitstorm… press… protest."

"Here?" someone asks.

"Incoming."

I pick up my pace, not slowing until the medical wing is in

sight. A handful of cubicles are full, the curtains drawn to conceal their occupants. There aren't any staff behind the nurse's station or in the corridor. Injuries incurred during the storm must still be keeping the medics busy.

Inside Raine's cubicle, he's curled up on his side. A strange pair of aviators are balanced on his nose so I can't see his eyes, but he perks up the moment I walk in. The man's like a damn bloodhound.

"Xan?"

"Yeah, it's me."

Drawing his curtain, I stride over to the small window to the left of his hospital bed. A quick peek outside doesn't reveal much. I may be paranoid, but I feel better, having my sights back on him.

"What's going on?"

"I'm not sure," I admit, studying the institute's grounds. "Some press video is circulating. Everyone is all riled up after what happened to Noah."

"Have you heard from Ripley or Lennox?"

"Still no sign of them."

"Maybe they're just in solitary," he guesses.

"You really believe that?"

I watch Raine rub his temples. He isn't stupid. As soon as I relayed the whispers I'd heard yesterday, it was clear he knew. Both of us did. Neither of them are coming back anytime soon.

"We have to help them, Xan."

"You think I don't know that?"

"Then what are we still doing here?" He winces, trying to sit up quickly.

Rubbing my face, I sigh wearily. "Because it isn't that simple. I don't even know where Harrowdean's Z wing is. No one does."

"Then we have to find out!"

Sitting upright now, he tugs at the needles and wires still attached to him. I grab his wrists to halt his movements.

"You're going nowhere."

"Don't start getting all protective just because Lennox isn't here to do it. We both know you don't care."

"I do care!" I hurl back at him.

Raine freezes, his wrists still caught in my grip. I clear my throat and look away, not that it makes a difference. He can't see the terror that admission has provoked inside me. But he can sure as hell sense it.

"I… I thought I was just a nuisance to you," he admits quietly.

"You are." My stomach flips. "A nuisance I care about."

Raine's mouth hangs open. He doesn't have a response. I don't blame him. I've spent my entire adult life not giving a flying fuck about anyone or anything including myself. This is new for me too.

"That's why you're going to lay back down in the goddamn bed, and let me handle this."

"I can help," he baulks haltingly.

"They both made this mess. But I'm going to fucking fix it."

"Xan—"

"Stay here, Raine!"

Cringing back into his pillows, he summons a reluctant nod. I pluck his plugged-in mobile phone from the bedside table then shove it into his hands.

"I'm going hunting. If any trouble starts, call. Got that?"

"What kind of trouble?" Raine's forehead wrinkles.

"I honestly don't know. But something's coming."

I quickly check around the medical wing, ensuring it's secured. Nina is on-duty again in the small office, preoccupied by her crossword book. She pays me no attention as I stride past.

I spend the next few hours systematically picking the

institute apart with my all-access pass. Checking every last locked door, storage cupboard and floor. There seems to be no security around for me to beat any clues from.

After breaking in, I'm picking through the filing cabinets in the warden's office, searching for records of any admissions to the solitary wing, when I hear approaching voices. Slamming the cabinet shut, I duck behind a thick curtain.

"It began as a handful of reporters, sir." Elon's annoying voice is unmistakable. "They're gathering outside each of the remaining institutes across the country."

"The corporation has released a statement," Davis responds.

"It appears the crowds are growing by the hour. The negative response to that leaked video is escalating fast. Security reports a large protest gathering at our front gates."

"Goddammit! Handle this, Elon."

"It's a rather large mob," he says uncertainly.

"I don't care. Send every man and woman we have out there. Go too. I will not be intimidated in my own institute."

"I believe Sir Bancroft intends to address the crowd himself. The leaked video is likely the work of Sabre Security. A distraction technique, perhaps."

"Then Bancroft can clean his own fucking mess," Davis spits.

Trouble in paradise?

The warden sounds less than enthused by his superior's actions. I haven't had the misfortune to run into Bancroft again since he agreed to our release from Priory Lane's Z wing. But I've heard whispers of his presence in Harrowdean.

"What about the patients?" Elon asks. "News has already spread. They're restless."

There's a thunking sound like Davis has slammed his forehead against his desk.

"Hold a skeleton staff back to keep the peace. We'll

declare an emergency lockdown for good measure. Send everyone else out to hold the crowd back."

"Yes sir," Elon acknowledges.

When I hear retreating footsteps and the office door close, I peek around the curtain. Davis is sitting at his desk, staring into space. I slide the pocketknife from my back pocket, creeping up behind him.

"Argh!" he startles as I press the blade to his throat.

"Warden. Where are Lennox Nash and Ripley Bennet?"

"Step away from me."

"No. Answer the fucking question before I make this throat a gaping smiley face."

"Think about what you're doing," Davis attempts.

Pausing, I take a moment. "Alright. It's thought about. Now answer."

"They're dead by now!"

Pressing the blade in, I feel his skin begin to part. "You continue to underestimate us all, Warden."

I can feel a weak tremble running over him. The mighty warden of Harrowdean, sweating like a pig in a butcher shop. Men like him shouldn't have power. Yet they always seem to covet it.

"Where is the Z wing?"

"You're on camera," he gasps. "Walk away now, and I won't report this."

"Why didn't I think of that?" I slash deeper into his throat. "Oh, wait. I did. The moment I cut the CCTV camera's power supply."

"Please…"

"Where is it?"

"I can't tell you! I won't!"

"Then what use do I have for you?"

"Please," he tries again, holding up his hands.

"Still begging, Warden?" I lean closer, scenting his sweat and fear. "Didn't you know I have no humanity to appeal to?"

His throat cuts like warm butter left out in the sun for too long. I ensured to sharpen my blade as I plotted overnight, preparing for whatever price finding Ripley and Lennox would demand.

The glinting steel slashes him wide open like a fucking piñata. Warm blood gushes forth in a hot, sticky spray. It pours from the deep wound and splashes all manner of paperwork, framed photographs and incident reports.

No doubt forged documents that are all dipped in the blood of Harrowdean's stuffed suit. His essence now stains the lies he's been paid to perpetuate.

Holding him close despite the spray, I watch every last droplet. Each satisfying spray and gargle. The agonal breath of a dying soul. Holding Davis as he bleeds out stirs some internal bloodlust that only grows.

When I release him, he thuds against the desk with an audible *smack.* Eyes blown wide. Mouth hanging open. Face waxy and a yawning gap where his throat should be. I can't help but stare for several peaceful moments.

The sound of distant shouts breaks my reverie. It floats through the stained glass window, emanating from the institute's gates. From the warden's office, I have a better view of what's unfolding.

A quick look outside reveals something I never expected to see. Elon's description was a gross underestimation.

"Holy shit," I mutter.

He was right about one thing—it sure looks like a protest. Reporters and press vehicles blur with the enraged general public. Placards are being waved, accompanied by shouts and screams.

Harrowdean's security is struggling to hold the protest at bay. Heading down the paved path beyond the gates, I recognise Bancroft's shrivelled form with Elon and a multitude of guards in tow.

He's dolled up in a fine suit, silvery hair slicked back and game face on. The crowd's rage only heightens at the sight of his approach. My attention is pulled from him as the emergency alarm blares.

It shatters the still air of the office and slams me back into reality. Davis's corpse is slowly cooling. But his orders still stand. A lockdown has been called.

Taking one last look around the office and its deceased inhabitant, I duck into the corridor. Emergency lighting flashes on repeat, reminiscent of an epileptic fit. Still, the silence is eerie.

I almost startle when my phone begins to buzz.

"Raine?" I answer hastily.

"What's that alarm, Xan?" His voice is high pitch.

"Everyone's going into lockdown. Hold tight."

"I can hear shouting. Sounds like patients."

"I'm coming now."

Hanging up the call, I keep the blood-slick blade poised in my hand as I enter the spookily empty corridor. Not many staff are around on weekends anyway, but it's deserted now the guards have been directed outside.

As I near the reception, doors are flung open. Chairs upturned. Brochures scattered. The sounds of screaming and yelling emanate from outside where the witching hour has fallen.

A quick peek outside reveals the growing commotion. With the majority of Davis's men sent to protect the institute's perimeter, few remain to hold the tension at bay. And damn, has it exploded.

All hell has broken loose. At first glance, it looks like Harrowdean's patient population has turned on itself. There are dozens of scraps taking place, fists flying into faces and blood spraying in all directions.

As I squint through the darkness, I can see the true reality. Beyond a few random fights, they're actually targeting the guards. Patients rally together, taking down black-clad brutes and stealing their weapons.

Guards are being tasered and cuffed. Pummelled with fists at every available opportunity. The mob is growing as sides are drawn. In the gloom, violence rules. And it's growing by the second.

This is an uprising.

A fucking *riot.*

CHAPTER 29
RIPLEY
SINNER – OF VIRTUE

"PLEASE!" I beg at the top of my lungs. "Stop!"

Arms shackled to a thick metal ring built into the wall above my head, I strain my shoulders each time I attempt to break free. Hours of agony and I'm still no closer to escaping. Every muscle feels like it's been pumped full of lead and torn to shreds.

It doesn't compare to the pain I've been forced to witness, though. There was a time when I would've enjoyed seeing Lennox scream himself hoarse and pass out. If I could go back to that mental place right now, I would. Anything to escape this.

"The suffering of others is a particularly interesting motivator." Craven's tone is conversational. "Most can have empathy for a stranger. But empathy for a peer? That's far more powerful."

His mouth frozen in an eternal yell that his vocal cords have long since stopped supplying, Lennox strains against his own shackles. He's bound in a similar fashion, but unlike me, the spotlight is all his.

"Again," Craven orders.

His partner in crime, the guard with a cap covering his

closely cropped hair, flicks a switch on the battery-like machine placed a few inches from Lennox. It's connected to several wires, each one secured to his bare chest by an adhesive pad.

The moment the lever is pulled, his body jerks. An intense electrical current is being fed into his torso, over and over, the shock far more powerful than a mere stun gun blast. This is brutal, repeated electrocution.

"What do you want from us?" I sob violently.

The professor deigns to look at me, his expression completely void of emotion. "Absolutely nothing."

"Then stop! Don't hurt him!"

"Believe me, I'm being paid a significant sum to hurt him."

When this round of electrocution ends, Lennox's head lolls forward, shining beads of sweat dripping from his skin. He's barely lucid, moaning and swaying during each brief reprieve from the torture.

"Why?" I blubber.

Craven shrugs nonchalantly. "Incendia has orders to fulfil. Machines without morals are in demand, but the mind must break first. Only then can it be wiped."

With that explanation, he crouches beside Lennox. Craven grabs a handful of his greasy hair, using it to wrench his head upright. I can't stop myself from wailing as Lennox's deep-set eyes struggle to open.

"Ready to comply, Patient Twelve?"

"Go f-f-fuck yourself," Lennox moans.

Sighing, Craven lets his head drop. "Again."

The process is repeated. Over and over. Each shock more horrific than the last. Lennox's screams may be silent, but my tears offer a constant soundtrack. I can't feel my own battered body anymore, only the fierce burn in my throat from shouting so much.

"What's your name?" Craven demands.

When Lennox doesn't respond, he nods to the guard who pulls a steel-tipped whip from the rolling table of instruments in the corner of the room. The guard retakes his position, the whip held high.

"Answer me, Patient Twelve."

Still, Lennox doesn't respond.

"Fine." Craven nods to his goon. "Go ahead."

I bellow as the whip strikes across Lennox's lowered face. Blood sprays from the deep laceration it leaves in his right cheek, reaching from earlobe to nose. His tears mingle with the blood, forming a red veil spilling down his neck.

"What is your name?"

He chokes on a phlegmy cough. "L-Lennox fuckin' Nash."

The professor's hands curl into fists. "Wrong answer. We can escalate if you insist on being stubborn."

When the next weapon of choice is unveiled, what little hope I had left in my heart fizzles out. It's a handheld drill, the bit sharpened to a gleaming point. Even the cap-wearing guard seems reluctant.

"Start with his hands and feet," Craven instructs. "That ought to get things moving."

The drill bit is lined up with his shackled left hand. I take the coward's way out. My eyes screw shut as the mechanism begins to turn, the metallic buzz drilling into flesh and muscle. Lennox's voice roars back to life with each ear-splitting scream he releases.

"Lennox Nash is dead," Craven elucidates. "Do you understand?"

It feels like an eternity before the drilling ceases. Ribbons of tears soak my cheeks, leaking from my closed eyes. I don't want to look. I can't. For all his faults, not even Lennox deserves to be unmade.

"No," his sonorous voice wheezes. "H-He's not."

I hear Craven sigh. "Such resilience. Perhaps we should focus on the girl to motivate him."

Daring to look, I find the professor staring at me in contemplation. His goon has halted drilling, leaving Lennox in a bloodied state. I can't even tell if he's still breathing after forcing those words out.

When Craven takes a step towards me, I close my eyes, preparing for whatever comes next. I just hope Lennox has passed out and won't have to watch my torture like I did his.

"Now then…"

The command to inflict more torture that I expect doesn't come. With my eyes squeezed shut, I await my fate. The sound of a heavy blow and body crumpling follows instead. I dare to peek a single lid open.

"What an absolute piece of work." Weirdly, the voice spilling from the guard now holding the drill upside down is light and feminine.

Eyeing Craven, he looks physically repulsed.

"You know what? The world won't miss you, Professor."

The guard repeatedly smashes the drill into the back of Craven's skull. Each collision causes a stomach-lurching crunch, yet the guard doesn't relent.

Thud.

Crunch.

Crack.

Blood pools around the professor's head, peppered with chunks of broken bone. By the time the guard halts, panting for breath, not much remains of Craven's skull but a semi-crushed shell.

He slumps, elbows braced on his knees. "Bastard."

"Y-You," I force the word past my constricted throat. "You killed h-him?"

Breathless, the guard shoots me a glance. "Sorry I couldn't do it sooner. I'm working on someone else's schedule."

Still gaping at him, I feel like I've already fallen into insanity. I must still be mid-torture because there's no way in hell this is really happening. I've hallucinated the whole thing.

"We don't have a whole lot of time." The guard lifts his cap to scratch at his short hair. "I can't fucking think straight in this stupid wig."

With each scratch, edges of dark hair lift, revealing a flash of lurid pink beneath. It *is* a wig. I watch in dismay as he taps a cleverly concealed, flesh-coloured earpiece slotted into his ear.

"Next time, someone else can pretend to be a man and help people get tortured to maintain cover. I do not get paid enough for this."

This isn't a guard at all.

She's a mole.

"Hello?" She taps her ear again. "Come in, Theo."

Seemingly getting no response, she curses. I watch the stranger stand up, tossing the drill aside with a look of disgust. She pulls a set of keys from her cargo trousers then heads towards me.

"Who are you?" I blurt.

"I work for Sabre Security."

"You're... one of them?"

"Unfortunately for me," she replies sarcastically. "I get all the glamorous jobs."

Squatting down, she works on unlatching the shackles holding me in bondage. The moment the metal slides open, I cry out. My wrists and arms have ballooned from all the abuse, so bloated and inflamed, I know an infection is brewing.

"My name's Alyssa," she speaks quickly. "And I'm really sorry, but I'm not here for you. My team is coming in fast, though."

"I d-don't understand."

"Bancroft took one of our own. I'm here to extract him." Alyssa pauses to locate the next lock. "We can offer you both protection, but you have to come with me now."

"Come?"

"Ripley." She frees my other wrist. "I know who you are. This is your chance to choose the right side."

My arms slumping, I lay lifeless as she moves to unshackle Lennox. He's unresponsive now. Alyssa cringes at the sight of his left hand, mangled and seeping blood.

"Sorry." She grimaces. "I had a cover to maintain."

"You h-hurt him!"

"And now I'm freeing him. A fair trade off, don't you think?"

Working fast, she removes his shackles then gives him a nudge. Lennox moans in response, filling me with relief. He's still alive, just completely out of it. Alyssa looks equally as relieved.

"It's time, Ripley," she declares as she stands. "I have to find Phoenix then meet the team for extraction. Come with me if you want to get out."

"I can't leave."

"We can take Lennox with us!"

"It isn't just him," I whisper through falling tears. "I can't leave the others behind."

Staring at me in disbelief, Alyssa shakes her head. "It's now or never. I don't know when we can free the other patients. Bancroft won't give this place up without a fight."

"I know." My eyes move to Lennox's battered state. "But I won't abandon them. Not even to survive."

"So what will you do?"

I watch his chest rise and fall. "Find the others. Then run."

She sighs, reaching into her trouser pocket to flourish a black keycard. I recognise it immediately. It's the same as the one that Elon used to unlock the Z wing's security system.

The matte black rectangle is tossed across the cell to me. Shakily, I take it, stashing the cool plastic in my bra.

"Wait for us to clear out." She bends down to meet my

eyes, explaining hurriedly. "This part may get messy. Stay hidden until it's over."

Before she can leave the cell, I summon my voice again.

"Thank you."

Alyssa looks over her shoulder. "Sabre will help you, Ripley. If you make it out… you know where to find us."

Then she's gone as mysteriously as she arrived. The cell door clanks shut but doesn't lock. I eye Craven's practically decapitated body for a second before starting the agonising process of dragging myself across the room.

Traversing his long, powerful legs and the boxer shorts he's been clothed in, Lennox stirs at my touch. I work on detaching the electrodes from his chest, tossing each wire aside. Some leave burned patches of skin behind.

"Talk to me, Nox," I throw his words back at him.

A low groan rumbles in his throat.

"Words, big guy. I need you conscious."

With all the electrodes discarded, I try to wipe some of the blood from his face and neck with my soiled shirt. The jagged slice across his cheek is oozing, his skin flapping open. When I accidentally touch one side, his eyes fly open.

"Argh!"

"That's it." I quickly pull the edge of my t-shirt back. "Wake up."

"R-Rip?"

"It's me."

"Where?" he asks woozily.

"Still in the Z wing. There's some kind of break in happening. We need to find the others and get away from Harrowdean."

"H-How?"

"There must be a way out. Xander will know."

"I c-can't make it…" He hisses in pain. "Leave me."

"Like hell. Thought we were allies?"

"Enemies," he whispers.

"Not anymore, Nox. Not in here."

Struggling to prop him up despite my own throbbing body, I search around the cell for anything I can use. The only items are the table of torture instruments and Craven's body. Biting my lip, I move to the corpse first. Warm blood slips beneath my bare feet.

"He d-dead?" Lennox mutters.

"Yeah. Looks a bit like a smashed egg."

"Good."

Searching his lab coat pockets, I find a folded handkerchief. A quick pat of his suit underneath reveals an old flip phone suitable for a dinosaur like him. Nothing else. This will have to do.

I shove the phone into my bra, stumbling back over to Lennox. He looks like he wants to yell at the pressure I apply to his bleeding face with the handkerchief, but it comes out as a tiny, child-like cry.

"Suck it up." I press down as hard as my own throbbing injuries will allow. "You're bleeding."

"F-Fucking bitch."

"That's more like it. Thought you'd gone soft."

"Not likely."

Lapsing into silence, I let him rest as I focus on staunching the bleeding. It feels like an eternity has gone by before I hear the first incoming noises.

Shouting echoes from the corridor outside the cell. A multitude of different voices. The wet thunk of repeated, frenzied stabbing. Someone grunting with exertion.

"Rip?" Lennox whispers.

"Shh." I hold him tight. "Be quiet."

Gut-twisting screams follow. They sound so close, I wonder what's unfolding just outside the cell we're cowering in. More shouts ensue. The words permeate through the steel door to reach us.

"You're going to fucking die for that!"

It's a female voice. Unfamiliar. I hug Lennox even tighter to me, like I can shield him with my own broken body if the owners of those voices come looking. I don't know if they're friend or foe. We have to stay hidden here.

Bang.

Lennox flinches in my arms at the sound of gunfire. It cracks through the Z wing like an almighty thunderclap. Anguished shrills follow, the shouts all intermingling to form a terrifying mental image of a battle unfolding.

My face hidden in Lennox's shoulder, I tune out the unimaginable sounds. Part of me wonders if we've both died when silence eventually settles what feels like centuries later.

"Are we dead?" he grits out.

"Not yet."

Lifting my head, I strain my ears for any noise. There's a far-off banging. It sounds like cell doors are being systematically opened and closed. Briefly releasing Lennox, I grab the first instrument I can find on Craven's trolley of toys. A scalpel.

"Someone's coming," I whisper.

Lennox grunts, attempting to move, but he can hardly crack an eyelid let alone defend himself. I stand with my back to him, ignoring every last protest of my body. The scalpel rests in my white-knuckled grip.

Another bang.

Another.

Inching ever closer.

"Nox?"

He groans in response.

"If this is it… I just want you to know that I forgive you."

His reply is drowned out by the sound of our cell door flinging open. Three figures step inside, all barefoot and clothed in rags. My eyes bounce from the misshapen caricatures of human faces until I spot a familiar sight.

"Ripley."

Rick pushes past the other two, stepping farther into the cell. Blood drains from my face at the gun clasped in his hands. It sure looks a lot like Harrison's gun, the one he jammed into the back of my head.

He takes one look at Lennox, half-dead and slumped over, then focuses his attention on Craven's caved-in skull. All eyes seem to be locked on that sight with varying looks of satisfaction.

"What are you doing here?" I hiss.

"Getting out." Rick lifts his gaze to me. "Some dude who isn't a dude let me out. You?"

"The same."

"Well, now's the moment. You need a hand with him?"

I tighten my grip on the scalpel. "You'd help us?"

Clothes dripping like he's only just been pulled from his icy tub, Rick shrugs. "The enemy of my enemy is my friend. Ain't that the saying?"

"We aren't friends."

"Doesn't mean we both can't walk out of here," he counters. "No one's stopping us. I handcuffed that sick fuck in the tub when he came searching."

"Harrison?"

"He's taking a little dip now." Rick grins to himself.

"Alive?"

"I didn't care to check. You coming?"

I'm hit by indecision. Even in the best of health, I have little hope of carrying Lennox's massive, over-muscled body alone. But certainly not like this. He's going to take some serious handling.

Resolved to my fate, I reluctantly place the scalpel down then pull the keycard from my bra. Rick lifts a brow.

"I can get us out," I explain.

"Well, no time like the present."

He gestures for the two others to help. Neither speaks nor meets my eyes. I recognise the woman, despite her bruises and sliced-up skin. She's Patient Three. The one Harrison and Craven were reconditioning.

The other patient is male, his hair long and untamed. I don't know how he's maintained his muscles in here, but his arms are corded. Enough to lift Lennox's dead weight with a bit of help from Patient Three.

"You know the way out?" Rick asks me.

"You don't?"

"They pounced before we even had a chance to poke around the building. Never saw them coming. That professor asshole told me the others are already dead."

"How can you be sure?" I limp towards the door.

"I checked. All the other cells are empty."

Looking over my shoulder, I watch the two Z wing patients struggle to manoeuvre Lennox between them. He's breathing unsteadily, his head still limp.

"They got names?" I whisper to Rick.

"Nah. Haven't said a word."

As we step out into the corridor, the smell hits. I should be used to it by now, yet nothing can prepare you for the scent of a bloodbath.

It's everywhere. Covering everything. Walls, floors, cell doors. There are signs that a body has been dragged through the spillage. I have no way of knowing if our mysterious saviour made it out alive.

Not a single soul, though.

We're in a ghost town.

"Where are all the guards?"

Rick picks his way through red spillages, heading where I point. "I don't know. Unless we're missing some secret society party down here, the place has been abandoned."

Not likely.

When I slide on a crimson pool, Rick has to lunge to catch me. My knees are knocking together, I'm so weak. Numbness has swept in as my extremities switch off due to the constant onslaught of pain.

"I'm fine," I struggle out.

"Yeah. You look it."

"No more than Harrowdean's whore deserves, right?"

He clears his throat. "Think we've both paid our dues down here, Rip."

Honestly, he has a point.

We move slowly, barely able to shuffle ourselves towards the concrete staircase leading upward. Tackling each endless step feels like running a marathon on an empty stomach. The thick steel door seems forever out of reach. I can hear the grunts of the pair behind us struggling.

At the top of the stairs, I use the special black pass to unlock the door. My heart threatens to explode when there's no response. I try several times, each failed attempt causing my breathing to hitch.

"Come on!" I hiss under my breath.

Trying one last time, I'm rewarded at last. The security system eventually buzzes, and I could cry from relief. The door clanks open loudly.

A cacophony of sounds immediately filters in, emanating from beyond. Sound can't penetrate the Z wing's fortifications, but it's clear that something is unfolding outside. I hesitate, listening to the distant screams.

"What is that?" Rick's nose is scrunched up, a divot between his brows.

"The reason why there aren't any guards watching us."

With that grim realisation, we inch out of the Z wing and into a lit corridor. The bare bulbs are illuminated, breaking up the nighttime shadows. I don't even know what day it is or how long we were below ground. I've lost all concept of time.

Hanging back, I let Rick take the lead as we break outside. Lennox has roused a little on the way back up, his teeth now gritted for each movement. I swipe hair from his face to check on him, my hand sticky with his blood and sweat.

"You with me?"

"Just about," he grunts.

"We have to find Raine and Xander. I don't know what we're walking into, but this is our chance to get out."

"Following your l-lead, Rip."

He slams his eyes shut as the two patients tow him onwards. I don't know how we'll manage to run let alone walk with Lennox in this state. We have to try, though. Bancroft won't let our escape go unpunished when the dust settles.

Blazing, bright-white lights temporarily blind us as we're greeted by the night air. Floodlights have been turned on, illuminating the perimeter fence and the manor itself. As we stumble through the trees to reach the quad, the racket intensifies.

"Holy shit," Rick exclaims.

It's chaos.

Violent, deadly chaos.

In all directions, patients run wild and free. Some armed with weapons, others battering the living daylights out of any remaining guards. It goes beyond mere beatings. They're being incapacitated and restrained, then dragged into haphazard lines.

"What is this?"

Lennox lifts his head. "Hostages?"

"What?"

"They're taking the guards hostage." Rick's head swivels as he gapes at our surroundings. "This is like a fucking prison riot."

The five of us huddled together in astonishment, we spend several seconds taking it all in. The still-blaring alarm only adds to the havoc unfolding. With a smile blooming, Rick pulls the gun he stashed in his ragged waistband.

"This is it," he proclaims. "This is how we take them

down. If we have hostages... we can make demands. The world will have to listen."

"They're just going to send reinforcements in and kill us all!"

"Not if we barricade the doors." The male patient holding Lennox speaks for the first time. "Secure every entrance and exit."

"We can toss them scraps of dead guards if they dare break our perimeter," Patient Three chimes in.

Looking between the three of them, I'm trying to summon a response when my name rings out. Rae's face is covered in splattered blood, her auburn hair in disarray as she runs towards me.

I warn her off with a raised hand, fearing I won't survive the collision. I'm barely remaining upright as it is.

"You're alive!" she squeals.

"Rae." I lock eyes with her. "What's happening?"

"We're taking over."

"Who is?" Rick interjects.

"All of us." Rae eyes the gun in his hands. "Is that real?"

He nods, clutching his weapon possessively.

Noticing our presence, a handful of other patients have gathered to gawk. We must look like we've swam through a vat of blood. Spotting Rick's gun, a few more converge.

"We're gonna kill the bastards!" Taylor is one of them, a ragged slice marring her brow line.

"No!" someone else protests.

"They deserve it!"

"But we aren't killers!"

Everyone is shouting and arguing, violence still unfolding all around us.

"We need barricades!" Hands cupped around her mouth and voice raised, Patient Three can be heard above the bickering. "Chains! Padlocks! Furniture! Every exit has to be blocked!"

Nodding, Rick waves his gun. "They're worth more to us alive. We can use the guards as bargaining chips."

"Why?" a patient calls out.

"Because if we don't have leverage, they'll kill us."

"Like Noah!" another person screams.

"We're animals to them!"

"I don't want to die in here!"

Rick begins to bark off orders, waving that damn gun around like a lunatic. It's the role he always wanted. A righteous mob at his beck and call. With growing horror, I realise they're all going to get themselves killed.

Backing away from them, I inch towards Lennox. Patient Three quickly surrenders his right arm to me, preoccupied by instructing the horde of patients growing all around us.

"What are you doing?" Lennox groans.

"I'm not sticking around for this. We'll tunnel out if we have to."

"We w-won't get far like this."

"Then we'll take our chances."

"Rip—"

"No! We have to run. Riots only end one way."

Tugging his other arm from over the male patient's shoulder, I'm almost crushed beneath his weight. Lennox huffs, fighting to regain his balance, but he can hardly hold his head upright.

"Ripley," he wheezes.

"Don't start! I'm not leaving you!"

"We can't run forever."

"Fucking watch me."

Half-carrying, half-dragging him, I manage two steps before my knees give out. We go down hard, hitting the ground in a pathetic tangle. Lennox tries to avoid smothering me, but his gargantuan body thwacks into mine.

I'm crushed beneath his bulk, staring up at the night sky with a war waging all around us. I don't even try to fight off the tears, turning cold by the time they drip into my ears. We're never going to get out of here. Not like this. I'm not strong enough.

"Ripley! Hey, someone help me."

Hands grab hold of Lennox then heave, dragging him to the side. I pull in a breath, my entire body wailing. Rae hangs over me, a couple of others helping her position Lennox into a seated position.

"Where are you going?" She kneels next to me.

"Leaving," I cry out. "We have to run."

Her mouth twists into a grimace. "You can't, Rip. There's a protest outside the front gate. We're surrounded. This is our only shot."

"They'll kill us all, Rae!"

"We're as good as dead anyway," she replies tersely. "Come on. We need your help."

"I don't help people," I admit shallowly, pain overwhelming me. "I hurt them."

Offering me a hand, Rae's gaze is oddly steady. "Then start hurting the right people."

In the growing madness, I stare at her hand. At the thick layers of cuts and scars peeking out from beneath her shirt sleeve. A mere glimpse of the evil I've inflicted here. The same evil I'm desperate to run from.

All I've ever done is run.

From memories. From mania.

From demons.

From my own transgressions.

Bloodstained hands clasping, I let Rae tug me to my feet. She offers a tearful smile that I can't return. Not yet. Not until I've earned that privilege back. And she's right—I'll never do that by running. None of us will.

Her eyes shift beyond me. "Incoming."

"What?"

"There!" a familiar voice yells.

Chest aching, I lean on Rae and turn. At the rear exit of the institute, two shadows stare across the quad at us. One in a crimson-splattered polo shirt, the other a hospital gown and aviator sunglasses. Both head towards us.

"Ripley!"

Hearing Raine shout my name is like seeing a tiny ray of sunshine peeking through this hellscape. His arm circling Raine's shoulders, Xander steers him through the half-destroyed quad. His stare flits from Lennox to me, searching both of us.

Fuck me gently.

Xander Beck himself looks bloody worried.

The pair awkwardly stumble closer. Between guards being dragged into line, their cuffs stolen then attached to themselves, and the bark of orders being given, it feels like a battlefield stands between us.

But then I'm in Raine's arms.

Freshly squeezed orange.

Sea salt.

Home.

"Rip," he says urgently. "Are you okay?"

"L-Lennox... He... We..."

Grasping handfuls of his hospital gown, I collapse against him. Raine struggles to hold me upright until Xander intervenes and takes me from him, a hand cupping the back of my head.

"Xan."

"Breathe," he orders. "I've got you now."

Shaking all over, I let Xander gently lower me to the ground. I'm placed next to Lennox, my back resting against his side. He stirs and looks up at his best friend surveying us both.

"Xan."

"Hey, man." Xander's mouth does this strange, curving motion. "Good to see you're... kind of alive."

Lennox blinks rapidly. "Rip… is h-he smiling at me?"

I sag into him. "Yeah, I think he is."

Lennox's mangled, still-bleeding hand finds mine. Xander watches Lennox hold me with a cocked brow. The pair exchange some silent words, their eyes locked for several seconds until Raine interrupts.

"Guys? Plan?"

Lennox hacks up a mouthful of blood. "Ripley wants to run."

"Run where?" Xander replies.

"I… I don't know," I admit.

"The place is surrounded."

We watch the hysteria growing all around us. Rick is gesturing towards the lit-up perimeter fence, directing patients who have stripped the captured guards of all their worldly possessions. Anarchy is spreading like wildfire. But in the pandemonium, I'm not alone.

I have my enemies.

Now… my only allies.

EPILOGUE

EVERYBODY'S DEAD INSIDE – ALISSIC

RIPLEY

Present Day

In the interview room, horrified silence reigns over my audience. I take a sip of my water, some slopping over the edge due to the incessant shaking of my hand. It does little to relieve my throat, raw from hour after hour of talking.

Staring down at his notebook, Elliot is speechless. It's an amusing sight. He brought me here, expecting a story. Boy, has he got one. Perhaps not the tale he thought he'd tell, though. The truth is never simple.

Relaxed against the wall, Hudson stares into space. He hasn't made eye contact once throughout the entire afternoon or evening. I'm sure his own bleak memories of that time are rising to the surface. We all lost something inside the institutes.

Elliot clears his throat. "Well. That was quite the tale."

"I warned you."

"Details of Incendia's experimental program are few and far between. Hearing a firsthand account… It is harrowing."

"The world ought to know. They still see us as monsters. Freaks. Criminals." I curl my lip in distaste. "The ones to *blame*."

"No one blames you, Rip," Hudson croaks.

Looking into his crystalline stare, I ignore Elliot observing us in my periphery. Hudson isn't one for emotions, but so much is simmering behind his blue eyes. All manner of rage and bloodlust.

"I blame me. It took experiencing the true extent of their evil for me to wake up to the truth. To choose the right side."

"You were trying to survive."

"So was everyone else," I refute.

Head hitting the wall once more, Hudson blows out a breath. "The world will never understand what we sacrificed to still be here today, able to tell this tale."

"And that's why we're here." Elliot caps his fountain pen. "So the world will know."

I'm not sure what good it will do, a whole decade down the line. Evil and atrocity continue to this day. Society has a short-term memory when it comes to injustice. What happened back then taught them nothing.

I don't care if anyone watches this interview. I don't even care if it's ever broadcast to the nation. Old Ripley resolved not to run, and this Ripley can't do it for a moment longer either. The ghosts I carry need to be excavated.

Only then can we find peace.

Only then... can I begin to forgive myself.

Elliot stretches his shoulders, chatting quietly to his cameraman. Taking another sip of water, I glance at Hudson who's taking a hushed phone call. He acts like he isn't studying me from the corner of his eye.

"You think I'm done?" I watch Elliot rise.

He startles, looking up at me. "Uh, I just assumed—"

Bitter laughter escapes me.

"That was only the beginning of the story."

"Would you like to continue?" Elliot asks, eyes wide with surprise.

"Well, I'm still here."

With a slow nod, he settles back in his seat. Hudson finishes his phone call then waves to grab my attention. He mouths an apology, stepping outside to let someone else in.

It's almost like he planned it.

Scheming bastard.

Warner takes his place, briefly clasping his arm as they cross paths. Over the last ten years, his dark hair has become peppered with silver. It looks good on him. Glancing around the studio with his attentive gaze, he gifts me a tense smile.

I return it. Somehow, it seems only right that he's appeared to witness the retelling of what came next. After all, it's his story too. We wrote the next chapter together.

Elliot turns to a fresh page, plucking the cap back off his fountain pen. "By all reports, Harrowdean Manor fell into violence. A riot broke out overnight. Incendia kept it quiet, though."

"They were losing the fight. That's why."

He nods, poised to take fresh notes. "Tell us what happened next, Ripley."

"Harrowdean wasn't just my kingdom anymore. It was all of ours." I look to Warner, still here all these years later. "Right, Langley?"

His baby blues twinkle.

"Right."

To be concluded in...
Burn Like An Angel (Harrowdean Manor #2)

PLAYLIST

LISTEN HERE:
BIT.LY/SINLIKETHEDEVIL

1121 – Halsey
Punching Bag – Set It Off
Hateful – Post Malone
Dead Or Alive – Stileto & Madalen Duke
I'm Not Yours – The Haunt
All The Ways I Could Die – Arrows in Action
Misfits – Magnolia Park & Taylor Acorn
Meet You At The Graveyard – Cleffy
Devil – LOWBORN
Rain – grandson & Jessie Reyez
Thnks fr th Mmrs – Fall Out Boy
Bipolar Rhapsody – KID BRUNSWICK
Monster – Fight The Fade
Hero – David Kushner
n/A – Bring Me The Horizon
intoodeep. – Dead Poet Society
Start a War – Klergy & Valerie Broussard
Street Spirit (Fade Out) – Radiohead
Pretty Little Devil – Shaya Zamora
Harder To Breathe – Letdown
Love Abuser (Save Me) – Royal & The Serpent

Chokehold – Sleep Token
do you really want to hurt me – Nessa Barrett
Love You Better – The Haunt
drowning. – Eden Project
Play Dead (Just for Tonight) – The Messenger Birds
ADHD – Two Feet
My Name Is Human – Highly Suspect
V.A.N – Bad Omens & Poppy
Sinner – Of Virtue
Everybody's Dead Inside – Alissic

WANT MORE FROM THIS SHARED UNIVERSE?

The timeline of Harrowdean Manor runs parallel to Blackwood Institute. Learn more about Brooklyn, Hudson, Kade, Eli and Phoenix by diving into the dark and twisted world of another experimental psychiatric institute.

https://mybook.to/TwistedHeathens
https://mybook.to/SacrificialSinners
https://mybook.to/DesecratedSaints
https://bit.ly/BIBoxSet

Dive into Sabre next. Set in the same shared universe, the Sabre Security series follows Harlow and the hunt for a violent, bloodthirsty serial killer. Featuring cameos from all your favourite Blackwood Institute characters.

https://bit.ly/CorpseRoads
https://bit.ly/SkeletalHearts
https://bit.ly/HollowVeins
https://mybook.to/SSBoxSet

Finally, follow Willow's story next as she flees an abusive

marriage and takes refuge in the small mountain town of Briar Valley, assisted in her hunt for justice by Sabre Security.

https://mybook.to/WBWF
https://mybook.to/WWTG
https://mybook.to/BVBoxSet

ACKNOWLEDGEMENTS

Wow! It feels so good to be back in the J Rose shared universe. Blackwood Institute is the story that started this crazy journey for me. Coming back to this world truly feels like returning home.

Sin Like The Devil has been in the making for a couple of years now. I've always wanted to write Ripley's story—the tale of a female antihero, a survivor. So often, we hold our heroines to exacting standards that we'd never apply to the "alphahole" love interests. But why is that?

The girls deserve to be baddies too.

Their redemption arcs are equally as valid.

This story is for those who love as hard as they hate. Everyone trapped in the throes of toxic love. A love so complex and irrational, life would be unbearable without it. I don't believe in uncomplicated love stories, and if you're here, I can only hope that you don't want to read about them either.

J Rose wouldn't exist without the incredible team of loved ones who support me.

Thank you to Eddie for loving all parts of me. It's wild to think that before much longer, we'll be husband and wife. I can't wait.

To Lola. My partner in life and crime. I wouldn't have survived writing this book without our late night breakdowns and plotting sessions while strolling down Parisian streets. I love you.

For my incredible wife and alpha reader, Kristen. You continue to be the greatest sidekick a girl could ask for.

My next thank you is to my phenomenally talented illustrator, Dily. Girl, you understood the assignment for Harrowdean's paperback formatting and holy fuck, it's gorgeous. Just like you.

I have to shout out Kim, my badass editor, for lovingly kicking my ass into shape. You're my person. And thank you to Ellie for beta reading this bad boy and offering unwavering love, support and enthusiasm.

Of course, I can't forget my best friend, the wonderful Lilith Roman. You support me, challenge me, console me and love me at my worst. The best thing to come out of this author gig is meeting pure souls like you.

Thank you to the amazing team at Valentine PR for running this entire show behind the scenes. You're all amazing. And not to mention my fabulous ARC and influencer team—I appreciate every single one of you.

Every day, I pinch myself that I get to live this life and career. That wouldn't be possible without you. The reader. Thank you for making my dreams come true with every book I publish.

Stay wild,

J Rose xx

NEWSLETTER

Want more madness? Sign up to J Rose's newsletter for monthly announcements, exclusive content, sneak peeks, giveaways and more!

Sign up here:
www.jroseauthor.com/newsletter

ABOUT THE AUTHOR

J Rose is an independent dark romance author from the United Kingdom. She writes challenging, plot-driven stories packed full of angst, heartbreak and broken characters fighting for their happily ever afters.

She's an introverted bookworm at heart with a caffeine addiction, penchant for cursing and an unhealthy attachment to fictional characters.

Feel free to reach out on social media. J Rose loves talking to her readers!

For exclusive insights, updates and general mayhem, join J Rose's Bleeding Thorns on Facebook.

Business enquiries: j_roseauthor@yahoo.com

Come join the chaos. Stalk J Rose here...
www.jroseauthor.com/socials

ALSO BY J ROSE

Read Here:

www.jroseauthor.com/books

Recommended Reading Order:

www.jroseauthor.com/readingorder

Blackwood Institute

Twisted Heathens

Sacrificial Sinners

Desecrated Saints

Sabre Security

Corpse Roads

Skeletal Hearts

Hollow Veins

Briar Valley

Where Broken Wings Fly

Where Wild Things Grow

Harrowdean Manor

Sin Like The Devil

Burn Like An Angel

Standalones

Forever Ago

Drown in You

A Crimson Carol

Writing as Jessalyn Thorn

Departed Whispers

If You Break

When You Fall